THE STONE OF MESA

Book Two of The Myriar Series

Frion Farrell

PLATFORM ONE

Second Edition 2021

Other books in the Myriar Series:

The Round Spear (Book One) Wordbranch 2013; Second edition Platform One 2017; Third edition Platform One 2021

The Auric Flame (Book Three) Platform One 2017

Email: platformonewriting@gmail.com

DEDICATION

For Alan, who taught me to find the jewel in
the stone.

GLOSSARY

Alleator- music maker

Amron Cloch – Song Stone

Arwres – Myriar stone of the Inscriptor

Chalycion- Myriar stone of the Creta

Chimera - part lion, part goat, part serpent

Creta- Seed of the Myriar- artist

Devouril- Once Mourangils, followers of Belluvour

Fossilia – tiny, butterfly-like light beings that facilitate movement between space and time.

Frindy- shortened version of Pont y Ffrindiau

Galinir – female Devouril

Irresythe- giant winged creature

Iridice– the Myriar stone of the Reeder

Inscriptor-Seed of the Myriar – translates ancient and modern language

Kejambuck - eel-like creature that directs the energy of the Undercreature

Lute- Seed of the Myriar- hears the melody of all things, manipulates sound

Mesa - mankind's origin and Moura's sister-planet

Mensira- mind control used for evil

Magluck Bawah – the Undercreature- malevolent energy

Mourangil- one of the bejewelled race

Ordovicia – the first human habitation on the planet

Perfidium- obsidian stone that has been refashioned to disguise a powerful evil weapon

Pont y Frindiau – means Bridge of friends- Welsh university town

Reeder- Seed of the Myriar- telepath

Reuben – inhabits an inter-worldly cavern

Stozcist – Seed of the Myriar. Can manipulate stone.

Tanes- a group of elementals in Dublin

Tenements- the name of the Rugby team populated by Tanes

Teifi- river in Wales.

Tinobar- healing place

Tolbranach – mythical sea creature inhabiting the Caher mountains in Ireland

Prologue

Two hands tapered around the bat shaped controller; fingers danced effortlessly across the hard, black surface. The left thumb darted up and down a raised cross, the right depressed a pliant, round key to produce a change of weapon. Skimming to the left, his index finger found a trigger that extinguished alien life in a shower of exploding, blinking reds across the screen. Almost at his goal of a hundred kills, the left index finger clicked a button to send a grenade hurtling at the alien enemy. Though he was tired and thirsty his fingers continued, piano like across the console: controlling, stimulating, emboldening.

He lowered the tool reluctantly as the game moved towards its conclusion. It was hard to see at first, amid the splintered debris of his triumph, but then, squinting, he spotted a door that had never previously shown itself. He had chosen a Marine to represent his alter ego, but only the strong, bare hand was visible as it pushed cautiously at the wooden door, out of place in the metal landscape. There was no part of the marine visible as he entered the concrete cell. There on the floor was an alien creature and yet he could make out the outline of a human face as he moved closer. It shrieked, loud and plaintive, with a human voice. His own shadow loomed large on the cave wall, but he did not register this as he bent towards the pathetic, writhing creature. Another soldier came behind him, a player who often piggybacked his online playing. A baseball bat was offered and taken; the small grey eyes of the other soldier appraised him, and he felt momentarily uncomfortable. He lifted his arm, the console no longer needed, the kinetic response of the machine instant. The crying was childlike now and for a heartbeat he hesitated, then the lust to kill this enemy, the pale face now fully human, consumed him.

Down and down came the bat, thirst and fatigue long forgotten in the killing sport. Blood tasted in his mouth as he bit his gum with excitement. At the end, the brutalised form lay sprawled on the floor of the cave, the other player now vanished. The huge screen became black, the power light extinguished and yet he thought he heard a woman laughing, slapping tidelike against his ears in the surround sound hotel room. He sat back on the oversized leather sofa and let his chest settle its tumultuous heaving. It was only then that he saw the wooden baseball bat, held tightly within his grasp; the rounded end occluded by fragments of blood and bone.

Chapter One

Gabbie was surrounded by glass. Cascades of rippling water tumbled lightly behind the mirror in the restaurant bar. White-suited waiters carried tinkling trays of Chardonnay as they passed the wall-to-wall window through which Darling Harbour was an impressive backdrop. Amidst the hum of relaxed chatter, a rock ballad manoeuvred expertly through the tight coils of workday stress. As always, unfettered by work, her thoughts made their way home. The old railway cottage in England, where she had lived all of her young life, had turned to rubble before her eyes almost one year ago. Gabbie felt that she would give all her new possessions to have it back.

The sound of Kier's voice broke her reverie. Gabbie's companion looked up from a wad of paper to address the Australian manager of their latest venture.

"I don't need huge profits Ed; the place will sell itself."
Kier was crossing out and adding to parts of a list. "And no need for the high costs for cutlery. The deposit's ok but keep it reasonable."
She placed the hostel contract on the table. Ed Saul, who was to manage the new business along the coast on Coogee Beach, placed the document carefully back into a briefcase and grinned.
"No worries," he replied, in a generous Australian accent. "Only wish this place had been around when I was back-packing!"

Ed was in his thirties with an easy manner and what Kier had called his 'well utilised' good looks. He was well travelled and as relaxed as any of his fellow countrymen. Except when he was opposite Kier. He chatted easily but his hands clenched fitfully as he studied her face across the table. Kier as always, seemed unaware of the impact she had on the men with whom she came into contact. Gabbie's employer had dressed for the celebration in a snug fitting black jersey dress. She wore an amber necklace that lifted the honey-brown of her eyes. Her long black hair was, for once, allowed to tumble loosely around her face. The full and generous mouth quirked upwards on one side and her eyes smiled mischief.

"No cricket though," Kier said conversationally, as she reached for her bag.

"What?" Ed's composure was shaken, as he looked from one to the other straight faced English women.

"You can't be serious ay? Gabbie!" he appealed.

"Bad for English digestion," Gabbie told him seriously. "And you know how we feel about healthy food."

"But you've bought a state-of-the-art screen for the lounge," he spluttered. Gabbie exchanged a glance with Kier and leaned her head to one side.

"Not really mate," she said in an Australian twang, picking up her bag and laughing as Ed shook his head.

"For a moment there I thought I'd have to quit the job before I started. And it's the opening tomorrow!"

He followed the two women as they walked towards the door and stepped out into the balmy Sydney evening.

"Don't forget the papers Kier," Ed told his new boss, as he handed her the briefcase. "You'll both be there tomorrow ay?"

Kier smiled and nodded, "Yes, see you then."

Gabbie blinked.

Ed afforded them his tanned, handsome smile as he waved and walked away, but Gabbie had seen something in his eyes a second before. Having walked ahead, she had turned back towards the other two. In that momentary tableau, as Kier moved her body to adjust the shoulder strap of her briefcase, Ed's brown eyes had darkened to venomous hatred. Gabbie folded her arms around a body that now felt as if it had been dipped in ice water. Kier's warm hand curled under her forearm, and she pulled it close to her side. "Shadow and neon," Gabbie murmured to herself. "A trick of the light."

"What's up?" Kier asked as they walked along the wide harbour front.

"Nothing," she replied, trying to shake off the dread that had so unexpectedly assaulted her. The city skyline pulled her eyes upwards and Gabbie managed to shape her mouth into a smile. The Sydney Tower stood aloof above a dazzling array of skyscrapers, its blue neon circle providing the eye of Darling Harbour. Luminous matchbox strips of light dotted the buildings, some dull, others intensely bright as they poured multicoloured reflections in sparkling stripes on the water below. Kier smiled as they weaved their way between streams of tourists, still busy shopping.

The recession that hung over England and the rest of Europe had no counterpart in the busy and opulent Sydney. It was no wonder so many young backpackers, from all over the world, flocked to the city's beaches. The experiences they had shared of being exploited by some hostel owners had prompted Kier's business venture in the city. A youth in a baseball cap powered his jet ski down the centre of the harbour and pulled alongside one of the many boats that were moored in various bays along the quayside. A stream of passengers disgorged from a cruise ship that had its own docking terminal and their excited voices echoed across the water.

"It's an amazing city," Kier commented, her eyes shining. Gabbie looked at her friend and noted that the shine was still only surface deep. Like her, Kier hid a well of emptiness that had refused to be filled by all the truly wonderful experiences that had been furnished by almost twelve months in Australia.

*

The apartment was at the top of a multi-storey building further down on the Westside and overlooked the harbour. Gabbie put her hands over her flat stomach and groaned as she opened the door.

"That seafood platter was gorgeous and huge! I still don't know the names of half the things I've eaten. I had to squish that red thing a bit, thought it was plastic!"

Kier laughed, "I had to guess a few," she answered making for her bedroom, "but it was superb."

It seemed so long, Kier thought, since she had any real appetite; the small succulent seafood had been ideal. When Kier returned to the lounge, in the long T-shirt she used as nightwear, Gabbie had switched on the TV. She stood motionless, the remote held stiffly in one hand.

"I thought they'd show it," she said tonelessly.

On the large flat screen ran a BBC world news report about Pulton on the coast of North West England. A three-storey building, with the words 'Forget me not' over the door, was stationed at the back of a garden, where wildflowers wove delicate colours between newly planted trees. The camera focused on the young saplings, beside each of which was engraved the name of an individual who had lost their life one year previously. Inside the building the camera moved along the corridors of the old bookshop, revealing alcoves that were once overstuffed with books but now contained quiet nooks of contemplation. It was fitting Kier thought, that the place that had provided sanctuary for their small group was now being used to give solace to others.

"They've rerouted the road," she commented, as she stood quietly behind her personal assistant. Unmoving, she watched the report in silence but could not prevent a sharp intake of breath as the camera flashed back twelve months to what had, to all intents, been a tragic freak of nature in the quiet seaside resort. The two women standing in front of the television, thousands of miles away, shared the knowledge that this had not been the case. The screen filled with clips of the devastating earthquake, as it sliced up the road and pulled down every building in the row apart from the old bookshop, now turned to a garden of remembrance for the victims and their families. Kier felt her knees give way as she remembered the shock of the ground opening beneath her feet, the torn rock screaming as she plunged into blackness. Gabbie's hand was firm on her arm as she straightened herself, squeezing the small fingers in thanks. Then the younger women flicked her wrist, and the screen was in darkness.

Gabbie's petite figure reflected back on the empty screen. Her straight blonde hair fell to her shoulders over a beautifully cut sapphire dress. The well-defined chin hinted at the unruliness that lay dormant beneath a tamed surface. Kier stood beside her in silence, their physical closeness a reflection of the friendship they shared. It had continued to deepen in the months since they had been first thrown together, amidst the turmoil of betrayal, attempted murder, and so much more.

"I can't believe that we're all so scattered," murmured Gabbie turning away, her eyes welling with tears. "Klim and Siskin chasing criminals in Nicaragua, Swift with Evan in Asia, Gally in America, Marianne and her family in Ireland and us miles away from them all!"

Her voice broke and Kier put an arm around her companion thinking of the days they had all spent together in the aftermath of the events on Whistmorden Scar, waiting for news that had never arrived. The phone rang. Gabbie frowned, it was after midnight and the call was an international one.

"Hello," she said tentatively, "Gabrielle Owen speaking."

Kier marvelled at the poise and professionalism that Gabbie had developed in the last twelve months. At just eighteen she had spent the last year studying long hours as well as working hectic days in the business, helping Kier to build her new portfolio. Adam's quirky face, sitting at his desk, a plate of toast beside him, made its way unavoidably into her mind. Even now however, she could not touch those memories, they were burning hot cinders that only time would extinguish. Kier glanced at her young assistant and realised that the colour had drained from her face. Alarmed, she moved towards her just as Gabbie put the receiver back in place and pressed the loudspeaker button.

"Seven Rivers," a young woman's light voice said quietly and firmly for the second time. It was the code word they had agreed, the name of the cafe and gift shop in Pulton from which had emerged the chain of events that had changed all of their lives.

"It's good to hear your voice," said Kier, carefully avoiding names as they had agreed.

"And yours. We need to meet," the disembodied tones told them.

"All of us?" asked Gabbie.

"All of us," came the reply.

"Are you still in Asia?" Kier queried.

"Not now," the light voice told her. "We've returned. The post code has been delivered."

"Ok, we'll try to be with you tomorrow," Kier told the loudspeaker and heard a sigh of relief in response.

"It'll be so good to see you both," the speaker said warmly and then rang off. The dialling tone buzzed and Gabbie reached over to end the call.

"Tomorrow?" repeated Gabbie. "That's pushing it a bit."

Kier shook her head, her face still deeply thoughtful.

"Don't forget we're virtually a day ahead. Just depends how far we have to travel from the airport."

"What about the hostel opening?" Gabbie asked her employer.

"Everything's in place. Ed can oversee the launch, he's up to it," she decided confidently. Kier moved towards the briefcase to retrieve her mobile. Gabbie turned as she heard her exclaim in surprise and lifted out a small, ribboned box. Opening it she laughed at the specially made iced cake, a replica of the new hostel.

"What a lovely thing. Ed's got even more charm than I gave him credit for!"

She put down the fondant and reached for the phone, sliding into an authority that was effortless and unconscious.

"I'll give him a ring now, so he has as much warning as possible. Can you try and get us tickets for the next flight?"

Gabbie nodded and headed for her laptop but turned back at a thudding sound behind her.

"Dam!" Kier's elbow had knocked the cake to the floor, where the white icing toppled sideways in the box. Peeping out from within the spongy mixture was something shiny and black. Gabbie pulled out the date like substance.

"That looks weird. Maybe it's some Australian delicacy."

She raised it tentatively towards her lips, only to find herself leaning back in shock as Kier swiped it from her hand.

"Jetra!" Kier's voice trembled in horror. "I've seen it before. Evan pulled it from the small boy that Jackson had poisoned. Even the slightest contact with the mucous lining of your mouth would absorb the substance and your throat would close over in minutes. Only a Stozcist can draw it out and neither Evan nor Swift are here right now."

"Ed!" Gabbie relayed to her friend the look of black hatred she had witnessed earlier that evening. "And I thought he liked you," she added. "I'll phone the police."

"No, wait."

Kier placed the dark stone on the table without speaking. She put the mobile phone back into her bag, checking there was nothing else hidden inside.

"Jackson was prepared to kill a child with this foul thing because there was a chance that he would find Swift. Instead, Evan was discovered, and it resulted in Jackson finding us in the bookshop."

Gabbie nodded mechanically, stunned at how close she had come to becoming another victim.

"We need to be on the next flight; our enemies are not the kind that the police can help us with." Kier carefully placed the jetra in an envelope. Whatever weariness they had felt disappeared in a shared urgency to leave the city. It took Gabbie less than fifteen minutes to make the arrangements.

"All sorted," she announced, collecting sheets of paper from the printer, "Five am."

Kier closed her computer.

"Ed had packed before he left the hostel. He never returned. We will have to take the offer of a sale. I've emailed Karen to handle it. It's a shame, a real shame."

Kier dragged two cases from a cupboard. "We'll have to pack and head straight for the airport; we can sleep on the flight."

Kier pushed away the fear that threatened to engulf her. Without acknowledging the fact, they had both retreated into the behaviour that had characterised the early months after

Whistmorden. Kier scanned the street outside from the side of the window. Gabbie checked the other rooms.

"I know it can't be good. It all seems to be starting again," Gabbie said quietly, her blue eyes soft, "but I still can't wait to see them all."

Kier smiled, "Klim, you mean."

Gabbie's response was the first easy smile she had seen her friend make in months.

"Not just Klim," she replied jumping up, then groaning. "How am I going to get all my stuff into one bag!"

It was Kier's turn to grin. As she dragged the case into her room, she buried any misgivings in the face of Gabbie's enthusiasm. There was, after all, a stirring of excitement in the pit of her own belly. He may not even come, she told herself. Evan, his rolling Welsh tones sounding in her mind, had made it clear that there was no predicting when and if Echinod Deem would return. "Their time is not ours," he had explained. "They blink away our years and our youth." And then he had looked up at Kier and smiled, "Though this time, perhaps it may not be long at all."

Chapter Two

The 'Barley Field' advertised itself as a quiet and secluded retreat in the village of Stromondale. The hotel was hidden away in a small valley only a short car journey from the famous lakes. It had lately become a favourite stop for a popular tour bus that was delighted to have found this out-of-the way gem. It meant that the tour company did not need to compete with a dozen others for parking and accommodation. The Barley Field was attached to a village shop and the owner of both was a young widow named Clare Armer. At the age of twenty-eight she had found herself, a transplanted southerner, trying to run her husband's family business whilst bringing up her small daughter, Juliette. Five years previously Clare had moved up with her husband Tom, after her father and mother-in-law had died in the same year. Three years later Tom had been the victim of a road accident when a drunk driver had failed to stop. Had they done so, he may not have died from his injuries, leaving a young wife and baby. Clare was utterly bereft.

A further tragic event had occurred last spring when a visiting group of holiday makers had included a member of a gang that trafficked young children all over the world. Juliette, Claire's three-year-old daughter, had been snatched from her bedroom. Clare thought she would lose her sanity. Miraculously, her daughter had been returned when her friend and sometimes lover, had tracked the child down to a house merely two hours away in Roust. The small fingers held tight, and Clare felt the distinct stickiness of jam as she led Juliette through the village shop.

Min was in her sixties; often she sat behind the small counter knitting. Clare tried to remember the last time she had seen Min free of the continued transformation of rolled wool into colourful small figures. Without stopping she looked up to smile at mother and daughter. The young hotelier often thought that Min would rival any mass production company. The dolls and tea cosies continued to increase until they competed for space with groceries and other gifts in the tiny store. Then the coach would arrive and clear most of them and the work of refilling the shelves would start again. Min's needles clicked away as they passed through the shop and out onto the road.

The strain of the last few years showed in the premature grey that was hidden behind the natural blonde of Clare's short hair. The weight she had lost after Tom's death had never been replaced and with Juliette's disappearance her thinness had increased, so that she dressed carefully in a maxi skirt that hid the protruding bones of her hips. Since her daughter had been rescued however, the pale skin had gained colour and the light had, at last, returned to her eyes. Throughout all of the tragedy she retained her love of the small village. The first day she had glimpsed the stone building set above the meeting point of two rivers, she had felt a sense of belonging. It was as if the place itself had accepted her, and the inhabitants seemed to understand this and accepted her in their turn. There was a water tap outside the shop and Clare stopped, peeling her hand from her child's gluey grip.

"Should we give our hands a rinse, Juliette?"

"Ok," her daughter agreed, her blonde head bobbing with laughter as her mum tickled the small palm with her fingers.

"Now, shake." Clare demonstrated and Juliette jumped up and down as her small hands fluttered, blinking as tiny flecks of water landed on her face.

Mother and daughter continued over the stone bridge and up the hill towards a patch of woodland. Since Juliette's return Clare had been terrified of losing her again, placing the pink 'princess' bed from which she had been taken, in her own bedroom. Juliette spurted forwards and ran excitedly along the narrow gravel trails, chirping noisily. Clare followed, her brow furrowing as she realised that she could no longer hear her daughter's chatter. The trees crowded around her, and the bitter taste of fear rose in her throat as it opened to scream her daughter's name. Quickly she closed her mouth, trapping the stale air, quelling the panicked cry. The small blonde head poked out from the bushes a little further along the trail, tipping to one side, listening, enraptured. It was intermittent at first, caught on the breeze and barely discernible. Clare, smiling widely now, reached out her hand as she approached her daughter and put a finger to her lips as they moved further into the copse of trees. As they drew nearer the notes of a classical guitar twined themselves around her senses. Then his voice began, and she and Juliette found a nearby fallen tree; without thinking, they sat down to listen. The song belonged to the earth that hummed in accompaniment; it belonged to the trees that rustled in chorus, and it belonged to the sky that illuminated its beauty. Tears fell down her face in its deep embrace and she felt her heart constrict with longing when the song ended. It was a moment or two before she realised that she was watching her daughter's tiny steps moving towards the sound. As the little figure rounded a corner she turned back to her mother and Clare again put a finger to her lips, signalling the little girl back to her side. Together they entered the copse where he sat on the ground, his back against a tall beech tree, his eyes closed, strumming the guitar with effortless grace.

Long fair hair was tied back off a strong face with a firm chin; a single circle nestled in his left ear lobe. The lashes were as long as a woman's and were blonde with the sun. Tanned, fine-boned fingers found their rhythm with the ease of long use, and he seemed unaware of his new audience, lost in sound. Clare knew, however, that this would not be the case, his senses were as alert as tripwire, and he would have already identified Juliette's quiet steps. Furthermore, Clare was one of the few people that understood that this man would know her melody, for he thought in terms of sound, could truly understand the music of everyday life. There was a small rucksack on the floor beside stretched-out legs in a pair of old denims, torn from use rather than design. The strumming ended and the eyes opened, acorn brown. He smiled at Juliette who immediately ran and deposited herself in his lap.

*

Klim knelt at the small square, upon which he had placed a bouquet of his mother's favourite daisies. He had been surprised to find fresh roses framing the remembrance plaque, beneath which the ashes of Eleanor Klimzcak were buried. It was hard to believe that he was back here in the garden of remembrance, unrecognisable now as the old bookshop in Pulton. Although his mum had not died in the earthquake, Evan suggested that she be laid to rest in its grounds. It seemed to Klim that the silver birch he had planted beside her grave had grown more upright and stronger than any of the others; already it was clear that the young tree would take ownership of the corner space. He came to his feet with a natural catlike grace, refined by Siskin as they survived critically dangerous situations in Nicaragua.

The group had still been together at the Mountain Inn, almost twelve months previously, when Klim sensed something was seriously wrong. He had returned to Bankside and spent the last precious days with his mother before she died. It was of special comfort to him that, during this time, his mother had been more lucid than at any period since she had been taken into care at his now deceased uncle's instigation. Not long after the funeral he and Siskin had left the country. Klim had jumped at the chance to work with the ex-soldier, who had become his mentor and friend. They had worked together undercover in South America, tracking those who, like his uncle, preyed on others. In the eyes of the traffickers, children, women, and young men like him were no more than commodities to be herded and abused for profit. Siskin had hunted them with complete focus and determination using Klim's latent telepathic talents to the full. Barely had their efforts finished, resulting in the round up of a vicious gang, when they were summoned back to England. He squatted back down and imagined his mother's face as it had been in health. Fair hair, worn loose, her eyes shining with love for him and his father. Fervently he hoped that they were together again now.

"Everything he made went to the earthquake victims." His voice was a whisper, even though there was no one else in the garden, as he recalled the aftermath of Whistmorden.

"He never thought I'd be living longer than him and inherit the lot!" His uncle's handsome but cruel face flashed across his vision, and he banished it away.

"I sold the Hunting Lodge that he stole from us," he continued apologetically. "In the end I didn't want it without you and Dad, and besides, I could still feel him in the place and the stench of the things he'd done."

He remembered the woman Sarah, initially employed by his uncle, Alec Jackson, and then murdered in the hidden cottage behind the main house. He remembered Marianne and Swift who had been captured and rescued and Gabbie who had been stabbed by their own friend, as a result of his uncle's sadistic manipulation. Klim turned his face towards the sunshine and allowed it to wash away the dark memories. Smiling, he told the daisies, "It'll be great to see her again." One of the flowers leaned sideways in the vase and he straightened it before he stood to leave.

In the old doorway of the refurbished building, he saw a familiar figure, grown taller in the last year. The sandy hair was neat and tidy and, in his hand, instead of the inevitable cigarette, was a small posy of roses. The other young man had been shocked at Klim's presence and stood quietly, his face pale, his eyes large and startled. Eleanor Klimzack's son probed the thoughts of the uneasy figure, shuffling to one side of the entrance. It was easy now for Klim to pick up the imprint of the boy, now turned man, who had once been his best friend. There he saw that this visitor was no stranger to the garden, coming as often as Klim himself would have liked to have done, had he not followed Siskin to the other side of the world. Klim understood why his past friend now braced himself for abuse; he had decided that Klim would see this as an act of violation to have someone like Luke tending his mother's place of rest. Equally Klim saw the tenderness that had been applied to the task, which had been undertaken in atonement for the terrible actions of the previous year.

Slowly Klim made his way towards the door and the figure shuffled to one side to allow him to pass, his eyes fixed on the gravel path. Klim turned and held out his hand. The other young man lifted his face where pain and guilt had erased feckless abandonment. The dreadful betrayal he had committed was a gaping chasm between them.

"Hello Luke," Klim said quietly, his deep, dark eyes holding those of his old friend, noting the tear-filled, speechless response as Luke pressed his hand into his. Walking on through the now hushed corridor, Klim allowed the familiar sense of loss to wash over him. It seemed less painful than the bitter grief and regret that now leaned so heavily on the young man who had once been his friend.

Chapter Three

Gabbie passed her companion a white stone from a small silk pouch, that obviously contained many others.

"Swift said it would take away the jet lag," she whispered.

"I'd forgotten how long this flight is," Kier said rubbing the milky white crystal upon her forehead and instantly feeling refreshed. "At least we're on the last leg now." They had both managed a few hours' sleep.

"It's not so bad," Gabbie commented cheerfully, finishing her breakfast. "I was getting pretty homesick to tell you the truth."

"Have you let your dad know you're on your way home?"

Gabbie's face lit with a mischievous grin.

"No, I'm going to surprise him!" Her gaze followed the stewardess as she headed up the aisle. "Besides, he wouldn't understand why I wasn't going straight there."

She sighed, "As soon as I'm free I'll go to Bankside. Are you coming with me? Dad would be made up."

A pretty Qantas stewardess leant over and smiled as she collected Gabbie's emptied tray and the barely touched meal left by Kier. The tiny blonde was irrepressible.

"It would be great if you could," she encouraged.

"Maybe."

Gabbie yawned as she readjusted her seat. She closed her eyes and seemed to grow in contentment the nearer they came to England. A blanket of cloud snuggled beside the window. Kier remembered the sensation of being wrapped in the air itself, enveloped by the wind when Tormaigh the Mourangil had transported her to Tinobar. Gabbie had been on the brink of death and her recovery could only have taken place in that unique place of healing. Kier glanced at the tanned face of her companion that now glowed with health. iPod in one ear, her eyes closed, Gabbie mimed happily to the music. Kier smiled, the lids of her own eyes were weighted with the long hours of travel, and she allowed them to shut.

A reflux of fear, bitter and sharp, brought her blindingly awake into the glare of a white sky. Gabbie was fast asleep beside her, but Kier's agitation had been noticed by the stewardess who moved towards her. Kier smiled reassurance that all was well, and the woman gave the faintest of nods in acknowledgement, as she passed down the plane. The images that had assaulted her dreams were muted in the calm drone of the aeroplane, the chatter of families and the crackling of crisp packets. She sighed her relief, a deep release of tense breath acknowledging that she was no longer immersed in the frozen torture inflicted by Nephragm the Devouril; that the pain-filled faces of Marianne and Gally were free of their imprisonment. Kier tried not to think how her brother would feel when he realised that she was returning without him. Swift, who had been responsible for the summons back to the

29

UK, undoubtedly presumed that she and her brother were still together in Australia. The main reason she and Gally had chosen to go to the Southern Hemisphere last September had been to see their mother, who had kept little contact since their parents had divorced eight years previously. Kier had asked Gabbie to accompany her to Australia on seeing her friend's distress when Klim had agreed to go with Siskin to South America. The visit by Gabbie, Gally and Kier to Darwin had been short and superficial. She pictured the beautifully preserved face of her mother organising her new husband and household. It was clear that Drea Morton's new life and family had taken precedence over her own children. Sister and brother left without imparting any real knowledge of their present life.

Kier and Gabbie had begun work in Sydney and Gally travelled to America to see their father; it seemed that he had fared better over there with their other parent. Both Gally and Sam were university lecturers and Sam Morton had arranged for his son to work with him in Los Angeles. Kier could see that a sense of well-being had begun to show in his face as they skyped each other. She had even started to rebuild a tentative relationship with her father, in the small snatches of conversation facilitated by her brother.

Gally, she reasoned, did not need to be with them right now. Unlike her, he had not been identified as a Seed of the Myriar; it was not his responsibility to answer this call. Kier's mouth set firm, she could not risk losing him again. Martha, their sister, had been killed in a chilling accident when Kier was still a teenager. She quelled the sensation that the events that had overtaken them last year were somehow linked to that tragic loss. "Do you think they're all okay?" Gabbie's apprehensive voice cut through her thoughts. Kier turned and smiled at the sleep-touched blue eyes.

"We all promised, Gabbie, that if anyone was hurt, we would use the codes and inform the rest. That was the agreement, remember?" Gabbie sighed with relief.

"I remember," she nodded. "Just making sure."

Kier was suddenly overwhelmed by the extent of her young friend's struggle over the last year. It had worried her that Gabbie seemed to stand remote from the lively crowd that frequented the clubs and cafés near their apartment. Her friend smiled but continued to hold the leads of her headphones in an apprehensive grip.

"Only another hour," Kier said gently, returning her smile, "and then we should be there."

Gabbie nodded. She popped the headphones back into her ears and closed her eyes.

Manchester, Kier thought, her home city. Where memories of Martha lifted in soft enveloping waves from the tapered gardens and pocketed playgrounds of middle suburbia. They folded into a soft blanket and smothered her with their nearness. And then later, there had been Adam, fiddling with purple glasses perched too big on thin features, the ever-present tapping of a keyboard and the baked smell of golden-crumbed toast. Kier allowed the painful realisation to course through her once again; a bitter acceptance that she had lost both these wonderful, benign influences in her life.

As soon as she was old enough, after Martha's death, Kier had taken herself away, letting new sights and sounds parade the grounds of a confused existence. In the ten years since she had left it, she had not visited the family home, even though she had continued to work from the city centre. The offices she had shared with Adam had been sold and she could not contemplate at this time, ever again kayaking down the Manchester Ship Canal. In spite of all this here she was, heading back again, launched into the unknown face of unfinished business.

Grey drizzle greeted them just after dawn as they made their way to pick up the RAV4 that Gabbie had arranged. Kier's spirits lifted with the sense of familiarity, but they could not match the ebullience of her companion who was fixing the satnav to the windscreen. Gabbie took out a piece of paper and typed in the postcode that had been messaged to an email address, used only for rare communication with the rest of the group; it had arrived in an encrypted attachment. The small, clever instrument listed the code as 'unknown destination,' but the map clearly showed that they were to head for Wales. The atmosphere of recession loomed over the city. Kier felt its damp grip as she drove, deliberately avoiding the motorway. There was a surplus of charity shops, several bleak whitewashed windows, in a suburb that had once been thriving with specialist, elite rows of colour. The contrast to the prosperity and sunshine of Sydney was overpowering. The summer was duller than the Australian winter but there was a taste in the air, a luminous light sneaking through the cloud. It reminded Kier that this was England, with its undefinable charisma and coalesced diversity, somehow fundamentally sound.

"My mum took me to the Trafford Centre in Manchester once," Gabbie said, a childlike expression on her face. "It was awesome."

It was perhaps the second time Kier had heard her friend mention her mother, who she knew had left when Gabbie was still in primary school. Kier had taken her shopping in London and Sydney, without producing the kind of reaction that the one trip to Manchester with her mother had engendered. The silence that followed was broken only by the Scottish tones of Sean Connery giving directions and Kier concentrated on steering the vehicle.

"Keep left," the Scotsman instructed suavely and Kier turned the wheel obediently.

"It's good to be home," Gabbie whispered, eyes shining with emotion.

Kier wondered if she knew where home was any more.

Chapter Four

It was no surprise that the directions took them out to the west and Wales but Kier had expected to be heading towards Snowdonia and the north of the country. Evan was from a small village in North Wales, and they knew that he and Swift had lived at his old home for at least part of the year. The James Bond-style insistence from the tiny screen however, perched firmly in their line of vision, clearly directed them towards mid Wales. The early morning fog closed in as they peered through the window at an empty country road dotted with signs for 'Trallwng,' the English name of 'Welshpool' supplied underneath. Rows of tall, shrouded trees loomed high on either side of the recently laid tarmac; their deep green leaves top heavy with morning dew; their branches leaning with casual curiosity. Red dragon signs were frequent and reminded Kier that this was a land apart, proudly displaying its distinctive heritage and the language of the bards.

Distances in Australia were massive and a four-hour drive to mid Wales should have seemed nothing in comparison to the long miles that separated towns, described as neighbours, on the southern continent. The long-haul flight had taken its toll and after only a couple of hours Kier felt exhausted. Gratefully, she pulled in at a service sign that advertised early morning breakfasts. They were the first customers of the day and the middle-aged woman at the counter addressed them in the rich, rolling sounds of the Welsh language. Kier opened her mouth to respond in English and then clamped it shut again as Gabbie leaned forward.

"Bore da. Dau coffees gwyn os gwelwch yn dda," she said smiling.

The woman behind the counter smiled back appreciatively and turned to fetch the two white coffees that Gabbie had requested. Kier was speechless and stood looking pointedly at her friend, eyebrows raised, her mouth curving in amusement.

"What?" said Gabbie turning red, "Evan taught me."

Kier broke into a grin as she paid at the till and picked up the tray that now contained two steaming hot coffees. As they took them to the table she looked up with respect.

"Can't believe you can remember. It's a year since you worked with Evan."

"He said I had a quick ear for languages," she replied, pleased.

Gabbie focused on her coffee, looking thoughtful, and Kier relaxed, sipping her drink. The windows were open, and she smiled at the sound of sheep in the nearby fields, inhaling the fresh earthy smell of early morning in the UK countryside.

The small car park was deserted as they made their way back to the RAV4, greeted by a break of sunlight through the mist. It seemed to bring with it fresh enthusiasm and Kier felt physically lighter as she approached the car. She pulled the driver door open, but her hand froze tightly around the handle. A sound rumbled underneath the surface and for a fearful moment her mind flew back to the earthquake as she thought the earth was going to break apart below her. She searched the ground frantically but there were no signs of stress in the concrete. The sound became louder, a deep shuddering that wailed mournfully beneath her feet and seemed to reverberate in the air around her. Gabbie, on the other side of the vehicle, hopped lightly into the passenger seat and looked over curiously at the empty driver's side, her eyes questioning why her friend was still outside the vehicle.

"Can you hear it?" Kier asked, pressing her hands over her ears. Gabbie frowned, puzzled, her mouth tightened as the edge of alarm crept into her expression. Her head rolled from side to side, searching for sound. "Nothing but sheep," she replied.

"It's underneath," Kier told her, eyes wide with horror. "Something moving, long and heavy, scraping and shifting."

A flock of crows flew up from a nearby tree, screeching loudly and forming a black shadow overhead. Kier jumped quickly into the vehicle and immediately the unnerving noise ceased. She searched for her keys, only to realize that she had dropped them outside on the ground and climbed back down to retrieve them. A deep menacing growl assaulted her ears and filled her with a sense of dread. Quickly she got back into the vehicle and pulled the door shut; her eyes closed in relief at the quiet inside the car.

Gabbie was searching the area for any sign of movement, her back tense, her eyes steeling.

"Let's get out of here," she said tersely. "Something feels really wrong."

Kier took a deep breath and started the engine. They were back on the main road within minutes. At first neither woman spoke and Kier glanced at the satnav that showed they needed to follow the same road for several miles.

"Whatever it was, it's foul," Kier told her.

"Did it feel like....?" Gabbie hesitated, struggling to say the name neither of them had spoken since the previous year.

"Like Nephragm?" Kier asked, her expression hardening. She shook her head, "No, I don't think it was Nephragm."

"Evan might know," suggested Gabbie thoughtfully and Kier nodded.

"Maybe it was nothing to do with us, there are old mines in this part of Wales. I could have overreacted."

Gabbie smiled, "That would explain it," she agreed, turning her face towards the side window, ending the conversation that had brought little reassurance to either of them.

An hour later blue sky had started to break through in earnest and the pair began to feel more at ease, as the fog disappeared to reveal a richly shaded patchwork of green fields that stretched for miles on both sides of the road. Hedgerows divided the pastures and the ground rose in the distance to form a steep hill, sharp-angled and firm against the undulating landscape. Gradually the road became more winding as it climbed higher and Gabbie let out a hoot of delight as a red kite circled in full view of the vehicle, its distinctive black wing tips and forked tail spreading out above them.

"It's so beautiful," she said, her eyes drinking in the wide expanse of rolling hills that allowed the light to play along waves of ridges and hidden hollows. Kier smiled her agreement and wound down the window to breathe in the fragrant landscape. It was obvious now that they were heading towards Aberystwyth and on impulse Kier turned off the road at a sign for Devil's Bridge. She leaned over to turn down the sound on the small screen that flashed 'recalculating' across its surface. Gabbie mimicked the satnav's Scottish drawl. "Continue straight on. Keep right," she repeated as Kier veered left up the narrow road. Kier laughed, "No fun, these satnavs."

"U-turn at the next opportunity," continued Gabbie in a good rendition of an early James Bond.

Kier winked at her friend, "You know I find all the best places getting lost," she told her. "Let's take a look and then I promise I'll get back on the straight and narrow!"

Gabbie laughed and pulled a baseball cap from her jeans pocket and muffled the sounds from the vocal square display. Kier steered them up the narrow road and then eventually downhill where she stopped in front of a large hotel, its tall stone covered in ivy. It was still very early as they got out of the car, spotting the 'Devil's Bridge' sign just by the building. Kier imagined that the place would later be packed with visitors; now their footsteps echoed in the empty valley as they made their way onto a bridge straddling over a spectacular gorge.

Peering through the metal trellising on either side of the narrow, wooden bridge, they were able to view a winding tumble of stairs that led to the bottom of the falls. In the centre of the gorge the high initial descent of the waterfall was occluded by trees. Kier guessed that there had been an unusually dry spell, as posters on the railings showed that a forceful rush of water was usually visible from where they now stood. Even so she was thrilled by the tumbling cascade that cut through the steep slope of the cliff and collected in foaming pockets at intervals along the way.

"What a shame, it's too early," Gabbie shouted over from the revolving metal bars at the entrance to the attraction, now firmly locked. A sign 'Mynach Falls' gave details of the separately named segments of the tourist attraction and Kier's fascination grew as it described 'Jacob's ladder', 'Robbers' Cave' and 'Ravens' Rock'.

"We wouldn't have had time now anyway," she said sighing, "but I'd love to come back another day and do the walk."

"Mm," agreed Gabbie staring at the plummeting melee of trees, stone, and water; each falling over the other in their descent to the bottom. "It seems so old."

Kier nodded. Moss wrapped roots bulged from the earth. Ivy dressed trunks, sturdy and weather worn, stood sentinel over the water carved passage that ran crooked down the mountain. Nearer to the channel long stretched fingers, leafless dark veins of wood, bent inwards on either side of the narrow gorge, creating a curtain of shadow that filtered the sunlight.

There was movement at the bottom of the falls and Kier leaned over, focusing on a patch of water that stirred with activity in the still morning. Gradually it became a dark whirlpool, building in intensity, finally spurting upwards and ejecting what Kier first thought was an eel, its black coils emitting a coarse, clicking sound. Instead of plummeting back into the water however, the twisted creature stretched its long body upwards until it was level with the bridge, its tail end almost touching the pool. Kier leapt back in astonishment and Gabbie turned, a puzzled expression on her face. Hovering in front of the bridge was a whip like creature, its body twisting continually beneath a calmly focused hooded head. Pale eyes stared dispassionately from a pouch of leathery dark skin, split by a fish mouth that did not struggle to breathe air. The sound, now risen to become an excited cackle, came from the intense agitation of the scaled, writhing body. The creature snapped forward as it spotted Gabbie, whirling quickly to where the young woman stood. Kier cried out and ran towards her friend but the long coils had already wound, helter skelter fashion, around Gabbie's slight figure and now hovered above her head. Kier reached her friend as the long body formed a concertina, before springing upwards to circle the gorge. There was a suspended moment when it hung Damocles-like in the sky, before plunging downwards, slicing through the water, back into the dark pool from which it had sprung. Kier reached for Gabbie's hand.

"Run," she said, tugging her friend across the bridge towards the car. As soon as they hit the road the sound Kier had heard earlier rumbled beneath her feet; the discordant cry sending both hands to her ears. She jumped as if the ground had become hot coals, pressing the unlock button on her key fob as they neared the vehicle. Kier hardly registered the moment of silence when it came, for it was quickly followed by the thunderous beating of hooves. She turned to see a massive black bull, snorting with rage, heading downhill straight towards a startled Gabbie at the back of the car. Kier yelled to her friend, breaking her frozen stare, and flung open the driver's door, flying into the seat. The key was inserted in the steering column as Gabbie launched herself into the vehicle, just as Kier hit the accelerator and pulled out onto the road. Gabbie banged the door shut and turned a fearful face to the back window where the bull was now inches from the boot. Kier had her foot flat to the floor as she negotiated the winding hill by the river but the huge animal, foaming and steaming, still raged behind them. Gabbie screamed in alarm as she turned to see the car heading too fast for a sharp bend, but at the last possible moment Kier turned the wheel. The vehicle lurched to the left, staggering on two wheels as it rounded the corner. The huge creature behind, its nose almost touching the boot as she turned, blasted into the shoulder high stone wall that crumbled beneath the force and weight of the beast. The animal wailed as it careered over the cliff edge down to the river below. Gabbie was yelling for the car to be stopped but Kier focused on checking her mirrors and looking up towards the sky, as she pushed the RAV4 too fast down the narrow road.

"Wo!" Gabbie protested as they rounded another bend and almost spun out of control. "Please Kier!"

She slowed the vehicle marginally and looked across at Gabbie's white face.

"We should have stopped, got in touch with the farmer," her friend admonished. She had grown up in semi-rural Bankside and knew that a bull of that size and strength would have been a major investment for the farmer. "The creature must have gone berserk!" Her voice was shaking.

Kier brought the RAV4 down to a normal speed, but her chin was still set, and her eyes flicked back and forth through the mirrors. Gabbie finally pulled on her seat belt and slowed her breathing.

"Thank God, you heard it coming! That animal was going to mow us down."

Kier's brow furrowed. "Didn't you see it?" she asked.

"Not 'til it was trying to get in the car with us!" Gabbie shook her head.

"Not the bull, the creature at the falls."

"What?" Gabbie's brow wrinkled, and her eyes squinted. She shook her head. "What creature?"

Kier grimaced. "It came out of the bottom pool, a bit like an eel, only longer. It had a face," she said, her mouth pinching in distaste, "and it coiled around you...I thought it was going to strike."

The colour drained from Gabbie's face. "Kier, I didn't see or feel anything," she said quietly, her expression strained and frightened as the RAV4 again slowed and they rejoined the main road. Kier, shocked, concentrated on steering the Jeep, still fearful that the strange creature from the falls would reappear. Deep down she had been expecting something. She knew that the events of the previous year had only paused and now she felt plunged again, not only into physical threat, but also into the internal confusion of experiences that seemed to single her out. The creature at the falls had the same tainted feel that she had known only too well in Whistmorden. What frightened her most was that it had ignored her completely and seemed so interested in Gabbie. The sudden attack by the bull had to be linked.

It was a matter of urgency now to get to Evan. The satnav showed another fifty minutes to the unknown destination, as she impatiently slowed her speed through Aberystwyth, barely noticing the university town that her companion seemed to find so appealing.

"We'll come back, I promise," Kier said apologetically, as Gabbie turned her head towards the rows of shop-filled streets; many businesses just opening their doors as they passed. A glimpse of coastline bordering the streets signalled that she needed to follow the road towards the southwest. Gabbie nodded, understanding, and smiling at her friend but Kier's eyes were still searching her mirrors as she manoeuvred, without stopping, through the beautiful seaside town.

The road widened and an earnest blue sky welcomed them to this popular tourist area. The sea was barely visible across the fields as Kier accelerated, but she could see the white line of light where water and sky melded together. There was no sign of pursuit, but she was grateful when the satnav took them inland on a more circuitous route through quiet villages and off the main roads.

"I think we must be heading for somewhere called 'Pont o Ffrindiau' commented Gabbie in a rolling Welsh accent. "Bridge of friends," she translated with a nod of approval. "The satnav is saying three miles left and that sign back there said it was three miles to the town."

"You're right," Kier said shortly afterwards, as the road took them into the centre of Pont o Ffrindiau, undaunted as she read the name that would be unpronounceable to most English people but she, like Gabbie had a quick grasp of languages. On their left, above a sloping lawn, was an impressive grey, turreted old building with rows of symmetrical latticed windows that might have been transplanted from Oxford. A sign told her that it was indeed a university.

"What an unusual campus," she mused as she negotiated the road into the small town and turned left onto the main street. Gabbie nodded absently, watching the route on the screen in front. A little further on the Scottish drawl took them off the main road and down a narrow lane with wooded areas on either side, where the voice finally announced, "You have reached your destination." Kier looked along the high stone wall to her left.

"There," Gabbie pointed. "I can see a driveway by that tree." White blossom covered the road, the trembling petals had been scattered by a large tree on one side of a wide gateway. Opposite the gap, on a metal plate attached to the wall, there was a name.

"Y Wasgod Oren." Gabbie laughed excitedly. "It means orange waistcoat," she explained. "That could only be Evan."

Kier smiled, remembering the flamboyantly coloured materials that the Welshman wore around his middle. Carefully she turned the car into the driveway.

"His wife, Bethan, made them," said Gabbie quietly. "She embroidered special words into the waistband, they were for luck when Evan entered the Eisteddfod. The orange one said 'Afon dawel' or 'Quiet river' in English," she sighed softly. "It was the name of their first home."

Kier looked over at Gabbie's thoughtful face, realising for the first time how close she had been to her old employer, who had lost his wife to cancer some years ago.

The track was shaded by overhanging trees and alongside it, to their right, was a narrow stretch of river that meandered its way downhill, burrowing underneath the road and out into the valley. A sudden flood of sunlight took them by surprise as they entered a wide space surrounded by sloping hills. In the centre of the space was a large, white stone building, three storeys high that rambled outwards into several small, attached dwellings. Immediately Kier was reminded of the old bookshop, which had spread out onto the street and was filled with rambling nooks and crannies, all of which she eventually realised were ruled by their own eccentric internal logic.

"We're definitely in the right place," announced Gabbie laughing.

Chapter Five

Evan came out of the panelled oak doorway as Gabbie reached the entrance and with a booming of Welsh greetings his strong arms easily hoisted the slight figure upwards, swinging her round in an enthusiastic circle. A golden retriever tumbled out alongside their old friend, eagerly bounding towards Kier.

"Come back Herald," Evan told the soft eyed, excited hound, who reluctantly lay down at his feet. Evan grinned widely as he turned back to his visitor.

"Hello Gabrielle," his rich rolling voice intoned, "I've missed my little blodyn." Gabbie hugged him fiercely and then turned back towards the car. Kier smiled warmly at the man who was to be her host for the second time. He moved forwards to meet her, enfolding her slim figure in a bone-crunching embrace.

In his mid-fifties, Evan Gwyn was still fiercely strong; it seemed to Kier that he appeared younger and leaner than when they had been in Pulton. His thick, dusted grey hair, was longer and even more unruly, giving him a boyishness that he had not possessed when she had known him previously. Grey eyes sparkled in a summer-brown face as he watched Kier lean over to his dog who was panting hard, straining to be noticed. Herald gave a small yelp as she stroked the soft head.

"You must be hungry," he said, his two arms perched around the girls' shoulders. "Come inside."

Herald waited dutifully until Evan had passed and then he followed, snuggling his face into Kier's open hand.

"Wow," exclaimed Gabbie entering the hall and discovering the beamed ceiling, through which wound a black metal spiral staircase. A series of wooden latched doors lined the walls either side. At the end of the corridor Kier glimpsed a large farmhouse kitchen with herbs trailing from a wooden rail above a modern central workstation.

"It's an old wool textile mill," Evan told them, "It was converted in the fifties, and I bought it about ten years ago. My daughter has let it out as a holiday home since and generally managed the place."

"It was definitely easier than managing you."

Kier smiled at the striking woman who came from the kitchen and spoke in an even more pronounced North Wales accent than Evan.

"My daughter, Angharad," he said proudly, placing an arm around her shoulder. She was in her thirties and looked at them with Evan's grey eyes. Short dark hair framed her face, and she was holding a tea towel in her hands. There was a homeliness and an air of efficiency about the stocky figure who wore a green tunic with a number of pegs attached to one side.

"Da said you might be arriving today, and you've made good time."

"It's lovely to meet you," Kier said warmly as she took Angharad's hand and allowed herself to be ushered into the kitchen. The smell of garlic and rosemary stirred her appetite and Evan went to check pans that were filled to the brim with a mouth-watering stew. He reached up to the rail of dried herbs and added a handful of basil to the pot. Evan nodded towards the other side of the kitchen where a large maple table filled the space.

"Get yourself seated," he instructed. "There's a pot of coffee and some of Angharad's biscuits to keep you going. We'll eat later when you're all here."

The two visitors sat down at the table that was set, Kier noticed, for eight people. Angharad reached over to the worktop behind and placed a jug of filtered coffee with a plate of oatmeal biscuits in front of them.

"I'll take you to your rooms when you've had a drink," she said.

"Mmm," Gabbie told Evan's daughter, "these are seriously good."

Angharad smiled, "It's quite a journey you've made," she commented. "I'm looking forward to hearing all about Australia. I'm trying to persuade Da to come with us on a holiday out there."

Evan looked at his daughter and Kier thought he would be hard pushed to say no to anything she asked.

"We'll see," he told her smiling.

"Australia was great," Gabbie told her, on her second biscuit, "but there's nowhere like home."

"When are the other's arriving?" asked Kier.

"Where's Swift?" said Gabbie before Evan had a chance to answer.

Content that the meal was on course Evan sat down at the table. Angharad excused herself to continue her preparations for their guests.

"Josh arrived yesterday, and he is with Swift in town. They're doing some shopping for me," their host explained.

"Marianne and Matthew?" asked Kier.

To her disappointment, Evan shook his head. "The lad has not told his parents he has been summoned. He says he will not risk his mother again."

Kier nodded, "Nor me Gally," she replied, and Evan's expression told her that he had already guessed as much.

"But what about Klim and Siskin?" Gabbie asked him.

Evan lifted his eyes to hold those of the young woman's and Gabbie placed her coffee carefully on the table, aware of a slight tremble in her hand.

"We were unable to reach them until a few days ago. Swift was lying quietly on her bed, and she heard Klim speaking. He has, it would seem, developed his gift."

Gabbie's brow dipped as Evan spoke of the link that Klim had forged with Swift, her initial ebullience now vanished.

"What did he say?" she asked tonelessly.

"That he and Siskin had succeeded in infiltrating an organisation operating out of a coffee plantation in Nicaragua. The organisation they work for is called *Red Light.*" Evan looked round at the two women who nodded their understanding. Kier remembered that Echin had initiated the setting up of this organisation to stop human trafficking.

"Well," Evan continued, "Klim told Swift that the organisation was trying to get them out of the country alive."

Gabbie gasped, her eyes wide with apprehension.

"It's alright," Evan continued, "I should have said first that they arrived back in England yesterday, but we don't know when they're coming to us."

Gabbie sighed with relief as Angharad entered from a utility area in the corner of the kitchen carrying a pile of clean towels and the young woman stood up.

"Is it alright if I go and clean up?" she asked Evan's daughter.

"Of course," Angharad replied, placing the laundry at the end of the table. "I'll take you to your room."

Evan began to rise, presuming that both his guests were leaving the kitchen but Kier reached up to touch his arm. He looked at the serious expression on her face and reseated himself at the table. Kier waited until the other two women had left the kitchen and then gave Evan an account of the journey from the airport, carefully describing the strange creature that she had seen at

Devil's Bridge.

"Ach, I do not know what this thing is," he told her, shaking his head.

"It was Echin who told us to gather here, yes?" she asked him tentatively.

"Yes," he nodded. "He sent me word to summon you all. He has a unique way of contacting me."

He pointed to a square frame on the wall behind Kier. She turned to view an unusual mineral-encrusted mural.

"It used to be in the bookshop cellar," he told her. "A Stozcist feels the vibration and alteration in the stones, to me it's as clear as if Echin were here in the kitchen. Though I keep telling him I prefer email," he added with a wry smile.

"And Swift?" she asked him. "As another Stozcist. She hears him too?"

Evan hesitated for a few seconds; his grey eyes inscrutable.

"She can do things I could never have contemplated," he told Kier, his face shining with awe.

"In Japan, I sat with her as the earth trembled beneath us and watched her reach to the ground and whisper to the rock so that it stilled again. She worked tirelessly, coaxing the earth to reveal the broken bodies of the earthquake victims." His eyes were pain-filled with memory. "Her gift far surpasses my own."

It was a simple statement of fact, without any hint of regret. He paused and looked up to the mural, "But no, strangely it seems that the glitter box was made specifically for me and only I can translate its meaning."

"Glitter box?" Kier repeated looking puzzled and amused.

"It's what Angharad named it as a little girl. Echin calls it a 'crysonance' but like me, she prefers glitter box."

He lowered his voice. "She knows nothing about the Myriar, nor about my work as a Stozcist. I made the decision long ago that my family would not be brought into danger because of my gift." There was a sadness, Kier thought, in his eyes.

"She'll be leaving tomorrow to get back to the children. When I said I was coming down here she wanted to show me everything she'd done with the house. All she knows is that you are friends from Pulton, gathered for a reunion."

Kier nodded, "I'll mention it to Gabbie," she reassured him. They had become so used to avoiding speaking about the events of last year that she knew that Gabbie would say nothing in response to the reserve that Evan had already shown. She turned to examine the strange mosaic, seeing the intricate way each mineral wove around the others, leaving no gaps in between the richly coloured gems. The pure white quartz that filled much of the background gave off a subtle glow that would be more pronounced, she was sure, when the room was in darkness. She remembered the last time that she had sat at Evan's table in Pulton, just hours before plunging into the darkest hours of her life. Evan was the last bastion against the tide of uncertainty. Impulsively, she leaned over and kissed his cheek. He sat back and put his hand where she had laid her lips.

"And now I won't be washing for a week," he grinned and there was the faintest hint of a blush.

"I'd best go and get cleaned up," she told him, suddenly feeling extremely tired, "and I might close my eyes for a bit if that's okay."

Angharad appeared on cue.

"Of course, it's ok," she told her. "I'll take you up."

Chapter Six

Kier followed Angharad up the spiral staircase onto the second landing. There were a number of latched, wooden doors mirroring those she had seen beneath; her companion nodded towards one on the right.

"Your friend is just opposite," she informed Kier, opening the door to reveal a room meticulously clean and cosy with hand-crafted rugs scattered over a wooden floor. The window was small, looking out over a woodland that toppled towards a large lawn at the back of the house. Kier was delighted to find a small vase of sweet peas placed on the mahogany dressing table, their scent fresh and welcoming. The room had its own simple en suite bathroom and was perfect for holiday letting.

"It's lovely," she told Angharad.

"It was Echin who found the place and showed it to Da. Of course, anything Echin liked Da was bound to find wonderful." Kier turned and looked sharply at Angharad, who sighed and shook her head.

"My husband left after Llinos was born." Her face did not invite sympathy or comment, she was simply stating a fact. Kier nodded slightly, trying to convey with her eyes that she understood the grief of rejection.

"All I know is I was without my Da, my mum dead and with little ones to bring up. It's great to have him here again but neither I nor my children will ever be able to compete with the wonderful Echin in Dad's eyes."

"Your father adores you Angharad," Kier said gently and her companion laughed self mockingly.

"I know, just ignore me," she said smiling. "It's just that you all seem so mysterious. I can't help feeling that everyone else seems to know more about my father than me. And Echin clicks his fingers and Da is suddenly hosting a reunion. He's only been home from Japan for a couple of weeks." Tension grated in her voice.

"He hasn't worked his magic on you then?" Kier asked gently. "Echin, I mean."

Angharad was vaguely aware that just the mention of his name had made Kier's eyes fill with emotion. The two women sat side by side on the bed and it was Angharad's turn to scrutinise her companion.

"Oh dear," she said smiling. "Another devotee."

"He's like no one else," Kier continued, somehow able to say to Angharad what she had not dared to share with even Gally, as if the other woman's distinct lack of enthusiasm made it easier. Angharad laughed, "Well someday maybe I'll meet this man!" Kier look surprised and Evan's daughter explained.

"He was around when I was little apparently, but I don't remember, and I've never met him since. But even so, he's been a major influence on our lives."

Angharad stood up, she seemed about to say something else but then appeared to think better of it.

"I hope we can talk some more before I go," she said, moving towards the door.

"Me too," replied Kier sincerely.

Within five minutes of being alone she was lost in sleep.

*

It was another dream that was no dream. The room was strange but innocuous, some kind of village hall where she might have been helping to serve a hotpot supper. It was the kind of event her mother would have organised. Kier was dressed in a blouse and skirt and had milled around the various families, chatting easily, ensuring the tables were cleared and having a sense that the event had gone as well as planned. Gratefully, exhaustion making her limbs weak, she came to sit back at the table, waving goodbye as people started to leave. It seemed so natural that the place opposite was taken by the long faced, small eyed woman whose hair was the colour of dried blood and whose dull, waxen face gave an impression of ill health. Kier barely registered the thought that there was something out of place with the stranger when the cold, colourless eyes rounded on her with shuddering, painful force. She felt herself floundering, dazed, as the woman scraped her being with talons of fierce will, searching to know her. Somewhere, beneath the dream, in the reality of attack, Kier remembered the way Alex Jackson had pummelled her mind. She recalled Echin's gentle instructions on how to shield herself from this kind of invasion. Slowly she visualised the protective shell around her mind, breaking away the groping tentacles of thought that had seized her, using her own power and will to repel the invasion. The forced waking brought a haze of light that stung wide open eyes. She sat up and raised her hands across damp skin as the noonday sun flooded the bedroom. It did little to relieve the chill within. Excited voices could be heard in the hall downstairs and Kier tried to dismiss a wave of sickness. She went to the bathroom and splashed water on her face, pale beneath the Aussie tan, and flattened down the stray hairs from her long plait.

Gabbie was already downstairs and Kier, descending the spiral staircase, could see her friend's face looking as vulnerable and unsure as she had been in the Seven Rivers, twelve months previously. As she reached the bottom, Josh and Swift turned to greet her. Josh, just a little younger than Kier in his early twenties, had lost the blond waves in favour of a closely cut hairstyle that emphasised even more the fine bones of his face. His easy smile was unchanged as he hugged her.

"Good to see you," he told her mid squeeze.

"And you," she replied.

Kier turned towards Swift and began to understand the lost look she had seen on Gabbie's face. The same age as Gabbie, Swift, who had been taken by Alex Jackson from her home in Peru, now dwarfed the other young women. She had grown at least four inches in the last twelve months and was simply statuesque. She wore skinny white trousers that emphasised her long legs and a pale green crop top revealed a slim brown midriff. Jet black hair dropped straight to her shoulders. Swift's eyes were dark orbs that flashed purposely in a face that was as beautiful as it seemed remote. Kier embraced the girl now turned woman.

"You've grown," she told her.

Swift smiled, "It's so good to have you both back." she said warmly, her Spanish accent emphasising the exotic sheen of her beauty. Evan appeared at the kitchen doorway.

"Lunch is ready," he announced, and they all huddled down the corridor into the kitchen.

Over the next couple of hours, they sat around the table exchanging news, but as Angharad was with them the conversation did not touch upon the Myriar, or the more dangerous aspects of their lives. Kier completely understood the resigned disappointment of Evan's daughter; she was an intelligent woman who was excluded from much of her father's life. Angharad was seeing strangers, like herself and Gabbie, laying claims of friendship with Evan that could only have been formed from a deep involvement about which she knew nothing. "We heard so much about your children last year, Angharad. How are they doing?" Kier leaned towards her over the table, smiling. The other woman smiled softly back as her father answered for her, detailing the characteristics of her young son and daughter. "Dylan bach," he said, his eyes bright, "is getting as tall as a tree."

The afternoon was rich with news of their lives, the activities that had shaped the last twelve months; all without reference to the real work that Evan and Swift had undertaken in Japan. They had come back with some rare books, the reason that Evan had given his daughter for their travelling to the East. Angharad spoke of the earthquake in Pulton the previous year that had brought her father home. Seeing the bleak look in Kier's eyes however, she quickly steered away from this and chatted more generally about the University of Pont o Ffrindiau.

"I 've had a lot of past students staying here." She glanced at her father, "Da said not to let it out this year because he might want to use it himself. How right he was." Her tone chided him for his secrets. Taking in each face she smiled warmly. "Most people hanker after their student days, but there's something special about Frindy I think."

"Is that what you all call the place? Great!" Josh laughed. "I can manage to say that!"

"Yes, it's a mouthful," Angharad smiled. "Everyone calls it

Frindy. The students say it's different from every other campus they've been on. It's old for a start, been around nearly two hundred years. It's also the smallest university in Wales. The ones that love it seem to be of a particular breed."

"Really?" asked Josh, his eyebrows raised. "What kind of breed?" Angharad's brow furrowed in thought, "Open," she told them.

"To what?" he asked her.

"To the place," she replied simply. She stood up and started clearing the table, ending the conversation but then returned to her seat when Swift spoke for the first time, Kier realised, since the meal had started.

"It's a place of deep stone. There are lines that meet here and rivers that protect, and those that knock on the windows can't come in."

Angharad smiled gently at Swift's idiosyncratic statement. There was a surprising deference in her attitude to Swift, considering that more than anyone else the young woman might be seen to be supplanting Evan's own family in time and affection.

"You're certainly right about the old stone," Angharad replied. "They say Stonehenge was cut from the rocks in these hills and there's something about Frindy being at the centre of a number of ley lines."

"What's ley lines?" asked Gabbie.

"I think they're some kind of connection between sacred sites across the land," Josh told her. "One of those New Age things."

"Not only New Age Josh," Kier found herself recalling from somewhere. "The theory's been around since the 1920s, I think."

"And probably long before," added Evan.

"Well, that's settled," Kier said. "Definitely some exploring on the cards I think!" Angharad shooed them away from the sink and refused offers of help as they left the table. Her glance fell on Swift who remained sitting after the others had gone, her eyes far away, her hand resting below her throat.

Chapter Seven

Josh drove and Kier opted for the back seat, happy to be a passenger. Gabbie, with her usual efficiency, had quickly arranged for him to be added to the hire car insurance. She sat in the front, commenting enthusiastically as Josh took them through the small market town and then out of the valley onto the hilltops. Swift sat in the back, content to say nothing, while Kier sleepily watched the panoramic views unfold.

"Why've we been brought back?" Gabbie asked.

"No idea," Josh replied, steering round a tight bend. "Since our three friends disappeared after Whistmorden, this is the first contact Echin's made as far as I know. Is that right Swift?"

He looked in the mirror, but Swift had not been listening and he had to repeat the question before she realised that he was talking to her.

"Has Echin been in touch with Evan since we left?"

She shook her head, "Not until just recently. He just said to pull everyone together and come down to the house at Pont o Ffrindiau. Apparently, he'd told Evan in Pulton that keeping the house free this summer would be a good idea, long before the earthquake. We've only been here a few days ourselves.

Angharad has worked really hard to get everything ready for you coming, as the house hasn't been used since last year."

"You seem to be close," Kier ventured.

"We are," Swift replied matter-of-factly.

"Hmm." Josh glanced at his mirror. "That Celica, the slick looking one."

"The Silver one?" Gabbie prompted, glancing back. Josh nodded in response, his eyes scrutinising the rear mirror. Kier turned towards the wing mirror, where she caught the glimmer of a silver car a little distance behind. Josh slowed the RAV4, pulling towards the inside of the wide road, but the Celica remained behind them.

"Looks dodgy," she agreed, leaning forwards, and pointing. "There's a left-hand turn coming up."

The Celica was much closer now, just one man driving, but Kier had the impression of lean and mean. Josh turned in without signalling and glanced back to see the Celica carry on past the junction. Kier realised they were driving through a small village that consisted basically of one road. A Welsh name registered somewhere in her brain. A little further down she pointed to an incredibly gnarled and tortuous tree, covered in ivy. It looked as if it had been chopped at one stage but then had regrown. The result was that it was stunted, topped by a mop of tightly closed leaves with one long, untidy branch, which pointed away from the road and above a small space.

"Pull in here Josh," she directed automatically, feeling a familiar prickling of the skin on her back.

The tree was in the middle of a paved courtyard between two buildings, both of which seemed to be derelict. In fact, there was little sign of life in the village as a whole.

"There's room at the back," she told him, her eyes scanning the small area. Josh manoeuvred the RAV4 behind a van that was parked sideways at the front of the courtyard, leaving space for a vehicle behind. It too looked abandoned, its colour a faded white with rust spots around the door.

"Look there's a gate into a churchyard." Gabbie pointed towards an entrance that was hidden from the road by the tree and parked van.

"Keep down," warned Josh as they tumbled out of the RAV4, now completely hidden from the road behind the white van. They gathered behind the bigger vehicle as the silver car made a hasty run through the village. Deep sighs of held breath were audible as the small group acknowledged the angry revving of the Celica's engine, loud in the quiet afternoon, as it ploughed onto the main road at the end of the junction. Gabbie straightened her small body and seemed intrigued by the untidy patch of land behind a short row of houses, into which the small courtyard gave entrance. She was heading towards the path when Josh called to her.

"Gabbie, come back, we can get back onto the road and head out of the village in the other direction," he suggested. "They might head back this way if they can't find us."

Swift had also turned towards the path and was almost level with Gabbie.

"We need to stay here," she stated simply, turning briefly towards Kier and Josh before continuing to follow Gabbie, who had not responded to Josh's call.

Josh shrugged his shoulders and locked the vehicle. Kier was already through the forlorn looking entrance gate that had seen better days. In moments, she had caught up with Swift whose dark, exotic face was alive with concentration.

"There's a stone here, it's calling us," she told them.

A small path led to a church that may or may not have been in use. Kier was intrigued by the mixture of recent care to the building and the abandoned impression given by the grounds. The main door was locked but in good repair. A polished wooden, as yet unused door had been fitted at the side of the building. Closer inspection showed that the windows had been repainted and the brickwork repointed, giving clear signs of recent care. Not so the small graveyard that surrounded the church. It was overrun with long established growth, unfettered trails of ivy and moss split the trunks of the older trees to form miniature forests between torn bark. There was no sign of any new graves, and the words on most of the gravestones were barely visible.

Kier felt her heart lift as she moved behind the church to

find that the small village was at the top of a valley. A soft green and gold blanket of grassy countryside unfolded beneath the mellow light of a clear blue sky. Swift called to the scattered group and led them round to the other side of the building. The peculiar sight of a cone-shaped rooftop, inclusive of an old weathervane, was sitting in an overgrown patch of grass. Looking back towards the old building, it appeared that the spire had been removed from the church to make way for a newer. castle style turret. The spire was approximately ten feet tall and surrounded by a makeshift wooden fence, easily straddled by Swift's long legs. She signalled to Josh and in moments she was on his shoulders, examining the weathered stone underneath the top of the now redundant spire. Kier and Gabbie watched with interest as she spoke to Josh and then lifted her feet onto his shoulders in a precarious balance, which seemed little effort to either of them. Swift leant against the wall and reached up to the top of the weathervane. A few minutes later she jumped down, her face triumphant as she held out a luminous ruddy brown, almost red stone.

"It was lodged in the eye of the vane," she told them.

"The spire was torn off two years ago in a gale and it's going to be moved next week. I said we needed to be here!" Swift's eyes were bright as she examined the stone, "Its jasper," she informed them.

"Swift how do you know all this?" Kier asked gently.

"I can speak to the minestraals," she told them. "Well, not exactly speak to them but I'm aware of what they know about the stone."

"Straals?" Gabbie repeated thoughtfully. "Echin said they saved me from the earthquake the night they spoke through my radio."

"Straals are alive. They're quicker than thought and pass through every substance on the planet, apart from what we know as living creatures. Even the things we think of as inanimate constantly have Straals passing through," Swift instructed. "Sometimes when they come together in big numbers, they can make things happen, but mostly they just reflect what's going on with whatever they've been in."

Once again Kier reflected how much Swift had grown. This statuesque woman seemed to have little resemblance to the fragile girl they had known last year.

Gabbie had not taken her eyes of the rust-coloured jewel in the other woman's palm. Turning towards her Swift held out her hand, "It's yours Gabbie. It's meant for you."

Gabbie shook her head as if she'd just woken up.

"What do you mean?" she said, her eyes wrenching themselves away from the stone to Swift's face.

"It calls for you, I just knew its voice."

She held out her hand further and the tiny blonde, her blue eyes wide, picked up the stone and then gasped as its colour deepened to a rich flame. Kier felt, for the first time, that she understood what Swift meant when she said some stones were alive. The only other time she had seen anything like it was the very one that Josh now produced from under his T-shirt, the rose pink Chalycion that had belonged to Marianne. The Chalycion pulsed with light that bounced in and out of the tiny pink veins that covered its surface.

"It's greeting 'Arwres,' that's what this piece of jasper is called," Swift explained. At another time Kier would have expected to see Gabbie's eyes roll in amusement at this statement, but instead they had come alight with a joy she had only seen on rare occasions and never whilst they had been away.

"I can't believe it's for me," she said haltingly.

"It knows your name and it's just as excited to find you, as you are to find it," Swift said, her momentary girlish excitement now lapsing to the grave seriousness that seemed to have become so characteristic of her.

Gabbie closed her hand tightly around the stone and put it inside her jeans pocket, her hand still remaining tight around it as they began to head back to the car. Kier put her arm around her friend's shoulder.

"Maybe there's a tiny sword going to come out of it, and you'll be crowned Queen Arthuria of all Wales," she whispered.

Gabbie laughed, "Well 'Arwres' does mean heroine in Welsh," she told her. Kier looked impressed. "And Swift's doing a friggin' good impression of Merlin," her companion added.

Kier let a smile touch the corners of her mouth as they headed towards the gate.

Chapter Eight

On the way out of the graveyard Kier noticed a particularly wide
weathered stone, almost hidden by the leaves of an ancient oak.
Even from several yards away however, the engraving on its
surface was clear. Steering Gabbie towards the oak tree, she could
now clearly see a double headstone beneath it, framed in ivy that
trailed down to form a V-shape in the middle. The stone looked
almost majestic amidst the array of its toppling and worn
companions. The script was copperplate and as they drew nearer
to the bold lettering, Kier felt the touch of that other world, one
that seemed to speak only to her. She read aloud:
"Here, unknown, and unnoticed we stand guard against those who
harvest shadow, the Virenmor. They will come with the
awakening of Arwres, their intent to crush the Seeds of Hope.
Know that where ivy and moss mark the boundary, they cannot
enter."
Swift and Josh had reached the gate as Kier 's command rang out,
stopping them even as Josh's hand rested on the wood.
"Stop! Stay within the churchyard," she shouted clearly.
Josh, hearing the note of alarm in Kier's voice went to turn back

but over his hand was suddenly another. Pock marked, thin fingers wrenched his wrist and pulled him back towards the gate. And then they were visible.

"What the?" Gabbie began, as she followed Kier towards Josh. Swift now stood with her hands around his waist in a gruesome tug of war. Josh had wedged his feet against the wall beside the gate but already he was in agony, as his hand was clawed towards the exit. Kier shivered as she saw the whole, loathsome bodies of the creatures that surrounded the small graveyard. If they had not been holding Josh with such fierceness, she would have thought them some kind of illusion.

Covering every space along the perimeter of the graveyard there stood grim figures scrolled in ash. Tall, man-sized bodies, covered in grey flakes of skin that hissed with movement. Black beaked heads on long, mobile necks framed eyes that were vaguely human, all vicious. Then the creature that held Josh's hand spoke with a human voice, excited with discovery.

"The Creta!" she yelled. "Take his hand off!"

Immediately they flocked around Josh's outstretched hand, and he screamed in pain as the razor-sharp beaks tore at his hand. Kier moved fast, digging her fingers in the soil by the wall and picking up a handful of trailing ivy and moss, mixing them together. Momentarily she looked into the small pale eyes of the blood-stained, beaked face. Shocked, she recognised the woman in her dream. Kier lifted her cupped hands full of the mixture and threw it directly into the creature's eyes. With a wail the figure disappeared, just vanished. Kier could hear the sound of screeching, a wreathed gathering of voices united in panic.

Josh floored Swift and Gabbie as he fell backwards, released from the hold. Kier was already putting together more of the soil mixture and instructed her companions to do the same as they scrambled towards her. Soon Swift and Gabbie were flinging the moss, soil, and ivy at the figures, managing to hit and destroy those who were not yet out of range. Most of the creatures had moved a little distance away from the wall, as Kier led the others back to the double gravestone. The lichen covered oak provided a canopy as they stood behind the stone, giving some relief from the malevolent gaze that now replaced the open view of the valley and covered every inch of the graveyard's border.

"Josh!" Gabbie cried as she saw the torn right hand that he cradled.

There were deep puncture wounds around his wrist, and the flesh on his hand was severely torn, down to the bone in parts. It bled profusely as Josh took off his T-shirt with Kier's help. Unable to hold the limb, as her hands were covered in soil, Swift peered intently at the swollen and damaged flesh.

"I don't think it's broken Josh. Thank God you were so quick Kier."

Josh turned to her and nodded his thanks, smiling weakly as he wrapped the T-shirt around his hand.

"How did you know?" he asked her.

Kier pointed to the front of the gravestone and they trailed round to read the inscription. It was no longer there. Only faded markings, slightly indented the worn surface of the old stone.

"I saw it," attested Gabbie. "I saw the writing, but it didn't make any sense to me." Swift put her hand on the stone and her brow furrowed in concentration.

"There's something there, very deeply hidden, and it's very strong. It won't be drawn, not now."

Kier turned to Gabbie, "We need to remember the words," she said, her lips silently recalling the exact content that had now disappeared.

"Maybe there was something else in the inscription to help us?" Josh offered.

Kier, her eyes closed, reciting the lines that she had read and then looked to Gabbie who nodded confirmation.

"It said," Kier explained, looking at the puzzled faces, "that when Gabbie was given the stone it would sound some kind of alert for the Virenmor," she quoted. "Which I guess would be our attractive friends! It also said that where moss and ivy bordered the graveyard they could not enter."

"So basically, the whole place then," commented Josh, relieved as his eyes roamed the perimeter of the graveyard. They all tried to avoid the oppressive shadow of the unwanted audience.

"You were quick to know the stuff that would hurt them Kier."
She had known instinctively, in a split second, the importance of
what she had read. She nodded and let her mouth curve into a
grateful smile.

"What now?" Josh asked.

Kier shook her head as she tried to concentrate her thoughts.

"We're losing the light," Swift commented as the sky became a
shade darker and a mild wind rustled through the tangled foliage.
The young Stozcist stiffened. She closed her eyes for a short time
and then jerked them open, her long limbs moving.

"We need to move towards the gate," she instructed firmly.
The other three, uncertain, followed her along the path as the
Virenmor crowded around the gate. Kier signalled to Josh for the
keys to the vehicle as he nursed his injured hand, passing the keys
to her with the other, grimacing in pain. The creatures by the gate
were hemmed in by the old van and Kier's car. Each one reeled in
shock as they were suddenly attacked from behind. Kier blinked
in surprise and joy as she saw Klim and Siskin heading towards
them.

"Run!" Klim yelled as he leapt, his feet connecting with one of
the gruesome creatures that had rushed in to block the gate.
He was dressed in a black vest and pants and looked leaner and
taller than when Kier had first seen him. He swirled a metal
chain, at the end of which were two heavy globes that decimated
the surrounding figures; one of which vanished with each

rhythmic blow. Siskin was there on the other side, hair hidden under a close-fitting black hat, holding a long rod that rotated smoothly and with a similarly devastating effect. Kier followed closely behind the others as they ran through the path that Klim and Siskin forged for them. As Kier raised the key fob on the hire car Siskin came close behind her, followed by Klim, both still wielding their weapons.

"Not yours," he told her. "Head for mine."

It was then Kier realised that the RAV 4 had been disabled, all four tyres were slashed. On the road was a long, black BMW four by four, windows darkened. Siskin raised his hand towards it just before Swift opened the door and jumped in. Josh was helped by the girls into the back of the vehicle as Kier saw one of the Virenmor lunge towards her. She covered her face, but Siskin swung the rod upwards to pierce the carrion features, giving her time to get in. She watched tensely as the two men fought their way to the front of the vehicle and sighed with relief when she realised that they were actually moving.

Kier braced herself for piercing glass and ripped tyres. The Virenmor had formed a tight circle around the vehicle. Siskin pressed a button and they all bounced backwards. The Virenmor jumped back in surprise and the car moved quickly forwards, manoeuvring through a gap. The Virenmor remained in position, clearly unaware that Siskin was now driving the vehicle back the way that they had first entered the village. Some part of Kier's mind registered that there were no lights in the small cottages, no people coming out to stare. The village was deserted.

"They're not following," she announced in amazement, as she turned towards the others sitting in front of her. "But our car!" she remembered.

"Sorted," answered Siskin. "They won't get in or be able to find anything that'll trace it back. I'll arrange for it to be picked up in a few days."

"How?" she asked.

"He has surrounded it with sound that they can't hear, and it distorts everything so that it can't be touched," Klim told her.

"Oh," she replied looking around curiously, having no clue as to what Klim meant.

Kier had climbed into the long seat at the back beside Gabbie, and until now had not noticed the interior of the car. It was like nothing she had ever seen before. Shocked, she realised that Klim and Siskin were perched on swivel seats, like those she had bought for the office. The dashboard was more like a plane's control panel than a car and she could see no pedals or handbrake. There were strange looking devices implanted into the roof and the doors, like tiny ceiling lights that flickered slightly. The engine was not only smooth, but it was also silent, the main sound being the tyres rolling bicycle like on the tarmac. Klim, on the passenger side was facing towards them, and he was applying a field dressing to Josh's hand. Kier noticed with surprise that already some of the torn skin appeared to have healed.

"It's the Chalycion," Josh explained, seeing her expression.

"Mum's stone. It means I heal really quickly." He winced as Klim finished taping the dressing.

"Doesn't stop it hurting though," he added.

"They can't see us, those things," Klim explained as he turned to lift a glass capsule and syringe. "How bad is it?" he asked the injured man.

"Not that bad," Josh told him, his eyes widening. Klim shrugged with a half-smile.

"Best take something," he was appraising Josh with an experienced eye and Kier remembered his ability to pick up the thoughts of others. He pulled out some oral analgesia and a bottle of water, offered it to Josh who swallowed the tablets, drank the water, and then handed it back to Klim, who lifted it upwards.

"Hi," he said, passing the bottle round to the others, his eyes resting on Gabbie.

"Hi," she replied, with a soft smile, taking a sip of water and handing it on to Kier. "Glad you could make it."

Siskin turned around to face them and they all cried out in alarm much, apparently, to the amusement of their two rescuers

"Sorry," Siskin looked shamefaced. "Suara, that's my vehicle, runs on sound. She can tune in and drive herself once I've given her the melody."

"But I can't hear anything," said Gabbie, puzzled.

"None of us can, apart from Siskin, and sometimes me," Klim explained. "What Siskin can do with sound and music the rest of us couldn't even dream of."

There was pride and affection in his glance over at his companion.

"He's used an overlaying melody to balance it out and it's played on frequencies we can't hear. He made it invisible to those things by changing the melody and the frequency. He's also played with the fabric of sounds to form a kind of force field."

"Awesome," Gabbie commented. "And the ninja thing," she added, raising her eyebrows, and making a face that made Klim laugh. "Cool."

A year with Siskin had brought out the potential in the youth turned man, who now had his own commanding and confident presence, but Gabbie was clearly undaunted.

Siskin laughed, "Sounds more complicated than it is," he said.

"It's amazing," was Swift's comment as she examined the flickering surface of the small objects in the ceiling.

"They're specially designed transmitters," Klim explained, turning towards his mentor.

"It's the first time it's really been in action," Siskin told them. "We had to wait for it to be flown back before driving down here. It was our project between coffee picking and chasing bad guys in South America. Klim made it kinetically viable. He amplified the melodies and helped make it mute."

Gabbie's forehead furrowed. "So, you made it move and keep quiet at the same time?" she queried, looking at Klim who nodded.

"Ninja," he smiled at her.

Gabbie's mouth twitched in a reluctant smile.

"But how did you find us?" Josh asked.

Siskin nodded towards Klim, "We went out looking for you and luckily headed this way. Klim felt Swift nearby and called to her telepathically."

None of them used mobiles under Evan's instruction but Kier doubted that they would have had any signal where they were anyway.

"That was lucky," Gabbie commented neutrally as Klim searched her eyes.

"I'll second that," Josh smiled, then winced as a stab of pain made him cradle his wrist.

"What were those creatures?" asked Siskin.

"We think they must be called the Virenmor," Kier told them.

"We're here," Swift said, as the vehicle smoothly pulled into Y Wasgod Oren.

The sun diffused a deep orange glow through the green net of forest that cradled the house. Kier's sudden intake of breath, however, was not a response to its undoubted beauty but to the person she had seen emerge into the garden. There, walking out from the trees, silhouetted in the sunset, was the distinctive figure of Echinod Deem. She lagged behind the others, as they dropped out of the vehicle and ran to greet the Mourangil. She struggled with the fact that he could be so beautifully human and yet not human at all. Her eyes drank in his tall, athletic figure dressed, like the first time she had seen him, in T-shirt and jeans. None of his amazing transformations that had happened in her presence changed her very human response to him. Even now, as she watched his easy smile lighting on each of her friends, she knew that she was bound to him in a way she couldn't quantify and hardly understood. He acknowledged her in the same way as he did the others, the intrinsic light of his eyes touching hers, banishing the horror they had just endured. Evan, always so light on his feet for a big man, ran past with a splurge of Welsh exclamation and enfolded Echin in an enthusiastic bear hug. As Kier turned with the rest of the group, she watched the fading sunlight bounce from the white stone set in his ear, as Echinod Deem led them all inside the converted mill.

Chapter Nine

One by one the visitors returned downstairs, having taken the chance to clean up before dinner. Angharad's eyebrows had risen when she saw the dirt-stained hands of the three women, Josh's naked torso and the bloody T-shirt that covered his hand. As she had begun to ask what had happened Evan steered his daughter away into the kitchen to help prepare the meal, speaking softly in Welsh. Shortly afterwards Kier had picked up Echin's distinctive voice from the room next door, along with Evans muted but still rumbling tones; she surmised that they had spoken with Josh and had been appraised of the attack in the churchyard.

The kitchen was crammed with activity as they gathered for the evening meal. The clean smell of mint was refreshing as Angharad poured ice cold liquid from a large pottery jug, which seemed to relax and revive at the same time. Kier had watched with interest as her father introduced her to Echin; she noticed the veil of Angharad's eyelids as he offered his thanks for her hospitality. Evan had covered their injuries with a story about 'foolish archaeological impulses,' but it sat uneasily with Kier, who saw a mixture of hurt and anger in Angharad's clouded eyes. The table was formally laid and punctuated by the soft glow of red candles. An extra place had been set at the top where Evan now presided over the table. A basket of freshly made bread was passed around and the ebullient Welshman served a portion of fragrant fish pie to each of them. Evan raised his glass in a toast. "Iechyd da," he told them. "Welcome home and good health to you all!"

There were smiles and laughter amidst the clinking of glasses as they each repeated the toast. Kier was aware that her "yaki da," in return failed to catch the rolling Welsh syllables. Her eyes widened in amazement as she saw Josh reach out with his so recently injured hand that, apart from appearing slightly red, seemed whole once more. Kier looked over at him, frustrated that they were unable to discuss the day's events in Angharad's presence. Instead, they discussed the remarkable building, Frindy, Angharad's children and everything that had little perceived bearing on the Seeds of the Myriar.

"Will you be here for long?" Evan's daughter asked Echin directly.

"I hope to be," was his reply, softly spoken, his eyes finally catching her roaming glance.

"Unfortunately, I'll have to say goodbye tonight," she told them. "I need to be back home tomorrow, and I'll be leaving early."

Evan looked at her and she smiled, "I'll be up to see you off," he told her.

"There's no need Da," she replied, her mouth tight. "I can see you'll be busy without me to concern you."

"I'll see you off," he repeated firmly, the smile gone.

Angharad nodded and the group made their farewells. Kier, suddenly aware that she felt exhausted, needed no prompting to raise herself from the table and climb the spiral staircase.

*

The popping of gravel compressed by heavy rubber woke Kier not long after sunrise. In an oversized T-shirt, and her hair a tangled crown, she peered down from the top of the stairs to see Echin watch Angharad's departure quietly from the doorway. He patted Evan's shoulder as the Welshman re-entered the building, his eyes brimming with emotion.

"I'm sorry my friend," Echin told him." Your years of service have cost you dearly." Evan looked at him, his grey eyes folding.

"She would never understand," he said softly. "She is not someone who can enter the world you have opened before me Echinod."

"Given the chance she may surprise you," his friend replied.

Evan shook his head.

"I love her for herself, but we are spectrums apart, Angharad and I. Truly I don't think things would have been that different if my work had not taken me so far away."

"She's strong like you Evan," Echin reminded him.

"I'm grateful for the times we are together but they're better taking place at her home in the village. I could never refuse her wish to come here but I won't allow her to be put at risk."

Echin nodded and looked upwards as they turned back down the hall. His slight smile was quizzical as he noticed Kier, who found herself understanding that Evan's daughter was an issue that concerned him as much as it concerned her father. She returned his smile, saying nothing, and retreated to her bedroom.

Later, after showering, she sighed with disappointment as she looked out of the window and saw the Mourangil walking towards the woods.

"He's coming back," Gabbie's voice piped as she followed Kier's eyes. She was at the door, having knocked just as Kier was coming out of the shower. She looked refreshed in cotton shirt and trousers as she perched on the bed. "I heard him tell Evan. He's only going for an hour or two."

Kier nodded, acknowledging the lift of her heart that Gabbie's words had produced. "What happened to summer?" she commented, staring at rivulets of rain as they trickled down the glass.

"Tell me about it," Gabbie replied. "Freezing after Australia. I'll leave you to get dressed and then we can go down together."

Kier nodded and smiled but as her friend closed the door her gaze quickly fixed on the point where the Mourangil had disappeared. To Kier, Echin seemed more human than ever, even though she knew in her heart that this could never be the case. Nevertheless, her eyes searched hungrily through the rain-soaked leaves until she was sure they had banished all trace of his passing.

*

Bookcases lined the sitting room walls, so diverse in height and width that Kier guessed they had come from the bookshop in Pulton. Evan's own peculiar style of arrangement meant that he would know exactly where to find a volume that he had shelved, even though this would remain a mystery to everyone else. There were two large couches, covered in patterned throws, and several armchairs in a room big enough to have formed the main working area within the mill. An oak beamed ceiling defined the space into a cosy living room. Kier tucked her legs underneath as she nestled alongside Gabbie and Swift, on a long settee that faced French windows. They would, in better weather, lead out onto a large patio. Bay and lemon trees, their leaves newly washed and vivid green, lined the edges of the paved area, where rain now pooled in natural hollows. A wood burning stove glowed in one corner of the room, blanketing them against the dim grey of the morning.

They had gathered together without formal arrangement,

drifting into the sitting room after breakfast, the ordeal of the previous afternoon fully present once more, now that the cloak of exhaustion had been removed. Echin and Evan entered last, the Welshman seating himself in what was clearly his usual place, in an armchair the size of a throne. Echin relaxed in an upright chair that he moved into the semi-circle of seating, crossing his ankle over one knee. Although they had not spoken as a group Kier was aware that Siskin and Josh had given the two men details of what had happened the previous afternoon. Kier found her thoughts returning to The Mountain Inn, after the events on Whistmorden Scar and the long hours of waiting for the Mourangils to return. Dispersing haplessly, this was the first time they had been together since, albeit without Marianne, Matthew and Gally. And Adam, she whispered to herself. She was startled to hear Gabbie voice her thoughts.

"Why didn't you come back after Whistmorden?" the young woman asked bluntly, sitting at the end of the couch, the tone of disappointment that they had all felt welling in her voice. Wide blue eyes looked directly at Echin.

"What happened?" nudged Siskin, his voice neutral as Echin did not answer straight away. "You sent no word."

"I am sorry," sighed Echin, unravelling his long legs, the deep blue of his eyes catching each of them. "It took all three of us, me, Faer and Tormaigh, the best part of the time we have been away to corner Nephragm. To destroy another Mourangil in our given form is not permitted and would result only in our own destruction. Therefore, Faer and Tormaigh still guard him, deep in the planet. It is vital that he is prevented from taking another innocent's form."

Kier dropped her head, tears pricked her eyes at the memory of Adam's amazing mind being ravaged by the dreadful Devouril. "Well, there we were, Kier struck dumb, all of us wandering round like dazed sheep and you super beings couldn't even use a phone! Don't you have helpers? Y'know elves or something?" Gabbie sat back in the couch, her arms folded.

Evan's eyes twinkled. He had long endured the unpredictable comings and goings of the Mourangils, but Gabbie was not inhibited by his reverence towards them. Echin shook his head and smiled lopsidedly, "And yet you have all fared well without us! I understand you Gabbie, yet we left you in good hands. The Mountain was protected in ways invisible to you. You won't feel so abandoned when you can access the mind-places once more." Before Gabbie could ask him to explain further Kier brought them back to the present.

"The Virenmor?" she began. "What or who are they?" Echin's eyes darkened, "Alex Jackson was part of the Virenmor." Klim's intake of breath was audible as he heard his deceased uncle's name. Kier could not suppress the ice-cold stab of fear at the memory of the man's invasion into her consciousness. On two occasions, had it not been for the intervention of others, she would have lost her life.

"Three thousand years ago in Mesopotamia we discovered that a scattered malevolence, fuelled by the influence of Belluvour, had shaped itself into a swarm of evil. So powerful did the Virenmor become that they wiped out a civilisation and delayed the progress of mankind for thousands of years."

Echin's words clanged liked fallen bells in the living space as the small group listened intently.

"The Virenmor consider themselves elite, above the masses. They have adopted the Devouril belief that mankind in general is unworthy to exist alongside what they consider to be superior life forms. They have bought into the delusion that only their breed of human matters. It's an attitude of mind they have replicated down through the ages, used to justify prejudice and atrocity. A virus fed by the depraved powers they have developed in Belluvour's service, which seeks to lay low the general body of man. Nephragm has been the dark force behind their success, keeping them hidden from the Mourangils, typically birthing them into families whose basic goodness masks the horror of a rogue individual."

Kier looked over at Klim who had spoken of his father's struggle to accept his brother's vicious nature; his dark head was bowed in thought.

"But they didn't look human," Josh pointed out and the others nodded in agreement. Gabbie made a gesture of an elongated beak and twisted her face in a way that produced laughter from the others, challenging the fear that the creatures had engendered. Echin's mouth twitched, "They were projections of themselves," he told her.

"No way," Josh replied, shaking his head, and lifting his hand, "but they were real enough."

"Oh, they had physicality," Echin told them leaning forwards, his elbow on one knee. "For some time now I've been aware of a group that has mastered manipulation through game play."

Siskin nodded, "Some games have been used to enhance not only dexterity but also aggression. Plus, in-game advertising's been around for years."

"Tchh," added Evan, "I am always telling Angharad to keep a close eye on the children with these computer things." Grey waves of hair fell over his face as he shook his head in disgust. Echin sat upright and sighed.

"I don't judge the media itself. There are many advantages and disadvantages, and it is a human issue to determine how this sits within your society. However, the Virenmor have taken this to a more sinister level, they have developed a way to place an element of their own physical bodies within images used for the computer game."

Siskin let out a long whistle. Josh and Klim who liked gaming together, were visibly shaken.

"But how?" Siskin asked. "You're saying they were there in the flesh as we saw them and also miles away in their own bodies?"

"The occult process is an extension of the player's will to do harm, abandoning moral perspective and any sense of consequence," Echin explained.

"If they were actually present does that mean they were struck down when we hit them?" asked Siskin.

"You may have injured them a little physically, enough for them to be wiped out of the game. The game wizard or witch, for want of a better term, will largely protect their physical bodies whilst enabling the character in the game to inflict fatal violence. I think the whole village was set up as a game, probably to be played only by the most vicious 'elite' gamers, who the Virenmor have recruited unwittingly, then manipulated and duped."

"So, this game controller can do this to anyone in any part of the world?" Kier posited.

"I don't believe so," the Mourangil replied. "The village set up is evidence of their work nearby but there are limits. Red Light," he nodded towards Siskin and Klim, "has recently reported the brutal murders of political prisoners without any visible sign of another human being. The murder weapons were devoid of DNA, prints or any other identifying matter, other than those belonging to the victim. Each case followed a visit from a female stranger, posing as a legitimate connection: journalist, prison warder, teacher."

"Pictures, ID?" checked Klim.

"All records cleverly wiped," Echin shook his head. "The

connection has only come to light very recently. In the last case the murder weapon, a baseball bat, was removed from the scene. A banker, family man, working in the Middle East, was found holding the bat covered with the victim's blood. He reported killing the prisoner, to whom he referred to as an alien, from his living room ten miles away."

"Did you manage to find the game? Track it back to the manufacturer?" enquired Josh.

Echin shook his head. "A colleague in the next apartment came in to find the man sitting with the bat, telling his garbled story. When the colleague went to get help the banker set fire to himself and his games, and so the hotel was evacuated. We only have the bat, as it had already been passed to the other man before the gamer became lost in despair."

The colour drained from Gabbie's face.

"So do you have any idea about this master gamer, the one who controls it all?" Siskin asked.

Echin's eyes were hard glints of blue stone. "It has the stamp of Danubin, the most powerful of all the Virenmor."

"Danubin." repeated Kier. Just saying the name made her feel that a sinister aspect had invaded their company. "What does this person look like?"

"I have no idea," Echin replied, shrugging his shoulders. "She is invariably female, likes to use the technology of the age and mix it with her own occult and brutal practices. But I think that she was caught off guard for once. "

"That's off guard?" muttered Josh, glancing at his hand.

"From what I've learned the whole village was being prepared as a trap," Echin explained. "Somehow, Arwres was tracked to the graveyard. They're snapping at our heels, but had the snare been fully in place the outcome may have been vastly different."

"Thank goodness for the ninjas!" Gabbie looked over at Siskin and Klim, whose mouth lifted into a smile.

Swift's tone was serious as she turned to Echin.

"So why bring us to a place where the Virenmor are so near?"

Echin stood up, hands in the pockets of his jeans, watching the rain.

"The summons wasn't mine; I was merely the messenger on this occasion. Arwres needed to be found and any later would have been disastrous."

"If not you, then who was it that brought us back here together?" Siskin asked.

Gabbie gasped as she felt a burning on her neck where she had fastened a small leather pouch. She reached inside and took out the flame-coloured stone, holding out her hand tentatively towards Echin. The stone flickered to life and Kier held her breath as she noticed a soft glimmer become a glow just in front of Gabbie. A moment later, to their astonishment, the figure of a woman manifested herself. Short red spikes of hair framed her head. Wide green eyes flashed against dark skin, and she was clothed in a leaf coloured, soft leather jumpsuit.

"So, where's Candillium?" the newcomer demanded of Echin as she scrutinised each of their faces. Her Asian accent clipped through the words, "Don't tell me you still haven't found her!" Echin ignored the question and said mildly to the group, "This is Silex."

Chapter Ten

About fifteen miles from the house, within the village of Capel Cudd y Bryn, a woman in her thirties stood looking at the abandoned RAV4 with interest. Dafyd had rung her, unable to follow the instructions as to how to tow the vehicle and she had been scathing, suspecting laziness on the part of the garage owner. She knew that he would be anxious to return to the game she had forced him to leave. She held up an umbrella over her immaculate suit and carefully navigated the cobbles in stiletto heels. Shreive had driven over from her estate agent office in Carmarthen, from which she had sold every house on the row to a religious Welsh chapel organisation, she helped to administer in North Wales. It had been her suggestion that the abandoned church would provide an opportunity to set up a new religious community in this part of the country, particularly after she had arranged a very generous, anonymous donation. It had not been difficult to persuade them to buy the old chapel and its grounds, plus the small number of surrounding houses, once the main members had been convinced by her religious fervour. It had been tricky though, when she realised that she was unable to enter the old ground; she'd had to manoeuvre with versatility to hide this from the congregation. Whilst directing the work in the old grounds she had led the chapel members to believe that she was focusing her energy on preparing the small cottages for those most in need.

She had been clever, cleverer than any of them. It was she who had tracked down Arwres to this part of Wales, and she who had discovered the abandoned churchyard. This was little comfort in the light of their abject failure to find the stone and destroy the Myriar Seed as planned. Worse, she now knew that there had been more than one Seed in the graveyard. The fact that they might have already gathered together produced an unusual sensation of fear, one that made her heel dig too firmly between the cobbles, so that she wobbled as she moved forwards. Irritably she snapped at Dafyd. "What's this nonsense?"

Unabashed, Dafyd pointed to the abandoned RAV4, as he began to pack away his things.

"Shreive, there's no way. It's as if there's a band of rubber around it. Everything bounces off."

Shreive quelled her temper, his game playing had shown her that it was never the way to handle Dafyd. She nodded and smiled, a painted splash in a tanned face. In his early thirties, Dafyd wore a black vest despite the rain. The droplets fell on rounded muscles that rippled as he moved. She bottled her lust, for now. She circled the vehicle noticing that the licence plate had been wiped clean and was now unreadable. There was no way she could get near enough to apply her own peculiar talents to trace its ownership. She decided that she would need to install 24 hr CCTV. Flicking back her short black hair, worn in a graduated bob, it was arranged within minutes as she spoke into the mobile phone. Then the red lips opened lasciviously as she turned her attention back to Dafyd.

*

Echin's expression was one of equanimity, completely unaffected by the querulous tone of the newcomer. The companions were too dumbfounded to speak as Silex walked over to where Siskin sat. He returned her gaze with frank curiosity, but as he went to stand up, she looked down at him expressionless.

"The Lute," she pronounced.

Turning to Josh she said sharply, "You should tell them what happened in the Wicklow Mountains, Creta."

Josh flinched, his eyes quickly masked, then lifted to mouth a reply. Silex however, had already moved on to meet the calm expression on Swift's face, as she stood to meet the Mourangil. The sharp face softened its expression, "Stozcist," she said reverently and bowed her head. Swift bowed in return and sat back in her place. Klim was next to face the scrutiny.

"For a Reeder you miss a lot," she told him curtly.

Finally, she faced Kier and leaned her head to one side, her eyes quizzical.

"An Inscriptor?" she asked, looking at Echin who nodded and then seeing Evan she frowned. "Two Stozcists, and no Candillium?"

Her tone was one of angry disappointment. Gabbie stared at the stone in her palm, sure that it still pulsed with life even though the Mourangil had emerged from the jasper and stood in the centre of the room.

"Why me?" she blurted out. "Why did you call to me?"

Silex looked around sharply and Gabbie shrank under the lightening gaze, but then straightened her shoulders and lifted her chin.

"Arwres," the haughty tone instructed, "in which I resided for a while, is yours." Her mouth softened as she seemed to pick up Gabbie's thought.

"I will not take its pattern again," and then seeing the puzzled expression on the young woman's face she added, "I will not be in the stone. It beats to your heart now Storekeeper."

Gabbie looked back puzzled, her eyes reaching to Echin who nodded. On her outstretched palm, there was a minute orange flicker at the centre of the stone. She closed her hand and then returned Arwres to the pouch around her neck.

"What's a Storekeeper?" Gabbie's words came in a rush as if she wasn't sure she wanted the answer. Irritably the imp like figure sighed, but the gaze Gabbie returned remained questioning. Silex reluctantly explained.

"It is foretold in Lioncera that certain stones will be placed in the hands of the final Seeds of the Myriar, when they are all gathered. I am the first Mourangil to have discovered such a gem, though many of us have searched through the ages of your time."

Her tiny figured swelled with pride.

"I guarded the stone in readiness for your arrival, but once I sensed the approach of the Virenmor I asked Echin to bring you all here. I did not know which of you it would claim as its keeper."

"Does this mean Gabbie's one of the Seeds?" asked Klim.

"We don't know," Echin told them. "Marianne held the Chalycion for many years. Marianne is not a Seed, but like her any human who holds a stone will have great influence. It may be that all the Seeds have gathered and that Gabbie is one of them, or it may be that she holds the stone in keeping for another."

"Oh!" Gabbie said quietly, glancing at Kier in confusion, her fist tightly curled around the pouch. It occurred to Kier that not once had she doubted that her friend was part of their unique group. Kier could see that Gabbie was about to frame further questions when Silex turned back to Echin.

"Candillium?" she demanded.

"I don't know," he said simply, without apology. "The Myriar has moved far beyond its original design on paths of its own making. Candillium could be here in this room but until she recognises herself, we cannot know her. Or it may be that we have yet to meet her."

"You mean she could be Swift or Kier or Gabbie?" asked Klim.

"Or any of you," Silex snapped. "Male or female, it would not matter," she told them impatiently. "But Candillium is needed and very soon."

Echin lifted his eyes and looked with compassion at the others, knowing, it seemed, what it was that Silex was about to communicate to the group.

"Magluck Bawah has been released."

"The Undercreature," Kier found herself saying aloud, as memory of the words that she had read in the bookshop flooded back to her. They had told of the land of Ordovicia. At first, she had imagined some futuristic place inspired by science fiction, but now she understood that this had been the original home of the human race on Moura; the name the Mourangils gave to the planet. And what she had read of the Undercreature terrified her. Silex glanced at Echin.

"She found the reference room," he explained, his expression unreadable.

Silex turned towards Kier who held her gaze, and then she

continued. "The release of Magluck Bawah signifies that Belluvour's power has reached a point where the bonds made by the Myriar are strained to their limit. We can barely keep balance on the surface. I feel him in the crumbling rock beneath and in the blinding storms above. If you do not find Candillium soon, it will be too late."

Echin stood up, his expression solemn as he held the eyes of the sharp Mourangil.

"She must first find herself, Silex, if she has come at all." Compassion crept beneath the harshness of her tone as her gaze swept across each individual in the room.

"Then the Undercreature will hunt the Seeds and, together with the Virenmor, will do everything to pursue your destruction." She sighed and turned to Gabbie, her voice softening.

"It has your scent, Storekeeper."

There was an audible intake of breath from all of the group. Klim came forward in his seat, tension in every muscle. Kier thought of the events of the previous morning and the whip like creature that had circled her friend in triumph.

"Devil's Bridge?" she asked Echin. "Was this what I saw? Silex turned to her in query once again as Echin nodded.

"Evan told me," he said evenly. He nodded to |Kier who briefly gave an account of the events at Devil's Bridge. Silex bowed her head, her eyes were an autumn green, full of faded sadness as she spoke.

"I think without a doubt it was the Kejambuk you saw, the guide of the Undercreature, created by Belluvour to direct its destructive power towards the Seeds. Magluck Bawah can sense its prey but not see as it pollutes the deeper tissues of the planet. Recently I discovered that the Kejambuk has been primed as a guide to the creature and to recognise the Seeds. It is an inhabitant of the Obdurates; living in water or air the creature is highly mobile and one of the world's oldest trackers."

"Obdurates?" repeated Kier.

Echin explained. "These are materials cast by Belluvour, more numerous now than ever before, areas within the deep where Mourangils cannot pass." His tone gave them to understand the terrific sadness this had caused.

"I don't get it. What is this Undercreature? What does it want with us?" Gabbie's face was strained with fear.

Echin looked towards Silex who sighed and perched on the arm of the settee before responding. The light and vibrant figure seemed suddenly to fold, Kier noticed glistening jade particles running across her jaw line and then they disappeared.

"Even we, as Mourangils, rarely speak of this creature, though it has been my study for longer than your human minds could fathom."

The room was picture still, and the clipped tones dropped into the silence.

"I believe that Magluck Bawah first came into existence at the point when Candillium accepted into her being, the centrepiece of the Myriar. At first the Mourangils barely registered its presence, it was a small tear in the fabric of the planet. We surrounded it with our healing vibration, but nothing that we did could fill the black despair that is at its core. Belluvour seemed to take pity on the strange entity that inhabited the deep reaches of Moura. He named it Magluck Bawah, the Undercreature, for he saw that it could not breathe air. It was he who guided the creature to the Waystation and showed it how to wear a form above the surface. We did not see that Belluvour had engineered that first transformation into that of an Irresythe, a winged huntress. It resulted in the murder of Erion, the beloved sister-friend of Candillium. Nor, as we grieved, did we understand that the raw and destructive energy of Magluck Bawah could not construct its own individual form. It took instead the life of any creature that it wished to inhabit. The same technique that Nephragm has since perfected."

The jade eyes glimmered in the rain shadowed gloom. All were silent with their own thoughts and Kier felt herself touching the outer rim of the dark hole into which she had fallen after Whistmorden. It took her a moment to realise that Silex had begun speaking once more.

"From all that I've learned I believe that hatred for human life, particularly for those connected to the formation of the Myriar, is the Undercreature's innate driving force. I think this was the case even before Belluvour's malign influence. For this reason, Candillium bound them both in the Secret Vaults. The ascent of the creature once more to the surface realms is the warning bell of Belluvour's return."

Into the strained silence came a soldier's voice.

"Above the surface," Siskin was calculating, "this creature is vulnerable to attack?" Silex nodded in response.

"I have tracked parts of its passage," she glanced towards Echin apologetically, "but I could not pass the obdurates to reach it. The distorted entity can only take an animal form," she told them. "Each manifestation requires a tremendous slice of it's being, but such is the driven hatred for the Seeds of the Myriar and the Stonekeepers that it will risk everything to hunt you down."

Josh placed his hand around the Chalycion and Kier guessed that he was giving thanks that the stone was no longer with his mother. Marianne had been tortured, firstly by Alex Jackson and then by Nephragm, just twelve months ago. Like Kier, Josh had hidden the summons to Wales from his closest family, unable to think of them in danger once again.

"I have calculated that the ravaging energy of Magluck Bawah can make five mortal lives on the surface," Silex told them.

"Yes," she turned to Siskin, "the creature is vulnerable while it assumes the form of whichever poor animal it decides to take, once it has consumed the original living being. Already it has used one of these lives."

"The bull," Kier stated with certainty, as she turned towards Gabbie whose face paled. Silex nodded.

"The next attempt will come soon, and it will be more dangerous," Silex told them.

"It was dangerous enough!" Gabbie piped up.

Silex ignored her. "Magluck Bawah is all distorted emotion, it has been searching for you since its release. It was a clumsy attack. Now the Virenmor will help direct its dark energy and it will feed information to the Kejambuck. Even the Virenmor will be wary however, for only Belluvour has been able to tame Magluck Bawah."

"How can we stop this thing finding Gabbie," Klim's tone was business like.

Gabbie rewarded him with a flash of her sapphire blue eyes.

"The River Teifi will deter the creature, for its channels run deep and its nature is strong. In the area within its confines the Undercreature cannot detect your presence without the Virenmor." Silex turned towards Klim, "You must establish Mengebara very soon."

"Menge who?" Klim turned to Echin.

"Mengebara is the mind place the human race established in Ordovicia," he explained gently.

Klim look perplexed. "But I don't know how to get there!"

"You're already there," clipped Silex.

Klim opened his mouth to ask what she meant, but Silex had

turned and was moving towards Swift, who was standing. Water particles hung suspended on the window and from them droplets of light bounced as the sun broke through the clouds, to reveal the diamond stone set against Swift's throat, sparkling regally, for once fully visible to all those in the room. It had been Swift's first creation and caused the discovery of her gift as a stone changer. She had banished the dark presence that lay within the stone to form the clear, and mostly invisible, jewel that she was never without. Silex smiled as if in greeting and then turned back to the group to take her leave. Echin took her hand and her eyes softened, as they exchanged whatever private thoughts they shared. She then walked towards Evan who stood up, his eyes brim full of emotion. Kier suddenly realised that he had remained uncharacteristically silent throughout the conversation. Silex reached out and took Evan's hands in her own.

"Blessings old friend," she said softly.

"Thank you Silex, and to you," he replied, his voice unsteady. Gently she detached herself from the Welshman and turned back to the group.

"You will need to grow quickly," she said to them, the steel returning to her eyes. As she opened the French windows sunlight flooded into the room and in its glare Silex disappeared from sight.

Chapter Eleven

Angharad stood in the garden she loved, for over its low walls could be seen the majestic Snowdonia mountains. Her son Dylan, his dark hair flopping over his face as he steered through imaginary rugby players, weaved across the lawn. Llinos, her long dark hair plaited tidily, easily moved her dolls out of danger as he passed, continuing the tea party that she had arranged around an upturned bucket. Angharad gave a sigh of satisfaction, acknowledging to herself that she had done a good job, mostly alone, in bringing them both this far.

The garden gate scraped, and she turned to greet Shreive, the chapel administrator. The chapel community had helped her through the worst of times and Angharad was part of its centre in the small village; still she had never felt comfortable with Shreive. Even though the woman spoke Welsh it felt as if she had purchased the language and was using something that belonged to someone else. Undoubtedly, she had demonstrated her tireless efforts on behalf of the chapel that, she had explained, were inspired by her Welsh mother. Still Angharad had to repress the urge to turn her back. Instead, Evan's daughter laid aside her misgivings and greeted her fellow chapel member with a smile, as she made her way along the path.

There was something intimidating in Shreive's impeccable wardrobe and youthful figure. Angharad was amazed that this highly fashionable woman took an interest in this remote community. Their minister, the Reverend Hammond, whom Angharad adored, clearly trusted Shreive to run parish affairs. There was no doubting the cleverness of the woman, who had arranged the expansion of their religious community to Capel Cudd y Bryn. It had been Angharad who had found the abandoned chapel a few months ago and mentioned it at one of their meetings. She had been flattered when the administrator took such an interest and then everything seemed to happen very fast, when money had been left to them. Angharad understood that the renovation of the chapel and the provision of housing began happening far more quickly than any of their community could have hoped.

"What can I do for you Shreive?" she said warmly. Shreive glanced at the children playing.

"They're such lovely children," she intoned and then rounded her voice into a soft whisper.

"I believe you have some concerns regarding your father?"

Angharad looked startled, "Pardon?" she blurted aggressively, stepping backwards. Shreive seemed not to notice.

"The Reverend Hammond mentioned that you felt he was being influenced by a non-religious sect." Shreive rested a supportive hand on Angharad's forearm, her eyes full of concern. "But I see it distresses you to talk of it. I'm sorry," she said, looking embarrassed that she had broached the subject.

Angharad closed her eyes for a moment, releasing the tension in her body that the other woman's touch had produced. After all, Shreive only meant well. Sighing she found herself explaining her worries about the 'sect' that had embroiled her father. The words tumbled out, released from the constraint of her tightly bound anxiety. The minister obviously felt that Shreive was the best person to help his distressed chapel member and Angharad reasoned that the woman's wider experience might be useful.

"And not only Da," she told her, brows furrowing. "There are others."

Shreive said nothing as Evan's daughter wrung her hands in indecision, her eyes refusing to meet those of the visitor. Shreive stepped back a little.

"There's no need to distress yourself telling me if you don't wish," said her perfectly shaped mouth. Angharad's hesitancy dissolved.

"There are young people involved. They all have their lives ahead, but that man will drag them along with him. They'll put him first, shut out their families. It's not right."

"And exactly who would 'that man' be?" Shreive asked quietly.

"Echinod Deem," Angharad told her.

She caught a gleam in the other woman's eyes as she released the name and immediately retreated to uncertainty. Even though she held in her mind all the right reasons she had for her concern, there was no feeling of lightness as she shared her thoughts. On the contrary, the sense of doom that suddenly swallowed her made her turn towards the garden and shout for the children. Shreive was asking her about Echin, where he lived, what he looked like, but all Angharad could see were the dark clouds that had arisen from the mountains, heading for the garden.

"I'm sorry Shreive," she said hurriedly, "but I need to get the children inside now, we'll speak again soon."

Without turning to her visitor again she scurried the two children into the hallway and firmly closed the door.

*

"Echin, you've had a difficult morning old friend, first little Gabbie and then Silex."   Evan's eyes twinkled with amusement as he walked with the Mourangil alongside the river that bordered his garden.

"You didn't help much I noticed," Echin commented.

"That's true," his companion replied unashamedly, "though I did rescue you from further interrogation."

Herald matched Echin stride for stride.

"Man's best friend, eh?" Evan complained, giving the dog a rueful stare. "When you're here I might as well not exist."

Echin laughed and bent down to the dog, who jumped excitedly and then bounded forward towards the forest. The woodland was surrounded by a stone wall at its outer rim, but Evan voiced Siskin's worries about attack coming from that direction. "How secure are we here?" he asked.

"Neither the Virenmor nor Magluck Bawah can enter," replied Echin.

"Ah, well then," began Evan relieved.

"Beware my friend," Echin interrupted him, "they are darkly devious. Any contact with them is perilous and they'll manipulate others to gain their way. The events at Capel Cudd y Bryn have shown us that they are near, far too near."

Evan nodded thoughtfully, "How did they track Arwres there?" He broke off abruptly as Herald disappeared into the woodland.

"Come back Herald," he shouted, running after the dog. He turned back to his friend, breathless as Echin responded to his question.

"It's part of the reason I need to go. The fact that Danubin has found a way to track the Stones of the Myriar is more than a little disturbing. She'll not be found easily."

"They'll be sad to hear you have left again," Evan told him. "The kids don't understand, they don't know what it costs a Mourangil to stay with us as much as you do."

Echin looked towards him quizzically and they stood facing each other, as the afternoon sun broke through the clouds and scattered shimmering sparkles along the water.

"I have been a Stozcist for over twenty years now," Evan said. "I know in your terms that the time would barely register but still I feel the heartbeat of the planet and have laid my hands upon living stone. I know that for you to be with us, like you are now, for so long as you have done, splinters your being in a way that is beyond my comprehension. It doesn't mean I'm blind to the sacrifice it costs you."

Evan's grey eyes were wide with compassion and Echin put his arm on his friend's shoulder.

"And yet you do not mention your own sacrifice and what our friendship has cost you?" Echin told him.

"Friendship?" Evan stopped moving and turned to his companion. "You virtually brought me up remember? I owe you, my life." Echin turned his serious eyes towards the man he had known from boyhood.

"You owe me nothing Evan, as I have said many times before."

"Then take my love Echin, and my loyalty, freely given," he grinned boyishly and Echin gave him a grateful smile as they moved forward together.

"It's quite a job you have given me to watch over these young ones," he said, scratching his chin. "They're all so different!"

"And yet the same," his face lit in a way that Evan had rarely seen. "The last Seeds of the Myriar, finally."

"Well don't be so long," Evan told him. "This is too precious a cargo for me to carry on my own."

"There's no one I trust more," Echin smiled, "but I really won't be long. I need to visit an old friend nearby."

Not reassured in the slightest Evan nodded, "Hmmm," he said quietly.

"Oh," Echin continued, "I have left an Ordovician manuscript for Kier in my room that will help Klim to re-establish Mengebara." He smiled at Evan's puzzled face. "It will fascinate you!" he said laughing, "but don't spend too much time there, it'll give you little peace."

Evan shrugged and shook his head. They had walked along a small track into the woodland where the remnants of standing stones stood in a clearing, long forgotten. Now all that remained was a circle of rocks, mostly hidden beneath moss and grass. Herald darted out from between the trees and Echin knelt down to receive a sloppy greeting. Evan came forward and caught hold of the dog's collar, he stroked its head as he watched the Mourangil reach the centre of the circle and place his hand on the soft earth. Then Echin was gone. The dog whined softly, straining to follow as Evan patted its head.

"I know Herald," he said, turning back down the path. "Let's hope he remembers to come back before I grow too old to notice."

*

"So, what do you think this 'mind place' is that I'm supposed to do something with?"

Klim addressed the small group now gathered around the kitchen table after lunch. Evan's hand slapped against his forehead.

"I have something for you," he announced, jumping up to leave the room. On his return, a few minutes later, he carefully removed a document from a cardboard tube and passed it to Kier.

"Echin asked me to give you this," he told her, "to help Klim do whatever it is he needs to do."

"How long will he be away for?"

Evan reassured her, "He said not long. He's gone to see someone nearby."

Kier looked at him steadily, "Which in Echin's terms could be Fiji!" Evan conceded. "But we will hope."

"It's like cloth to touch," Kier told them, her attention turning to the document that she had carefully removed from the tube.

"Looks like an old scroll," Siskin commented.

"It's a remnant from a book I think," she replied, unrolling the soft material that she had seen before in the reference room.

"How old is that!" Gabbie hunched her shoulders. "It gives me the shivers."

"It's probably the oldest record of human existence on the planet," Evan said softly.

Kier looked up startled, she was in the process of placing the corners of the sheet under various condiments.

"No pressure then!" Gabbie quipped.

Swift carefully removed the salt cellar and replaced it with her slim fingers. Gabbie, Klim and Josh followed her example, gently touching the other three corners. Siskin came to stand over Kier's shoulder, who was coming to terms with the fact that she had handled such material so many times before, without knowing its age or significance.

"Should I wear gloves?" she asked Evan.

"I don't know, should you?" he returned, shrugging his shoulders. Kier shook her head thoughtfully and then closed her eyes for a moment, summoning the sense of peace she had always felt in the reference room. Slowly she leaned over the table and scrutinised the ancient document.

"It looks Arabic," Gabbie said, screwing her face up as she tried to make sense of the distinctive shapes. Kier looked up at her. "You know, the first few documents I looked at in the reference room seemed to be written in a different language. But I was so taken by the drawings that I kept on looking and then I discovered other passages written in English." She paused a moment and then, understanding the truth of it for the first time added, "It was me and not the language that changed!"

"Pictures would be good!" Gabbie announced ruefully, failing to find any meaning in the characters that remained bold and clear despite their age. Kier grinned in response but then her expression changed, fixed in concentration as she leaned over to examine the writing more closely.

"What does it say, Kier?" nudged Josh, as she scanned the whole sheet.

"It's an extract from a journal," she replied without looking up.

"I've read bits of it before, but I'm guessing this is much later." She bent over the table, flicking her long hair over her shoulder so that she could scrutinise the words more carefully.

"I think it's written by Candillium," she told them, her voice unsteady. She paused for a moment and then began to read clearly, transporting them to a time and place with which she was already familiar.

"It was the Chalycion stirring, flickering deep purple, which brought me to the doorway."

Josh gasped and reached for the stone around his neck. The group turned towards him, awestruck as tiny strands of white light pulsed in the pink stone. He placed his hand tightly around it. Then Josh said quietly, "Go on," his throat constricted.

"I was filled with fear for Erion. From the hilltop I could see the blue water of the lake remained undisturbed, but the air tasted unwholesome. I visited Mengebara," Kier looked up as she

emphasised the word, "*and saw that her mind print was no longer present.*"

"It's what Echin said," commented Swift, "it's a mind place."

"And Erion," remembered Siskin, "was the first to be murdered."

Kier nodded and looked at the others who were all deep in thought. She continued,

"*In my distress, I called for Toomaaris. In moments, I was lifted by an arrow of light, folded in the air, traversing its currents in the embrace of his being.*"

"When we came back from Tinobar with Tormaigh," Kier said quietly, "that's just how it was."

Klim, Siskin and Kier exchanged a smile as they remembered the incredible experience and then she continued to read.

"*Together we crossed over the city, and the Visperaals…*"

"Straals of the air!" chirped Gabbie and Swift nodded solemnly.

Kier refocused on the document.

"*The Visperaals pointed us towards the pale shore where the land received the ocean. A mighty winged Irresythe…*"

Kier looked up for confirmation that she had used the correct pronunciation, but Evan again shrugged his shoulders in bewilderment, and she turned back to the parchment.

"*A mighty winged Irresythe…*"

"The winged huntress," Klim interrupted.

Kier nodded seriously, as her attention again refocused on the elegant lettering.

"A mighty winged Irresythe lay hunched over its prey, it's massive body spanned black against the pebbled surface as we reached the shoreline. The creature turned towards me as I steadied myself, remnants of torn flesh still in its beak. The black eyes spewed hatred but then the bright light of Toomaaris the Mourangil shone before me, and the foul thing was gone."

"This bit's difficult to read," Kier used her fingers to stretch out the material further.

"Even now my tears fall as I record the moment when we turned to find Erion, Alleator of Ordovicia and Sisterfriend, dead on the ground beside us. A deep wound gaped in the centre of her forehead; her expression fixed in vivid terror. It was to her that I had prepared to give the last Seed of the Myriar. The fingers had been torn from her left hand; the hand that had moved up and down the pipes of Alleth with such ease, and with which she had won the title Alleator, principal music maker. I wept over my friend's mutilated features and sought our community in Mengebara."

Kier paused and looked at Klim, who nodded his assurance that he was listening carefully. She read on.

"Before long the boatmen came, their vessels lined in tribute along the edge of the sea and gently they lifted the torn body of Erion and brought her home. It gave us comfort, her mother Durane and I, to weave the blanket of passing. We poured our sorrow into the lilac flowers of yesterday and wove golden

blooms of tomorrow on soft green alu cloth. Then in Mengebara,
where the past lives again in memories shared, we heard once
more the fathomless sounds of the Pipes of Alleth made infinitely
eloquent by Erion."

"How sad," Kier choked.

"You really think that it's Candillium?" Swift asked, her dark
eyes huge.

Kier nodded. "Who else would be imparting the Seeds of the
Myriar?"

"I think the girl was to be the first Lute," Siskin said and then he
looked surprised that he had used the term that had been applied
to him by the Mourangils. Kier gently rolled up the document and
returned it to the cardboard tube.

"She adored Toomaaris," she found the syllables sweet on her
tongue. "Toomaaris," Kier said softly, "was her star."

"How do you mean?" Josh asked. "Like a shining light?"

Kier held on to the thought, for it had come with the familiar
certainty of a truth already present in her mind.

"Maybe it's from all that I've read but I think that he more than
shone a light for her, he was its source."

Evan's eyes welled with tears. "And it has never grown dim," he
added softly.

Kier's eyes widened with understanding, "Echin?"

"Echin," he confirmed, "the lonely Mourangil. That's how I see
him," he added, seeing the look of surprise in the faces of his

friends.

"I don't think the Mourangils can really be lonely, they are so immersed in the fabric of the planet," said Swift gently.

"It's still how I see him," said Evan, turning away from the table.

Chapter Twelve

"Klim and I will recover Kier's vehicle tonight," Siskin said conversationally.

Evan glanced over at him, "Can't see that it'd make much difference to wait a bit longer."

Siskin stood in the doorway of the annexe, a converted stone barn with whitewashed walls where Evan was going through what appeared to be boxes of junk.

"The longer it's there the more chance the Virenmor have of finding a way round my devices that are shielding the car. We can't allow them access inside. I suspect they already have DNA samples from around the gate."

Evan looked up in alarm. "There's no records of any of us in the main databases, but I've no way of knowing what internal information Jackson kept." He nodded thoughtfully and then turned back to the overstuffed room. Siskin spoke gently as he rearranged the boxes that Evan had discarded in his search.

"Evan, we need a way forward, we can't just sit here waiting to be found by the Virenmor or this other thing Silex spoke of. It's three days since she and Echin left, and we've practically achieved nothing."

"There it is," the Welshman announced, pulling out an easel from a cupboard. He turned to rummage in another drawer and found an engraved wooden box.

"That's it," he told his companion, placing the box in Siskin's hand and lifting the easel, "Come on."

Siskin shook his head in resignation and followed his friend to the two-storey building, a little nearer to the house. Gabbie was pulling a face as Josh completed his charcoal sketch.

"Can't you see what the lead thing really looks like? Y'know, doing your Creta stuff."

Josh smiled ruefully as he pushed the sketch pad into the centre of the table.

"Afraid not," he replied. "There has to be a full physical connection for the first drawing. It was too distorted by whatever means she used to engineer the game."

Siskin whistled over Josh's shoulder. "That's her alright."

He placed the wooden box on the desk, his eyes picking out every detail of the sketch. It was a perfect depiction of the lead Virenmor that had assaulted Josh at Capel Cudd y Bryn. Siskin frowned with distaste.

"Hideous. But it's also remarkably powerful. To pull off that a hundred times over!"

The ex-soldier swept back his hair as he stared at the screen, taking a black hat out of his pocket, and fixing it over his head. He squatted beside the desk.

"What name did Echin use?" Gabbie asked.

"He called her Danubin," Siskin answered, his face implacable, "but that won't be the name she's using. From what he was saying I suspect she makes Alex Jackson look like a choirboy! And we need to be doing more to find her," he announced firmly, straightening his limbs.

"I don't think going after her is the way forward for us," Evan said calmly. "Echin's looking for her. He said she won't be easy to find, even for him. And there are other things we need to do." Evan set up the easel and shifted the wooden box in front of Josh, whose eyes glowed as he opened it.

"Beautiful," he said as he took out a set of brushes and oil paints. "These are the best," he explained, looking at Evan with interest. "They're Chungking. Where did they come from?"

"They were a gift from Angharad," Evan told them uneasily. "I never found the time to use them." He pointed to the easel. "I think you should paint whatever you saw in the Wicklow mountains."

Josh had been relieved that no one had mentioned Silex's comment to him. He looked as uncomfortable now as when she had addressed him.

"No," he said flatly standing up and with uncharacteristic hubris walked out of the building.

*

Kier was alone by the river, sitting on the bank, her long legs underneath her.

"Josh," she said softly with a smile as he came towards her.

Josh turned his face, appearing startled at the sound of her voice. The close-fitting Guinness T-shirt and jeans emphasised his wire-tight movement. For a second his left shoulder angled away, and she thought he was going to ignore her, then his mouth relaxed, and Marianne's son came over to sit on the bank beside her, both elbows on his knees.

"Are you ok?" she asked.

"Nope," was the reply, the normally soft eyes now ice blue.

Kier said nothing, watching his rapid breath begin to ease. A splash of orange and blue sparkled on the opposite bank as a kingfisher launched upstream. Both of them gasped and jumped forward to see if they could catch another glimpse but Kier overreached towards the river. Josh's quick reactions pulled her towards him, and they tumbled beside each other onto the bank laughing. He leaned on one elbow and picked at the grass.

"Why is it that the most beautiful woman I've ever known happens to feel like my sister?"

Kier laughed, "How do you know you haven't just broken my heart?" she said seriously. "I might be languishing with passion."

Josh looked keenly into her eyes and then broke into a grin. "Nah," he said shaking his head, "the only time you look remotely interested is when Echin's around."

Kier dropped her eyelids and didn't comment.

"You feel like my brother too," she told him, Gally's image crossing her mind. "And I think Gally probably feels much the same way," she added. "So little bruv, what's eating you?"

Josh, thumbs on his cheekbones, ran his fingers across his brow. Taking a deep breath, he turned to face her.

"What Silex said?" She nodded understanding.

"Evan wants me to paint it."

Kier sat up and hugged her knees. "You mean what you saw in the Wicklow mountains?"

Josh nodded, "I can't do it."

"Then don't," she said simply.

Josh smiled at her and then leaned over to kiss her cheek. For a fleeting second, she was reminded of Adam and her stomach churned bittersweet with hollow longing. By the time Josh had sat back the pain was wiped from her face.

"I don't get it Kier. I don't get what we're meant to do."

"What do you mean?" she asked, though she knew exactly what he meant.

"Why are we saddled with this bloody awful responsibility? And is it all real?"

Kier lifted her chin and let her eyes follow the soft flow of the river.

"What's already happened has been real enough, I wish it hadn't been," she replied. A touch of the walled in emotion that had left her unable to speak in the days after Whistmorden groped at her mind, its shadow made her eyes blur. Breathing deeply, she pushed the memory aside.

"Echin," she hesitated, "or Toomaaris, is the most deeply real person I have ever encountered, human or not."

Her gaze caught the patterns of light as they shifted in the water, and she felt Josh's keen focus on her face. "And I have never met another group of other individuals that I love the way I love each of you."

She turned her head and Josh's eyes were shining, "So," she continued, "I can only believe that what we are stems from good. And that the most important thing we can do is to allow ourselves to be truly whoever we were meant to be."

Josh leaned over and hugged her. He pulled himself up and headed back towards the outbuilding, where Evan had set up the easel and paints.

*

The voices were soft and intimate, tones that discussed things that mattered. Gabbie knocked but didn't wait for a reply before entering Klim's bedroom. His things were packed into a rucksack, placed on a chair by a bed that was perfectly made. Swift sat cross-legged on the bed and Klim was opposite, his knees folded underneath him. They had been holding hands.

"You don't look as if you're staying?" Gabbie's voice was a challenge and she completely and deliberately ignored Swift's presence. Swift unfurled her long graceful legs and slipped from the bed onto the chair. Klim looked puzzled and then nodded at the already packed rucksack.

"Just a way of life now," he told her. "We had to be ready to run at any minute in South America and we often did."

Gabbie nodded, her mouth tight.

"We're trying to see if we can find this Mengebara place that Silex wants Klim to sort out," Swift said equably.

"Oh," Gabbie responded, somewhat mollified, "the Facebook thing."

"What?" Klim asked her.

"Well, that's how I see it from what I've read, kind of a Facebook without computers. Everyone agrees what they want to post there for others to see and you only share it with your friends."

Klim stood up and hugged her, Swift hooted out loud. "Gabbie you're right! How could we be so dense? We've been killing ourselves all afternoon trying to find a place that doesn't exist. Klim, you have to start it. You're easily strong enough now."

The conversation was losing Gabbie, but she was pleased that she had said something that caused them both so much excitement. Klim's arms around her had left her aching for more contact but he seemed unaffected. She perched herself on the bed.

"Okay, let's give it a go, the three of us," Klim said as he leaned over and placed a fruit bowl in the centre of the bed.

Swift climbed back beside him and shuffled to make the top of a triangle. She reached out and took Klim and Gabbie's hands and all three sat cross-legged facing each other.

"Okay," instructed Klim, "the fruit bowl represents Mengebara, now close your eyes."

"Frigging barmy," thought Gabbie.

"Shush," Klim said aloud, "that's a shared thought, can you see, you pushed it outwards."

Surprisingly, Gabbie thought that she did see. She was sure her thoughts were her own, and private, as she watched an amalgam of images pass through her consciousness. 'Just as well,' she reflected and quickly heard the response from Swift, inside her head, 'What's just as well?'

Gabbie broke the triangle, sweating and pale.

"You were in my head," she told Swift. "It was your voice in my head."

"But that's it!" Klim told her. "That's how we start it, Mengebara. It's like there's a house where your mind and personal thoughts live and that's pretty well locked up. But outside there's a garden and that's where people passing can look in, and where you can look over the fence and talk with those you want to."

"But you have to live in the village to be able to see the gardens," added Swift. "I get it!"

Gabbie didn't. She motioned to get up.

"Wait please," Klim told her in a tone that made her melt inside, his dark eyes holding her still.

"This time I'm going to place a memory in the garden, see if you can both access it."

Once again, they held hands and this time Gabbie vividly saw herself and Swift sleeping not far from each other, by a small waterfall, in a place of beauty and yet also great pain. Klim's voice whispered 'Tinobar' but she was certain he had not spoken aloud. She opened her eyes and looked in wonder at her friends.

"It's where we were healed," she said softly.

Klim nodded, he had not succeeded in removing his own emotion completely from the picture and Gabbie had felt his utter relief at finding them.

Gabbie's voice was gentle, "It's like a photo on the Facebook page."

"Exactly like you said," he smiled. "Facebook without computers. Now I have to provide the mental software so that it can be used more widely but not breached by any unwelcome visitors."

"That's easy," Gabbie said intuitively. "If they're not one of us they won't be able to see anything, the gardens won't exist."

"Great if I can make it happen," Klim told her.

"It's already built in," she told him, surprising herself. "You did it without any deliberate thought."

Klim closed his eyes and opened them a few moments later. "It's done," he said, his voice tinged with awe. "We've established Mengebara. Gabbie you're completely right, it can only be inhabited by those who we let in."

He paused, his dark eyes smiling directly into hers, "You always surprise me," he told her softly and for a moment Gabbie was transported back to under the old oak tree on the shore road.

Swift smiled, "You're still in Mengebara," she told Gabbie who quickly removed her thought. "Deleted," she told them, amazed how easy it was.

"Daft cow," Klim said derisively and Gabbie's temper flew. Immediately thorn bushes erected around the 'garden' that they had created.

"Can't see the Virenmor getting past that one somehow," Klim smiled, but the thorn bushes stayed in place as Gabbie saw that Klim had deliberately goaded her.

"Let's hope not," Swift agreed getting up. "Let's go teach the others."

Chapter Thirteen

A solitary streetlamp splashed out a circle of light as Siskin manoeuvred Suara along the abandoned street. Klim checked for any signs of life, his mind reaching out and finding no others hidden in the darkness. The deformed tree pointed towards the graveyard; a gnarled finger barely illuminated by the waning moon. The cloaked vehicle slowly pulled in alongside the damaged RAV4; the old white van now removed. They waited and observed, both in combat gear, their faces blackened, focused on the vehicle they had come to recover.

Klim found Siskin's mind print, uniquely translating image into sound, in a way that the younger man could barely understand. It had been a huge relief for Klim to find that each of his friends, with relative ease, were able to touch the mind place that he had created. Evan had told him that this was due to his own contribution, amplifying the way the others were able to connect. As for himself it meant that he could disentangle from any thoughts that he did not wish to be privy to, connecting instead through the controlled process of Mengebara. They were all there at the house, each focusing on the mind place, where Klim and Siskin deposited their impressions of the lonely village and the night-time vigil.

It was almost dawn when Klim and Siskin finally left Suara, their minds focused on their surroundings, every sense alert. All four tyres on the RAV4 needed replacing and Klim made his way to Kier's vehicle. He climbed into the driver's seat to gain access to the central reservoir used for storing tools. Siskin focused on releasing the vehicle from its protection, shocked by the layers that had already been removed, relieved that he had followed his gut feeling and come tonight instead of waiting. He doubted that they would have still been able to recover the vehicle had they left it any longer.

The ex-soldier moved quickly to the back of Suara, where they had stored the replacement tyres. The solitary CCTV camera pointing at the RAV4 had given him little concern, in fact he was surprised to find only one in his sweep of the village beforehand. Siskin, tyre in one hand, managed to pull out a small tube from his pocket that was akin to a dog whistle, but of his own design. He blew into it sharply and then glanced with satisfaction as the camera cracked. Moments later he was on his knees, the new tyre flung back into Suara, and his hands pressed tightly over his ears to shut out the roar of sound that shook the ground beneath him. It seemed to come from inside the earth, grating and heaving. Klim turned anxiously, as he felt his friend's mind fill with pain and horrendous sound. He pushed opened the door of the RAV4 to get back to Siskin, but the other man's alarm sounded loud in the deserted village.

"Go," he ordered.

Klim banged shut the half-opened door and turned on the engine. The vehicle swung wildly into the road, metal pressing against the remains of the slashed rubber tyres, sparks flying as he headed in the direction of Pont o Ffrindiau.

Siskin pushed aside the persecution of vibrating sound and dived into the front seat of Suara. Once in the vehicle the cacophony died, but only to be replaced by a rattle, high pitched and ominous. Siskin blinked as he saw what appeared to be a thin wire, whirling in the air directly above the RAV4. He launched Suara into motion, shrouding it in the protective, invisible cloak he had constructed for the vehicle. He forced aside his anger at having been caught so easily in the ambush that had been laid. Klim obeyed Siskin's urgent mental command to keep driving away from the village and was relieved to see the sun rise above the valley, as he hobbled the car to the end of the lane. They had already agreed to quarantine the vehicle in a barn outside of Pont o Ffrindiau and Klim, taking a left turn, hoped that there were no police on the deserted main road. He was at a loss to understand why they were damaging Kier's vehicle further and making themselves vulnerable, as the squeal of metal sounded loud on the deserted road.

Without warning the sky blackened and Klim thought at first that a plane was off course and was heading towards him. Then he saw that it was a creature, something like a pterodactyl, and his quick mind thought back to the Virenmor and their use of game figures. He slammed on the brakes and the vehicle careered across the road smashing into a fence. The creature barely altered direction, its massive black wings coming to fold over the car whilst dead grey eyes held him, stunned. He felt the ancient evil of the thing seep into every pore of his being and knew that this was something vastly different and old, so old. 'The Winged Huntress,' his terrified mind recalled, the enemy that had murdered Erion. Klim felt his heart freeze as dead space swallowed his thought and the pitch-black cape of a giant wing lifted further towards the door. Siskin's voice yelled inside his head and quick reflexes jumped back to life as Klim shoved the door open and threw himself beneath the vehicle, in the gap between wing and door. He barely noticed the hot metal of the exhaust burning against his skin, as his top slid upwards in the scramble to get underneath the car. He felt Siskin silently positioning Suara about twenty yards behind the RAV4, as the repulsive figure nudged its head against the doorway and pushed. The car shook and the wheels lifted but fell back into place with a discordant clang, any rubber that had been present was now shredded or melded onto the metal wheels. Klim shuffled to the far side with difficulty. The further destruction of the tyres meant that the body of the car was lower in the grass, challenging even his slim figure. He shuffled across, coughing as exhaust fumes filled his nostrils and reached for the other side. A greater push from the creature almost caught his arm between the edge of the vehicle and the ground before slamming back into place, the exhaust rattling just above his chest.

The massive hunter had shown no signs of noticing Suara and Siskin. Klim followed his friend's mind-print as Siskin descended behind the driver's door and reached a hand towards his belt. 'When I say,' Siskin said softly inside Klim's head. The trapped youth closed his eyes and breathed deeply. "Now, Roll!" Siskin demanded, this time aloud, as the creature turned, becoming aware for the first time of Siskin's presence. It screeched in anger before turning back to the RAV4, but it had been enough time for Klim to roll out onto the road and to get to his feet. He dived into the opposite field as Siskin expertly threw a grenade, blasting the vehicle and the winged creature into flames. A wail pierced the atmosphere, an agony of existence that was consumed in the flames, as they plumed upwards from the entangled remains of mechanical and organic demise. Suara pulled up on the other side of the road and Klim pulled himself into the car.

Siskin's relief was profound as he saw only superficial

burns on his friend's arm and back. Klim, his eyes shut, pressed his head back against the top of the seat and swallowed as they glided along the empty road. Then he opened them and looked back over his shoulder at the smouldering remnants of the car he had been trapped underneath minutes previously, and the shocking creature that had pursued him.

"Way too close," he told Siskin. "Way too close!"

*

Gabbie ran into Kier's bedroom, but she was already awake. Out in the corridor Swift and Josh joined them, as they made their way down to the kitchen. Evan came in seconds later and it was clear that they all had seen the images that Klim had placed in Mengebara. Ten minutes later they heard doors banging in the courtyard and went out together to help. Klim was pale as he dropped down from the car and Gabbie was quick to offer her arm.

"I'm okay," he told her, but still placed an arm over her shoulder, as they herded together towards the house and into the kitchen. Evan had taken out a bottle of brandy and both men drank from it.

"Hey, Mengebara's better than mobiles," Klim said with a half-smile.

Swift had brought dressings for his arm and back; gently she helped him take off his sweatshirt. He winced as she cleaned the areas and smeared on antibiotic cream. Gabbie stood aside, picking up the dusty top, her hand outlining the two areas where the sweatshirt had been torn away, two holes edged with burnt material. She deposited it in the utility area.

"What in God's name was that thing?" asked Evan, drawing up a wooden chair.

"An Irresythe," Echin's voice came from the just inside the back door, in front of the crysaline mural.

Siskin gave a sigh of relief as he turned towards the Mourangil. Echin looked different, noticed Kier, there were flecks of grey in his dark hair; his calm, oceanic eyes were more remote than ever. He was dressed in a soft dark green shirt of some cloth she couldn't quite place, with over trousers of the same material but an even deeper leaf colour.

"You found Mengebara," he congratulated Klim who nodded, pleased.

"And Magluck Bawah found you," Echin continued, casting a penetrating glance over the two men.

"The Undercreature," Klim said as he recalled the document that Kier had translated.

Echin nodded sadly, "The Irresythe was the very last of its kind, hidden for centuries in Scotland and found by Danubin who brought the creature nearby and waited for you to arrive. When you triggered the prepared device Magluck Bawah was released into the doomed body of the ancient creature."

"She knew I'd use sound." Siskin's voice was tight, "My defences on the RAV4 were almost unravelled. I underestimated her and I wasn't prepared."

He looked over apologetically at Klim who shook his head.

"There was no way you could have known what was going to happen. You stopped me from ending up as that thing's main course."

Siskin gave a half-smile, but his eyes remained troubled.

"Yeah, that's great," Gabbie said, pointing a finger at them both, "but what am I gonna tell the hire car people!"

Siskin put an arm round her and glimmered a smile.

"Sorry," he said unapologetically.

Evan, with Kier's help, made coffee for them all as they chatted out the strain of the night before. The day was well established as Echin said softly, "Josh, its time."

Josh hesitated, "Everyone's so tired," he commented looking around at the puzzled faces, but Echin held his gaze. "I'll go and get it," the artist told him.

The group remained silent as Echin took Josh's place beside Kier, waiting for his return. As he came back into the kitchen Evan went to help him carry the easel he had brought. Josh positioned the tall wooden frame at the end of the table and carefully placed upon it a painting that in itself, Kier thought, was as much a masterpiece as she had ever seen. There was a white path in the middle of a steep incline and to either side was a vast heathland.

Josh had painted the small wildflowers, heathers, and gorse so that they formed an intricate part of the landscape and their colours pressed against each other in a tight-fitting garment that covered the whole mountain. The eye was drawn to the horizon and the softly illumined sky. A solitary figure stood at the top of the path and on closer inspection she realised that Josh had painted himself. At the same time as she identified him in the painting, she realised he was no longer standing by the easel. Gasps of amazement came from around the table and Swift, who had been sat at the edge, opposite Evan, jumped up and examined the area around the easel. Turning back to the group she stated what they had all realised, her hands held up in a gesture of helplessness.

"He's gone!"

"Look more closely at the painting," Echin instructed.

Swift bent over and her dark eyes widened in shock.

"He's moving! He's in the picture."

In moments, they had all scrabbled around the painting as the pictorial version of Josh climbed the last few steps of the ridge. Kier felt Gabbie's small fingers press against her palm, and she took her friend's trembling hand in hers, as they fixed their eyes on the scene that Josh had created. The side of the mountain had vanished to be replaced by the view from the ridge onto which Josh had climbed. Mountains circled a lake that shone blue in the afternoon sun. On the surface were reflected autumnal golds and greens that still hung on to the trees that bordered the lake. Josh turned towards them, but they were unable to hear any of the words that he was saying. Kier glanced at Klim who shook his head.

"There's no mind print, I can't reach him," he told them.

Josh looked uncertain. Within the painting he reached to the ground and picked up a pencil and pad. Facing the lake, he began to draw.

"The lake, look!" Siskin pointed to a movement in the centre of the water.

"It's like Swift's diamond," Gabbie said.

"Yes, but a different shape," commented Kier.

Kier could see that the clear jewel flashing before them in the sunlight was increasing in size until finally it hung huge in the air, suspended above the lake and just short of its diameter. There were intricate engravings over its surface, apart from the centre where there was nothing.

"It's a five-pointed star with an empty circle in the centre," Evan noted.

"The Myriar." Kier hardly recognised her own voice hushed in awe. "Around the edges are words but they're not all clear."

"There's writing around the centre circle, Kier," Gabbie said, peering at the engravings.

Josh in the painting, bowed his head and the image dimmed and began to reduce in size. Evan produced a pen and notepad,

"Quickly Kier."

Wordlessly Kier took the pen and paper but her eyes continued to search the jewel. Concentrating hard she whispered the words to herself, as the image began to fade, and committed them to paper without having time to fully appreciate what she had written. Josh turned away from the lake, his eyes infinitely sad and the drawing dropped from his fingers. The view from the ridge was lost.

Slowly they watched the forlorn figure as he made his way back down the mountain. At the bottom of the white path, he stood looking back at the heathland and then abruptly he was in the kitchen again, the painting returning to its original form.

Echin caught Josh, cupping his head as he fell to the ground. The Mourangil looked towards Evan, who came towards him as the others looked on anxiously.

"He'll be okay," Echin told them, "he just needs to rest."

Echin and Siskin carried the unconscious Josh towards Evan's cottage that had been converted from stables to the right of the main building. Evan and Klim went before them, opening doors and clearing obstacles. Swift followed, collecting a bag of crystals from one of the cupboards. Kier and Gabbie remained in the kitchen and Gabbie reached for the notebook and pen left on the table.

"I can't read it Kier."

To her surprise Kier saw that she had written the words exactly as they appeared in the script of Ordovicia. Somewhere along the line she had divided the two languages and was able to move easily from one to the other. She had written down the words that had appeared at the centre of the Myriar. She tore off the sheet, on which she had been writing and placed it in the centre of the table. Reaching for the rest of the notepad she ripped three further pages from the pad and wrote on each of them, placing them around the original sheet.

"It's like trying to catch a dream," she told her friend. "It's not just like being able to translate a different language, it's like it speaks to you at the time. As if it were a conversation."

Gabbie looked puzzled and Kier was frustrated with herself, at her seeming lack of ability to describe the process of being able to transcribe the hidden inscriptions.

"It's not like a dead thing, there's an interaction," she sighed. "It's hard to explain."

"It's okay Kier," Gabbie told her, "just get it down."

Kier stood back, "I think I've got it now."

"It's still all in the funny writing," Gabbie told her, screwing her face at the unfamiliar characters that Kier had drawn.

"What's the matter?" Gabbie asked, as Kier tried to suppress the fear that had risen to her chest, making her breathing shallow.

"I couldn't see all of what was written around the edges," she edged. "I feel that it was really important."

"Well at least you've got some and those around the middle," Gabbie reassured her. "Can't you change it to English?"

Before Kier could reply they both turned towards the back door from which could be heard footsteps returning from Evan's cottage.

"How is he?" Kier asked, as the rest of the group filed back into the kitchen.

"What he did took incredible courage," Echin told them. "He made visible and entered another plane of existence. Had his concentration wavered he wouldn't have been able to return."

"You mean he would have been trapped in the picture?" Gabbie looked alarmed.

"He would have been unable to cross the veil back into this dimension," Echin replied cryptically. His eyes peered over the shoulders of the two women. He smiled approval at Kier's distinctive copperplate script, a legacy from her over-traditional primary school.

"What Josh has brought to you is a vision of the Myriar as it now exists," he explained to the small group. "A validation that all five Seeds have been brought together."

"Does that mean one of us is Candillium? There's seven of us," Siskin asked.

"Remember this is a human struggle and the Myriar has evolved with your people. Even though I walk beside you, yet I am not the same. The Myriar revealed itself through you and to you. It may be that we have yet to meet Candillium in this life or it is possible that she has not come at all."

"She's come," Gabbie said with finality.

Echin laughed, "I hope so," he told her.

Siskin seemed exhausted, neither he nor Klim had rested properly since the previous morning. He straightened his shoulders and looked at Echin.

"What happens if we never find Candillium?" he asked the Mourangil.

Echin nodded, his face a solemn mask. "Then we must face Belluvour, at the moment of unbinding, without her. He will seek the destruction of all living things on the surface of Moura and the planet will darken in mourning if he succeeds. Already you have witnessed his intentions through Nephragm; should he succeed, there would be no more life as you know it upon the surface of the earth."

There was utter silence as each of them tried to process the unthinkable outcome.

The Mourangil turned to the table and picked up the three outer pieces of paper that Kier had written out. He gave the first to Klim, translating the words.

"*Into Mengebara will pour the army of the Iridice.*"

"I think we need more gardens," Gabbie looked at Klim, her eyebrows raised.

Klim nodded, his face wire tight as he slipped the notepaper into his pocket.

"What's Iridice?" she asked, trying to identify the memory of having heard it somewhere before.

"It's my father's kingfisher stone," he told her, looking stricken. "Don't you remember how we found his cave on the crag?"

"The one your uncle stole?" she replied.

He nodded, his jaw line lifting.

"I remember," she said thoughtfully, recalling the milky white moonstone that appeared like a cat's pupil when it moved. It had been used to unlock the secret cave that Klim's father had built as a hiding place on the crag in Bankside.

"Where is it now?" Echin asked him.

"Safe," said Klim, not meeting the other man's eyes.

Echin waited until Klim finally looked up.

"It helped her when she was dying," his dark eyes were haunted. "She said she could see him, my dad, whenever she looked into it. She was holding it when she died, I buried it with her ashes." Kier's heart went out to him as she saw the rigidity in the muscles of his back and his two fists clenched tight. Echin walked to the glitter box and placed his hand on the surface. The stones glittered in a pattern of light that suffused the room. Then he turned back to Klim.

"It's no longer buried in the garden of remembrance, nor anywhere in its vicinity," he told him.

"No!" Klim was outraged, his face darkening as his fist banged on the worktop. "I'll find it!" he announced, striding from the room. Before anyone could react, there was a loud banging at the front door followed by Klim's return to the kitchen, his face adopting what Gabbie had called his 'ninja look.'

"There's a whole crowd of them," he announced. "They're shouting for Evan; I've barricaded the door."

Evan suddenly seemed to grow straighter and taller as it became clear the voices were speaking in Welsh, "I'll deal with this," he told them, leading the way into the hall. Echin called Kier back, handing her the folded papers from the table.

"Look after these," he said softly before following the others.

Kier placed the papers securely in her jeans pocket. Herald barked furiously in reply to the demanding attempts to ram open the front door. Evan stamped his way forward and easily moved the heavy chair that Klim had placed by the entrance. Echin moved just behind the Welshman and Klim and Siskin followed. The shouting became an irritable hum as Evan demanded quiet. He held the dog by the collar and opened the door fully. Half a dozen people tumbled into the hallway led by a spokesman.

"What are they saying?" Kier whispered to Gabbie; Swift turned back to catch Gabbie's reply.

"Just a minute," she told them, dragging a chair nearer the doorway, and standing up on it so that she was able to see over the others, to the chaotic melee of people at the foot of the staircase.

"I think the bald headed one at the front is a minister, he's wearing a dog collar," she explained. "They're trying to save

Evan and the youngsters, guess that means us, from the pagan perversions of Echinod Deem!"

The name was in stereo as Gabbie echoed the words of the minister, which would not translate into Welsh. Then they heard Evan's irate reply.

"Better not translate that," Gabbie's said, with eyebrows raised.

Kier glanced in the hallway to see Echin move forward. He put a hand of restraint on Evan's arm and also spoke in Welsh.

"He's asking them to calm down," Gabbie continued to translate, then in the silence that followed Evan's rich bardic tone echoed ominously.

"You have no business in my house Joel Hammond," he said coldly in English.

Gabbie almost toppled with concentration and the other two supported the chair. All three were concentrating so hard on the scene in the hallway that they were unaware of the back door quietly opening. In fact, they only noticed the female figure that had entered when she strode past them and pulled the kitchen door closed, locking it from the inside. Kier hadn't even noticed that the door had a lock and Gabbie's face was stunned with surprise. In a second, she had jumped down from the chair and stood side by side with the other two women. They were inches from the intruder's face as Swift, shocked and puzzled, spoke her name.

"Angharad!"

"What are you doing?" Kier demanded, but it was already too late, there was a clinical smelling cloth over her mouth and nose. "Don't hurt them, Terence!" Evan's daughter was saying. The blurred image of her pale face was the last thing that Kier saw before she slipped beyond consciousness.

Chapter Fourteen

"Shreive said to keep them tied up until we got back to your village." The voice was male.

"I don't care what she said," Angharad replied in high pitched fury. "They're not criminals!"

There was a hesitation and Angharad added, "What, can't you manage three unconscious women?"

"I'll free their feet, but the hands stay tied," grunted the man. The tightness around Kier's ankles had flipped her back to awareness but she was careful now not to react as the rope was loosened. The vehicle started moving and Kier heard the echo of one of her companions banging involuntarily against the side of the vehicle, producing a booming sound. It appeared they were travelling in a large van. The indented button of a mattress pressed against her right cheek and her shoulder knotted beneath her. One knee had made contact with the warm feel of flesh, though whether it was Gabbie or Swift, she was uncertain.

Concentrating hard she sought Mengebara as Klim had taught her, and left images there of what she had heard and felt. She dared not risk opening her eyes, as she was convinced that the man called Terence was watching her. This was confirmed moments later by Angharad's scathing tone.

"Stop leering Terence, for God's sake. Remember you're a married man!"

"Just making sure she's still out," he countered. "Thought I saw a flicker of her eyelids."

"Really," she replied. "No doubt Shreive'll be fascinated by your diligence."

That name again, Shreive. Kier filed it away. Their best chance of escape had to be before they reached wherever they were being taken. She felt another connection in Mengebara, Swift. She was conscious then. Klim, Siskin, Echin, they were there too. Unlike the others Echin seemed physically present in Mengebara. Rather than seeing images that he produced to reflect his experience or thought, he was a glowing light that washed Kier with its flame. He held out his hand and there in the centre of his palm was a gleaming lapis lazuli stone. Seconds later came the feel of the small jewel in her hand and its warmth tingled against her skin. Her fist closed tightly around the stone and the sick sluggishness of the chloroform left her. Strangely, in the discomfort of the van, being knocked against the walls and unable to open her eyes, Kier felt more at peace than she had done at any time in the last twelve months.

*

Mist had gathered around Y Wasgod Oren. Siskin approached the broad back of Evan as he sat hunched over the kitchen table. The musician had slept fitfully for a few hours, but the disturbing melody that was Evan Gwyn had awoken him. Evan's song had always been a vital rhythm, a deep echoing drum beat that told of the stone and the earth. Now it was as if blades scraped against rock, the grating and harrowing sound of shame and regret.

Siskin, through long experience, could envelope the sounds he did not wish to hear, but his friend's sorrow he could not overcome. The half-smile that Evan attempted, when Siskin pulled up a chair to the table, was negated by the desolation in his eyes.

"It was not your doing, my friend," Siskin told him.

Evan's heavy lids opened to reveal bloodshot eyes above a glass of brandy.

"It was exactly my doing," he stated.

Siskin waited until the older man chose to continue.

"I never tried to include her or even explain. I never gave her the chance to understand. She loves Swift and would want to do what is right for the girl. I suspect it was really her that she came for."

"Echin does not blame your daughter."

"Angharad knows that Echin has directed my life and for that I feel no shame. How could I tell my young daughter that the man who looked no older than her father had been as a parent to me!" Fingers worried his brow, "But later I could have tried to help her understand. I failed them both."

"Evan!" Siskin was firm now. "Clearly Angharad's concerns were manipulated."

His words however only produced more agitation in the

Welshman, who pulled himself up from the table. "Echin didn't say, but I know he suspects Danubin has been involved. Into what peril have I placed them all?"

His anxiety had soared to a crescendo of pain and Siskin knew no way to appease this man whom he had come to respect and who commanded such affection from them all. Klim entered the kitchen door, his lean and intuitive face distorted with anxiety.

"Another trap," he said, his eye wide with realisation. "Danubin stands calling us from the gateway. She has Gabbie."

Evan looked up alarmed as Siskin groaned, "It's my song, she has my song!"

The Welshman looked at him in confusion, trying to throw aside the lack of sleep and awaken senses dulled by brandy.

"Stay inside," he said firmly. "She can't pass the perimeter that Echin has drawn."

It was too late. With ease of long practice Siskin and Klim had gathered their resolve and headed for the gateway, swift as arrows.

"Come back!" the Welshman shouted; his eyes filled with tears as his sluggish mind began to understand.

The two friends had almost reached the gateway when Josh appeared beside them. The Chalycion around his neck pulsed a pink glow that made visible the figure that emerged from the mist and was now only a few feet away. She stood at the centre of the entrance to Y Wasgod Oren. Dressed in a long gown of gossamer she appeared fiercely beautiful. On either side of her began a row of men and women, whose concentrated presence pressed heavily upon the two men and continued in a line on the other side of the river. It was to Shreive however that they were both drawn and only Josh's light figure barred the way. He turned towards the would-be intruders.

"Go Danubin," he said firmly. "There's no place for your kind within our walls."

Shreive screeched in laughter and Klim gasped as he witnessed the transformation from the fragile beauty to a being of red flame, her cape billowing to fire, her pink eyes shrinking to malicious gleams of hate.

"But I have you all," she told them. "As soon as you leave this space." There was an uneven cackle, "And you Lute!"

Siskin turned his head.

"I found Amron Cloch," she told him, her voice a harsh whisper. "It calls for you, but it is mine."

Siskin was stock-still and he allowed her eyes to settle upon him. He did not stir as she came closer, peering into his being, trying to ravage what she could. Siskin looked into the eyes of Danubin and spoke with a coldness that Klim had come to know well. He had heard Siskin use the same tone dealing with the deadly influence of those they had opposed in Nicaragua.

"I know your melody now Danubin and it is the cold sprite of disaster. You will never find me unaware again."

Danubin faltered slightly, her red cape billowing behind her in the mist. Klim heard her call inside his mind and found himself heading towards the gate. Josh barred the way, his voice steady and firm.

"She doesn't have Gabbie," he told his friend. "It was an implant in your consciousness. She used the fact that you are a Reeder, making it look like you were picking it up from Gabbie."

Again, Danubin cackled, her gaze resting on the quiet figure of Josh who was now surrounded by the pink glow that emanated from the Chalycion stone. The malign figure appeared to shrink before it but then as she stepped backward from the gate she was just as fierce.

"Magluck Bawah knows each of you," she said, her voice low and malicious. "You will not live long enough to fulfil whatever foolish dreams the Mourangils have instilled within you."

Josh turned towards the gate and Danubin came nearer.

"I will have you Creta," she told him. "When you no longer have that filthy pebble round your neck!"

Josh did not react. Klim and Siskin came to stand at either side of him. Spitefully Danubin placed her hand upon the cherry blossom tree that adorned the gateway. In minutes, it had disintegrated with disease. A moment later both she and her followers had vanished.

Chapter Fifteen

Kier awoke to the cold air that fanned across her face; the doors to the van were wide open. On either side of her Gabbie and Swift were also rousing. She shook herself free of the loose rope around her ankles, noting that she had lost the jewel that had rested within her palm. She tackled the ties around her wrists with her teeth and loosened the remaining ropes. The free hands checked the hollow of the mattress nearby, but she could not find the stone. Turning to the other two she quickly undid the ropes, whispering to them to keep as quiet as they could. Gabbie looked grey as she clambered down from the van, her eyes blinking. Swift squatted, placing both hands on the ground, looking around her.

It was mid-afternoon and the soft light that peered through the cloud revealed a landscape that was both bleak and beautiful. They were very high up on a mountain track that seemed barely accessible. The van was perched on the last broad space of road before it became a pedestrian track. The path stretched above them, a narrow ridge on either side of which was a sheer drop; the dark brooding shapes of the surrounding mountains poked elusively through the mist, allowing transitory glimpses of their summits. Alarm tightened the faces of Gabbie, and Swift, as harsh human sounds bounced alien across the valley. Quickly, the three women moved to the front of the van where they could follow the muffled screams that had their source high above on the narrow track. Kier could just make out two figures writhing together at the edge of a dangerous precipice.

"Angharad," shouted Swift. She was already moving, followed immediately by Kier and Gabbie.

As they came closer, the male figure defined himself into a man of middle years and build. He was dragging Evan's daughter further up the side of the mountain, pulling her arm while she kicked and flailed in an effort to shake off his grasp.

"Hold on," Swift screamed, scrabbling like a leopard on all fours, holding her balance confidently on the treacherous path. Kier identified the half groans, half bullish commands, as the male voice she had overheard in the van. Terence, Angharad had called him. Swift had reverted to a tirade of Spanish, exhorting the man to release Angharad on pain of death. As he reached a bend in the track, he looked directly down at Swift; a long, leering, predatory gaze over the top of Angharad's head. The face of his victim was now turned towards the other women, her dark eyes filled with tears as she frantically pulled against her captor.

"Go back," she yelled to Swift, as the man's hand yanked her hair, pulling her face back towards him. He stopped moving and adjusted his footing on the narrow ledge.

"Let her go!" Swift commanded in English.

The skin on his face was torn, his nose bled slightly, oily hair hung limply down across his cheek. The short gasps of his hot breath, like puffs of poison in the cold mountain air, changed shape as his mouth distorted into a cruel sneer. Angharad jerked violently to release her arm just as he swung his own out over the silent panorama, casting his victim over the ledge, snapping his fist back as she frantically tried to gain some hold. Angharad flew outwards, her dark hair and pale face captured in disbelief as she fell into the vast abyss.

The three women screamed, their appalled faces barely registering what they had seen. Swift, now upright, gathered her long limbs and sprung towards the man she had watched murder Angharad. He strode arrogantly towards her.

"Saved me the job of going to fetch you," his mouth arched cruelly as Swift reached him. He caught her arm, ready to fling Swift over the edge but Kier's stride prevented this. She found a foothold in a hollow by the path edge and leaned inwards, lending her weight so that the man was wedged against the rock. Kier was now perilously close to the edge of the cliff; she looked around for a handhold, tensing against the expected push. Abruptly, she slumped inwards against Swift's slight but strong form. Her eyes opened wide with horror as she heard a chilling gasp from their assailant. Swift's dark eyes were livid and her arm ramrod straight as her hand pressed the man's face, pushing it deep inside the rock cliff. The expression of terror was lost as the stone seemed to melt around him, but Swift now used both hands and their combined weight to press what was left of his leg into the unforgiving tomb. It was only the sound of Gabbie arriving that finally cut through her rage and made the young woman release her hands from the grim surface. Rock scree fell beneath Kier's feet; she stumbled backwards but Gabbie was there to stop her falling.

"We need to get down from here," Gabbie shouted against a rush of wind.

Kier nodded and stepped in behind her friend. Looking back, the shape of a face was just visible, until Swift passed long fingers over the rock surface, erasing his impression forever. Her dark eyes were a mixture of triumph, shock, and fear as she turned back towards her companions.

"He killed Angharad," she told them fiercely.

"Evan," Gabbie bowed her head. "Poor Evan." Her words were lost in a gust of wind that pinned the women against the rock as carefully, holding hands, they descended the track.

The van, its back doors wide open, banging in the wind, stood where they had left it. Forlornly Gabbie and Swift tumbled into the back of the old vehicle and Kier sighed with relief when she found the key left in the ignition. The wind had risen to screaming pitch as Gabbie reached forward to close the doors that clanged shut with a violent echo. Kier frowned as she worked out the controls. There was no choice but to reverse down the single track until she reached a level where there was room to turn. Sweat tickled her forehead as she brought the rear tyres to the edge of an overhang and finally lurched the vehicle forwards. Glancing in the mirror Kier could see that Gabbie had her arm around Swift, who sat dazed and silent. Rigid with tension, she fixed her hands on the steering wheel as they descended through twists and turns down the treacherously steep road. They were still high up on the mountain, where only a flimsy rail gave protection, as the road skirted alongside a precipitous gorge. It was only after another mile that Kier was able to relax, as they reached a wide enough road for two vehicles to pass, with a densely wooded area to their right. She slowed, intending to stop, if only to release the tension that wound around her neck and shoulders. Gabbie and Swift were kneeling on the mattress behind the passenger seat. The two girls screamed in warning; Kier slammed her foot on the brake as a female figure stepped out from the woods and placed herself directly in front of the vehicle.

Chapter Sixteen

Siskin breathed a sigh of relief, hearing the strong melody beat out its determined pace as he followed the Welshman through the twists and turns of an underground tunnel. The walls were dense granite and smoothly finished, as if the tunnel had been carefully maintained. Crystals were spaced along the roof, giving off a soft glow that allowed the four men to see that the stone floor was gradually ascending and that they would have to lie flat on their bellies for the stretch ahead.

"It's only this part," Evan told them. "Where we won't be able to stand up, is where the tunnel bridges the river beneath."

He was squatting in front of the narrow space, his voice raised above the rumbling river below.

"On this side our protection holds, but the stretch on the other side of the Teifi will be vulnerable to the Virenmor." The grey eyes were serious. "From here until we get underneath the college we'll be in danger of discovery if they sense us from above the surface, and I have no doubt that Danubin has the ability to do so." Evan raised his head so that he could see Klim at the back of their small column, "I need you all to think granite."

"How?" asked Josh over Siskin's shoulder.

"I've placed in Mengebara how the stone feels to me," Evan told them. "You need to hold that impression in your minds as much as you can. Klim, can you amplify it?"

Klim nodded, he was breathing deeply, already lost in concentration, searching for the stone's impression in Mengebara. "Are you alright?" Siskin asked Evan, seeing that his face was grey with strain.

"I get weaker the longer I stay underground," the Stozcist replied. "It's possible you will have to help me during the last part. You should lead once we're on the other side."

Siskin nodded and they joined together in Mengebara. There, in the centre of the 'garden' was a structure that had no semblance to granite whatsoever.

"Danubin and Magluck Bawah are out there," Evan had 'messaged' to them all. We have to enfold ourselves in the stone for the last half mile to the college, so that our presence can't be easily seen. Danubin has already shown far too much insight into how we think and feel, unless we get this right we'll be at her mercy."

Siskin thought about the way she had spoken so directly to him. The moment she had spoken the name 'Amron Cloch' he had felt it reverberate in every nerve fibre. He knew instinctively that it was a vital part of what he was searching for. With tremendous effort, he pulled in his concentration and observed the separate parts that made up the image of granite stone in the centre of Mengebara. It had its own vibration. Reaching out mentally he found and amplified the finely different tones of mica, feldspar and quartz that made up the whole. At the same time Klim's mind took the material and clothed each of them with its imagined substance. Josh looked towards the pulsing stone beneath his throat and the Chalycion dimmed its glow in response as he placed it beneath his sweatshirt.

Evan nodded. Breathing deeply, he led the way forward through the narrow tunnel and out to the other side. Siskin squeezed past Evan to take the lead as soon as they were able to stand up in the damp darkness. Slowly they trudged on, aware of the different feel of the stone on this side of the bridge. Evan had explained that the tunnel had been excavated at the time the college was built; the successive inner circles of theologians had maintained its secret down the years. There was no light, as they crept quietly along the same path as one of the ley lines that gathered at the town's epicentre. Siskin calculated that they had been walking for twenty minutes, when he felt Evan stumble against him. Turning he gave his arm for support but then Klim's voice rang out sharp in his head.

"STOP!"

Immediately they were still. Above in the distance Siskin heard the discordant cry that he knew to be Danubin. The snake of awareness coiled around him as he began to respond to the seeking energy above, feeling a momentary tug of attentiveness from the creature, whose pernicious energy weaved above the surface. A loud rumble shook the tunnel, and he began to fear that he had alerted the Virenmor. Immediately Klim's mental energy suffused him and blotted out every thought, apart from the granite that surrounded them. There was a second booming sound somewhere nearby. They each breathed a sigh of relief as the sound became more distant and they felt the malignant influence pass them by.

Evan slumped forwards but Siskin was quick enough to prevent him falling. Josh came quickly to his assistance and between them they inched their way along the damp tunnel. Finally, they rounded a bend where crystals glowed once more within dry walls.

"We must be under the college," Josh said confidently. Klim did not respond. He held his mind in focus, holding the barrier to detection in place. Ten minutes later they reached what had to be the entrance to the chapel. The door was locked. Siskin turned to Evan whose melody had become the low hum of detachment. Klim was still in deep concentration. The ex-soldier had brought none of his tools and he feared that a physical assault on the door would create too much noise. Evan had instructed that they bring no attention to themselves once inside the college. Josh, his voice a soft whisper suggested, "Sing to it."

Siskin turned to the younger man who had seemed so remote, and yet also more fully present, since his sojourn to wherever he had really been, when they were able to see him in the picture. The Chalycion seemed more in tune with him, literally; it throbbed softly to his heartbeat. Undoubtedly Josh seemed to have accessed an insight that was heightened by his strange experience. Evan's large frame pressed against him, and Josh looked pointedly towards the door. Siskin placed his hand on the wood, which was solid oak. To his surprise, he began to understand that the wood fibres gave off a distinct vibration. The tune rose within his throat, barely a sound but it echoed gently in the underground tunnel, three notes close together, modulating in the musician's voice. Siskin filled himself with the vibration of the sound, channelling it to his fingers that pressed against the door. He felt the internal locking mechanism shift and the heavy oak door creek open, allowing them to file into the darkness behind.

The scent of wood and worship was pronounced as Siskin led the way through a narrow passage that climbed upwards and opened out into the back corner of the chapel. Once they had all exited the passage Siskin noticed that from within the chapel the door appeared as a decorated panel to hide its existence. He quickly closed the panel that aligned completely with its neighbour, noting its position carefully. They helped Evan as they made their way to the back of the chapel, where each of them slumped into one of the tall individual seats that provided a cocoon of meditative space. Neither Siskin nor Klim had slept properly since the attack by the Irresythe and Klim was grey with exhaustion. Evan was weak with the effort of travelling underground and Josh seemed content to rest his eyes. Siskin looked upwards at the ornate ceiling, where a rich patchwork of burnt orange and green engravings embroidered a domed roof. He was so tired that he knew he had to focus in order to keep functioning. His methodically examined the pews, ending in the back corner of the chapel on the other side of the aisle from where they were sitting. He started as he realised that his gaze was being returned by a pair of dark eyes, which watched him steadily from behind small round glasses. Immediately Siskin was fully alert once more as he returned the impassive stare of the cleric, for a cleric he judged him to be. The stranger was middle aged and wore a white T-shirt underneath a dark jumper; he was small, and his jet-black hair curled around skin that was the colour of the elegant cello that Siskin sometime played. His melody was the peaceful ebb of a windless lake, which the musician associated with those who spent long hours in prayer. This particular melody seemed to echo an ancient theme but there was no hint of a threat within its notes.

"I am Samuel," the stranger said quietly.

Siskin noted that the Irish brogue seemed out of place with his overtly Jewish features. He nodded in response but said nothing, wondering how he could have missed this man sitting quietly in the rear of the chapel. If he had been deeply in prayer perhaps, he had not seen them enter. Klim and Josh had opened their eyes at the sound of the other man's voice and Josh look surprised. Getting out of his chair he went over to stand in front of Samuel.

"You were in the Wicklow Mountains last autumn," Josh said

neutrally.

"Yes," the other man replied simply.

"You walked with me to the lake," Josh said, his face furrowed in concentration. "You were the figure in the first painting I made. You walked back through the gateway with me."

"You answered the call of Samuel," replied the other man cryptically.

Josh stood scrutinising the small, unabashed stranger but it was Evan who spoke.

"That's in the Old Testament," he told them. He seemed to have recovered quickly, though his voice was still gruff with exhaustion. "He was known as the man who let none of the Lord's words fall to the ground."

"You know your Bible, Evan Gwyn," said Samuel smiling.

"What does it mean?" Klim asked, scrutinising the stranger. He turned, his expression alarmed and said quietly to Siskin, "He has no mind print."

"How do you know my name?" queried Evan, standing and coming over to place himself next to Josh.

Siskin and Klim followed so that all four now stood facing the stranger in the next row. As each row descended in height however, they were merely level with the small man whose eyes continued to sparkle; they showed no sign of being intimidated by the intruders in the chapel.

"When Eaman Keogh rang the bell as it were," he looked at

Siskin and smiled, "I was aware of each of you. You could not have entered, even with your song, had I not allowed it."

The four men look stunned at his words, but none spoke, and Samuel continued his explanation. "But Toomaaris said there were seven and you are only four. Where are the women?"

His eyes grew serious as Evan sighed and leaned back against the wooden rail.

"You know Toomaaris?" the Welshman asked.

"Whom you know as Echinod Deem?" Samuel asked in return and Evan nodded.

"That he is Toomaaris the Mourangil, once guardian of Ordovicia, is not unknown to you I think."

"Still, it feels strange to call him that," said Evan, an edge in his voice. "He has always been Echin to me."

Samuel nodded, "Then Echin it was who gave me your names and told me that you would soon need to escape through the tunnel of Judges."

"Judges?" questioned Siskin.

"The original Samuel judged for his people; he related the word of the divine. I judge when and how the passages are used and to whom they are closed."

"And you judged that we should be allowed into the college?" Klim responded.

"I judged that you were in part the Seeds of the Myriar," the small man replied.

"Is there anything you don't know?" asked Evan with an exasperated sigh.

"I don't know how I am going to make you look like a student!" replied Samuel laughing. "We will need to use the passageways. Sadly, the college is beset with agents of Danubin. They cannot enter here however, and it is a short way to my rooms above." He stopped talking for a second; there was a hum of activity outside the entrance to the chapel. "We should go now," he told the others, turning around to touch the rectangular, carved panel behind him. It opened silently into a dark tunnel and Samuel signalled them to enter.

"I need to go last to close the entrance behind us," he explained. The four friends exchanged glances. Klim messaged in Mengebara, 'Do we enter it?'

'Certainly,' Evan messaged back.

They found themselves bending into the small doorway and shuffling along until Samuel stepped behind them and closed the door, plunging them into complete darkness. Klim felt Siskin, tired as he was, tense for a fight but Samuel's laughter tinkled into the confined space as he squeezed past each of them to reach the front. At first Klim thought that he had lit a lamp. He was therefore startled to see that in fact light was emitting from the top of Samuel's index finger. The small man moved rapidly ahead of them, revealing the rich red and gold of carpeted murals that lined the walls of the passageway. Brief glances seemed to reveal biblical pictures of a man who looked much like the one now leading them through the darkness. At the end of the corridor was a circular stairway and as Samuel reached the top of the steps the soft glow was replaced by a flood of light. Klim gasped in surprise as he found himself emerging from a square trunk. In front of him was a board held out to the side by steel hinges, to the right a suspended assortment of books, and to the left was the trunk lid. Klim turned to step into the room and watched as the others followed behind him. Once Siskin had joined the others, the square board smoothly became the floor of the trunk once again, followed by the assorted contents and finally the lid, as they moved noiselessly back into place. Automatically Klim had noted the small area they had entered and that it contained two doors, both glass, providing light for the small windowless hallway. The clink of cups sounded, and Samuel popped his head round the nearest door.

"Come, come through," he urged. The main room proved to be a good size with a small kitchen to the rear. The four men sank gratefully onto two sofas as Samuel produced mugs of tea and a plate of sandwiches. Klim could do no more than briefly realise that the walls were lined with bookcases filled with very old hardbacks, the kind that Evan collected. The companions gratefully reached for a sandwich and a mug of tea, which had a peculiar but pleasant fragrance. Klim's stomach gurgled, he felt hollow with hunger and exhaustion and the sandwich was good, though he couldn't identify the filling. Some hummus thing that Gabbie was eating these days, he registered vaguely. He carefully put down his empty mu of tea and saw that like him, his friends were fighting off sleep.

"Now rest," Samuel said softly moving around them and removing crockery. It was if the words placed an unseen heavy cloth over Klim's eyes, occluding all waking thought.

Chapter Seventeen

Kier was assaulted by screeches inside and outside the van as she stopped within centimetres of the woman who had stepped into the middle of the road. Swift scrambled over the handbrake into the passenger seat and was out of the door within seconds. Tears fell down her face. A garbled thanks to St Rose of Lima sounded in choked Spanish, as she ran to the woman who had somehow filled the void left by her mother. Angharad stood dazed, her arms comforting Swift, whose head was buried in the older woman's shoulder. Kier helped Gabbie climb out of the vehicle; she held the other woman's gaze over the top of Swift's head.

"Where is he? Terence?" asked Evan's daughter.

"Gone," answered Kier quietly, with an expression of finality that Angharad seemed to understand, as she looked around now for another. "And Echin, where is he?"

Kier circled, searching, innervated. There was no sign of the Mourangil.

"He saved me," Angharad said quietly. Then as her companions looked puzzled, she continued, "Echin caught me as I fell."

"But where did he go?" Kier could not help the disappointment in her voice.

"I don't know. He said that Terence would never come back into my life and that you would be arriving soon in a white van. I was not to come out of the forest until I saw you."

Swift was holding Angharad's hand with an expression of grateful incredulity, as she continued to tell her story in a tone that told of lingering shock.

"It was like being held in a cloud. I felt out of time, I thought I had died," Angharad continued. "I saw myself as a child, him standing beside me, holding my hand. I saw how my father struggled between his love for us and the important work he has done. The way he tried to keep me safe by telling me so little. I heard my mother's voice singing."

Her tears flowed freely now and then her mouth tightened, "We have been so deceived." She bowed her head, "I am so sorry, so very sorry," she whispered.

Swift held her close and the other two women joined the embrace, standing together on the Welsh mountain, for the moment oblivious of all but the comfort they gave each other.

*

A deep booming pounded relentlessly inside Kier's head as she carefully drove the van away from the mountain. She had been aware of it from the moment they had begun to descend, but the treacherous drive needed all of her concentration and she could not let herself be distracted. Once they were down onto the road again the sound seemed to fill the vehicle but none of the others appeared aware of it. She tried to quell the tremble in her voice as she spoke.

"We can't go to your home Angharad," she took a left turn off the route that Evan's daughter had given her automatically. "We need to think. And hide."

Angharad, in the front of the van, nodded quietly. Swift said nothing, Kier saw that she was now gazing sightlessly out of the window, kneeling on the mattress behind Angharad. Kier continued to follow the road she had taken for several miles before Gabbie spotted a lay-by with a tea wagon.

"We could all do with a hot drink Kier," she said, catching her friend's eye in the mirror.

"I'd love a hot cup of tea," nodded Angharad, pulling her purse out from the glove compartment.

"I'll go," Kier told her as she stopped the van. "You might be known."

As she jumped down from the vehicle, she registered that the sound had lessened a fraction. It was not the fearful growl of the Undercreature, of that, she was sure; nevertheless, it remained highly disturbing. She had parked at the furthest edge of the lay-by and Kier, concentrating on the strange sound was startled to feel an arm slide under her own. Echin's voice whispered in her ear, just before they would have come in view from the interior of the tea van. He steered her back round towards the vehicle she had left.

"What are you doing? We need a drink." Kier told him.

"It's not worth the risk. Danubin has scouts all over this area."
Kier shivered, "I can hear a booming sound, like a really low
bell," she said, resisting the impulse to look backwards.

"Swift. Unfortunately, her moment of rage has done just that.
She's rung a bell that will be heard across the planet by all those
who are able to tune into its frequency, including the Devourils
and the Virenmor."

Kier blanched, her shoulders tensed as she quickly scanned the
empty car park.

"They know we're here?" she asked him.

"Not yet," he told her. "I diffused the vibration so that they'll
only be able to pinpoint Snowdonia and not the location of the
attack. But it won't be long before the mountains are swarming
with Virenmor."

Kier tried to suppress the surge of fear engendered by the memory
of the hideous creatures.

"Do you mind if I drive?" Echin asked her. Kier shook her head.
She joined Swift and Gabbie on the mattress in the back of the
van. The other two looked a little bewildered as Kier came to sit
beside them and the van door shut quickly behind her. Gabbie
smiled as she looked at Kier's face, "Echin?" she guessed.

Kier gave her a wry grin as the Mourangil started the van. To her
astonishment, he did not use the key or accelerator, only the
steering wheel.

"We need to get up on the ridge," he told them as the engine started of its own accord. Smoothly he steered the van out onto the road, continuing in the direction Kier had taken. A few minutes later, after a sharp bend, he turned left up a barely visible track that led higher into forest. Echin pulled the vehicle off the track without slowing down and manoeuvred the van faultlessly between the conifers, as Angharad shifted uncomfortably in the passenger seat. It was as if the trees were gliding out of the way. When he finally stopped the vehicle and indicated that they should all get out with him, the women let out gasps of surprise as they found themselves completely encircled by the tall conifers. He led them back down towards the track, which he crossed, to bring them to a steep ledge.

Kier breathed in the scent of pine as she bent down and peered with Echin through the trees. He had brought them almost directly above the lay-by, where the tea wagon had now closed its shutters and a middle-aged couple were disengaging it from the Land Rover to which it was attached. Hastily they got into the vehicle and in a few minutes were on the road heading in the same direction that Echin had driven their van.

"You we're right," Kier said quietly. "Or maybe they just happened to leave by coincidence."

"No coincidence," he told her as the Land Rover accelerated.

"Will they head up here?" she asked.

"It's possible," he replied, standing up.

"We're going to have to walk some distance," he told them,

glancing at their footwear. Only Angharad was not in trainers, but her shoes were low heeled.

"I'll manage," she told him, following his line of sight.

Echin turned and headed back to the van where Angharad removed her purse, placing it in the pocket of her light jacket. Echin signalled that they step back and put his hand to the ground. Kier saw his athletic form crystallise momentarily, until he seemed to exist somewhere between man and rock. The van started to shake as the land on which it stood became boggy; the vehicle started to descend. Blue flashes of light streamed from Echin's statue-like figure as the women stood in wonder. In minutes, the van disappeared, and the dry, sparse grass reformed. The space that had previously been wide enough for the vehicle was now just sufficient for them to wind through the trees into the depth of the forest.

"Achh!" Angharad whispered, making the sign of the cross.

Echin straightened his tall figure.

"Let your heart decide on evil Angharad, it's the only true barometer," he said gently, as he led them across the tree-lined space that the vehicle had previously occupied. Angharad looked shamefaced.

"I don't think you're evil," she stuttered.

Echin turned and held her eyes for a moment. He nodded. The women followed him up the steep slope where the towering pines filtered the sun to mere strands of light. Angharad suddenly looked scared and uncomfortable, but Swift came next to her and held her hand. Evan's daughter turned towards her with gratitude. Gabbie nudged Kier's elbow, her eyes signalling towards Echin as he strode ahead. "He is cute," she whispered, "just in a very strange way."

Kier smiled, trying to quell the singing in her heart that always occurred when she was with Echinod Deem or Toomaaris as she had now begun to think of him. Putting her arm around her friend's shoulder, her eyes lifted to the solitary figure who was already a good way in front. Gabbie looked up at her in incredulity as Kier began to hum softly to the tune of 'I've got the whole world in my hands.'

The walk became a trudge, it was Angharad who suffered the most as her ankles strained, unsupported. She struggled to keep up with the others as the climb became steeper though the women had taken to holding hands as they continued upwards. Angharad sighed loudly as they finally left the trees and found themselves in a semicircle of space, bounded by a huge wall of blue-grey slate. As they drew nearer, Kier saw that there were pockets of fine shale that created ledges, upon which it was possible to climb. She turned to the others, noticing Angharad's ripped tights, badly scuffed shoes, and the sheer exhaustion on the older woman's face.

"You go on," Angharad said in Welsh, perching herself on one of the rocks. "I'll wait here."

Angharad had spoken in weariness, not realising that she had lapsed back into her first language.

"Nid yw'n gwneud unrhyw synnwyr i ni wahanu nawr Angharad," Gabbie told her. "Makes no sense for us to split up now."

The Welsh woman looked at her in surprise but when she spoke again it was in English. "I can't climb that wall."

They looked round for Echin, but he was nowhere to be seen. Kier walked further into the semicircle, noticing that her footsteps echoed on the stone floor of the natural amphitheatre. There was a barely visible gap in the wall. She signalled the others across and then squeezed through the small space. Echin's hand reached out to catch her own and she felt the thrill of his touch, a charge of energy that coursed through her weariness.

"Come no further," he said softly. "I'll reach for you one at a time."

He helped each one pass through the small gap and in turn they gasped in shock as they found themselves perched side by side, to his left, on a narrow ledge on the other side of the slate wall. Down below was a sheer drop that ended in a picturesque mountain lake. Kier glanced once. but decided that none of the women were able to appreciate the scenery just then. The wind blew into their faces and kept their backs pinned to the wall as Echin led them to his right, holding Angharad's trembling hand as she stepped across the small gap; he waited until all had carefully bridged the opening before carrying on. Gabbie turned her head sharply, tugging at her friend. Kier's eyes widened as she watched the slate slide into place to seal the opening. Gabbie's fingers released hers as they rounded a curve in the rock. Kier followed and found herself falling backwards into a natural hollow that had been carved out of the south facing slope. Echin caught her and guided her into the small space.

The slap of the wind had left red marks on all of their cheeks as the women reached out for each other in relief. Angharad was still trembling, and Swift looked anxiously at the floor of the cave. Kier remembered Swift almost dying inside the cave on the crag at Bankside and she reached out her hand. The young woman let her small fingers be squeezed in reassurance but Kier caught the hint of despair in her eyes and it alarmed her. None of them had eaten or drank the whole day and they had been up most of the night. A neat pile of twigs was matted with the remains of some kind of organic material and Kier realised that this small cave had made a perfect bird's nest. A big bird's nest, she decided, seeing long feathers lying at the back of the cave. "Okay if you can fly," Gabbie said into her ear, "but where do we go now? I could murder a drink of water," she added, licking dry lips.

Echin had his head bowed in concentration at the opening of the cave; the wind was much less inside the hollow shelter, but the sound of its restless movement still made speech difficult. Kier watched as Echin passed his hand over the front of the opening, taking it away a few moments later to leave a film of white gauze-like material covering the entrance. Like a door closing, the sound of the wind died away and they were protected from the chill. Only Swift, shifting uneasily, looked less comfortable. "I can't stay here," she told Echin.

Echin nodded, "It's okay," he told her gently, and then turned to include the others. "I've created a portal," he glanced at the cave mouth, "and I'm afraid it's going to take a large leap of faith from you all."

He reached out his hand to Kier and she took it without hesitation, trying once again to ignore the exquisite sensation that his touch produced. "Just push your hand into the crystal cloth and let it take you to the cavern," he instructed. Swift took a sharp intake of breath at the word cavern, but Echin reassured her.

"You can come to no harm in this place," he emphasised and Swift nodded acceptance.

At Echin's instruction, Kier stood beside him on what seemed like the edge of the world. She looked at the white gauzy film in front of her and saw that it was alive with tiny lights that flickered like stars. Echin let go of her hand and she stepped forward, tumbling into space. Instantly she was aware of the fossilia surrounding her with the luminous fluttering of their tiny wings. She remembered their sparkling presence in Lioncera, their ability to transport matter seemingly without any effort. Kier's heart lifted in delight as she recognised Ortheria speaking directly into her mind; some part of her awareness registered that she was still moving through space. Whether this was above or below the earth she had no idea.

"Welcome Kier," the light voice said. "You have reached Reuben's Cavern."

In what seemed only moments, she found herself seated on the floor of a large space, where the walls were ingrained with an array of coloured minerals that reminded her of Evan's glitter box. The base rock was a smooth luminous green and in the centre was a small pool of oily liquid encased in a marble dish. Arising from this liquid was a white flame that flickered with reflected colour and whose warmth reached each part of the unusual room. Blocks of white crystal made windows of light on each wall and small, white, leafless trees flourished within their glow. Wood from these trees had been formed into chairs, a table, and various cupboards. Measured drops of water trickled from a small fountain at the back of the cavern into a stone bowl and back again by mechanism of a small spring. On the table was a colourful array of fruit and vegetables, fresh salad and different breads that set Kier's mouth watering. By this time, her thirst was overpowering, and she reached gratefully for one of the cream-coloured wooden cups that were perched on the edge of the bowl. The water was cool and clear and immediately refreshing. Even as she replaced the cup, she heard Gabbie's exclamation of delight.

"Wow! They're so beautiful, did you hear them? She called my name!"

"They're called fossilia," Kier told her, turning to her friend, "and the one you could hear inside your head is Ortheria."

Gabbie's eyes were wide saucers as she took in the amazing cavern, the indoor trees, the virgin white wood and light sources that seemed to enfold her.

"Where are we?" she said softly, her eyes still circling the space and gratefully reaching for the cup of water that Kier offered.

"Reuben's Cavern is what Ortheria called it," Kier said, allowing her eyes to roam once more around the unusual space. "I feel as if I'm in a dream," Gabbie replied, looking at the cup of water she had just gulped down, "and this stuff's dynamite! It's like I've just woken up!"

Kier was already filling her own cup again.

I don't think any of us have had a drink in twenty-four hours," she noted, filling three further cups, and placing them on the table.

Angharad arrived in an uncertain stumble and her face smiled relief as she saw Kier and Gabbie. She was trembling as she looked fearfully around at her surroundings. Kier took her hand and led her to one of the chairs where Gabbie placed a wooden cup in her hand. Once she had slaked her thirst, she seemed to relax a little.

"I think I blacked out for a moment. The next thing I knew I was here!"

Swift arrived a few moments later, her eyes filled with tears.

"They said they understood that it was okay," she told the others.

"Who, dear?" asked Angharad.

"The tiny creatures that brought us here," answered Swift. "Oh Angharad," she cried as she stepped towards the puzzled Welsh woman. Angharad reached out her arms and folded the young women in an embrace as her tears spoke an agony of regret.

"He would have killed us all," Kier said quietly, relieved as she realised that at last, they could speak of the morning's events. She remembered Swift's intractable passion that had forced the criminal into the surface of the rock face.

"I thought he had killed you," Swift muttered between her tears.

"I know Cariad," Angharad replied, patting the dark hair so like her own. "I know. And had it not been for Echinod Deem that would have been the case."

"Where is he? Echin, I mean," asked Gabbie.

"He has business elsewhere," answered a voice that did not belong to Echin.

Chapter Eighteen

Klim knew from the stiffness of his limbs that he had slept for hours. Stretching out his back, he realised there was space around him that he didn't expect to find. Abruptly he came to full alertness and saw he was alone. The training that he had undergone the previous year allowed him to push away the initial climb of panic and he concentrated on his surroundings. There was no sound, nor any hint of movement, but he was sure something had awoken him. Moonlight filtered through the small round window of the old building, where Samuel had led them through the hidden passageway. His mouth felt dry, and his head had the woolly sensation of sedation; had he been drugged? All traces of the light meal had been removed and there was not so much as a ruffled cushion on the other settee to show that others had slept here as well. He told himself that his friends would not have left him deliberately, but he could not prevent the slice of fear that cut through his insides. He sank into Mengebara-nothing. He searched for the mind prints of the other Seeds, but again nothing. Now he was afraid. The door rattled insistently, no knock. A voice that was more of a hiss, a whisper that crept inside the room and grew to a vicious vibrating threat.

"I have you now Reeder." The disembodied tones of Danubin

reverberated from each corner of the small space. Catlike he slid from the couch and made his way into the hallway that had been the initial entry into Samuel's room, or trap, he thought to himself. Then he reasoned that if she could enter these rooms she would have done so already.

The sound of scuffling came from outside the door. He heard the sickening thud of blows as Josh's voice cried out and Evan swore in Welsh. Siskin yelled for help and in a flash Klim was at the door. He was moments from opening it when he stopped himself and allowed his mind to reach to the other side first. There was no trace of his friends beyond the door. If they were truly present, they were already dead. Whatever else lurked behind it was shielded from him.

"Very good Michael," hissed Danubin, in the same eerie whisper that smoked underneath the oak that divided them.

The use of his Christian name punched hard against his will and revived every cruelty that his uncle had committed against him. Klim retreated back to the small hallway. He remembered that Echin had told them that his uncle was also Virenmor. Danubin's was a different evil, an almost primeval force that seeped under his skin and disestablished every belief, every solid good that he had ever known.

"Of course," the insidious voice continued, "you know she loves the Creta, I've seen her dreams."

Klim's control finally left him in a thud of sickening rage, though he never asked himself if it was because of his response to the creature's cruel mind games or the violent jealousy it had engendered. Without thinking he picked up a nearby walking stick and marched purposefully towards the door, but three feet before he reached it Samuel appeared out of nowhere to block his exit, one finger against his lips. In his rage Klim reached out to push him aside, his mouth intending to express all the pent-up anger of years, but he was unable to speak. Even as he absorbed the horror of his dumbness, Samuel had grabbed the raised stick and thrown it onto the couch. In another instant, he was propelling the youth through what Klim saw as a gossamer curtain, which had appeared at the back of the L-shaped room.

The space was filled with light. He was unable to see Samuel but was immediately conscious of the tiny fossilia that had been in Lioncera. They crowded around him, soothing his anger, calming the blind rage that had briefly possessed him. Even his shame at allowing Danubin to manipulate his emotion was swept away quickly by the incredible creatures.

'Klim,' they sang, 'Reuben is waiting for you.'

It seemed only moments later that he was surrounded by the soft glow of a light that defined itself quickly into a large cavern, where he was greeted by Gabbie's relieved cry as she simply said his name. It was enough to turn his knees to water, but he caught her eye only momentarily, as her small figure was lost in a throng of greeting. Evan's rough embrace was accompanied by exuberant Welsh castigation that he had taken so long to waken.

"I think I was drugged," Klim told them, confused.

"By exhaustion and camomile only," Samuel's voice said from behind.

Klim turned towards the smiling Irish Jew, "I'm sorry I doubted you," he said softly. Samuel brushed his apology aside. "Had I known that you would have woken up alone to face Danubin I should not have left you to sleep."

"What is this?" Evan demanded as the others crowded around.

"I do not know how she found my room and knew that you were inside. To get so far, she would have had to dismantle a number of protections that have been in place for centuries. The strongest held however, and she was unable to get into the room itself." Siskin voiced the concern they were all feeling. "How is she getting so near?" Then his eyes fell as he recalled Angharad's presence.

"I know what you are thinking," Angharad's dark head was bowed but she lifted her chin. "I did tell her the names of those staying at the house but that's all. I had no idea," her voice trembled, and she bit her lip.

Swift and Evan were quickly on either side the Welshwoman. Siskin turned, sighing, "We don't blame you Angharad," he said gently, "but there's something allowing her to wear down our defences and find us so uncannily."

"You are right Eamon Keogh," said a voice with a German

accent, from the back of the room.

"This is Reuben," Samuel explained to Klim, his arm sweeping around the large and unusual space, "and this is his cavern." Klim's first thought was that the man was wearing a costume from another age. He remembered watching films about Roundheads, short haired and severe, opposed by Cavaliers, the ones with the hats and ruffles. This was Reuben then, a Cavalier with dark curling locks that reached down to his shoulder, underneath a wide brimmed hat. He wore a high lace snow white collar that extended across a green velvet cape. His eyes twinkled sharp hazel, above a smile half hidden in a thick moustache and beard.

"Reuben was once a Creta," explained Samuel; Josh's eyebrows lifted in interest. "Come, let's be seated," he told them. "I for one, am in need of some refreshment."

"Where are we?" Siskin asked, seating himself around the strange table that had grown bigger and sprouted more chairs as their numbers had grown.

"It feels like inside the picture," Josh said thoughtfully. "Only not quite the same."

Samuel glanced at Reuben who produced a tiny harp from a nearby shelf. "Each strand is separate," he told them, "and with its own distinct note. Only the musician can bring them together and even then, they retain their separateness."

Klim caught Gabbie's eyes twinkling, she had no patience for anything that was not direct enough to be understood. But then she surprised him.

"So, we're not where we were, are we? In our world I mean. I feel as if this is a kind of dream."

"If you stay here too long," Samuel explained, "then the world you have left will become the dream; that's why we have contained you here in Reuben's halfway house. He has created several spaces within the different strands of reality, where human beings can be protected and healed without losing touch with the world in which they live."

"Tinobar," remembered Klim. "That was kind of out of everything and yet still there, and time moved slower there. What seemed only an hour was like a day in real time."

Reuben nodded and smiled, "I constructed Tinobar in the seventeenth century," he stated simply.

Kier looked more closely at the middle-aged man who was indeed, from another age and time.

"It saved my life," said Gabbie, serious now as her open face expressed the gratitude that she felt.

"And mine," added Swift.

Reuben smiled and bowed, sweeping the large hat from his head, and looking up towards the two young women.

"Madeleine informed me. We were greatly honoured."

Gabbie's eyes squinted as if she didn't know if she should take him seriously, but Swift bowed in return and Gabbie followed her lead. Kier's eyes twinkled.

"Thank you, Reuben," Swift said formally and Gabbie muttered her agreement. Klim checked to see if there was a sword hanging on the jewelled belt that hung diagonally over leggings and long boots but here was no weapon.

"We have brought you here as an extreme measure for extreme times," Reuben went on.

Klim sipped at the water and felt refreshed but was unable to eat.

"Should you venture to the other doorway of this cavern, it is unlikely that you will ever return to your former lives. That is a choice I can offer each of you, given the enemies that pursue you."

Klim looked around the table, even without his gift he could clearly see that his friends reflected his own thoughts.

"We are Seeds of the Myriar," Kier said firmly, "and we have to be here for Candillium."

"And yet," said Samuel, "it seems she is not here for you." It was Kier who removed her gaze first as Samuel fixed his eyes on her.

"I know she will come," said Gabbie confidently.

"Do you?" asked Reuben, "Even when Toomaaris himself cannot be certain?"

"Sometimes, foolish as it may seem, we have to hold on to our faith," Kier stated simply. "We don't always see the links between us. We have only known each other for twelve months and most of that we've spent apart, yet the bonds between us are stronger than blood."

The others nodded their agreement and Swift stood tall and dark eyed. "You are all my family," she said with unusual emotion, including all those around the table.

"And I," said Angharad reaching for her father's hand, "am not a seed, as you call it. I do not know who Candillium is, and I have no wish to know." She turned to her father. "I should have trusted you Da, but I thought . . ." Evan hugged her as she cried into his shoulder.

"It wasn't your fault," he whispered, and then he spoke in soft Welsh for her ears alone.

Angharad straightened up and brushed away her tears. "My place is with my children," she stated simply.

"They have been removed from the reach of Danubin, or Shreive as you know her," Samuel explained gently.

Alarmed now, Angharad's voice was shaky. "I left them with my friend. My God, have I put them all in danger?"

"Echin will watch over them until you arrive," Samuel told her.

"Then I will take you to a place of safety. All your things have been moved; you will tell your friend that you are going on holiday to Southern England."

"But our home!" Angharad protested.

Evan held her hands. "I will go with you," he told her.

"I have already sent Herald to a place that Danubin will not find," Samuel told them. "There are hollows along the Teifi river that she and her kind cannot see."

Angharad looked around at the small group, sorrow was etched on her pale face and there was a lost expression in her grey eyes.

"We should go now," Evan said gruffly.

"So be it," Samuel told them and rose towards the point where Klim had first entered Reuben's cavern.

Evan and Angharad made their farewells, embracing each one; Klim could feel his old friend's anguish at the parting. Gabbie and Swift were in tears as Samuel led Evan and Angharad through a barely visible sheet of light that shimmered its presence as the trio disappeared from the room. Their absence was palpable, and no one spoke as the group shuffled around the table.

"You need to eat," Reuben instructed them all.

Klim picked up some bread and cheese and realised that he was now very hungry indeed. The others were also taking advantage of the laden table, the food and drink seeming to lift their spirits. After the meal Reuben suddenly let out a cry of amazement. Klim turned towards him to find that his eyes were gazing at Swift's throat, where those who knew of its presence could see the faint outline of a clear diamond, pure and perfectly formed.

"Ah! I spent many long years searching for the Stone of Silence," he told her.

Swift's small fingers automatically reached for the jewel at her throat.

"I've never said to anyone the name it spoke to me when I first found it," she said.

"May I?" Reuben asked, holding out his hand.

Tentatively Swift removed the diamond from her neck, as she did so the glistening chain and translucent stone became visible.

"Where was it hidden?" asked Reuben, his voice filled with awe, as he took the stone and held it up to the light.

Swift looked a little uneasy at Reuben's attachment to the stone, and her eyes stayed focused upon it as she explained how she found it on the beach 'El Silencio' in Lima.

"Of course," she told them, "it was coal black then and it was the first time I changed a stone from its original form. It was... malevolent," she nodded as her curved Spanish stumbled over the angles of the word.

"Ah, the inscription had the right of it after all," Reuben said thoughtfully, his eyes sparkling in wonder.

"The inscription?" questioned Kier.

"Tormaigh found the words carved into a marble slab beneath the clay and ash that had once been Ordovicia."

"And it spoke of Swift's diamond?" asked Gabbie.

Reuben nodded and after a pause recited from memory.

"Diamond light will shine upon the face of the last Stozcist, when the Stone of Silence is released from the shadow of hidden intent."

"I don't understand," Swift told him, tense with concentration.

Reuben's tone was one of deference as he explained. "We heard of the destruction of Galinir the Devouril, though we did not know how it had occurred. It was from her that I sought to hide the stone."

Swift said nothing, her dark eyes flinching with memory.

"She was in the stone?" Kier asked softly and Reuben nodded.

"Somehow she found you and was waiting for the Stone of Silence to confirm your identity. Not even she guessed that you had first to create it and that her 'hidden intent' would be so completely banished."

Swift looked stunned.

"I couldn't speak of it to anyone until I met Klim. And Gabbie," she added a moment later.

Klim checked to see if Gabbie had noticed the delay, but she gave no sign, seemingly engrossed in what she was hearing.

"Remarkable," Reuben said softly. "I looked for it for many long years, always watching for Galinir at my shoulder. Once, in Rome, she almost destroyed me." His sigh was as long as his cape. "Toomaaris saved me, and I realised obsession had made me blind. I gave up the search. I was convinced that one day it would be found beneath a symbol of silence, a wordless tribute."

"I thought the name the Stone of Silence just described where it was found!" Swift said simply.

"Of course, it did," Reuben replied, his self-mocking laughter tinkling around the cavern.

Chapter Nineteen

"Kier!" Gabbie's voice was shrill. "Please don't go!"

Kier turned her face reluctantly from the breeze, so deliciously fresh and lemon scented, that feathered across her skin. In another step, she would have been through the gateway. It was not visible and yet she had found it, in a little nook that there had been no reason to enter, save her habitual curiosity.

Then another voice said gently, "You have choice."

Echin. Somehow the words sent her reeling, she touched another world, another existence, and sensed that it might be even more real than the one she had been living. She turned towards him.

"I'm not going anywhere," she said softly and Gabbie's arms were around her waist, her head buried in her shoulder.

Kier's arms enfolded her friend, but her eyes were focused on the lapis depth in the unfathomable face of Echinod Deem. Gabbie extracted herself and wiped her eyes.

"It's like a rabbit warren," she said irritably. "I nearly didn't find you!"

Kier had wandered when the others were resting after the meal. Reuben's cavern was in fact an extensive, interconnecting maze of caves and passages. They had only been in the 'porch' so to speak.

"We've all been looking for you for ages," Gabbie admonished. She put her fingers to her mouth and whistled sharply, bringing the others running towards them. Josh's eyes lit up at the sight of the shimmering gateway that glimmered more visibly at their arrival. Echin spoke to Reuben at the back of the group.

"I think our time here has almost come to its limit," he told him. Reuben nodded and led them back towards the cavern they had first entered.

"What's happened?" Gabbie asked Echin. "I mean, outside?" Echin smiled, "Many would say that it is we that are on the outside right now."

"Are Evan and Angharad safe?" interrupted Siskin.

The musician's sharp tone gave voice to the restlessness that they all seemed to feel. Kier was certain that if they did not leave soon, they might not leave at all. They had reached the original cavern and Echin showed no sign of offence but nodded towards the smiling figure of Samuel that greeted them as they entered.

"Angharad and her children are safe," Samuel told them, "but they will have to stay in hiding for now."

"And Evan?" asked Gabbie.

"He is also hidden," Samuel replied.

"How long for?" asked Swift. "They'll hate it."

"Until you deal with the threat of Danubin," answered Reuben. Swift's back stiffened but before she could reply Reuben added, "All of you."

"Do you have any suggestions?" Siskin asked him.

"Perhaps now would be a good time, Kier, to translate what you saw written around the centre circle on the Myriar," Echin suggested.

It took Kier a moment to realise what he was talking about. With a start, she remembered the inscriptions she and Gabbie had scrawled on the paper that she hoped was still lodged in her jeans pocket.

"O my God!" Gabbie exclaimed. "I'd forgotten all about that."

As Kier pulled pieces of paper from her pocket and began straightening them Klim turned to Josh.

"What went on there, Josh? How did you find the Myriar?"

Josh smiled wanly, "Samuel helped me when I first met him in Ireland. He more or less led me into the picture I'd created in the Wicklow mountains and helped me back out again. We walked together to the ridge and then we found the lake. It was only when I came out and he disappeared that I began to get really spooked. When he turned up beside me that afternoon, he made it feel like the most natural thing in the world." He turned to his friend and continued, "Echin helped me to understand when we met up in Frindy; it wasn't until then that I realised I'd found a plane of being in between other existences. He also told me that if I was not fully committed to making my way back, then a portal, into one of those other planes of existence, would act like a vacuum and pull me out of my present life altogether."

He glanced at the hidden gateway that Kier had so nearly entered. "It's a bit of a pull here but a hundred times worse where you're in places on your own, literally following a dream. When your sense of anything happening back where you were can fade with a moment's lack of concentration. It seemed the most natural thing in the world to draw what I knew to be hidden in the lake. Did you make that place?" he asked Reuben.

Reuben shook his head, "No, you made it Josh," he replied.

"That doesn't make any sense," Gabbie's brows were furrowed in puzzlement.

Echin explained, "Samuel helped you to slide in and out of the doorway that you created to a different dimension. Only you could have opened that particular doorway, behind which the concept of the Myriar is hidden."

"So, it's not the real thing?" Siskin asked.

Reuben shook his head, "You, all of you, are the real thing," he said solemnly.

"But what about me?" Gabbie interjected. "I'm not a Seed!"

Kier passed one of the papers to Gabbie, "It was around one of the points of the star." Gabbie read it aloud.

"The *voice of Arwres will soothe the calling crowd.*"

"We know that stone is yours, Silex said so," Kier said gently. Gabbie looked both troubled and pleased.

"But she also said I could be holding it for someone else."

"As I said once before, I cannot predict how the Myriar has evolved," Echin explained, "although its structure looks essentially the same as when Moura first gave the task of taking her gift to the Ordovicians."

"What else does it say?" enquired Siskin. "You said there was an inscription around each point of the star."

"But I could only read three," Kier replied looking towards Klim, remembering that Echin had given him the sheet of paper referring to his father's stone. Klim caught her eyes and nodded. "The last of the three is for you I think Siskin." She scribbled a translation underneath the strange lettering that she had copied and passed him the notepaper. As he spoke, the small harp in the cavern gave a thrill of gentle notes to accompany his words.

"To gather the chords and play the song of Moura, to remake the music of the earth, comes the Lute to Amron Cloch."

Siskin looked up, his expression a mixture of dazed wonder and apprehension.

"Danubin taunted me in Frindy. She said she had possession of Amron Cloch, the Song Stone."

Reuben rocked in his chair and sighed. "There have been many of us who have gone before you, paving the way, evolving the gifts that you are now discovering. Aided by the Mourangils we found a way to transmute our knowledge and power into particular pieces, living jewels to hand down to you. However powerful your gifts are right now, once you have a jewel of the Myriar in your possession you will begin to harness all that human endeavour, its brightest and most enlightened history that has been kept in safe storage for you." Reuben's head bowed, "It was not conceivable that one such as Danubin would discover these sacred gems, let alone use them for her own purpose. It was inbuilt into each jewel that no Devouril, or those whose dark hearts were committed to them, would be able to touch the stones."

"And yet my uncle was able to use it for evil for over three years." Klim stated, his voice terse.

"Nephragm fashioned pieces of baryte," Echin explained, looking sympathetically at Kier, who had given an involuntary gasp at the memory of the substance that had been used to paralyse her beneath Whistmorden. "It would seem like ordinary glass, but we know that the stone was used by the Virenmor to protect themselves from the destructive influence of the Perfidium. It also nullifies the ability of a Stone of the Myriar to repel the Virenmor, though it would be still very unpleasant for them to touch. Jackson was even able to use some of the power of the Iridice to amplify his own malicious Mensira, or mind control. I believe that Danubin must hold another piece of the restructured baryte, for I am certain that she now holds both Amron Cloch and the Iridice."

"But how?" Klim stuttered and Kier knew that he would be trying to still the picture of his mother's desecrated resting place. "And why?"

It was Swift who answered. "These stones have been especially fashioned for us as part of the Myriar. Find one and they can, in the right hands, lead to another and also to the person for whom it is intended."

"Luke," Klim muttered. He was staring into space, remembering his friend's dreadful remorse as Klim probed his thoughts in the Garden of Remembrance. He saw now with perfect clarity that Danubin had trapped the memory of her visit in a shadowy fold of grief. He could recognise now, through his contact with her, the subtle touch of burnt ash that marked Danubin's presence in another's mind; the dark void left by potential destroyed. He did not doubt that through using Mensira, she had manipulated his old friend into bringing her the Iridice. Klim, at the time of burying his mother's ashes, drowning in a sea of grief, had not cared that Luke had been watching silently. Rage, dark and dangerous, rose from the pit of his belly; he sucked air in, unaware that he was now standing.

Reuben's hand rested on Klim's shoulder, and he turned towards the old Cavalier, seeing infinite understanding in his gaze. The rage he had felt only moments before was quelled in the complex depths of long experience. Klim allowed the image of Luke's manipulation to seep into Mengebara. It allowed him to communicate the event, without having to use what he knew would be the sound of his own choked voice. Echin's eyes glinted hard in the filmy realm of Reuben's halfway house. "We must recover both these stones," he stated firmly.

Siskin nodded, "Do we know how?"

Echin shook his head, "Not yet."

Siskin glanced at Klim who stood up, ready to leave.

"Wait," Gabbie said softly. "What was in the middle inscription Kier, the one you found the hardest to remember?"

Kier felt her fingers tremble as she smoothed out the last paper on the table. The lines loomed clear and forbidding as she translated. *"Look for the Stone of Mesa in the toxic residue of grief."*

Swift's voice was rich with excitement. "The fact that this was in the middle, do you think we could use it to find Candillium?"

Swift turned to Echin who nodded, "It's possible," he confirmed.

"Mesa," Kier repeated. "I seem to know that name."

"Mesa was mankind's original home and Moura's sister planet," Reuben explained. "Many previous Stozcists have stated that they felt the presence of the Stone within Moura. It is a powerful fragment of Mesa, believed to be embedded in the foundation of Ordovicia and lost in the original devastation."

"Do you think it means that we should look in the ruins of Ordovicia?" queried Kier.

"I really don't know," Echin replied.

Reuben shook his head thoughtfully, "I think you should concentrate on recovering the stones Danubin has taken."

Siskin turned business like to Echin, "What do we really know of this woman Danubin? Can we find out more from Angharad?"

"I'm afraid her identity as Shreive has already been dismantled. She hasn't been seen in Carmarthen since Magluck Bawah was released. The people in the church community in Angharad's village have found themselves without an administrator and without funds."

Swift's eyes lit with anger, "That would be for spite," she said. "They were planning to do a lot of good work with that money." Her jaw steeled, "The man sent to kill us on the mountain. Who was he?"

"Terence Mace," Echin replied without emotion. "One of the Virenmor for many lifetimes. He was well chosen by Danubin for his task, as he specialised in the destruction of good women. His methods varied from physical attack to psychological abuse, but the outcome was always the obliteration of his victim."

Even hearing the appalling history of the man, Kier repressed the nausea that she felt at the memory of Swift's retribution.

Sighing deeply Echin stood up.

"Josh!" he called, as his friend turned with a surprised expression from the back of the cavern and the invisible gateway.

Echin turned to Samuel, "We should leave now."

Samuel looked at Reuben who nodded as Kier gently held Josh's hand and led him back to the group. Kier saw that Reuben had already created the gleaming doorway that marked the end of their time in the remarkable place. The ageless Cavalier gallantly removed his hat and bowed.

"Sadly," he told them, "this particular space can be used only once by those such as yourselves. It has been an honour."

One by one they said goodbye and gave their thanks to Reuben as they stepped through the portal that would remove them, reluctantly, from the sanctuary of his cavern.

Chapter Twenty

"Don't sulk, my pet." Shreive's finger followed the outline of a long, serrated limb on the other side of the glass. The giant black spider flittered sideways, as the perfectly manicured nails tapped the polished surface. The terrarium virtually covered the large marble table that stood on a white tiled floor and reached high towards a domed ceiling. Slowly she stretched her fingers into red leather gloves and removed the lid of a jar, just bigger than her hand. Carefully, she removed an oval shaped amethyst and placed it inside the tank. The walnut sized stone shimmered against the pebbled floor; purple strobes of light shot from its centre and a resonant humming filled the room. The huge arachnid shrank back, towards the furthest corner of its allotted space.

"To think that you were once some part of the Devouril that was Galinir!" Danubin scolded. "Now a ragged remnant left by a Stozcist!"

Her mouth twisted in hatred and then reformed into a callous grin as the spider's black shape drained of colour to become a ghostly grey. The baryte amulet she wore cracked against the tank as she removed the stone and waited for the spider's colour to return. Satisfied, she took a number of live crickets from a nearby pot and placed them inside the tank, fixing the lid tightly. She watched patiently, fascinated by the lingering process of arachnid feeding, the slow transformation of an animated cricket as the spider injected enzymes that would render them liquidly edible. Unhurried Shreive made her way to the writing desk against the far wall. Deliberately there were no windows in this, her private study. She placed the amethyst on the table and picked up another stone, this one milky white and smooth. Satisfied that the feeding was done she carefully placed the new object into the tank. Once again, the spider tried desperately to avoid the jewel. Within a short time, the dark shape visibly lost its colour. Slowly, just as the giant creature was brought to the brink of death, the red glove descended to remove the object responsible.

The clunk of the metal gates opening outside brought the perfectly shaped brows together in a frown of annoyance. A quick glance at the tank showed her that Galinir looked almost back to normal. Satisfied that the stones were still indeed the genuine articles, she placed them carefully into the table drawer, and added the baryte amulet. The drawer gave no outward sign of its existence as it slid closed, the locking mechanism automatic. Klim would have recognised the triumphant lift at the side of her mouth as she congratulated herself again on having possession of two of the Myriar stones. He had seen the same cruel sneer when his uncle had locked away the Iridice. A few minutes later Shreive entered the foyer of the immaculate mansion house, fifty miles from Pont o Ffrindiau. The door to her study was hidden by its perfect alignment within the marble wall and could only be opened by a remote device under the rim of a heavy ebony table in the centre of the hall. Aled managed the day to day running of her unique business. On the opposite side of the foyer was a corridor that held a string of individual offices, each one housing a member of the Virenmor. At this time of day all would be busy observing and preparing the most elite and vicious gamers, manipulating their participation in the constructs that she had created. Since the error in the Middle East, resulting in a banker's suicide, she and Aled had personally supervised the selection of all newcomers. She breathed in deeply, her mouth twisting in frustrated anger as she prepared to vent her feelings on the manager, whom she chiefly blamed for their failure to destroy even one of the Myriar Seeds. It was clear now that they were facing the gathering force of the outer points of the gift that Moura had foolishly tried to bestow on the first generation. Even without Candillium they were a serious threat.

Shreive knew that Belluvour was the only hope for the planet, and that he would tolerate only the Virenmor, his enhanced humans, to survive. The spider's response had shown that the two stones were still genuine. Why then did they no longer direct her to the two Seeds for which they were intended? She had used them as divining rods to find the Reeder and the Lute. Not only that, but she had found a way to extract some of the information they held regarding the two individuals. It felt uncomfortably strange that one of the Seeds should be the nephew of the now deceased Jackson. The engineered, politically motivated murders had provided an outlet for the rage and frustration that came with the knowledge of so many lost opportunities to destroy the Reeder. At least she had been able to use the information Jackson had left concerning the boy. The brat Luke had been surprisingly resistant to her methods. It was sheer good fortune that the Reeder had been stupid enough to bury the stone with his mother's ashes, Luke watching unobserved. Not only that, but the boy had given himself the job of protecting the grave! Ironically in the end, it was because of this that she had been able to find the Iridice. Had she not taken the baryte with her of course, she would have been unable to touch either stone. That had been Nephragm's gift, the glass like baryte that enabled the Virenmor to handle the Stones of the Myriar. The Iridice, held in Jackson's possession for a time, was a powerful amplifier of her own skills in thought transference and illusion. Together with Jackson's long file on his nephew, it had allowed her to come frustratingly close to capturing the boy called Klim.

Shreive licked her lips as she remembered her great triumph, the wonderful discovery, that each stone pulled towards another. The Song Stone, waiting for the Lute, had revealed itself in the forest of Stromondale, residing in the trunk of a large oak. She used the two stones to find Arwres and then began to develop the village as a construct. Her foot tapped habitually in suppressed rage at that failure. An edge of fear clawed at her groomed shoulders, as they tensed in the knowledge that she had also failed to draw out the Seeds from Evan Gwyn's house and that she had so nearly enticed the Reeder into her grasp at the college. Aled had found a way for her to break down some of the constructs that Samuel had engineered in the Old Building, though she had not managed to enter the rooms that were hidden within its walls. His thin, black-suited figure now strode purposely into the hall. Danubin turned and took a deep intake of breath, ready to fuel the tirade that had built inside her, ready for vitriolic release. Instead, her voice collapsed into a spluttering gasp as she caught the eyes of her employee. Like the spider she had just finished taunting, her skin lost its colour. Stumbling into a clumsy bow she caught her breath and lowered her eyes.

"Lord," she whispered, her voice trembling, her legs barely able to hold her. Nephragm stared coldly from Aled's body. He did not reply as he walked beyond the ebony table and flicked his eyeline towards the back wall. Fumbling, she opened the hidden door, just as his determined stride reached the entrance.

*

"Swerve!" Klim yelled.

Samuel let his left hand fall down the steering wheel as the bus horn blared and a fist of light passed angrily close to their right.

"Where the hell are we?" demanded Siskin.

"Dublin, at a guess," "Josh replied, his tone tense. "That's the

River Liffey."

Klim looked ahead, where all he could see was the outline of a stone bridge as Samuel weaved through the traffic.

"Where's the girls?" he asked, shifting round to discover that only himself, Samuel, Josh, and Siskin were in the vehicle.

"They're with Echin," replied Samuel, crunching down a gear.

"Er, when's the last time you drove? Maybe we should change over?" suggested Klim, his voice rising as they lurched round a corner on the other side of the bridge.

"Lebanon," Samuel told them smiling. "It was a few years ago but I think I'm back in the hang of it now."

The vehicle climbed the pavement causing a couple to jump backwards and Klim turned to see the man pick himself up enough to run out into the road and scream abuse at them. He choked for a moment, in disbelief, as the side of a yellow Volkswagen Beetle gleamed in the passenger wing mirror.

"Discreet," he muttered and pulled across his seat belt. Josh and Siskin followed his action in the back seat. They rocketed around a few more bends and then, to their relief, Samuel slowed the car into a cobbled gap behind a number of terraced properties. He tucked the VW into the backyard of a house, where a line of motorbikes leaned against the stone wall. On an ordinary night, the yard would have been pitch black once the car lights were extinguished. Tonight, the curtained windows and stone steps, leading up to the back door, were clearly visible in the fierce glow of a full moon. As Samuel turned off the engine a black van pulled up behind them, blocking them in. Klim turned sharply to see several hard looking men emerge from the vehicle. He glanced at Siskin who had already placed a black woollen hat over his blonde hair, and the pair exited in unison, moving towards the back of the VW, where the occupants of the van had formed into two rows.

There were six of them ranging from maybe his own age, Klim reckoned, to about thirty-five. Most had some sign of a fighting life. The big stocky one to the left, with curly hair, had two prize misshapen ears and the flat nose of the straight-haired tall lad at the back hadn't come naturally. At the front of the group, possibly in his mid-twenties, a man stood with his hands in his jean's pockets and Klim looked, but did not find, the shape of a knife or gun. He was as handsome as Josh, with shoulders bigger than those of Siskin and his eyes glinted wolf like in the light of the moon. Klim was unable to read his mind print, as it was shielded from all of them. He messaged the fact to Siskin, who realised that they were not dealing with any ordinary thugs. Siskin's almost imperceptible nod acknowledged the mental observation, as he faced the newcomers with a deceptively relaxed stance. Samuel emerged unhurried from the VW and the wolf smiled perfect teeth at him.

"Jasus Sammy, will you stop driving that disgusting yellow thing. You're a friggin' menace!"

Samuel was grinning widely as he stepped across to the barricade of individuals, shaking them each by the hand and letting their mickey taking surround him like a favourite coat. Klim and Siskin watched the thuggish group transform into long lost friends and let out a simultaneous sigh of relief. They turned as Josh exited the car, Klim seeing the uncertainty in his friend's face smiled reassurance.

"They're on our side," he whispered.

"Allithwaite!" It was the wolf who shouted, staring at Josh in amazement.

"Mactire," replied Josh, his jaw jutting towards the other man. They held each other's eyes warily, as Samuel turned back to his companions.

"It's time we went inside," he said, looking up towards the blink of light in the house next door. He took Josh's arm and led them up the stone steps to a solid looking door that opened at his touch. They entered a shabby narrow kitchen, where a light bulb hung naked over a collection of unwashed pots that filled the sink. Klim headed for the dark hallway, but Samuel signalled him towards the tall, old off-white fridge that occupied the corner of the room. It was virtually empty apart from a few beer bottles, a half-eaten pack of butter and some milk. Josh raised his eyebrows and shook his head as Samuel signalled him towards the inside of the fridge. The Irish Jew shrugged his shoulders and laughed, then he stepped inside and disappeared. Josh leaned forward and held open the door for Siskin and Klim's inspection.

"Straight in boys," said the wolf behind them. "It's a projected light illusion, is all." Josh closed his eyes, bent, and disappeared into the centre of the shelves, which were in fact merely a passageway. As he followed the others Klim realised that they were in some kind of porch that was as high as the house itself. The back of the house, inclusive of the blinds on the windows, was clearly a façade. He suspected that the front of the place was also false.

The central building was a column of stainless steel at least three floors high. Klim likened it to a castle with a dry moat; they were in the moat now looking up at the real building encased within. Siskin whistled. Josh's eyes shone wide as the steel shimmered blue in the light of a series of wall lamps. The wolf took out what looked like a laser pen and pointed it at the convex doors in the centre of the column. They moved apart with hardly a sound. Klim followed Samuel as they entered the building that would have sat more comfortably with NASA than in a Dublin street. A number of individuals, who barely looked up at their entry, worked on computers that surrounded a central transparent pillar, occupying over half of the room's space. Klim's eyes quickly became captivated by the dance of light that was occurring within this enormous tube, of what seemed to be hardened clear glass, and reached upwards to disappear within the roof of the building. He noticed that there were glinting threads, running in straight lines every few metres or so around the outside of the tube. Whole spectrums of colour leapt like flames and roiled in waves of glorious light that plunged downwards and upwards in a sea of constant change. A young woman who had been circling the column came over to greet them. She was very slight, with long auburn curly hair that had been carelessly pulled back so that strands feathered her face. Her hazel eyes shone intelligence but as she came nearer, they were fixed solely on Josh who had visibly paled. Samuel stepped across towards her. "Loretta," he said. "Good to see you."

"And you Samuel," she returned, her eyes tugging away from Josh as she shook Samuel's hand.

Cheerfully he introduced Siskin, Josh and Klim to Loretta and to the group of men with whom they had entered. "Welcome to the best kept secret, almost, in Ireland. This room nicknamed the 'Vortex,' has been maintained by these good people for the last two years. Loretta here is one of our key engineers and Mactire over there is responsible for the whole concept. Apart from playing centre for the Tenement Rugby Team he also lectures in quantum mechanics."

Klim followed Siskin to receive the firm grip of the man he had already come to think of as Wolf. Josh simply nodded with his eyes focused on Mactire who returned his nod with a fraction of acknowledgement. Loretta's cool green eyes stared frankly at Josh without expression. Samuel moved on quickly to the others who were Mactire's rugby teammates and who had also helped build the 'Vortex.' Killian was the tall, dark-haired man with the flattened nose. Aedan turned out to be the name of the stocky lad with curly hair. Danny, Oisin and Lorcan were the remaining three, all solid athletic builds with wide grins.

"We're just known as the Tenements mainly," Danny explained. "Great to have yus on board."

Klim decided that he appeared to be the youngest and the most easy going of the group, as he shook the proffered hand. Mactire looked towards Siskin and Klim.

"In my research at the university I've been working with underground detectors for some time now to help understand what's out there, so to speak, in the dark matter of the universe."

"Why underground?" asked Siskin.

"Too much cosmic noise otherwise," Mactire replied cryptically. "Anyway, with Loretta's help, myself and the boys fashioned a way of amplifying the locations of certain in-planet energies that we've been tracking over these last few years. What you can see is the translation of these energies into light imagery wherever the focus of the Vortex is arranged."

"It's stunning," commented Siskin, who was examining the construction. "What's it made of?"

"A material of my own concept that uses diamond conductors." He turned towards the unruffled figure who was circling the column.

"Sammy there is our sponsor, a private commission; he should be a politician for all the questions he's dodged. We are hoping, as our first ever visitors, you might be a little more enlightening." Siskin shook his head. Lorcan and Oisin had never left their side since entering the building, the threat was mild and subtle but still existed. "We didn't even know the Vortex existed until tonight," he replied truthfully.

Mactire searched the other man's eyes and seemed satisfied with what he found.

"A few weeks ago, a strange and sinister image emerged. In my branch of physics, you expect the unexpected, but this is something else. It's immense for a start but holds no mass underground. It seems to travel in wave patterns that can change direction at an instant; where it does so there is an effluent energy left behind and its only function appears to be death. Where this energy is discharged any organic matter within that location is destroyed in seconds. A few weeks ago, part of it separated from the main body and seemed to emerge on the surface twice, a few days apart, in South Wales. We could find no evidence of any effect in the immediate surroundings. "

"Apart from a bull breaking through a hedge, racing down the road and flinging itself over a cliff," added Loretta sardonically.

"I may have some more information for you," Samuel told the Tenements, nodding towards Klim.

Klim swallowed as the whole group turned their attention towards him. Hesitantly, seeing a further nod from Samuel, he began to explain. "I think whatever it is nearly killed me in Pont y Ffrindiau a few nights ago," he stated simply.

Loretta shook her head.

"Then it's not our Undercreature, as Danny here named him. It's been all over the place but left South Wales three weeks ago." Samuel finished his circumvention of the Vortex and joined them as Loretta finished speaking. He offered an explanation.

"You have spent three weeks away Klim, though your condition may have made you feel it was only a few nights."

All three friends took on board the fact that Samuel did not mention Reuben's cavern, even as they struggled to come to terms with the time lapse. To a lesser extent, Klim had experienced a similar shift when they had entered and left Tinobar, in what now seemed like a lifetime ago. Samuel went on to explain that both Siskin and Klim had been recovering from their interaction with the creature. There was an air of excitement engendered by this news. The Tenements began a bombardment of questions about the incident, effectively pinning the two friends to the couple of steps that led up to the tube.

As Siskin began to tell the story of the attack by the Irresythe, Klim noticed Josh moving nearer to the central hub, in seconds he was joined by Loretta. The woman's face was tense with questioning anger, as the two spoke quietly to each other.

"So, you think this Irresythe was the same entity that we've been tracking?" Mactire asked Klim.

Klim was about to say, 'According to Echin,' but realised he had no idea how much the Tenements knew. Instead, he nodded towards the swirling lights within the tube.

"I don't know about the science, just that the creature that attacked me felt primeval almost, filled with anger and hatred; it had the stench of death."

Mactire held him with a probing stare for a moment and Danny asked, "So any chance of getting tissue samples is pretty much out of the question?"

"I'd say that was a safe bet," Siskin replied. "It was incinerated in the blast."

Mactire moved towards one of the screens and tapped into the keyboard, "It fits, Loretta," he said, looking round for her. He glared at her as she came back to the group, Josh moving to stand beside Klim.

"If we could have your attention for a little time," he said to Loretta, his tone acidic. She ignored it.

"There was a massive particulate activity before the separation from the main body underneath. It's feasible that it would be able to permeate an organic life form on the surface."

"And explain why we couldn't track it," Killian added.

"The question is, where is it now?" Josh stated.

Loretta moved towards the keyboard and tapped in different sequences, though her eyes never left the swirling colours of the

Vortex. It was like watching weather maps from different countries, Klim decided. Finally, an image appeared where a fog of dense grey overshadowed the whole tube. The atmosphere, even outside the Vortex, dimmed as an air of depression gloomed the space. Klim felt physically cold, and Loretta lifted an eyebrow as the visitors automatically closed in together.

"Even just tracking this thing is dangerous," she told them. "Its energy is such that even our force field cannot entirely shield us from its destructive nature. We only allow the image to stand for a few minutes, otherwise we'd be all killing ourselves or each other. Except Samuel of course," she said, seeing the one smile left within the room. "It appears that he's the only one unaffected."

Samuel inspected the image more closely, even as the others were repelled. Klim began to sense the will of annihilation that seeped from the grey fog; fear chilled him to the core at the thought of encountering this entity another time. Samuel nodded to Loretta who tapped again at her computer and the shadow was replaced with wing like shapes of white light that weaved through the Vortex.

Samuel's look of surprise drew a wry smile from Mactire. "Yes Sammy, we found them too."

Samuel afforded him a long stare of admiration and something else, possibly apprehension. Klim acknowledged that he was unable to read any of the mind prints in the room, apart from

Siskin and Josh who were tense and distrustful.

"How's the melody?" Klim whispered to Siskin.

"Nothing from the Tenements or the girl," was Siskin's equally quiet reply.

"Loretta," Josh said firmly. He repeated his question as she turned her spitfire eyes upon him, "Where is it now?"

"About twenty miles outside of Dublin," she told him tonelessly.

"Is that why we're here then?" Josh questioned Samuel, whose face remained expressionless. "Or has it followed us?"

Samuel looked at the three visitors and then at Mactire.

"Let's talk out the front," he said heading purposely towards an exit on the opposite side of the room from which they had entered. "Loretta, I need a location audit please. The Undercreature's movement in the last three weeks."

Mactire nodded his permission to Loretta and the other Tenements took their places on computers around the Vortex. The small, dark haired figure of Samuel had already disappeared from view.

Chapter Twenty-one

Lines of sweat tapered through a film of make-up and trickled towards her ears. Shreive dragged the discarded body of Aled into the vast and empty cellar beneath her mansion home. In the centre of the stone floor, she set a match to the husk that Nephragm had left behind, after he had used the body to ravage her own. Still, she lusted after the absent Devouril, even as she ached from the extremes of his demands. Shreive watched coldly, with a faint tinge of regret as Aled's remains turned to ashes. Satisfied, she turned and made her way from the tomb like space.

*

Klim followed Siskin and Josh through the silent doors that sealed the Vortex from the rest of the building. A few strides behind was Mactire who raised the laser pen towards the steel entrance and then caught up with Klim as he reached the bottom of a stairwell. The narrow staircase was spiral and brought him to a small cupboard that was underneath a further set of stairs. He bent down in the enclosed space and clicked open the door to emerge into a hall covered in family pictures.

"Stay on the ground floor," the wolf instructed from below.

Klim turned to his left, away from the next flight of steps, and waited for Mactire. Once the other man had joined him another light illusion covered the hidden doorway at the back of the understairs cupboard. It portrayed a grubby wall complete with spider and web. The couple of coats and a pair of wellies that hung on the opposite wall were genuine. It was an ingenious way to use illusion to maintain privacy and one he filed away for the future. The front of the house was not, as Klim had thought, false. The hallway brought him to a point where, to his left, it joined the passageway, slanting downwards to the back door where they had first entered the building. Klim turned to the open door on the right that led directly into a comfortable study space with leather seating and a work desk. On this were scattered, what appeared to be, Mactire's papers from the university, including a marked pile of essays. The only other piece of furniture was an antique sideboard from which the aroma of rich coffee welcomed them.

"Sit yourselves down," instructed Mactire as he closed the study door behind him. "There's a pot of coffee on the sideboard." Klim was nearest to the coffee maker and poured himself a mug, moving to the leather couch to make way, as the others did the same. Samuel perched himself by the work desk. There was an adjoining door and Mactire explained that the house at the front was basically a two floored construction, with a long connecting passage to the back kitchen. He had used light, imagery and incline to secrete the space where the Vortex was hidden.

"Clever," nodded Siskin. "That's very clever."

"To tell you the truth," the wolf smiled, "I don't want for

cleverness. Loretta and I moved our work to a point where science became art, even when we were still kids."

He glanced meaningfully at Josh. "Then we discovered that what we may not lack in technique, we don't have in makeup. Josh on the other hand is a different matter. He lacks nuttin' at all."

He stood up, his expression sad but not acrimonious.

"But like you Sammy, he doesn't want to share. And I don't know yet about your friends," he added turning to Siskin and Klim, "but I suspect you're both a little more of the same."

Samuel remained silent as Mactire sighed his frustration.

"Why work with us for six months Josh and then disappear? Loretta withdrew into herself; she was just coming back to the sister I knew when you and Sammy turn up here again together. I don't get it. Jasus Sammy, money or not, either close us down or give us heads up as to what the hell is happening!"

"You knew of this?" Klim turned to Josh, who shook his head in reply.

"I was looking for other answers, to other questions." 'Not here,' Josh quickly messaged in Mengebara to Siskin and Klim.

"Why don't you have a mind print?" Klim's question broke abruptly into the room.

"A what?" asked Mactire, taken aback by the change of direction.

"A mind print," repeated Klim. "Neither you, nor any of the Tenements, can be read telepathically."

"You can do that?" Mactire's attention was that of a researcher finding an unexpected sample in his lab.

"Usually, and very few have been able to shield against me. All have been more than they seem on the surface."

Klim knew it was showing his hand, but his heart had decided what his gift could not tell him. Mactire was silent.

"They're fae, all of them," Josh said quietly. "It's a different pattern of thought."

"Fae," Klim repeated. "What's that?"

"We're not the only ones who choose not to share, Mactire," Josh said simply. The wolf smiled his retreat as he sank into the armchair beside his desk.

"You're in the most elemental realm of the planet," Samuel explained. "Mactire and his sister are Tanes, descended from the beautiful Etain of many transmogrifications."

"Er, many what?" asked Klim.

"Shape changes," answered Siskin absently, concentrating on his host's reply.

"Only one is now available to each of us," Mactire sighed. "How long have you known?"

Josh looked at him, his face expressionless, as he explained.

"I drew you one night as you and Loretta were coming over the Halfpenny Bridge. Danny had been painting all day, but he had to leave early, and I volunteered to take back his stuff. There you two were, talking on the bridge just as the sun was bedding down. I did a quick sketch. My pencil was driven by myth and legend.

I'd drawn a beautiful white unicorn and a dam scary cross between man and wolf that I've since discovered is called an Adlet. Described somewhere as a werewolf vampire originated from the eskimos."

"Adlet I may be," retorted Mactire, his green eyes glinting fiercely, "but I'm neither werewolf nor vampire."

He bared his teeth in a lopsided grin, "Scary ha? Maybe I should let that side of me out a little more."

He stood up and came nearer to Josh, they were both of the same height. Josh did not flinch under the other man's cold-eyed scrutiny.

"The Creta then after all," Mactire's voice held a reluctant edge of awe. "Loretta had the truth of it."

He turned away from Josh's pale face and settled himself into a leather armchair. Josh eased himself back down between Klim and Siskin.

"So, you can transform into animals, is that what you're saying?" Siskin quizzed him.

"So, you three are the famed last Seeds of the Myriar?" countered Mactire.

Samuel looked closely at the relaxed figure of Mactire, his eyes glinting in the dimly lit room, "Now it's my turn to ask how long you have known?"

"Since Danubin approached me six months ago," Mactire said into the silent room. "Clever woman that, and hot."

As he spoke the room began to fill with the other Tenements from both exits. Loretta entered last. Klim glanced at Siskin, they had allowed themselves to be completely outmanoeuvred, trapped. Josh leaned forward towards Mactire.

"I've met her. She's not your type," he told him. There was a heartbeat of uncertainty and then the wolf laughed.

"Jasus, you got that right. Shit the hell out o' me!"

"What did she ask you to do Sean?" It was the first time Samuel had spoken Mactire's birth name.

Mactire looked uncomfortable as he turned towards the cleric and spoke quietly into the dimly lit space.

"She was careful what she told me and she'd no idea we were friends, the three of us." He glanced towards Josh. "She was after an artist; young she thought, and from Northern England. It took us about five minutes to figure out it was Josh she wanted."

"She'd tracked me to Dublin?" There was shock in Josh's voice. "What did you tell her?" He stood up, his fists balled, "Was that how she found us in Wales? How she followed me across the sea?" Killian slid in front of Josh and eased him away from Mactire. Josh looked around at them all. "What did it buy you then, selling me to Danubin?"

"Well, there's the thing," Mactire said easily, "Loretta here wouldn't let us do that. And if we had you wouldn't be back in Dublin now for this little tirade. It's your thanks you should be giving instead of your anger. The Virenmor left empty handed."

"They never leave empty handed," Samuel stated simply. "What did you give them Mactire?"

Loretta turned towards her brother, scrutinising his face. "What does he mean?" she demanded.

It was Killian who answered. "Sammy's right. They never leave empty handed and with our research just building momentum here it was imperative we get shut of the foul creature as soon as we could. We don't want the earth upturned on its ass any more than you do. But we're no man's friend either, we have our own interests. We gave them you Sammy. We told her where you were and that we thought you had something to do with the Myriar; having no actual idea that you did."

Loretta opened her mouth to protest but Samuel nodded and brought up his hand in a gesture that silenced her.

"Ah," he said without rancour. "I thought as much."

"You nearly got us all killed, "Siskin said quietly. "Or was that what you really wanted? Not just to give her Josh but throw in a few extras in for good measure."

"That wasn't the way of it," Killian replied angrily.

"I'm the only other one who knew of the Vortex before tonight," Samuel said calmly. "I also financed it to a point where it's only the paying back they have left to do."

"Is this so?" Loretta looked around at Lorcan, Aeden and Oisin who all nodded confirmation.

"What gave you the right to make such a decision without me?"

she demanded angrily.

"There was no time," her brother told her. "Danubin was on my heels, and I didn't want you involved."

"You didn't want me involved. . .!" Loretta's fury took her voice to a discordant pitch.

Siskin interjected before her anger could gather the words she was seeking.

"The question is where does this leave us now?" he challenged.

"Why is Magluck Bawah in Ireland?"

"That's what you call this thing?" Killian commented.

Siskin nodded. "That's what we've called it from the start."

Siskin too, Klim noted, avoided mentioning Echin.

"At first, we thought it was drawn here by the Vortex," Mactire said, looking troubled now.

"There was no evidence to warrant that proposal," his sister explained. "The location audit I've just run was compared to our tracking of the creature and there's still no correlation in its movements."

"So why then?" Josh asked her. "Why Dublin?"

Loretta shook her head, "We were hoping you might tell us," she said, shrugging her shoulders.

Samuel reached his hand out to Loretta, who glanced at Mactire before passing over the location audit. The cleric's face was expressionless as he read the document, folded it carefully and placing it inside his jacket.

"It's time we left," he said simply. His companions lined either side of him.

Oisin's stonewall glare and rock like stance barred the passageway to the backyard. Samuel looked back at Mactire, his gentle face set in firm lines of implacability. Mactire nodded and Oisin moved aside as the three men passed, Siskin at the rear, every sense alert. "Nice seeing you again," Josh said to Loretta as he left.

Klim wanted to run once they were in the passageway, but he kept his pace steady with his friends. Once in the yard Samuel signalled to the VW and threw the keys to Josh. As the others quickly dived into the yellow car, he went over to the black van that blocked their retreat. A flick of his finger propelled it backwards through the gate and into the road. Josh backed out the VW, picking up Samuel on the way. As he straightened up to head in the opposite direction from where Samuel had placed the van, the cleric raised his hand and the van followed behind. The three friends turned to watch it concertina, until it wedged itself with a crush of metal into the entrance to the yard. Klim whistled, eyebrows raised as he looked at Siskin, who was staring at the gentle cleric with renewed respect. Josh revved the engine and shot out of the cobbled alleyway into the Dublin traffic.

"Down O'Connell Street and head for Dun Laoghaire," Samuel instructed from the passenger seat.

Josh accelerated once he was clear of the main thoroughfare, which was still busy in the early hours of the morning.

"I'll take the Dock Road," he said as he swerved off the dual carriageway and onto a nearly deserted route, lined by a sea wall.

"You can't put your feet on the ground, any of you," Samuel told them.

"What?" Siskin exclaimed. "Why?"

Samuel pulled out the sheet Loretta had given him.

"Magluck Bawah in the last three weeks has been to Snowdonia, Wicklow, Pulton, Sydney, Cumbria, Nicaragua and now Dublin."

"All the places that we've been prior to meeting up," commented Klim.

"The speeds it reaches are faster than air flight," Samuel stated, still examining the notes.

Siskin leaned forward between the front seats.

"It's tracked back to where we all were before Frindy. How?"

"I've frankly no idea," Samuel told him, "but I'm pretty certain you to need to make contact with the earth for it to register your presence. Mactire's house and yard are protected but I daren't risk you setting a foot elsewhere in Dublin."

"The girls!" Siskin and Klim said together.

"Yes, message them in Mengebara and share what we have learned today," Samuel instructed. Klim closed his eyes and concentrated on transferring his most recent memories to images in Mengebara.

"Samuel, I can deal with this, but I need the Tenements," Siskin said thoughtfully. "I need to study the Vortex."

"They can't be trusted." Josh's tone was neutral.

"Wait. Pull over Josh please," Siskin's tone was commanding. Josh did as he was asked and pulled the vehicle into a small cul-de-sac, bordered by the shore, and rolled down the windows. The sky was lightening to a tearful dawn and the Irish sea slapped against the shale, slinging its pungent odour of seaweed and fish into the vehicle.

"Done," Klim told them, opening his eyes. "Why have we stopped?"

"It's tuning into our individual frequencies," Siskin told them and turning to Klim he explained, "Magluck Bawah, I know it."

"How?" Samuel asked.

"It's to do with the vibration of the frequency once we connect with the surface, underneath which the creature's access is unimpeded."

"How can you be sure Siskin?" Josh asked tersely.

"You read the Vortex visually, but it was filled with sound and musical motion." the musician replied.

"The creature sings?" Klim was sceptical.

"It moans," Siskin told them, "giving the densest of sounds, unrecordable with our current instrumentation. Kier could hear it in connection with the ground but if we do that, we become vulnerable to attack. I need to get back to the Vortex and find a way to tune into it without connecting to the surface. I could go back with Klim," Siskin added, seeing Josh's face set in rejection of the proposal.

"We can trust the Tenements only to look after their own interests," Samuel told them. "I pulled us out of there because I sensed that their interests were no longer convergent with our own."

"You think they'll give us up to Danubin?" Siskin asked.

Samuel sighed, "I think they already have. Otherwise, we wouldn't have left without a fight."

"And we're travelling in a bright yellow VW," Kim sighed.

"Look again my friend," Samuel told him.

Through the passenger window Klim saw that the yellow had disappeared.

"We're now in a blue Ford, a bunch of lads after a night out in Dublin. Mactire's not the only one who can play with light and illusion." The cleric laughed as he spoke.

"Great job Samuel, but what do we do now?" Siskin asked.

"Firstly, we will head to the ferry," was the reply. "Once we're on the water we'll be able to move around safely and then we can decide."

Chapter Twenty-two

Kier stood, her feet firmly planted on the ground, as she gathered the information that Klim had 'posted' in Mengebara. It seemed that once again, the creature had failed to track her presence. Strangely, only Siskin and herself had been able to hear the mauled sounds of its energy nearby; or see the whirling Kejambuck before Magluck Bawah made the transformation to animal predator. She held onto the rail nearby as she reeled with disorientation, the fingers of her other hand tightened over the strap on her left shoulder. Echin had managed to bring their things from the house in Frindy, her belongings were packed in a lightweight rucksack. Unsettled, she wondered why they had been split up again without discussion and tried to push away the growing resentment that she seemed to have so little control. Reuben's cavern had already taken on a dreamlike quality, though she could still smell on her skin the distinct flower like fragrance of the natural spring water that she had found in an alcove in that strange place. Even now the pull of that other portal filled her with both dread and delight. The fossilia had once again cushioned her journey and she could still hear their collective song as Echin's words whispered in her ear to make for St Paul's.

It was easy to recognise her location by the River Thames in London as she made her way through tourists along the riverbank. The water traffic was just beginning to gather momentum and she glanced at the experienced boatmen making ready for the first tours of the day. The landmark of St Paul's Cathedral stood gloriously on the other bank, as she approached the Millennium Bridge. It was the least crowded she had ever known the steel construction, which was hoisted by what reminded her of two stone goblets, conveying its constant pedestrian movement towards the magnificent domed building. The south face of St Paul's dominated the skyline and was just a short walk away once she descended from the bridge. The sun made an appearance through the cloud as she approached the architectural splendour of the cathedral. She caught her breath in salutation to its enduring beauty. A distinguished looking man with silver hair leaned against one of the pillars, looking in her direction but disappeared as she approached. To her relief Echin emerged from behind the adjacent stone; even his strong figure was small against such a background. As she approached, he nodded and slid his arm in hers to lead her around the building towards Cheapside. It was only as they reached the tube station that he spoke.

"Nothing?" he asked, looking towards her feet.

"Nothing," she confirmed, relieved. There was no sound or vibration to indicate that Magluck Bawah was nearby.

Echin manoeuvred her through the tube station producing tickets that allowed them access to the platform and within minutes they were standing hemmed against all nationalities on the train.

Kier's eyes roamed across the faces, old and young, black, and white, impossible to know if any were there with the purpose of their destruction.

Echin nodded towards the exit as they reached Bank station and she followed him towards the Docklands Light Railway where they jumped on a train minutes after their arrival. It was only when he signalled her to leave at the City of London Airport that her eyebrows raised in uncertainty. Echin however simply made for the desk where a flight to Dublin was checking in. Kier searched her bag for her passport to present to the soft-spoken assistant when Echin had submitted their tickets, hiding her surprise that the Mourangil possessed such a mundane thing as a valid identity document.

"Why didn't we just go with the others in the first place?" Kier asked, as Echin returned from the cafe bar with two hot coffees. He was looking around at the other passengers and she saw the slightest shake of his head.

"More fun this way darling, don't you think?"

A passport and he called her darling! A smile of amusement lit her face as she nodded that she understood they had to play the part of a couple. No problem there she thought, turning her head to see some quizzical glances from a group of middle-aged travellers in the corner seats. There was so much she wanted to ask him, but it was impossible, he looked and acted like any ordinary guy just now and it felt completely unfair. He chatted about London, a show that was currently playing at Her Majesty's Theatre, and she smiled and nodded, interlacing his narrative with the odd comment of her own. The travellers in the corner left the cafe and they watched the group disperse, leaving just two women who were heading towards the boarding gate for Dublin. Echin waited until boarding was well underway before picking up Kier's rucksack and edging into the last two seats on the flight, in the middle of the plane. He was chatting easily about sport, as he stowed the rucksack above their heads and took the aisle seat beside her. The two women from the cafe had taken the seats in front. One, the younger by a good few years Kier thought, was particularly smartly dressed, with a slimline business suit and expensive, though discreet jewellery. Her hair was cut smartly short and was very dark, the diamond drops in the centre of heavy gold earrings made a perfect accessory. The second woman was grey haired with a pinched jaw line; she saw neither of them speak on the short flight.

Echin closed his eyes and Kier did the same, seeing that her companion had posted in Mengebara that she was not to fall asleep. Once told that she could not sleep however it was exactly what she wanted to do, to the point where she had to visit the bathroom at the back of the plane to splash water over her face, in order to prevent her eyes from closing. On the way back she almost missed her seat as a silver haired older man of slight build seemed to be sitting in Echin's place. She checked that the two suited women were in front and then looked back at the seat behind to find Echin smiling at her as he stood up to let her pass. Kier hid her confusion and smiled back.

'Don't understand anything anymore,' she posted in Mengebara, where she received a 'ditto,' from Klim. There was still no message from Gabbie or Swift.

It was lunchtime when they finally left the airport and Kier walked beside Echin as he followed the two women from the cafe into the main arrivals area. There was a joyful shout as one young girl threw her arms around a man in his twenties and Kier smiled as she realised that they were sister and brother. Inevitably her thoughts flew to Gally; her eyes fell as she realised how long it had been since she had last seen him. Echin's attention was still focused on the two women, who had been seated in front and were now walking briskly towards the exit. Kier thought he was going to approach them but as they drew nearer a tall, well-built man with a misshapen nose appeared. He nodded towards the two women, "Good to see you again Esther," he said smiling towards the older woman. "And you Sonya," he added to her companion. The younger of the two turned to greet the man who was now stood at her side and Kier saw the daub of red lipstick and hard mouthed smile.

"About time Killian," Esther told him irritably, passing him her bags.

The younger woman swung her head round and her eyes met

Kier's. Had it not been for the feel of Echin's hand over her wrist, turning her towards him, she would have cried out. Even though she had seen the beautifully made-up features and large green eyes and knew that this was how the world saw this face, Kier was assaulted by the small dead eyes of the woman in her dream. The woman who she now knew to be Danubin, leader of the Virenmor. Kier found herself gasping for breath, but Echin stood in front of her, blocking any contact between them. When he finally stepped to one side, the two suited women and the man who had come to meet them, had disappeared.

Kier let out a long breath and stumbled against the Mourangil. Echin's arm came around her shoulder and she let her face lean against his muscled chest, seeking support but also allowing her to whisper for his hearing only, "It's her!"
"I know," was the quiet reply.
It felt the most natural thing in the world to let him hold her hand as they made for the exit. There was no sign of the two women outside the airport, as they emerged into a wet, blustery Dublin afternoon. Unhurried, Echin led them to the car park where he explained that Samuel had arranged for a vehicle to be waiting. In ten minutes, they were heading towards the city centre, where Kier had no doubt Danubin would also be found.

Chapter Twenty-three

"Kier!" Siskin turned to greet her as she descended the couple of small steps that led into the cosy interior of the narrow boat. Echin had deposited her on the roadside, above the Dublin canal, "It's called the 'White Arrow,' it's a muddy yellow colour, in the design of a longbow, can't miss it."

He had been right, it sat lazily, resting against the towpath in the afternoon sun. The lower body and both ends of the long narrowboat had been painted wood brown. The bowstring was a thin line of gold that highlighted the rim of the barge, with a white central funnel making the arrow. Siskin had been stoking the wood burning stove in the centre of the dimly lit space. Red leather seating blushed in the glow of carefully placed oil lamps against mahogany walls. Closed red curtains added to the sense of cosy secrecy. Siskin kissed her cheek in greeting as they both eased themselves into the old coach seats, knees sliding underneath a compact table.

"How did you get here? Where's Gabbie and Swift?" he asked her.

Klim entered from the cabin at the back of the boat, dark eyes full of sleep. His long torso had a natural tan, and he was dressed in loose jeans. He reached a long arm over her shoulder and smiled in greeting, his eyes scanning the space behind for the others.

"Just one rose amongst you thorns I'm afraid," she told them.

Kim's face looked troubled, "They haven't messaged, are they okay?"

"Echin says they're with Evan," she told them.

He nodded, "It'll be safer there, just don't understand why we've heard nothing."

"It's only hours since we saw them last Klim," she reassured him. "No doubt Evan will be keeping them busy."

"But we don't really know how much time we've been away from them. After all who'd have thought we spent three weeks in Reuben's cavern?"

Kier looked perplexed. "What do you mean? What day is it?" she asked him. It hadn't occurred to her to check the date when she had been with Echin, and she had barely glanced at her boarding pass.

"It's Wednesday August 31st," Siskin told her, as Josh shouted her name from the back of the boat. He was carrying a pile of wood.

"Not much like August today," he said cheerfully as he chucked the last log on the fire and came over to greet her.

"Good to have you back," he said, sliding alongside and pecking her cheek.

"Three weeks?"

"Crazy," agreed Siskin, pouring coffee in the kitchen area that comprised the first part of the boat.

Klim disappeared back into the cabin to find a black T-shirt and shortly afterwards joined them again as they sat around the table exchanging fuller details of what had happened since they had last been together. She told them of meeting Echin in London and the sinister encounter with the woman she was sure was Danubin.

"He followed her here. With you? What was he playing at?" There was anger and strain around the acorn eyes.

"He may have wanted to see if you recognised her," Josh commented thoughtfully.

"Or her you," added Klim.

"He took a major risk." Siskin turned his head towards the curtained windows, his shoulders taught with tension.

Klim glanced at his friend as he continued to quiz Kier.

"You said that Echin had quickly broken the contact between you and these women? Do you think she recognised you?"

Kier felt her stomach lurch remembering the glassy eyed woman of her dream and the hideous shape that had appeared in the graveyard at Capel-Cud-y-Bryn.

"This sounds daft," she told Klim the Reeder, "but I felt in my dream that she was looking, probing."

Klim nodded understanding, his dark eyes encouraged her to continue.

"Echin helped to protect my mind," her eyes lifted towards Klim, whose expression remained even, "after Jackson succeeded in implanting suggestions. Mensira, Echin called it. She must have broken down something to appear in my dream at all."

Again, Klim nodded but did not comment.

"I was certain she didn't get hold of my...... what do you call it? Mind print?"

Klim reached across the table and held her hand, a slight smile softening his thoughtful face.

"The point is," Klim told her, "that you got Danubin's!"

She pulled away gently and placed her hand in the fold of her arm. There was an uncomfortable sensation of alarm as she acknowledged the truth of Klim's comment. Siskin's torso had visibly relaxed, though he addressed her as if he were conducting an interrogation.

"You said the two women met someone. Did they use a name?"

"Killian." Kier gave a description of the man she had seen.

Klim whistled, Siskin looked dangerous, and Josh sprung to his feet.

"Samuel was right. We were already sold to her, even as we left the Vortex!"

"The Tenements?" Kier recalled Klim's message in Mengebara. "You think this Killian is one of them?"

Josh clenched his fists, his jaw tightened. "He's one of them. I drew them all in the end. Killian takes the form of a chimera when it pleases him."

"A what?" asked Klim.

"A chimera is part lion, part goat, part serpent. A mythical creature that is obviously no myth at all. I wonder if Danubin knows what she's dealing with?"

Siskin filled out the brief account that Kier had received of their meeting with the Tenements the previous evening. He described in detail their discovery of the Vortex. "It's incredible, as are the Tenements themselves."

"Incredible and utterly untrustworthy," Josh added bitterly.

Kier slid to the end of the bench. "I need coffee." An unexpected sense of claustrophobia had suddenly overwhelmed her. Waiting for the kettle to boil, she opened a door at the end of the boat, which led to an area of decking with a couple of chairs. Gratefully reeling in the fresh air, she looked up and down the still water of this deserted area of the canal. The afternoon had become sombre, rain hanging once again in the air.

"So, what's with the narrowboat?" She had returned to the table with a jug of coffee and was trying to inject some cheerfulness into her voice.

"As far as I know," Klim explained, "this is just a way of keeping our tiptoes from bringing the creature to us."

"Why didn't Echin challenge her? That's what disturbs me."

Siskin brought the discussion back to the question that troubled him so much.

"The Virenmor are human," Josh replied, "however grotesque they've made themselves. How many times has Echin said that this is a human story, our story?"

"Why get involved at all then?" argued Klim.

"I'm not saying he's not involved but I don't think he, or the other Mourangils, would willingly harm any human, no matter how bad."

Kier nodded her agreement.

"What about my uncle, he turned him into a mindless idiot," argued Klim.

"I got the impression that Echin only rebounded the intended destruction that your uncle already possessed, if you see what I mean," Siskin replied.

"Kind of. Like you said though, seems odd just to let her go." Kier spoke quickly in his defence.

"Without Echin and the other Mourangils we wouldn't have survived Whistmorden," Kier reminded them, her voice soft. "And by now that Magluck Bawah would have destroyed us if he hadn't taken us to Reuben's cavern."

"Your right Kier," Siskin sighed, "and I don't think it was a matter of letting Danubin go. I think they needed to know who she was going to meet."

Gratefully Kier acknowledged that Siskin seemed to have lost much of his anger.

"Would make sense," Josh nodded, regret in his eyes.

"Hey, how come you can walk outside without attracting Magluck Bawah?" Klim asked.

There was a long moment when Kier formulated many banal explanations in her head, opened her mouth to throw the question back at them and then closed it, deciding at last to share the fear that had begun to shake the foundation of her new and deep sense of belonging.

"I don't think I'm a Seed," she told them quietly. "I've been thinking about it. It was Gabbie that thing was interested in, that day at Devil's Bridge, not me."

Kier shivered as the thought revived her fear for her friend.

"But you see the words we can't see, you're without doubt an Inscriptor," Siskin pointed out. "The Tomer and Silex both said so!"

"Do you know Gabbie's already worked out the language of Ordovicia?" she replied.

The three men shook their heads and Klim looked amazed and proud.

"It took her no time at all, and she already speaks fluent Welsh and Spanish, with hardly any opportunity to learn. I think it's Gabbie that's the real Inscriptor."

"There are two Stozcists, why not two Inscriptors?" suggested Josh.

"I did wonder," Klim said softly taking her hand in his "Do you think you could be Candillium?"

Kier laughed and shook her head firmly. "Nope," she replied with certainty.

"Why not?" It was Josh who spoke but all three looked earnestly towards her.

Kier took a long breath in and then let it go, she looked at each of them in turn. "Well, in the first place, I imagine if Candillium was on the surface it would send some major bells clanging for Magluck Bawah!"

Siskin opened his mouth to reply but Kier raised her hand to silence him. "The other thing is that piece of parchment that Echin gave to us in Frindy?" The others nodded and she continued, a resigned look in her eyes. "Like I said it was part of a kind of journal I'd read in the bookshop. Candillium's journal. There were lines in it directly addressed to Toomaaris, as if she knew that the Myriar would not come together as they had planned." Kier closed her eyes and began to recite the passage she had committed to memory:

"*Wherever I must be, it will never be far enough to break the bonds between us. Though you are Mourangil, and I am not, yet we are the same and you will always know me.*"

There was silence in the narrowboat and Kier slowly opened her eyes, now glistening with tears. "I don't believe that there's any way that Echin, who we now know is Toomaaris, would not recognise Candillium in whatever shape or guise she may now walk."

"Perhaps," acknowledged Siskin.

Klim and Josh exchanged a glance but said nothing.

"Or it may be that the type of love that Candillium had for him could simply not be reciprocated by a non-human," Siskin suggested quietly.

Kier shrugged her shoulders with a self-mocking half smile that signalled the end of the discussion. She stood up to root around in the cupboard, hiding her face, but Josh reached up into the one over his head and placed four mugs on the table. Kier fixed her attention on finally pouring the coffee.

"I have to agree with Klim," the artist told her, his tone light. "I had you pegged for Candillium."

"And me," agreed Siskin.

Kier sipped the strong coffee, allowing the familiar aroma to saturate her senses. A moment later she put down her mug and smiled, "My money was always on Klim!"

Klim spluttered out his drink; Siskin and Josh hooted with laughter.

"Why not?" Kier shrugged.

Klim's eyes held hers, "Thanks," he told her sardonically, in the tone of a man who had just been hit with the bullet that she had dodged.

Chapter Twenty-four

It was late evening, after supper, when Echin and Samuel finally joined them on the boat. Kier had become drowsy with the slight motion of the canal and the closeted atmosphere of the barge. Klim had given up his room for her and was preparing bedding on the couch that lined the opposite wall from where she was sitting. She was just about to head for the small cabin, which was used as a bedroom, when Samuel entered soundlessly, Echin a few moments behind him. Kier nodded towards Samuel, who smiled in greeting. The implacable cleric looked tired she noticed, his skin was waxen, and his lively eyes seem to have lost a little of their shine.

"Did you find her?" she asked.

"Unfortunately, yes," Echin replied. "She's with the Tenements at a house that belongs to Killian, in Griffiths Avenue."

Josh's expression was bleak, but it was Klim who reacted angrily. "I got it wrong then, in my heart I didn't think they'd sell us out to Danubin."

"We don't know the whole of it yet," Samuel told him sadly, "but our chances of getting back to the Vortex are slim."

"Does she have the stones with her?" enquired Siskin.

"Amron Cloch certainly," Echin replied. "Its vibration is distinct, but the Virenmor held the Iridice for a number of years and as a result its nature is disguised so it will not reveal itself easily. In all likelihood she has both stones, at least she did not take Arwres from Capel-Cud-y-Bryn."

"She would have found Silex waiting," smiled Siskin.

Echin raised his eyebrows. "Now that would have been an interesting meeting!"

"We need to get after Danubin. What about roller skates?" suggested Klim.

"Eh?" Josh returned him a look of complete amazement. "That was a bit random!"

"I mean, do our feet have to be in contact with the ground? Couldn't we use some other way of getting around, or maybe Siskin could fashion us some kind of vibration cushion?" Klim's words tumbled out in his desire to be freed from inactivity.

Siskin shook his head, "Too risky. I need to get back to the Vortex and pick up its frequency, as that is the only way I can get to know its weaknesses, how it works, how we can survive it!"

Samuel looked carefully at Siskin.

"There's something else we need to do before then."

Siskin's eyebrows came together questioningly. Samuel did not react, and the question hung in the air as Echin spoke.

"Magluck Bawah is raw emotion, without rational thought," he told them. "Through the Kejambuck it will be able to direct its attack, but the vast energy of hatred means that it will attack completely savagely without any thought for the beast it is inhabiting." Kier pictured the huge bull plunging over the cliff edge and nodded.

"It will use whatever is in the vicinity but Danubin, as we have already seen, is capable of bringing it into contact with the oldest and most efficient hunters, creatures such as the Irresythe, that have hidden away in the recesses of the world. Silex has determined that there is enough energy within it for five manifestations, you have already survived two. My heart tells me that we must meet the other manifestations of this creature and defeat them. It will not be enough to cut off its method of detection or even to take away its link to the Virenmor."

"So, it comes back to the issue of bait again!" was Siskin's clear-eyed response.

"I'm afraid it does," answered Echin apologetically.

*

Echin drove through O'Connell Street, which was busy even at 3 am. Kier, in the passenger seat, watched him patiently manoeuvre through a chain of staggering youths, making their way from one venue to another. As they came out of the city centre, he took them through a maze of narrow empty roads.

"You can pull in here," Samuel instructed from the back of the car as they reached a row of terraced houses.

"That's the one," he pointed to the end as the car edged into a parking space.

Kier was fascinated to discover that the building gave absolutely no sign of containing the Vortex she had heard so much about, it just looked like the others along the terrace.

"Kier, you go to the door with Samuel, and I'll head round the back," Echin told her before quietly opening the car door.

"It's in darkness, looks like they're in bed," Kier commented as they crossed the road and noticed the drawn blinds in the upstairs windows.

"Mactire has it all on a timer," Samuel told her, "as he and Loretta often work during the night. He also has the front and back covered by CCTV."

He nodded towards the discreet cameras at the front of the building. Echin disappeared towards the end of the row and Kier felt the first edge of nervousness as Samuel knocked on the front door.

"There should be fewer of them here at this time," he told her, "especially with their visitors in town."

Josh had objected when Echin disclosed his intention to take Kier to the Vortex, calling it madness to allow Mactire to have any contact with her. Siskin had strongly vented the feeling that it was he, and not Kier, who needed to get near to it. Klim had looked at her and shook his head but said nothing. Kier had felt more fascination than fear at Echin's suggestion and pointed out that she was the only one of them who could move around freely. Samuel had taken the others to the barge by boat and Echin stressed the importance of the Tenements believing that the three of them had left Dublin on the ferry.

Standing next to Samuel on the lonely street, she realised that she was still at a loss as to what exactly she was supposed to do. Echin had said that she needed to see the Vortex and that the best thing to do would be to knock on the front door and ask; the programme, after all, was still owned by Samuel. The door was answered by a startlingly handsome man, a little older than herself, fully dressed. His mouth was set in a hard line as he looked at Samuel and then he simply stood back to let them in. The image of Little Red Riding Hood crossed her mind as she entered. Klim's nickname for Mactire as 'the wolf,' made him instantly recognisable. His predatory green eyes flickered in the lamplight as they entered the sitting room and widened as they fully noticed Kier. He loped around the room as Samuel quietly explained that he had brought his own engineer to see the Vortex. If her shock at being referred to as an engineer showed on Kier's face, Mactire gave no sign that he had noticed, though his eyes never left hers. She waited, remaining still as the silence grew and Mactire deliberated. In those moments, she felt the full force of his animal magnetism, but she knew, like camouflaged prey, that she must give no sign of fear or movement.

"No." He snarled the syllable, and in that instant, the chiselled human form altered. Josh had used the word 'Adlet,' an ancient standing wolf from the cold worlds of the North, to describe the essence of this man, the one he had painted on the Halfpenny Bridge. The room was charged with raw energy as he blurred from human to something else. The bottom half of his body comprised of the jagged and powerful hind legs of a large wolf. The top was Mactire with subtle differences: his features more canine, his teeth longer, his ears pointed, hair shadowing more of his face. The small figure of Samuel, his mop of curls tight round his head and cleric coat reaching to the floor, stepped in front of her. The disparity in size seemed to have no effect on the equanimity of the cleric as he reached inside his coat at the same moment that Mactire sprang across the room.

Kier screamed, noticing for the first time the long, clawed forearms and her hand reached automatically across her throat. A silver cord flew across the room from the inner doorway and the helpless creature yelped in pain as it lassoed around his body and brought him thumping to the floor, howling, and writhing. Echin, holding the end of the cord came up behind him and gently placed his hand on Mactire's chest. The fearsome creature shimmered back into the human form of Mactire, unconscious. Samuel, with equal gentleness, slid further silver cords from his coat. Echin removed the lasso from around Mactire's neck and Samuel bound both his hands and feet. Echin looked at Samuel, who nodded. Kier watched in amazement as the small man reached his hand towards the unconscious figure. Mactire rose in the air, propelled without effort by Samuel who followed closely behind.

Echin smiled, "He's going back with us," he told her. "Samuel will make sure he's safe."

"How's he doing that?" she asked, her eyes never leaving the bizarre sight of the cleric moving Mactire and opening doors without any physical connection.

"He's been around a very long time," was Echin's enigmatic reply.

"But he's not a Mourangil?" she asked.

"No, he's not," Echin confirmed in a tone that now wasn't the time for this discussion.

"That was the easy bit," Echin said ominously, as he guided her through the peculiar light illusions that made her feel that she was literally walking through walls. When they arrived at the steel doors, he closed his eyes for a moment and then reached across their centre; they slid open soundlessly. The room was empty apart from the fragile female figure that sat absorbed, tapping at a keyboard as she registered the changes within the central column, which Kier recognised immediately as the Vortex. Loretta turned as they entered, clearly expecting to see her brother.

"Where's Sean?" she demanded, turning from the computer, and striding out towards them. "Who are you? How did you get in here?"

Kier felt her skin tingle, she was responding to the auburn-haired Irish girl at some other level. There was a sheen to her skin that gave her an ethereal look, her leaf green eyes seemed filled with deep sorrow. Without thinking she stepped forward.

"You must be Loretta. Josh spoke of you."

The mention of Josh stopped her in her tracks, but the edges of her mouth remained tight.

"And you?" she challenged.

Echin answered before Kier could speak. "We're friends of Samuel and Josh," he told her.

"You are non-human," she stated matter-of-factly looking at Echin.

"And you…." she hesitated, scrutinising Kier, "surprisingly, I really don't know." She shook her head. "Where is Sean?" she repeated.

Her eyes moved to the steel doors as they swished apart, and Samuel entered the room.

"Mactire's safe." He turned to Echin and Kier, "We haven't got much time."

He nodded to Kier who walked to the left of Loretta, avoiding her gaze, and made her way up the few steps to the Vortex.

"Can you show us the creature's location Loretta, please?" Samuel asked and then he sighed as she shook her head.

"No need," Kier told him.

The descriptions that she had been given had not prepared her for the impact of her connection with the diamond threaded column of light and darkness; the twisting shapes of matter and space that were caught within. It was a universe, she thought, feeling the space around her, as she propelled her thoughts through the screens to plunge into the vast portal of the Vortex. Immediately she sensed the fearsome creature that broiled in an agony of hatred, permeating a space very near, but oblivious to her presence. She knew with great certainty that it would sweep her away in the course of its fermented emotion, should she try to get nearer. And then, in the swirling shadow that blasted across the whole of the Vortex, seeping its malevolent energy across the diamond boundary, she saw the stone. A large grey pebble, consumed in the belly of the beast.

Without warning Kier was plunged back to the scene of Martha's death. She gave an audible gasp, as she had done that day when she recognised the four circles of her dreams, etched on the back of the ancient stone depicting a bound devil. The same four circles were now clearly engraved on the innocuous looking pebble in the turbulent Vortex. Three small and one large circle, and for the first time she fully understood its meaning. A three-mooned planet. The stone had been swallowed by this terrible energy and would be lost forever in the inner realms of the planet; unless they defeated whatever creature manifested from this roiling anarchic entity that moved so disastrously below the surface.

"We need to go," Samuel told them tightly, looking at Loretta whose expression was a mixture of shock and suspicion.

As Kier glanced towards her she saw two forms, the outer woman and the inner Tane. The pure white unicorn had the same deep sorrowful eyes as those of the auburn-haired woman. Loretta looked from Samuel to Echin and then seemed to make a decision. She calmly went back to the keyboard and resumed her work. Samuel nodded to Kier who accompanied them through the sliding doors, just as they heard the sound of doors opening on the far side of the room. They ran, throwing themselves into the waiting car.

Mactire's unconscious body slumped against Kier as they rounded the first bend and Samuel drove out along the street. Minutes later he turned sharply into the car park of a local restaurant, easing the car alongside many others whose owners, Kier surmised, had left their vehicles and taken a taxi home. He had barely switched off the lights when a number of motorbikes tore angrily along the main street towards the city centre. As soon as they had passed, Samuel eased out the blue Ford and turned in the opposite direction.

"Why are we taking him with us?" Kier asked Echin.

"Because I don't think he would have come if I had asked him," replied Echin shrugging his shoulders.

"Right then," Kier said, looking at the compellingly handsome man beside her and trying not to think of claws and wolves.

Chapter Twenty-five

Gabbie saw what was happening in Dublin through the messages that Klim had left in Mengebara. She ignored his pleading that she message back, because whatever she imprinted in the mind place would be open to Swift as well. And that would not be a good thing just now. She noticed that Evan had also avoided Mengebara and wondered if he, like herself, was worried about showing too much of his thought in a place where façade was not possible. Gabbie was sure that it had not even occurred to Swift to use the mental network that Klim had created. She was embroiled in a disturbing world that neither she nor Evan could share. Echin had brought them to the remote island off the west coast of Wales, where they awoke every morning to the sound of sea birds. He had explained that the island constituted an uninhabited nature reserve but at the present time unusual currents around the harbour had closed it to visitors. Gabbie had no doubt that the 'unusual currents' would have been engineered by the Mourangils for their protection.

Swift had spoken only Spanish since her return from

Reuben's cavern, but this was not a problem for Gabbie, who had easily grasped the language. She had made it part of her purpose on the island to learn and speak as much of it as possible. Evan, however, was puzzled and disturbed. Swift responded and listened to his bardic English, but she spoke only in the language she had grown up with in Peru. The Welshman had reluctantly left Angharad in the new home they had begun to make along the River Teifi. Despite Danubin's quick exit from the church community in North Wales, Echin had felt it was too much of a risk for the family to return there.

Gabbie had come out that afternoon to her favourite spot on the cliff tops where the sea birds bartered noisily and the waves, cornered in a V-shaped channel, sprayed white plumes of water high against the rocks. She was delighted by the colourful puffins that populated the island and the seals that bobbed so unexpectedly in the waters nearby. Evan had pointed out the red campion flowers that inhabited sheltered coves and the swathes of purple heather that coloured the landscape. Growing up in the small semi-rural town of Bankside in the North of England, Gabbie had always felt at home where nature was most in evidence. Sometimes she thought people were like flowers, you could plant them in the most amazing places but if it wasn't just the right soil, they wouldn't grow. She thought of her dad and felt her eyes fill with tears of longing, wishing she'd gone up to see him straight away on her return to the UK. Then she thought of

Klim, and the others, and hugged her arms tightly around her knees. It took her a few seconds to catch Evan's rich 'Gabrielle' singing along the cliff top as he came towards her. He looked older, she thought, and thinner.

"She's gone again," he stated, his eyes roaming the landscape, as if Swift would appear beside them at any minute.

"She won't be far away," she told him with confidence. It was, after all, a small island.

"I'm worried Gabrielle." She knew Evan was not just speaking about Swift's absences.

Gabbie nodded in agreement, her eyes lost in the rhythmic motion of the sea. "I wish Faer and Tormaigh could be back with us. I miss them," she said, surprising herself. Until now she had not acknowledged her disappointment that the two Mourangils, who had been so instrumental in saving their lives, had not returned with Echin.

"It's so hard for us to understand that practically our whole lives can pass in what constitutes only a relative blink of their eyes," Evan explained, not for the first time.

"To keep Nephragm contained as they are doing, means that he cannot be here to add his evil to that of the Virenmor. We must miss them a little longer, blodyn."

Gabbie tilted her face towards the rugged Welshman, and he reached out a hand to her shoulder. She smiled and pulled herself to her feet, leaning on his arm.

"Let's go find her," she said, as Herald came bounding towards them.

"Where is she boy?" she asked the dog, who greeted her so enthusiastically, even though she had been gone for only half an hour.

Swift had left at sunrise and had not returned for lunch; had it not been for her companions she would not have eaten or drank all day. Gabbie automatically gathered water and sandwiches from the kitchen and then joined Evan in the courtyard of the small cottage. She took out Arwres and held the stone in her hand. It tugged, as it always did, towards the Stone of Silence, the diamond that Swift was never without. This time it led her towards the east of the island where they scrabbled up a tortuous path to reach a flat, grassy area in the middle of which stood a standing stone. Evan had once told her that the stone was often confused with the religious imprints of early settlers, and she could tell that it made him uncomfortable. Swift sat cross-legged, her arms around the stone, her head leaning against it as if she were asleep. As Gabbie and Evan approached she turned her face towards them, without removing herself from its embrace.

"Que me dice de tanto dolor," her voice was a low moan of pain.

"It tells her of so much sorrow," Gabbie translated.

Evan bent over and gently eased her limbs from around the stone. He put his own hand against if for a moment and his eyes looked troubled. Quickly he removed his hand and began to shepherd both girls towards the crumbling stone steps that he and Gabbie had just climbed.

"It grieves," Evan told Swift, "but it will soak in the sun again my dear. Come with us now."

Swift, her dark eyes sunken and haunted, her face pale beneath the natural brown of her skin, was content to let him guide her to a patch of grass. Gabbie encouraged her to take water and food and she saw, with relief, that today was one of the days that she would do as they asked. On other days, her eyes would blacken in anger, and she would refuse to go back to the cottage. On those days, Evan and Gabbie would bring blankets and make a fire beside her until she was ready to return.

Later, after they had gently guided Swift back to the cottage, Gabbie whispered to her old employer. "What's happening to her Evan?" She turned wearily towards him, secure that Swift was finally upstairs in an exhausted sleep.

Evan had lit a fire in the grate, but the room never really felt cosy. The place had been too long without human habitation and the whistle of the wind through the old stone walls continually protested their presence.

"As I understand it, she has destabilised her powers by giving into rage when she buried Terence Mace on the mountain."

"But he would have killed us!" Gabbie protested.

Evan nodded heavily, "Even so, she announced herself to the Devourils."

"But they already knew about her, Jackson used her to release the Perfidium."

Evan shifted uncomfortably looking for a way to explain.

"Because she used her gift in anger to wreak revenge on Mace, she has allowed Belluvour a way in."

The candles flickered and the wind hissed through the fire. There was no electricity on the island, and outside the dimly lit room there was total darkness.

"Don't mention him!" she pleaded, reaching for the blanket on the chair nearby.

"I'm sorry blodyn, I don't mean to frighten you," Evan told her, his grey eyes shining in the firelight.

"It's okay," she said, pulling at her lip. "Go on."

Evan glanced towards the bedroom upstairs where Swift slept.

"The part she played in releasing the Perfidium was done in innocence. Now she has committed an act of destruction, which may also have destroyed part of herself. The whispers of…" he hesitated, "the Secret Vaults, will be audible to her."

"What do you mean?" Gabbie asked, dreading the answer.

"It's not words or voices in her head," Evan sighed in frustration, trying to explain what he meant. Gabbie waited patiently.

"He will amplify the guilt that she feels until it becomes a worm that winds through her self-belief, her sense of who she is."

"I don't understand," Gabbie knew that she never wanted to understand.

Evan looked towards her, and his eyes smiled. He reached to pat Herald in front of the fire, and the dog snuggled against the outstretched hand.

"I don't think our dark thoughts will help her," he made to get up from his seat.

"What if she's Candillium?"

The words came out like rapid gunfire in the small room. The wounded look on Evan's face told her that he had long deliberated over the same thought.

"We can only do what we are already doing, trying to help her heal whatever injury she has inflicted upon herself."

Gabbie nodded. She picked up the blanket and headed towards the spiral stone staircase, carefully feeling her way against the cold wall in the darkness. When she looked back towards the dimly lit room she could see Evan, hunched over the figure of Herald, his head upturned towards where Swift was sleeping.

In the hallway above Evan had fixed a couple of oil lamps and Gabbie was able to distinguish the small basic bedrooms. It was a matter of course for her now to check on Swift, who slept in the room next to her own. After a quick glance, she ran back to remove an oil lamp from its bracket, checking the small bed and each corner of the room. She shouted to Evan who grabbed the candles and together they checked the tiny kitchen and the other rooms upstairs. Stumbling in the darkness they came back to the living room and Gabbie took out Arwres. Immediately the stone tugged at her, but this time taking her only a few steps. There on the chair cushion, where she had been sitting not twenty minutes previously, was the Stone of Silence.

Chapter Twenty-six

"Samuel," Mactire's voice croaked, his tone plaintive enough to bring Kier towards him with a bottle of water. Samuel watched dispassionately as Kier held the liquid to Mactire's mouth and the Tenement drank thirstily. As he emptied the bottle his head pulled up and Kier moved away from eyes that jabbed angrily in the gloom, broken only by a couple of candles. He looked towards the silver cords that bound his arms and then his smouldering rage burst into a tirade of Irish that Kier took to be a string of curses. Samuel merely turned back to reading the document he had lifted from Mactire's front room. Kier had presumed that they would head back to the barge but instead Echin had directed northwards, to a place he called Druid's Den. They were now in a small cottage, within metres of the remains of several standing stones. "Interesting," Samuel declared, bringing the document from the table into Mactire's vision.

Seething, the prisoner pulled uselessly at the cords.

"I take it, this is for Danubin." Samuel handed the document to Kier who saw, to her shock, that Mactire had produced something very similar to the image of the Myriar created by Josh from inside his painting. It was a five-pointed star but there were two differences. The circle in the centre was solid, not empty, and there was nothing written on any part of it. The green eyes of the Tane softened into something like regret.

"I have to give her something to pin her stones on. Belluvour's already had a bitter taste of the Myriar; they're worried that Candillium is, after all, amongst us. Danubin told us that at least one of the Seeds is dead, if not Candillium herself. She thinks that if she gathers the Myriar Stones in a similar arrangement to the Seeds, that Nephragm will act as the centrepiece and destroy whatever the Myriar intends to create."

"And where did this shape arise from?" Samuel demanded acidly.

"I'm not like you Samuel, whatever the hell you are, but I can slip in between the folds from time to time, especially when young Josh opens the door, so to speak."

"You followed me to Wicklow?" Samuel was the sternest Kier had ever seen him. Mactire didn't bother to confirm it.

"A Tane doesn't have the same propensity to end up there forever, and in that environment, we are virtually part of the landscape. Josh struggled with himself and whilst you were watching him, I slipped into the lake. I took a chance that I'd have a bit of time to look around. I had faith in the boy's ability though, to keep the way open, and what I found was truly fascinating."

Kier glanced at Samuel, her back turned to Mactire. He was unaware that what he had found had been more fully revealed when Josh drew his picture a second time.

"Danubin wants insurance, just in case she doesn't get to kill you all with the creature after all."

"And you provided her with it." Kier turned back towards the prisoner.

"And would you be Candillium by any chance?" Mactire challenged.

"And would Samuel bring me near you if I was?" she replied calmly.

"One of the Seeds then," he probed, "but I suppose not, if you're able to stand on open ground."

Just as Samuel was about to interject, his attention veered to the open door on the far side of the single roomed cottage. Echin looked relaxed as he entered, his hair damp from the soft shower of rain that had started as they arrived. After helping to deposit Mactire in the cottage, he had disappeared among the standing stones. The Tane turned his head as Echin made his way to stand by Samuel.

"Well, Mactire, now we've had a chance to chat I think you can be on your way."

He reached out his arm and the silver cords came apart, softly joining to become a long rope of silver that wound itself round his sleeve. Startled, Mactire jumped up dangerously and came over to

Echin, changing his form into the fearsome Adlet once again. Kier, with effort, found herself following the grave stillness of her companions as they watched the transformation with interest, but who showed no hint of fear or aggression. The creature turned suddenly and ran through the open door, into the night.

"You heard?" Samuel asked.

Echin nodded thoughtfully, "He's sick, his Adlet form is dying but his human form is not."

He glanced towards Samuel who shook his head, puzzled.

"I thought that was an impossibility."

"There are no impossibilities Samuel, but it goes against the pattern."

"Has it got anything to do with the Vortex?" asked Kier.

"Possibly," Echin replied. "As always the Tanes play both sides for their own ends."

"They are never straight forward," Samuel commented, "and Mactire and his sister Loretta more so than the rest."

"Yes, I think you're right there. No sense in us staying any longer, he'll have to recreate his drawing to give to Danubin." Kier felt herself squirm in revulsion as she visualised the terrifying figure she had seen in her dream and at the graveyard. The groomed and attractive woman of the aircraft overlaid what she recognised as a profoundly distorted personality. Echin put an arm around her shoulder, guiding her towards the door, his touch igniting her growing sense of need for his presence. Irritated with herself, she walked quickly towards the door and climbed back into Samuel's blue Ford.

*

Klim looked drawn and intense as they arrived back at the barge. He was stood on the deck, his shoulders set, arms folded, turning his attention from the rising sun to greet his friends.

"How'd it go?" he asked, following them into the cabin.

Echin gave a brief summary of the evening's events, and the youth nodded thoughtfully.

"So Danubin is creating her own version of the Myriar?"

Echin nodded.

"What is it Klim?" Kier asked, intuitively realising that another factor had contributed to the anxiety in his expression.

"It's Swift," he replied, anxiously. "I keep getting this cry for help but its swirling in shadows. I think she's underground again."

Echin glanced at Samuel. "It may take us both," he said quietly, "as there's only one place on the island that would allow her entry underground and she must have removed the Waybearer to get there."

Samuel looked with concern at Kier and Klim. "It's not us that will bring her home, you know this."

Echin looked troubled as he glanced at Kier and then turned to

Klim.

"We'll take Klim," he decided, "that is if you will come with us?" The youth, despite his anxiety, seemed reluctant to leave. He looked at Kier and she thought he was about to say something. Then he nodded and sighed, turning toward the bedrooms from which he returned minutes later, holding a small soft leather rucksack over his shoulder. He hugged Kier and then followed Echin and Samuel as they exited the cabin to the deck above. A moment later, as she reached the top of the narrowboat steps, Kier caught the barely visible outline of all three, wrapped in the soft rays of a gently rising sun. Exhausted, she went back into the narrowboat and lay on the first bed she came to.

*

"Klim," it was Siskin's voice, as he entered the small bedroom. "Er, sorry Kier," she heard him say, retreating, as she shook herself awake.

"It's okay," her eyes adjusted to the gloom of the cabin and the covered window.

"He's gone with Echin and Samuel," she told him, rousing herself with difficulty.

"I'll make some coffee," he replied looking perplexed. "We'll chat when you're up."

Ten minutes later, after she had washed in the tiny bathroom and changed into a sweatshirt and jeans, she joined both Siskin and Josh in the middle of the narrowboat. Over coffee and cereal, she related to her companions everything that had happened the previous evening.

"But where are they?" Josh asked.

"I don't know," she replied, shrugging her shoulders. "Something serious has happened with Swift. Echin said it would take both him and Samuel to help but that one of us needed to be there too."

Josh had stood up and was pacing the floor. "Didn't he say what had happened to her?"

"Something about her going underground again, and removing the Waybearer," Kier recalled.

"Underground!" Josh repeated horrified. "Has she been taken?"

"I'm sorry Josh," Kier said, trying to soothe his anguish. "Klim's connection with her only gave a sense of her being underneath the ground and in great need. I really don't know any more."

The disappointment on both faces made her realise how much tension had built up in the period of their confinement. Siskin pulled a black hat over his head that brought the angles of his face into sharp relief. For the second time, he had been left behind. The tight lines around his mouth were a silent protest. Then, it seemed, he picked up her concern and sighed. "I think we need to concentrate on what we can do here." He placed both elbows on the table, interlinking his fingers as he leaned forward, a look of concentration on his face. Josh, about to continue to express his worries for Swift, took a deep breath and pressed his lips together. He nodded and joined them at the table as his friend continued.

"Inside the Vortex, you saw this creature, and it had a stone inside it. Is that what you're saying Kier?"

"I saw the stone," she said. "It was right there at the centre."

"But Loretta said the creature has no mass," Josh pointed out.

"Nevertheless, I saw it and I am sure it is the Stone of Mesa." Neither of her companions asked how this could be and Kier was aware of a fearful realisation of their faith in her. She put aside her own doubt and remembered the clarity that she had felt as she stood before the Vortex.

Josh looked perplexed, "So Mesa was our original home, the one that gave us up for adoption before it ceased to exist. Maybe that's why so many of us feel so lost, even after all this time."

"Isn't that what the Myriar was trying to fix? Helping us to integrate into Moura?" Kier replied. "It's crucial that we find the stone," she told them, her voice hardening in certainty.

"What do Echin, and Samuel say?" enquired Josh.

"We didn't speak of it," Kier replied, realising this fact for the first time, "but I got the impression that the whole point of bringing me to the Vortex was to see if the stone lay inside Magluck Bawah."

Siskin nodded agreement, then his eyes widened in alarm as a scream reached them from the tow path.

"Siskin! Siskin!" a child's voice pierced the morning.

"Juliette?" Siskin turned white.

He ran the length of the narrowboat in seconds, ignoring his companion's cries for him to wait, but by the time they had followed him onto the deck it was too late. Siskin was already tearing up the gravel path in pursuit of a hooded runner in the distance, over whose right shoulder fell the blonde head of a small child. As Siskin drew near, the figure threw the child into the canal and made for the bridge steps, leaping up them, several at a time. Siskin had already launched himself after the small body and was in the middle of the water, where the canal was at its deepest. Kier and Josh had followed and were almost in line with their friend as he swam, reaching the small, limp figure that was face down in the water. Siskin cried out in a mixture of anger and relief, as he overturned the dummy that had been used to goad them into the open. The blonde wig was skewed around the plastic face that bobbed sightlessly in the water in response to Siskin's urgent examination.

Kier looked towards the bridge, where the hooded figure was now standing. As the hood was drawn back, she saw the well-groomed woman from the airport flash a red rimmed smile as Siskin pushed the dummy towards the towpath. The musician pulled the lifelike plastic doll from the water, his expression as black as the day they had walked amongst the atrocities of Roust. Only then did Kier acknowledge the rumbling of which she had been aware from the moment she had stepped onto the ground.

There above the bridge, the Kejambuck circled Danubin and Kier caught a flash of fear in the counterfeit perfection of her face. Her arm struck upwards towards the writhing figure and then fell, like an executioner's axe, long fingers pointing directly to Siskin. The Kejambuck arrowed sharply towards her friend as he stood waist-high in water, manoeuvring the small imitation body to one side. Kier screamed at him to get out of the water as she saw, beneath the surface, the shape of the creature that the Kejambuck had directed to attack Siskin. Passing the bridge, the monstrous outline headed train-like towards him. It charged down the centre of the canal, its squealing sound finally making Siskin aware of its presence.

It was pale as death, white fleshy eyes circling madly, its giant eel's head tunnelling the water as a ringed, elongated body thrashed wildly behind. Josh and Kier reached down frantically to pull Siskin from the canal, only then aware that his legs had become caught beneath the surface as they tried helplessly to free him. Kier saw the pinched face of the Kejambuck, it's body tightly coiled around the ex-soldier's legs, preventing any escape. She bent forward towards the malicious whip like creature, but its tail coiled up behind her and knocked her into the water beside Siskin. The canal bridge cracked as the summoned creature ploughed into the narrower stretch of the canal, gasping in the shallower water but yet continuing relentlessly towards them.

Josh jumped in beside them and the malicious eyes of the

Kejambuck winced in pain as the Chalycion stone flashed its presence. Siskin sighed in relief as the wire tight hold on his legs was released. Kier saw the malevolent Kejambuck uncoil and head towards the barge, but it was too late. The dark maw of the frantic monster was now upon them. Kier fell backwards into the water as both Siskin and Josh tried to shield her from the impact of the wide-open jaws. The dark cave of the huge creature's mouth, with rows of cliff like spears of teeth and the stench of rotting fish, surrounded the trio as it descended towards them. Kier was filled with a sense of outrage, a vast emptiness of unfulfilled purpose that brought tears to her eyes, as the jaws closed towards them, the creature's head knocking her defenders to either side. Even as she braced herself for the terrifying impact of the enclosing jaws, miraculously its head recoiled from the impact of another creature.

Kier knew immediately it was the Chimera that Josh had described as Killian's other self: three animals bound together in one body, its lion head tearing at the flesh of the predator that was determined to destroy them. She scrambled to the surface aided by Josh, who had jumped lightly from the canal. Siskin joined them once he was sure that Kier had cleared the water; he directed them both to the patch of grass beside the towpath where all three turned to fix their concentration on the battle that was still ongoing. The Chimera, fearsome as it was, looked small against the powerful creature that had caught the serpent tail in its mouth. It roared, battering the body of the Tane against the concrete walls of the canal. Abruptly, the creature released its prey as it was unexpectedly attacked from behind by the Adlet Kier knew was Mactire, now biting savagely into the pale flesh that reached out beyond the point where the small bridge had stood. It seemed to Kier that within moments this remote stretch of the canal had been filled with the sights and sounds of mythical creatures. A Griffin ghosted its way over their heads, its huge wings darkening the sky. Its eagle head dived beneath the water to lift the limp form of the discarded Chimera, bringing it to lie beside the companions on the tow path. The three faceted creature lay twisted: Goat, lion and serpent intermingled in death. Slowly, like a movie special effect, Kier watched the Chimera alter to the human form of Killian that she had seen at the airport.

"Oisen," called Josh, as the river monster reared its fleshy head towards the Adlet. Immediately the eagle wings of the Griffin spread, lifting its lion body, then swooped down in fierce attack at the enraged beast. The Adlet hung on despite the thunderous threshing of the elongated body. At the same time, the Griffin's sharp beak bit into the rolling head, circling and dipping, barely avoiding being crushed by the beast that seemed to be swelling in size as the canal waterline lowered. Kier could see that the two Tanes were tiring as the beast grew and she stood up ready to enter the fight. Josh caught her hand, "You can help him," he told her. "You can help Killian."

Kier looked at him puzzled and then she saw that Killian was miraculously still breathing. Anguished Josh told her, "The Tane side of him has kept him alive but without help it won't be for long."

She wanted to protest, to ask him what difference she could make but Kier knew in her heart that she could reach out to this creature, now returned to its pale human form. She put her hand on his chest and felt the heartbeat, faint, irregular, fading. Her hands travelled to his right lung and the laboured air vibrated beneath her fingers. As she closed her eyes, she saw his three faceted Tane form inlaid beneath his human exterior. It was to this form that she directed her consciousness, seeing again the proud lion's head, its mane torn; the goat, horns broken and bent, the snake's tail lifeless. Slowly she lent her will to returning the creature back to its original shape. The moment stretched beyond time, but she did not let go of the fragile connection that she sensed was Killian's only chance of survival. Then beneath her palm his human heartbeat in tandem with her own and Kier shut her eyes, fully connecting with the delicate process by which, in all that turmoil, Killian was finding a way to remain alive. As his heartbeat became strong and regular and his lungs fully expanded, she nodded at Josh who bent over his old friend, nodding, and smiling.

The three companions turned their attention back to the gruesome battle that was still taking place, as the high-pitched squealing of the monster wounded the air. Sensing that the two Tanes were defeated, it launched itself towards the three companions on the tow path in a ferocious attempt to claim its prey. Josh was knocked backwards against Kier, who saw a wall of dark fur shape itself into an enormous black bear that was bounding from the embankment behind them, forcing the creature into the centre of the narrow channel. Its head rolled back, and the long body reared in frustrated rage as it turned to destroy this new threat. At that moment, the Adlet and Griffin rallied as a second bear and a startling, oversized fox, entered the canal from either side, springing simultaneously into the water. The large bear was pure white; its huge teeth ripped into the throat of the thrashing beast, as it was harried by the scurrying fox. The brown bear stood upright pawing at the pale, leathery head until it poured a sickly, serous fluid that steamed against the cold water of the canal. The Tanes jumped from the water, as the defeated creature's death throes scattered its entrails and made the canal a sink of obnoxious flesh and fluid. They once again shimmered into their human forms as they reached the towpath.

Mactire bent over Killian who smiled wanly. "I was almost gone," he whispered. His head turned painfully towards Kier. "You saved me. Thank you."

Mactire raised his eyebrows as Kier shook her head in response. "You saved us all, Killian, thank you."

Killian's eyes closed, and Mactire bent over his body, concerned.

"He'll be okay," reassured Kier, to her surprise, but confident that she had spoken the truth.

"What was that thing?" Josh asked him.

"We know it as the Tolbranach," replied Mactire sadly. "It's lived under the Caher mountain since the Tanes first arrived. In its own life, it would never have harmed any of you."

"And now it'll be pawed over by the media and the scientists forever," added the handsome young man, who had shortly before leapt to their defence in the form of a black bear.

"No Danny, we'll not let that happen," Mactire announced firmly. "Come on lads, I know you're tired but between us we can swim her out to the open river and then the sea where she can lay in a place that she would choose to be, unseen in the ocean."

"Sean!" called Josh as the Tanes moved along the path. "Thank you."

Mactire nodded and tilted his head to one side.

"Look after Killian," he told them, breaking into a run, and becoming an Adlet once more.

In the glare of the rising sun, the Tanes escorted the despoiled creature through the remains of the broken bridge out towards the river, which would eventually connect with the Atlantic Ocean. The strangest of visions, Kier thought, to greet the new morning that had very nearly become their last.

Chapter Twenty-seven

Klim, brow furrowed, bent over the remnants of the standing stones that were scattered over the grass. A dark tunnel, like an open grave, revealed itself where one of the stones had stood. A lapis jewel shone on the granite rim of the gaping hole, moments before the figure of Echinod Deem emerged onto the grass beside him.

"Obdurates," he stated grimly. "I cannot pass any further. I have scoured the spaces that could hold Swift but cannot find her." Samuel walked back from the cliff edge where he had been standing deep in thought as the gulls screeched their morning hunger.

"Where is she Klim?" he asked tensely. The young man, gathering his concentration, did not reply.

"Klim!" Gabbie's voice, snatched by the wind, was there, outside the circle of his focus that burrowed to build the tenuous link between his own mind and the confusion of painful thought that was Swift. Eyes closed; he scattered his awareness until he felt it. Cold threaded its way down the back of his neck and soon his limbs shivered in response to the frozen and desolate place where Swift was hidden. Klim opened his eyes, he had put his hand without knowing onto a broken piece of the standing stone.

"She went underground here," he told them firmly.

He lifted his hand from the stone and saw that Samuel was watching him with concern and also something like clinical interest. Evan and Gabbie now stood quietly beside him and Klim regretted that he had not been able to receive the effusive greeting that he had heard, albeit distantly, in Gabbie's voice.

"Hi," he smiled at the girl who had grown so confident and womanly. He had always been unable to read her, apart from that one terrible time when she had been attacked by Luke and he had felt as if his own life was ended. Now she stood, her blonde hair spiked with the wind and the soft blue of her eyes saddened by dark rims. His heart sighed, even in this short time away she had become still more beautiful. Evan stepped forward, shaking his hand.

"Thank God you have all come," he told them all. "Has she contacted you Klim?"

He saw Gabbie turn away as he nodded.

"We've searched all night," Evan continued. "Gabrielle wanted to look here but it was too dangerous to climb these rocks in the dark. We waited till sunrise."

"I don't understand," Gabbie said peering into the dark tunnel, "why would she go underground? It'll kill her."

"She's still alive," Klim felt certain.

"She must have gone down there for whatever purpose and then surfaced again, either here or elsewhere," Evan surmised.

Klim looked around, increasingly disturbed, suddenly uncertain what to say. He saw that Echin had realised his confusion.

"You are certain she is still on the island," Echin asked gently, encouragingly.

"Yes," he answered immediately. "She's still here somewhere. I'm certain."

"Echin!" Gabbie cried with horror. Soon her distress was shared by the others as they accessed Mengebara.

"Danubin!" Echin's cheekbones glimmered blue crystal as he watched the recent memories that Siskin had placed in Mengebara. Together they each saw the image of the musician sprinting along the canal and jumping into the water after the figure disposed of by Danubin. The heart-rending moments when he believed that the child was dead were shrouded in the musician's dreadful sorrow. Klim reached for Gabbie's hand as tears streamed down her face and then they covered their ears at the booming anger that had followed as Siskin discovered the dummy. Horrified they watched as the Undercreature, in the shape of the terrifying Tolbrannach, attacked their companions. Wonder, like a rainbow, leapt into Gabbie's eyes, at the sight of the mythical Tanes. When the whole scene had played out, Echin glanced at Samuel who nodded.

"A Stozcist and a Reeder are better placed to find Swift than we are at this moment," he told them, moving towards the cliff edge. "We'll head back to Dublin."

The small group nodded their assent as the Mourangil, and Samuel disappeared in a fold of air.

After their departure Klim was filled with a sense of the island's bleakness and he suddenly felt assailed by grief. The loss of his mother and father cut through him once again, unbearable. The small fingers that squeezed his hand stopped the tears that threatened, and he breathed deeply, stepping back towards the gaping tunnel.

"I should go down," Evan was saying with deep resignation.

"That would be stupid!" The voice, it's eastern accent distinctive, brought a leap of hope to Klim who turned smiling to see the elfin figure of Silex making its way towards them.

"Silex!" Evan cried in greeting, his ingenuous face showing his delight, then he bowed respectfully. "Do you know where Swift is?"

The irascible Mourangil shook her head ruefully.

"She is likely dead." Silex spoke matter-of-factly and somehow that made it worse. Klim heard the sob break from Gabbie's lips. Silex ignored her, pondering,

"The obdurates would scream the presence of the Stone of

Silence to another Stozcist. If the girl had been here, you could not be unaware," her eyes turned hard as she focused on the Welshman, his genial smile of greeting now wiped from his face.

"But she didn't have it with her," Gabbie told the Mourangil, bringing the perfect diamond from the pouch around her neck. She went to hand it to Silex who stepped backwards.

"Keep it safe, Storekeeper. Clever Stozcist," remarked Silex.

"I have never tried but I will see if I can learn anything from the obdurate," said Evan, looking towards the dark tunnel.

"You will not," Silex told him without emotion. "She was truly the last Stozcist, born to the Myriar, but in her absence, you are the only one who could take on her role. Stupidity to risk you and you would not succeed; the obdurate would trap you below the surface and we would be powerless to recover you."

Ignoring the set of Evan's mouth, and before he could reply, Silex turned determinedly towards Klim. "Our hopes of finding her lie with you," she told him sharply. "Use the Stone of Silence."

Gabbie responded to the blunt instruction and immediately held out the stone towards him. It glimmered in the early morning light; Klim took the stone but then turned away.

"Not here," he said firmly. "I need to be in her room."

Silex looked impatient then sighed irritably. "Very well then," she agreed, "we will do as you say."

Klim deliberately fell behind the others and let his awareness reach towards Swift once more. Evan was talking to Silex, as her assertive stride made short work of the scrambled rocks leading off the hill.

"Wrapped in ice and cold as death," he whispered as his hands softly caressed the diamond in his pocket. "Deep below," his voice quietly expressing what he now knew. As he continued to hold the stone, he saw that it was not ice but a kind of cold crystal that surrounded her. He felt his insides lurch as he remembered what Kier had told him of her ordeal under Whistmorden, but he decided that Swift did not feel caught or trapped, this place was of her own making, and she was deliberately hiding.

The distress of his friend, the reason that had brought them all from Dublin, was no longer present. He guessed that somehow Swift had managed to pass through the obdurate but that it had caused her great pain. Klim located the fact that was really troubling him. Swift knew that none of the Mourangils could pass through the obdurate to help her. Why would she hide there? Until he could find the answer, he made the decision that he would not share what he knew of the Stozcist's location. If he felt a stab of guilt at prolonging Evan's and Gabbie's anxiety he put it to one side. Every instinct he had ever trusted told him to remain silent.

*

Gabbie felt Klim release her hand with regret, but she avoided looking back, so tired and bruised by the last few hours that all she really wanted to do was eat and sleep. Although she had been glad to see Silex and presumed that Echin had sent her, the Mourangil angered her. She got the fact that she had no idea really how to talk to them. Echin had explained that Silex had only recently (a hundred years in his terms), spent much time in her human form! Still, if it meant they found Swift she could handle it. The idea that Swift was no longer alive had not occurred to her and she had the feeling that Klim knew more than he was saying. Since when had he ever had to go to anyone's room to do his mental linking up thing? Without thinking she placed her hand on Arwres, worn in a pendant under her sweatshirt, it itched against her skin. Gabbie brought the stone out to rest on top of the black material and was shocked to see that it had turned blood red. Quickly she returned it underneath her shirt, finding that she was now very much wide awake.

Chapter Twenty-eight

Exhausted, Swift released her concentration from the last grain of crysaline that she had painstakingly created from the surrounding surface. Only once before had she touched the white material that had been used to hide the hateful Perfidium, but it had been enough. Now she had encased herself in the substance, understanding that it would prevent her from suffering the same sickness that had occurred when she had been forced underground on the crag at Bankside. She knew that Evan could not follow her and fervently hoped that he would not try. Over the months her powers had grown and far surpassed those of the man she had come to think of as a father.

Above her was the foul obdurate stone that had grasped at her being, attempting to solidify the molecular entity that she became, once she was inside the stone. It was the standing stone that had warned her, calling to her in subtle vibrations as she lay in the small bedroom of the cottage. Gabbie and Evan had been totally unaware of her presence as she slid easily within the stone wall of the sitting room, listening as they discussed their fears. Swift had not dared to reveal herself, knowing that the enemy was nearby and was coming for her. That the peaceful island had been breached by the fearful being who had nearly destroyed them on Whistmorden. Nephragm, she knew, would not show his hand until he had found the Stozcist. Evan had been right, she had left herself open to the Devouril, her rage and guilt leaving a trail for Nephragm to follow. Now she had to protect her friends. When Gabbie had shouted down to Evan in alarm, finding the empty bed, Swift had carefully removed the Stone of Silence and ran across the island, finding her way in the dark by following the vibrations of the stone.

It was strange for her to think that the monolith had stood for so long but that those who had lived nearby had no understanding of its significance. It had communicated to Swift that it was a Waybearer, a point at which Mourangils could transform from their natural mineral 'embeds' to a new form. It aided the first transmutation of a Mourangil into human or animal form, a kind of costume wardrobe, Swift decided. The standing stone held within its structure the imprint of all living forms that came within the radius of its indiscernible vibration. The Mourangils could use the recorded observations to help understand the beings on the surface and to shape forms that would allow them to pass among the creatures that inhabited the earth. In this way, they had studied and guided the living beings of the planet.

Swift discovered however, that very few Mourangils now used the Waybearer, for doing so was not entirely without cost for this indigenous race. Once the unique form had been taken, the Mourangil would no longer need the Waybearer to alter its appearance, it was then available to them at will. However, Echin, who chose to remain in human form for an unfathomable period, could no longer embed in the deeper tissues of the planet, only the outer rings were available to him. Slowly he was becoming less Mourangil and more human. All this she learnt in her first contact with the stone, barely noticing that Evan and Gabbie had kept her warm by lighting a fire and accompanying her long embrace with the Waybearer. Once again, her mind went over the events she had found recorded in the stone from the previous evening. Silex, the feisty Mourangil they had met in Frindy, had come to the Waybearer to study the happenings on the island since Echin had deposited the small group in the cottage. Swift saw the strip of silver that was her Mourangil signature and watched it transform into the striking, impish redhead. Unexpectedly a cormorant alighted on the grass nearby. Silex gasped as her green eyes held those of the long necked, hook beaked bird.

"Nephragm," she whispered, her voice filled with compassionate sadness.

The wide wings fanned out and the bird shook itself into the terrifying form Swift had seen once before, drawn by Josh at the Mountain Inn. The body was neither animal nor human but a mockery of both. Powerfully muscled feline limbs were oversized for the black body that was covered in red shimmering threads, which criss-crossed the coal like surface and rimmed the dark tunnels that comprised his eyes. The Waybearer had recorded the sense of horror that Silex had felt.

"Join me Silex," the hoarse whisper held a note of pleading. "We were close once." The green eyes softened as she shook her head. "Why are you here?" she asked the hideous form.

"I have another little service for our new Stozcist," he rasped.

"You can't have her," Silex told the predatory creature with a lift of her chin.

Nephragm did not answer. Cat like he inched a huge limb towards the slight figure and Swift saw Silex prepare to take flight. In an instant however, the map of red lines left Nephragm's body and formed a sinister net over the Mourangil. Swift had recoiled towards the Waybearer as she realised that the thread like lines that criss-crossed the repulsive form were not veins of fluid, but funnels filled with insects that radiated blood red light in the darkness. In seconds, they had tracked down Silex's mouth and throat, poisoning her human form. Swift had cried out as she watched the vibrant figure turn a deathly purple. Nephragm raised his paw like appendage and the voracious insects reasserted their symbiotic relationship with the hard surface of his body. He stepped forward and Swift saw the perverted look of pleasure as Nephragm merged his hideous body with that of the vivacious redhead. A moment later Silex's body rose once more and headed towards the cottage.

A rush of anxiety sent Swift into breathless panic, and she began to feel her life force threatened by the long stay underground, as the crysaline she had created began to disintegrate. Slowly she pursed her lips to slow her breath and push away the memory of Nephragm's embodiment of Silex. Instead, her mind sought comfort, as it so often did, in thoughts of Klim. She remembered his serious dark eyes as they had walked together along the shore road, after he had risked his life to rescue her from his uncle. Only Klim's mind, and the connection they had previously shared, could pierce through the obdurate to discover her hiding place. Swift dared not reach for Mengebara in her present form, she had to prevent herself being taken by Nephragm. Slowly she manipulated the molecules of her body and the surrounding material to bring the crysaline tightly around it, her heartbeat almost imperceptible as her human needs became immersed in hibernation. Here she would stay and ponder what she had learnt from the Waybearer about the nature of Nephragm. She breathed in deeply and thought she could sense Klim's mind searching for her. That awareness automatically triggered the deep well of longing that she could not erase either above or below the earth.

*

The spillage of blood-stained puddles littered the tow path, remnants of the struggle that had transformed the canal to a broiling stew that still emitted the stench of violent death. Exhausted, Kier raised herself to standing so that she could watch for Siskin's return. Once the Tenements had started on their funereal journey with the ill-fated Tolbranach, he had powered up towards the still intact steps of the broken bridge, searching for Danubin.

Josh's voice was weary beside her, "Let's get Killian onto the boat," he suggested. Kier nodded, transferring her eyes to the figure laying on the grass, the dints in the many times broken nose emblematic of his battered state. She knew from their shared contact that he had broken several ribs and his right shoulder in the struggle.

"We'll need to find some kind of board to act as a stretcher," she said, her eyes scanning the boat.

There was a half-painted narrowboat door alongside the shaft of the chimney. Josh had followed the direction of her gaze and in moments his nimble figure was atop the narrowboat and manoeuvring the door free. Kier moved to help him bring the makeshift stretcher beside the unconscious form and gently they lifted Killian onto the board. Kier sighed with relief when Josh hailed their returning friend and she looked over her shoulder to see the ex-soldier making his way towards them. She flinched at the bleak anger that had extinguished any artistic softness in the gun barrelled eyes of her friend.

Without speaking Siskin joined them, and together they lifted Killian safely onto the barge and placed him carefully in one of the cabins. Siskin's sigh of relief, as they returned to the main body of the narrowboat, brought her attention to his face, ragged with emotion. She placed a hand on his arm and felt the rigid tension that resonated throughout his body. It was with great relief that she heard Echin and Samuel returning.

"Claire and Juliette!" Distressed, Siskin's voice was tight, his acorn eyes darting to the door. "She must know where they are! I have to leave," he shouted and was already making his way quickly down the passage.

Kier and Josh immediately stepped forward to follow but Samuel halted their progress, his hand raised, his voice calming. "They are safe, I promise," he looked towards the Mourangil, "removed from danger when we first discovered Amron Cloch had been stolen."

"Where?" Siskin demanded, his voice catching.

Echin nodded sympathetically but his voice was firm, "We must tend to Killian."

Siskin stepped to one side, Kier felt he was like a steel cable about to buckle.

"He's in Klim's cabin," Josh pointed to the back of the narrow-boat.

Echin glanced at Samuel, who slid past each of them and entered the cabin. Siskin sank into the leather seating and the others joined him, He bowed his head and then lifted strained eyes towards Echin. "I shouldn't have reacted that way, she played me." He had the tone of a soldier who had cost his side the battle. "She has been playing this particular game for uncountable years Eamon, and there is no longer any doubt that she does indeed hold Amron Cloch."

Kier saw Siskin wince but further discussion was interrupted by Samuel, emerging from Klim's cabin with Killian's unconscious form floating behind him.

"Killian needs to be in Tinobar," he turned to Kier, his normally serene expression edged with concern. "If you hadn't intervened, he'd be dead, but he needs Madeleine now."

"If you will come with me," Echin looked towards Kier, Josh and Siskin, "we will take him together."

All three nodded their acceptance and with a flick of his wrist Samuel positioned the injured Tanes in the centre of the narrow-boat and wordlessly, Kier took her place in the circle around him. The small cleric stepped backwards.

"I'll stay and wait for Mactire and the others," he told them. Seconds later his face distanced and disappeared as she became enveloped in Echin's cloud of being. Kier felt she could sense within it the strong pulse of the Mourangil's existence, his long-hidden sorrow, and the crystal resonance of his essential nature.

*

Kier surmised that it was over a year since she had last stood in awe at her first sight of the healing place of Tinobar. It inhabited a picturesque dell, somewhere in the folds of reality between the concrete world she knew and the level of existence in Reuben's cavern. Where Reuben's cavern seemed to offer removal from physical life, Tinobar was tightly tied to the earth, its filmy substance a reflective essence of the life forms that lived on the planet. Here the ministrations of Madeleine and her helpers offered healing for those who had come into contact with the destructive power of Belluvour and his followers. Madeleine's square figure bustled through the golden gates, her keys tinkling, accompanying the gentle rhythm of running water in the distance behind her. Though her shape was ghostly, lacking substance of the flesh, Kier knew that the chief healer of Tinobar was fully alive in the body of a being, thought to have the mental age of a young child, physically imprisoned by severe disability. Her gaze fell on Killian and Kier saw the stern features soften in compassion as she assessed his condition. His body was suspended at waist level as she passed her palm above its contours.

At one point the healer raised her head and looked sharply at Kier, her eyes showing interest and respect. A necklace, previously unnoticed, motioned at Madeleine's throat emitting a series of harmonics. Each piece, Kier now noticed, was like a tiny golden organ pipe. Siskin looked up in surprise and pleasure, and for the first time that day her friend's expression lost its harsh edge. Killian's body was quickly swept inside by a small army of shadowy healers who had been summoned by Madeleine. Once the gates had closed, a shrewd glance of assessment motioned across her face as she noted the pale features of the human trio.

The smile of endearment she reserved for Echin transformed her stolid workaday face to beauty.

"You were right to bring them Toomaaris," she told him.

Kier found herself taking a sharp intake of breath, hearing Echin's true name confirmed by Madeleine. The healer's face retained its softness as she turned to the companions.

"Kier, you have shimmered in the folds of Reuben's cavern and its light is a flame within you. Josh, you have in your gift the crossing keys and felt the breath of the hidden skies. Though both of you have walked alongside shadow, it has not touched you as it has Eamon Keogh."

Siskin's strong face appeared almost boyish as Madeleine cupped an unsubstantial hand around his face.

"Please," she asked softly, "stay awhile in the music of Tinobar."

The gentle tinkle of the harmonic necklace began once more. Kier was aware of a small orchestra of sound within it, complex layers of melody and vibrant chords that complemented glowing strands of the setting sun over Tinobar. Siskin looked towards his friends and Kier saw the dangerous turmoil that was lodged behind his eyes.

"They are safe," Echin told him.

Almost imperceptibly he nodded his agreement and Kier knew that this was the most telling feature of the musician's critical mental state.

Madeleine guided Siskin within the gates of Tinobar and Kier felt a keen pang of loss as she watched her friend, now more like a brother, pass into the hidden place of healing as it disappeared from their sight. Echin turned to them, his voice containing an edge she had not previously heard.

"Now we hunt Danubin."

Chapter Twenty-nine

Toomaaris was cloud and air. Only the faintest touch of shimmering blue gave any clue as to the presence of the Mourangil, as he floated above the Irish sea. The dark waves beneath disseminated the light of a full rich moon as it bounced from a rocky mound that reached up above the water, nor far from the Welsh coast. Within the folds of his aerial form, he could feel the beating hearts of Josh and Kier, deeply sleeping. How many times had he watched, in this way, over the creatures that wandered across the earth? Only once before these recent weeks, had he lifted a human being in the fabric of his own energy, and that had been long ago, even as measured by his kind.

He felt Moura's embrace and remembered the glowing richness at the seat of her energy in the planet's core. The sigh he emitted gathered raindrops towards him, and he shook them away. He had made his choice, for too long now he had elected to inhabit a human body. Though he would always be Mourangil he had omitted to nourish his being in the form fire of Moura. Though the time needed was of small consequence to his kind, whole generations of human existence would have passed when he returned. Instead, he had continued to walk the earth as Echinod Deem, watching for signs of the Seeds and awaiting the return of Candillium.

The time span allotted to a Mourangil was from birth to the last days of the planet. Now however, he would diminish and give up his existence on Moura long before that time. His life had become finite and through his choice, would mirror the survival or extinction of mankind. Toomaaris found again the place in time, his internal record, of the day that Belluvour engineered the dreadful destruction of Ordovicia. He summoned to himself the images that had long gone unseen, records kept in the standing stones. The pain was still poignant as he saw once more the wasteland of volcanic ash that had once been the lush and beautiful land of Ordovicia. At that time, in the days of his youth, only a few centuries of mankind had passed. He felt again the toxic fumes that had torn at his human throat, made ragged his cry for help as he began to uncover the bodies of those destroyed. He saw and felt once more, his own despair as he searched fruitlessly for Candillium, to whom he had given the centrepiece of the Myriar. He acknowledged now that they had formed a bond, a love that transcended the differences in their race. All he knew then was that without her, existence had lost its meaning.

The relentless images continued. Toomaaris watched as spasms of his breath echoed in the cavern where the natural light of countless minerals made visible his underground retreat. Outside, the land heaved and vomited in its efforts to still the violent trembling of the malady that had come from within. The moving kingdom of Lioncera had found him in his need, stricken by loss. For two hundred of their years, he had watched and nurtured the elegant men, women, and children of Ordovicia. He had worn his human form, with its tough sinuous limbs, and moved quietly amongst them. At that time, his skin was a soft brown, and his long, dark hair was a knotted stallion tail down his back. Only the deep lapis lazuli blue of his eyes marked him as different from the new race. Toomaaris watched his younger self sink to the ground and remembered the feel of his back scraping against the stone gateway. He saw exhausted eyes close, a forehead deeply furrowed, and his chin lift towards the vaulted ceiling. Fatigued beyond measure, his body began to transmute into living rock. The exhausted limbs merged into veins of deep blue crystal that glittered in the rock face and as they did so he remembered hearing a thousand interwoven whispers bemoaning the lost race of man.

On either side, the wall shimmered with minerals that, a moment later, gave up their energies to stand beside Toomaaris in human form. On one side was Faer, fair and strong, and on the other Tormaigh, green-black hair draped over his needle thin frame. Both were clothed in loose trousers of alu cloth, an Ordovician fabric. With great effort Toomaaris roused himself and in the way of men, embraced his companions. They turned their attention upon a central pillar of limestone as it shifted and turned. The whole column was effused with diamond light as it became inhabited by their beloved Tomer, father of all Mourangils, and first guardian of Moura.

The Tomer spoke aloud in the language of those who had been betrayed.

"It is as you thought Toomaaris; Belluvour has altered the pattern and flow that was his charge."

The black cloak of loss descended upon Lioncera, but Toomaaris also remembered the bitter taste of guilt; he had failed to protect the new race. There was a silence within the cavern. For the first time in the existence of Lioncera the walls and pillar shook and all those within stood amazed and afraid. But then the central pillar was solid again, the diamond centre shone brightly and only the small white shards scattered along the floor of the great hall, gave witness to the tremulous moment when Lioncera itself threatened to collapse. The voice of the Tomer was weary and stricken but nevertheless firm. "You do not know that Candillium, her instinct strong, sent each of the fragments of the Myriar across the earth with a small community of her race. There is still hope, Toomaaris for Belluvour has not yet sought them out."

The Tomer paused for a moment as the young Mourangil lifted his head. "And the centrepiece of the gift is still intact, Candillium is alive."

Toomaaris, even now, felt his human heart beating loudly in response to this news. Then he had barely allowed himself to hope as the solemn voice continued.

"Renew yourself Toomaaris and take Faer and Tormaigh into the wilderness of Obason, where lies your brother diseased in spirit and intent. There he holds Candillium."

The central pillar resumed its limestone form as the Tomer removed himself from the hall and accompanied by his brothers, Toomaaris approached the column. Reaching out he cupped his hands beneath a silver stream of liquid that ran down the pillar and raised them to his lips. Watching the memory, he felt once more the transfer of energy into his beleaguered form, feeling grief and fatigue wash away. Despite dreadful sadness, memories of joy had returned and the young Toomaaris smiled at his brothers as they stepped together towards the middle of the chamber. The rock floor beneath their feet began to tremble, a crack slowly widening to reveal a torrent of water. Without pause the brothers dived in and began to traverse the waterways in the way of their kind.

Enveloped within the fluid streams of Moura the three Mourangils merged into the ocean currents. The sun had not yet set when they reached the dark pool at the outer edge of Obason.

Here the waters changed, becoming choked with tentacles of neglected foliage, harbouring malformed creatures that could no longer recognise the Mourangils, so blind had Belluvour made them. Belluvour had been at work engineering unnatural change for his own purpose, gathering around him living beings that were outside the laws of the Tomer. Grim had been that day on Moura as the three guardians emerged from the waters to move as men upon the single path that cut between the towering mountains of Obason. It was here that Belluvour had resided as one of the most powerful Mourangils, eldest after their father. Through his influence turbulent forces of the planet had been placated and, in this way, had Belluvour protected the life on its surface as the planet changed and grew. He had been strength and explosive laughter, the surge of new shape, the blanket of forgetfulness and most passionate of all the guardians, had been unable to accept Moura's decision to foster mankind. Earlier Toomaaris had felt that all was not right in his brother's attitude towards this new and cherished occupant of the planet. It seemed to the youngest Mourangil that he alone amongst his brethren understood the changes that were occurring in his most powerful brother. At that time, the Tomer had faith that Belluvour would eventually come to care for mankind. It was however, to Toomaaris, the youngest of their kind, that he turned in order to implement the task of delivering Moura's gift to the Ordovician race.

Concentrating on the task entrusted to him Toomaaris had

rarely left his human form and failed to see that Belluvour had also become increasingly engrossed. He studied man, not as Toomaaris had done in order to aid, but to destroy. He used and manipulated Nephragm's talent for imitating individual Ordovicians, until he was ready to commit the most heinous of crimes, the murder of the new race. At the path's end, the three guardians separated without speech of any kind and each one meandered through the dark passes of Obason. It was Tormaigh who had found him at last. Faer and Toomaaris answering the silent call, finding their brother at the edge of a cave, his skin a mix of green and black crystal, as he struggled to retain his human form in his anger and grief. A deep and musical human voice called to them from the depths of the cavern.

"Enter, my brothers. I will become human for a while to please you, for I know how dear they were to you."

The three brothers entered the opening and were assaulted by the stench of decay. The cave hummed with insects; distorted and bloated they created individual mounds around torn pieces of flesh. All around them the dead carcasses of warm-blooded creatures lay impaled on basalt spikes protruding from the cave's floor. Toomaaris once again surveyed the gruesome scene with a sick horror.

"Toomaaris!" Faer called out, pointing towards the furthest corner of the cave. There, beyond the carnage, in a silver cage that glinted as it turned, was the dying form of Candillium. Suspended and barely conscious, her long dark hair was grey with ash. Her body hung limply in the centre of the cage, covered with torn remnants of alu cloth. Toomaaris had cried out, moving forward, his enraged voice shaking the dark rock around him. Faer was ice cold, a silver dagger against black night.

The far wall of the cave began to hiss and steam as a jagged fissure broke the surface and Belluvour emerged from the molten lava beneath. Fluid fire hardened to become a black obsidian human sculpture. Never had Toomaaris seen such beauty corrupted so. The eyes, large and lidless, were colourless and cruel. The skin of his face was darkly smooth and flawless, an inhuman perfection without expression. When he spoke, the words reverberated from the walls around them.

"Did you think I did not know of your plans Toomaaris? Did you think I would let you give up our secrets so easily? That I did not know of those sent elsewhere to nurture your prize? By this creature!"

He lifted his sickly eyes towards Candillium, and tongues of flame leapt into being beneath the cage.

"No!" Toomaaris screamed and lunged forward.

Tormaigh and Faer moved to hold him back. Belluvour's laughter echoed around them. The three Mourangils moved forward to face their brother in the cave of Obason. He had severed the link of minds between himself and the other Mourangils and was already unable to recognise the sorrow etched on the faces of his brothers.

"Why?" Toomaaris asked.

Belluvour opened his mouth and his words seeped like pus from a raw wound. "I, Belluvour, was to care for such creatures as these? I, who created mountains and shaped the seas. I have scourged Moura of their presence, all but a few droppings that this one scattered. They will have no centre and without Moura's gift they will remain in narrow tunnels, blind and stumbling where I will seek them out. Let them begin again in the hidden corners to stagger in the dark and discover the baseness of their own true nature. I, alone, know the darkness within the race of man."

Slowly Toomaaris began to move towards the centre of the cave, his eyes constantly veering towards the suspended cage that held Candillium. Ignoring him Belluvour spoke directly to Faer and Tormaigh. "Toomaaris prizes her more than his brothers, he sets this creature above us all in his affections."

Candillium screamed as once again the travesty of human form turned his shape towards her and flames licked her heels.

Tormaigh spoke quietly, stepping into a gap in the centre of the carnage ahead of Toomaaris. "It is for jealousy and greed that you would destroy them Belluvour, you were to guide and aid what you have now murdered."

For a moment all were stunned, for this word had never been used on Moura and came to him from hidden annals of dark history on other worlds.

"Look at you all in these human forms!" Belluvour spat his contempt.

Black flame, cold yet burning leapt from his fingers as he pointed towards Tormaigh, who shrank to his mineral form to avoid the blow and was then quickly standing again. Toomaaris created a dome of light that encircled the three Mourangils as they closed towards the centre. Without warning the ground beneath their feet began to vibrate and cracks appeared, spewing molten lava all around them. Faer leapt across the gaping wounds that Belluvour had created in the earth and Toomaaris, winding his way towards Candillium, looked in horror at the black flame that flickered through the rocks; it was the Odiam. Tormaigh blinked at his brother's audacity, for the Odiam had been banished by Moura to the most hidden parts of the planet. An oil like substance, it was toxic to the Mourangils and to all living creatures. The shadowy fingers reached everywhere apart from the solid surface where Belluvour orchestrated their destruction.

"You shame us." Tormaigh's voice was a deadly weapon from which emanated a vibration that shook the dark figure that had been his beloved brother. Belluvour, unsteady, roared in anger. A whirling hurricane whipped all into a lake of black shadow and Tormaigh dropped in agony as the shadowy fingers crept towards him. Faer and Toomaaris moved in unison, lifting the still human form of their brother, one on either arm, as they leapt across the void to bring him to the remaining ledge high above.

Platinum shards rained downwards onto Belluvour as the two Mourangils fought to conquer his black will. Belluvour made a white ball of their weapons, hurling it upwards to the roof of the cave where it exploded outwards into Obason. The lost brother turned to deliver his final blow, one that would sweep the last ledges of his previous self away forever and send his brothers plunging beneath him. In that moment, the wind died and Belluvour heard behind him the gentle tinkle of a silver cage opening. Faer and Toomaaris looked in amazement at the tall and glowing figure of Candillium who faced her captor. Lit within by Moura's gift, Candillium was more spirit than body as she stepped towards Belluvour, her eyes deeply sad.

"Why do you bear us such hatred?" she asked, her voice gentle but still the words echoed around the cave.

Belluvour turned, "Do not speak your tuneless sounds to me." The volcanic timbre of his voice was hot with rage. With grating malice, he bent his will to crush Candillium. Fire hissed from a fissure that opened beneath the last leader of Ordovicia and Toomaaris leapt downwards. Even before he reached the surface a blast of violence flung his form upwards again in a hail of rock. Candillium's eyes followed the Mourangil she loved as he was helped in human fashion by his brothers, their upper limbs entwining his as he was eased onto the remains of the ledge. She had reached and finally found the power that had lain dormant inside her since Toomaaris had first imparted Moura's gift.

Balancing effortlessly on the edge of the abyss below, she was unaffected by the fierce flames around her as Belluvour raised himself to destroy the human forms of his brothers.

Toomaaris, watching, even down the untold ages, clearly saw the separateness of Belluvour as the tempestuous force of his rage whirled blindly around him. He had ripped the fabric of Moura and though his power remained, he had lost the integral embrace of the planet. Implacable hatred emanated from the black figure as he suddenly became aware of Candillium, now clothed in the Myriar. Turning towards her he raised his arm and black shadow rose to swallow her. Her eyes followed its course as it shrank from her figure, folding itself back into the cleft from which it had been torn.

Belluvour bent towards her, but Candillium stood unmoved.

"Leave my world," he hissed." You are almost dead."

"So, I am," she replied softly, "but you also can stay no longer on the surface of Moura."

With the gentlest flicker of her eyes the ground fell fully from beneath them, at the same time as Candillium reached towards the dreadful shape of Belluvour, plunging them both beneath the earth.

Long ago they said Toomaaris's cry reached the skies and was heard everywhere on Moura. Now, countless years of human time later, he still felt its raw, animal pain. He continued to watch as the ground reformed and the walls of the cave fell inwards. The

Mourangils had reeled in shock as they discovered that the black rock of the cavern would not allow them passage. Belluvour had created the first obdurates. It left them unable to transfer their energy below the surface. The poison that Belluvour had seeped into Obason meant that the attempt almost resulted in the destruction of their human forms. Toomaaris remembered the vacant exhaustion that had assailed them. Hours later the brothers found themselves lying on the basalt rock. Tormaigh woke the others as dawn inevitably came to find them. He had brought water from beyond the valley where he could trust its source. His voice was hoarse with sadness.

"I do not think Lioncera can enter Obason, we will have to make our way out of this place." Still Toomaaris would not leave, and they would not leave Toomaaris.

More hours passed and their bodies recovered themselves. Then, from below the surface, came a soft breeze that tickled their faces. The rocks began to crumble apart and the three Mourangils moved outwards, not knowing what other horrors they would have to face. To their utter astonishment, the form of Candillium rose above the surface without earth stain. When she reached out her hands were flesh and Toomaaris smiled.

"Candillium," he whispered.

Her face and figure were translucent and Toomaaris could feel the power of the Myriar radiating from her; beneath this he also saw that her human life was all but extinguished. Toomaaris did not speak for he knew that her time was short and that she needed to impart to them the dreadful events of her missing hours. Candillium walked forward to the edge of the mound on which they stood overlooking Obason. The air shimmered around her as she turned back to her companions and spoke quietly, her voice resonant with the accent of pain.

"Beneath the oceans in the secret vaults of Moura, there have I bound him, but his power and will clawed at me as we sank beneath the boundaries. Even as we fell, I saw his magnificence, all that has been tainted and spoiled beyond recovery."

Candillium bowed her head and Toomaaris could see her extreme duress and moved to comfort her. Before he could do so she raised her chin and spoke again.

"I willingly accepted Moura's gift and it has become sewn into the fabric of my being. Little could we have known that the first touch of its power would be to bind Belluvour in the Secret Vaults. His rage and hatred has changed the course of all our lives. The Myriar will not form as we planned for my body is broken and I am only held for this short time because of its power. When its light grows dim beneath Moura then he will seek to begin the unbinding. And long before that time the blackest poison will attempt to corrupt our race, or as Belluvour would have it, to bring out our true nature. I cannot enter the cycles of rebirth for unlike the other fragments this is not a seed to grow stronger the more it is nourished. I must leave Moura and take with me the centrepiece that remains lodged within. If the seeds I planted come to fruition, then I will return. That is my promise. But now I will be separated from you, beyond even the cycles of the spirit and I fear that the evil that Belluvour has created may mean that never again will we meet on this world."

"Candillium!" Toomaaris reached out to her.

The slight form grew dim, but she stretched her fingers towards his, the gentlest whisper of touch.

"It is strange now how I see you three, who I have known all my life in Ordovicia. Tormaigh, you are the blade of grass and the night sky. Faer is the wing of an eagle and the snow tipped mountain. And Toomaaris, my gentle Mourangil, whom I have loved with all of my capacity to love, you are the first breath and the last hope, my beginning, and my end. And I will remain Candillium and return when you need me."

And then she was gone. Completely, from this earth and from the human cycles.

A swan, floating on the water by the harbour, looked with interest at the spray of rain that drummed upon the water around him. His long white neck unfurled itself to find the source of this sudden shower, but already the cloud had passed.

Chapter Thirty

Kier awoke in a small, lamp lit room lined with shelves of books. Many were heavy, leather-bound tomes, others wore the finely strained binding of ancient texts. It reminded her a little of the reference room in the bookshop, a magical place that, until the dreadful day of her capture, had allowed entry to only herself and Echin. She recognised some Latin titles and suspected that others were written in ancient Hebrew. Gabbie, she now realised, would have had little problem mastering either of them. The thought of her friend brought her upright, seeking any messages in Mengebara. Relieved, she saw Gabbie's image, messaging briefly that Silex had joined them. Josh blinked widely at her across the small space, running his hand through his hair, the cornflower blue of his eyes still full of sleep. They were sitting opposite each other on two easy sofas and her rumbling stomach became aware of the fragrant smell that was coming from a covered pan in a small kitchen at one end of the room. Echin emerged from the door behind her and made his way towards the kitchen.

"Madeleine's prescription for you both was food and sleep. I could only give you a couple of hours rest, but this should help." He gave them an apologetic smile and poured out two bowls of soup, adding a mound of different, freshly baked, and mouth-watering breads. Kier leaned forwards gratefully towards the table, which had been placed between the two sofas. Echin took a seat beside Josh.

"I feel like I've slept all night," the artist told him, through a mouthful of soup. "This is great."

Kier nodded her agreement, she too felt as refreshed as if she'd slept much longer. "Where are we?" she asked.

Josh raise his eyebrows mid-spoonful. "Samuel's place," he informed her matter-of-factly, "in the college."

Echin poured himself some water from a jug on the table and Josh got up lightly, helping himself to another bowl of soup from the pan. He lifted the ladle towards Kier who shook her head laughing. "I think that must be one of the best soups I've ever tasted," she complimented Echin.

"I'd be a bit sad not to have picked up some skills over all this time," his grin was self-mocking. "I once spent three years as a cook in Constantinople."

Kier raised her eyebrows in interest and surprise, he shared so little of his long life in human form.

Echin shrugged, "Another story," he told her, "and if Josh has finished guzzling the soup, we can get started."

Josh managed to push in another slice of the unusually spiced bread as he nodded his readiness and leant business-like towards his friends. "So just why are we here then?" he asked Echin, glancing around the quaint flat.

"Firstly, although Danubin has found it after all these years, and I attribute that to the Tenements but also her possession of Amron Cloch, she is unable to enter these rooms."

"Siskin's stone," murmured Kier as Echin nodded. At the thought of her friend in Tinobar her eyes fell.

Josh commented, "He seemed really shaken when Danubin taunted him about the stone." The memory brought a grimace of revulsion to his finely boned face.

"As she intended," Echin agreed. "Amron Cloch is the Song Stone. It belongs to Siskin though he has never seen it, and Danubin has been using it to gain insight into his mind. We need to get it back, and also the Iridice. The stone that Jackson had in his power for of a number of years will undoubtedly amplify her power. It also gives her some link with Klim, though he has already created a barrier to any invasion."

"But how do we get them back?" Josh asked him anxiously. "She's a powerful enemy and we aren't exactly big on numbers right now! Siskin and Klim are our best fighters."

"And the most vulnerable," Echin stated.

Kier saw the tension in his face as he stood up quickly and crossed to the small passageway behind one of the doors. Kier and Josh turned to each other, and Josh lifted his hands in a shrug. Seconds later they both jumped up in response to the loud banging and sound of voices behind the door. Just as the two friends had stepped forward to investigate, Tormaigh and Faer walked into the room. Kier laughed with joy and relief as she hugged the two Mourangils that had come to their aid the preceding year. Josh shook hands, his face beaming.

It seemed that neither of them had altered greatly. If anything, Tormaigh's thin frame seemed a little thinner and his green-black hair stretched further down his back. Faer's handsome, well-defined face, glowed with the light of his sky-blue eyes and smiled his joy at seeing them both once more. Echin served up more soup and bread and it was well received. He laughed as Josh took the opportunity for a further helping. "When we have not been in our human forms for a little while it's easy to forget to eat," Faer explained to Josh and Kier, his voice thick with exhaustion. "We've travelled a long way through the oceans and then on foot along the banks of the Teifi." He placed his spoon back in the dish and looked solemnly around the small group. "We followed Nephragm to Wales but then we lost him. He's back on the surface and will have taken human form again by now." His tone was an expression of infinite sorrow and guilt. Kier noticed that he had eaten only a mouthful of the bread Echin had given him. Tormaigh bowed his head.

Kier choked. "You mean Nephragm is nearby?"

Tormaigh looked up towards her, lines of strain shadowing the almond shaped eyes.

"I am sorry Kier. He was cornered in the sunken pockets of Obason, so filled with obdurates that we could not pass to find him. But we did hold him there, captive."

The grief in the Mourangil's voice made Kier place her hand over his; he squeezed it tightly in grateful response.

"We were attacked," Faer told them, his voice unsteady as he spoke directly to Echin. "As the bonds have loosened, Belluvour's influence has grown. Some of our kind, saddened by mankind's neglect and abuse of Moura, have turned against us."

"Who?" Echin demanded, his face drip white.

"Sellonir, Geoden," the list went on as Echin listened, grief-stricken.

Gently Faer delivered what was clearly the most painful blow.

"They approached the Tomer to cast you out of Lioncera, Toomaaris."

The use of Echin's original name once again sent Kier's head spinning but her heart plummeted as she read the look of despair in his eyes.

"Instead, it was they who left," Tormaigh told him. "The Tomer holds true to our promise to nurture the human race."

Echin sank down on the edge of the settee by Kier's left arm. His silence echoed in the small space. A tilt of his head was all the warning they received before he disappeared in a soft, blue-tinged glow of light that blinked momentarily as he transmuted into his Mourangil form. Immediately Kier's hand flew to the smooth lapis lazuli stone that had appeared in an amulet around her throat.

Faer sighed, "Keep the stone safe, Kier, it's his route back to you. He has gone to speak in the hall of Lioncera, as we have exhorted him to do long before this, lest more of our kind turn towards Belluvour."

"When will he come back?" questioned Josh, the edge of alarm in his voice.

"You know that time shifts in a different pattern in Lioncera," Tormaigh reminded him. "We, like you, are physical beings, and Toomaaris must be there and not here. I do not know how long it will take him."

"But Echin said we have to get the stones from Danubin!" The colour had drained from Josh's face.

Faer's chin hitched upwards, and he sent a troubled glance to Tormaigh. The thin Mourangil looked gaunt. "Does Danubin have them in her possession?"

"She has Klim's stone, the Iridice, and Amron Cloch," Kier explained.

"The Song Stone!" Faer was clearly distressed by this news.

Kier felt a strong impulse to cry but it was quickly dismissed. She breathed in deeply and relaxed her shoulders so that her body felt taller. "We have to find a way to get them back," she repeated Echin's words. "Should we contact Samuel?" she added.

Tormaigh smiled, his green eyes like dew on grass, "Samuel! He has been with you? You are indeed blessed!"

"Has Echin…." Kier stumbled, "Toomaaris, told you nothing?"

"We could exchange very little so near the obdurates and with so many of our kind altering their allegiance, we had to be careful. Our links are shared with any in Lioncera that wish to see them in our Mourangil form, but it is only as humans that we can isolate our thoughts. We managed to exchange some, but not all, of the events that have happened in our absence."

"Can you share Mengebara?" she asked.

Tormaigh nodded. "If you permit it," he replied.

Kier looked towards Josh, who nodded.

The group closed their eyes and found that they were stood in the garden of Mengebara, which was the result of their collective thoughts. Klim had built a high yew hedge that surrounded a grassy garden. It had begun as a few square feet and now expanded to an acre of land, where Josh and Kier found themselves walking. Kier could smell the grass and feel it tickling her bare feet as she wandered towards an area of washed stone aside a deep well. This place had become the accepted repository for very recent events. Tormaigh and Faer glanced at each other with interest as they saw Gabbie's image of Silex, striding along with the group on the island.

"She's just arrived," Josh told them.

The two Mourangils looked relieved. Josh pointed to a row of what looked like individual allotments, divided from each other by a line of rope. Each one represented the way that each member of the group stored their collective memories. Kier had never actually visited Mengebara in this way, where she and Josh were guiding other beings around a creation that had been drawn from their collective consciousness. Each section seemed to perfectly represent its owner.

The first contained terraced rows of bonsai trees. Gently she put her hand on one of the magnificent branches to find that it immediately brought forth a melody that reminded her of the mournful passage of the Tolbranach. Undoubtedly Siskin, she decided. Swift's images were arranged into rows of stones, which glittered in an array of different crystalline colours. It occurred to Kier how little Swift had used Mengebara to share her thoughts, the collected gems would almost all contain the images she had collected from other members of the group. Gabbie's gathered images were grouped into pots of fragrant herbs and flowers. On each one was stamped a different national character. A vivid Welsh dragon splashed in sunlight on one terracotta pot that was crowded with daffodils. On touching the stem of one flower, Kier heard the unmistakable lilting sounds of the Welsh language. Although she could not follow the words, they brought to her mind the windblown mountains of Snowdonia. Shivering she saw that Klim's images were buried within a reed bed. Even here he would not trust people easily. She smiled as she saw the amount of bird life he had attracted, a small marsh tit with a distinctive sneeze like call, chirruped as she watched. It perched on top of a reed and swayed delightedly, but it gave away no secrets. Kier's own patch of garden was no easier to enter. She had stored the used images and messages in the only building along the rows. Surprised, though it had obviously been of her own making, she had conjured a small version of the white church in which Martha had died. The door was padlocked, and the rest of its land covered in yellow evening primrose, the flowers now sleeping in the daylight and revealing nothing of their centre.

"Here," Josh guided the two Mourangils, as he opened an ornate gate in the adjacent row. Light bounced against the dense patch of white poppies as Kier closed the gate behind her and gently moved around the area that depicted Josh's stored images. Her attention was caught by the centre of a tall flower that leant across her path. It contained a pencil sketch and she jerked backwards as she saw Danubin's vulture like face peering at her as she had seen it in the graveyard. Kier then realised that another image was melded and alternated with the repulsive visage in the centre of the poppy: the coiffured and sophisticated woman she had seen at the airport.

Faer and Tormaigh were busy gathering the images that

Josh had left over the last year, including his incredible ability to open another seam of reality in order to discover a reflection of the Myriar. Josh signalled to Kier, and they edged their way towards the gate, passing the small stone area prepared for new images, which remained empty.

"I thought Evan and Echin would have stored memories here," Kier commented.

Josh looked up and glanced around frowning. "I know Evan's used Mengebara, he showed us the way to become like the stone, when we were escaping from Danubin," he said thoughtfully.

"I saw it. Strange," Kier mumbled, still scanning for any hint of memories stored by Echin.

"He won't store them here," Josh told her confidently, correctly guessing the reason behind her line of enquiry.

"Yes, I can understand that," she replied, watching Faer and Tormaigh crossing the grass towards them.

"That was quick," she smiled, standing up.

Josh followed her lead as they emptied their minds of Mengebara and found themselves once again on the comfortable sofas in Samuel's living space.

"Good to have you in the room again," Samuel's brogue softly welcomed them back.

Chapter Thirty-one

The meeting between the two Mourangils and Samuel was one of
intense joy that lifted Kier's spirits and made her feel that their
task might not, after all, be so overwhelming. He listened to the
story of Nephragm's chase and Echin's return to Lioncera with an
expression of quiet compassion.

"Echin said we have to find the stones," Josh told him.

Samuel did not reply but looked carefully at each of them.

"Much care is needed," he said. "Josh, you need to draw us all,
now."

Josh looked puzzled and unsure, "Seriously?" he replied.

Samuel's provision of pencils and a sketchpad soon made it
obvious that Josh was being asked to verify that Nephragm had
not succeeded in taking over their bodies and identities.

"But he can't wipe out a Mourangil. Can he?" Josh directed a
sharp gaze at Faer whose response was a sad fall of his shoulders.

"In our human form it would be possible," he admitted.

Quickly Josh set to work and his sketches revealed a green shard of tourmaline, in which was shaped the figure of Tormaigh as a weeping young Mourangil within the mountains of Obason. He raised his eyes towards the Mourangil who nodded sadly, "The moment that Belluvour was truly lost to us," he explained.

Josh drew glistening feldspar as his inner vision directed his drawing of Faer. Within this his human form was clearly seen and was overlain by a soaring eagle. Kier felt that Josh had perfectly captured the way that she envisioned Faer. Samuel's image was clear and strong, a mirror image of the person that stood before them, but at the centre of his abdomen was a golden flame. As Kier turned to his physical counterpart she thought she could now notice flickers of light in the dark liquid eyes of the cleric. Kier proved the most difficult. Josh used his artist's inner eye and the Myriar's gift to reveal a young girl, weeping over the body of her sister whose chest was pierced with a shard of glass. A dark shadow overlooked the body, rising from a stone, inches from them both. Shocked, Josh found himself trying to move the pencilled drawing out of sight.

"It's all right Josh," Kier told him, "you found me."

Samuel nodded satisfaction.

"Josh himself is verified by his gift. Nephragm is incapable of seeing each of us in the way that the Creta would perceive our true selves. Now we find Danubin and take back the missing stones of the Myriar," he said simply.

*

The echoing staccato of stiletto saw the massive spider shrink to one side of the tank. The baryte amulet flickered in the artificial light as Danubin, now with no further use for the name Shreive, threw down the stones onto the desk, disgust and anger flaring her nostrils and flickering a pink heat into undressed eyes. Again, she felt a stab of unease that their old enemy, the man they called Siskin, who was in fact Eamon Keogh, a Seed of the Myriar. It had taken her weeks, from that first glimpse in the graveyard, to track him down. Red Light had shielded his identity from the Virenmor; Deem had barred her attempts to connect the stone and the man. She reflected venomously about Jackson's failure to recognise that Keogh was a member of Red Light.

It had been Killian, at her instigation, who had unravelled the complex strands of sound emitted by the Song Stone. Shocked, she saw the link with the woman called Clare and the child named Juliette. It had, after all, been a member of her own organisation who had kidnapped the child in the first place. Through the stone and with Killian's help, she had discovered the deep link between Eamon Keogh and the woman. She knew that the woman and her daughter were protected by Mourangil constructs in the Lakeland village, but she had gambled that the

Lute did not. She had them all! Fed to Magluck Bawah in the shape of the lumbering Tolbranach, but how could she have foreseen the interference from the Tanes?

"Where are they?" she seethed out loud, seeing the inert stones that gave her no further clue as to the whereabouts of the two Seeds. She had shrieked with rage when Killian had told her that she could not use the so called Myriar stones to connect with those already in use by the Seeds. With infuriating calm, he showed her the way that the energies of the Iridice and Amron Cloch retracted, reserving this further feature of their nature for when they were held by the living Seed. She banged the side of the tank with her red gloved fist and the huge spider skittered across the pebbled floor.

"Danubin!"

The call came from the hall outside, and she pressed a button underneath the desk. A door in the back wall opened soundlessly. A young woman in her early twenties stood in the doorway, her long legs displayed perfectly by a short green dress. Abigail, Aled's unruffled replacement, had been found in Dublin. Danubin recalled that Mactire had tried to hide her, to keep her for himself. He had been furious when the girl had chosen to return with Danubin to Wales. Her straightened copper hair fell to her breasts and framed the unblemished white skin of an intense face. She had been persuaded to move from the college in Dublin and Danubin discovered that she was an invaluable source of information, observation, an IT genius and most importantly, infinitely corruptible. Soon she would be persuaded to indulge her employer's personal pastimes. Abigail's game playing had revealed a ruthless thirst for power and Danubin intended to feed it like a pet snake.

"What is it, Abigail?" she demanded, the rule was that she was never disturbed in her study if it was not urgent.

"We have visitors," she informed her calmly.

*

"How long have you known she was here?" Faer asked Samuel as they crouched beside an eight-foot wall that completely enclosed the acre of land.

"These are painted obdurates," Tormaigh commented, his thin lips pinching in distaste as he stood in the shadow of the thick stone. "On the surface!" He seemed horrified.

"I know," Samuel told them, "that she had been virtually invisible until a month ago, when she and some of her guests decided to use the river."

"Where she knew you would find them," Faer sighed. "We play a very dangerous game Samuel; I hope it does not cost the lives of those we are trying to protect!"

The Mourangils and Samuel remained still as Kier and Josh crept stealthily towards them. As requested, the two friends had stayed on the riverbank for five or ten minutes before following their companions. Approximately ten minutes after Josh's feet struck the paved drive, Kier heard a rumbling sound beneath the ground. Josh seemed unaware but Samuel and the two Mourangils stopped and turned towards them.

"We don't have much time," Samuel urged. "We need to get inside."

He flicked his finger towards a hidden camera and smiled as a broken screen clinked in reply. Faer led the way, inching along the wall, careful not to touch the stone. A set of huge electronic gates presided at the front of the property. Samuel, overtaking Faer, guided them towards the back of the building; here a single locked gate barred their entrance. Carefully, he examined the stone inlays, forming the spear tips that peppered its surface.

"Obdurates," he told them. "Try the Chalycion Josh," he instructed.

Josh came forward, the pink stone in his hand, and he pressed it against the only area that remotely resembled a lock, a gaping indent within one of the spikes. The gate flew backwards noisily, the Chalycion thrown from its chain and fired over his shoulder. Josh chased to find it as they all dived inside.

"What's that about?" he asked Samuel, placing the stone back in his pocket.

"The Myriar stones and the obdurates are polar opposites so they repel each other," the cleric explained.

"They know we're here Samuel," Faer said calmly. "Someone

should have reacted to that noise."

"Maybe there's no one home?" suggested Kier hopefully.

The ground underneath her feet began to moan again, she put her hands to her ears at the agony of sound that seemed more tortured than ever.

"Inside quickly," Samuel instructed, dismantling with a touch the three locking devices on the back door, positioned to their immediate left.

Their footsteps echoed on the tiled floor of a long corridor as they filed past a number of open utility rooms including a laundry and waste disposal, the latter filled with IT equipment. Kier tried to picture the brief sketch that Samuel had scribbled, reassuring them, without giving details, that his information had come from a reliable source. The sketch had mapped the four corridors that branched off a grand central hall. Samuel had impressed upon them the layout of the circular building. The passage that they were in contained the utility areas. The one to their left housed a lounge, kitchen, and dining room while the bedrooms were housed in the corridor that reached outwards from the opposite side of the central hall. To their right, was a passageway containing the entrances to a number of offices. It was within these small, densely packed spaces that what Samuel referred to as 'remote mensira' had been engineered. Kier remembered that Echin had used this word to describe the sickening suicidal suggestion that Jackson had once implanted in her own mind.

"Ordinary marble tiles," Faer commented, running his hand along the wall. "Clever Danubin, placing the obdurates outside to obscure its presence for the Mourangils. Inside and no Devouril could ever hide in this place in their natural form."

"It's eerie," Josh's voice was hushed but the sound reverberated around the stark brightly lit passageway.

The group were a few metres from the point where the corridor joined the central chamber when a loud bang signalled the outside gate clanging shut. At the same time, all light within the building was extinguished. An echoing thud brought Kier's heart rate to an accelerated pace as she stopped moving, trying to establish the physical presence of the others. On one side Kier's hand was squeezed by Josh's long narrow fingers. Samuel's distinctive smell of tallow reassured her from the opposite side. Kier noticed, for the first time, the absence of windows. No natural light could enter this tomb like structure. They inched forward and Kier gasped at the whirring rattle of sound that she had last heard in Dublin and at Devil's Bridge before that. There was no mistaking the presence of the Kejambuck, and it was right beside her, just above where she knew Josh was standing. Knowing that her friend was unaware of the malign creature's presence, she turned towards Samuel, shouting his name. With no effect. Frantically Kier reached for Faer and Tormaigh, only to find that they too had silently disappeared. Above her head appeared a medieval style torch. She could smell the burning, oil-soaked rag, twisted around a wooden rod, in a bracket that had not previously existed.

"We're in a game set," Josh's tense voice told her.

Other torches flickered around the circular hall, a medieval chamber with a stone floor. A number of huge spears, axes and other weapons were pinned to the walls. Solid arched wooden doors appeared at the edge of each of the corridors, bar one. From the dark tunnel directly opposite, emerged a row of figures; Kier counted ten in all as they gathered in a semicircle. The Kejambuck was now visibly hovering above Josh; it's sick rattle providing the introductory signature for the cruel and malevolent individuals they now faced. Kier's attention was caught directly by the pale skinned woman who visited her dreams.

"We have saved you the trouble of drawing us, Creta," the same voice she had heard in the graveyard ground out the words in a tumbril of malice. Kier could see a faint image of the chic woman in the airport. The only jewellery now evident was an amulet of a material that Kier had seen before beneath Whistmorden. She gasped in horror at the memory of the baryte substance Nephragm had used to immobilise her. Anger and determination made her ignore the desire to flinch away from the woman who stood in front of her, the dead eyed murderess. Kier faced Danubin, seeing plainly the history of atrocity in her repeated lives and the grasping hatred that motivated her current existence.

And so, it went on down the line. A faint image of well

groomed, 'tick-all-the-boxes' men and woman overlay the gruesome realities. Each distorted face told its own story of a brutal history. One long nosed, dark faced man was dressed in the long gown of the inquisitor, marked in personal memory as his finest incarnation. Another, his red spotted butcher's apron, livid cheeks, and bloodshot eyes, told of sadistic violence against the most vulnerable. Only the last figure, totally cowled in a black robe, was not visible to them. The catalogue of deliberate inhumanity to man, was as disabling as a physical blow. Even as Kier feared for herself and Josh in this dark and dire place, a sense of dreadful tragedy, lost years, and opportunities for the human race, overwhelmed her. It was at the very last second, she heard the faint rustle behind. Glancing back, she saw that a giant spider's web now stretched tightly across the width of the passageway from which they had just emerged. An immense arachnid came forward from the centre, its eight eyed stare gleaming in the torchlight. The stench was overpowering. Death, insanity, ancient savagery. Kier screamed, backing away, pulling at Josh who took out the Chalycion. The spider retreated momentarily but the screech of triumph from behind showed that this had been the moment that Danubin had been waiting for. She was there in an instant, her red gloved hand snatching the beloved stone from Josh's raised hand. A hail of cackling laughter infected the chamber as she paraded the stone above her head, exiting with the other Virenmor through the tunnel entrance.

An echoing boom sounded as the opening was sealed with an implacable oak door, in the instant that the last follower disappeared into its black shadow. Josh hurled himself against the wood, desperate to retrieve his mother's stone. The flickering light of dying torches enlarged the bulbous orbs of the great spider that skittered across the floor towards Josh, bent on its prey. Kier launched herself towards the spider's shiny, egg-shaped abdomen, brushing the rough hairs on the creature's legs as she manoeuvred in between, bouncing from its impenetrable surface. The sharp serrated edge of one of its long limbs lifted and fell close to her face as she wriggled frantically, sick with the creature's stench, to move out of reach. Josh, nimble, had seized the chance to circle the giant spider, heading for the only possible exit. Kier watched in horror as he ran into the web, his hands tearing at the toughened silk fibre. Even as she leapt to help her friend the triumphant predator barred her route, its hideous clatter screaming in her ears as it finally cornered Josh, trapped in the mesh of web.

Kier was suddenly absorbed into another scene. Erion lay dead and the black cape of a winged Irresythe covered the Alleator's body. Its long beaked head turned with vitriol and murderous intent. Without thinking Kier's hand found the amulet at her throat. "Toomaaris," she called. Blue luminous light poured from the lapis stone, travelling across the stone floor, and materialising between the now cocooned Josh and the huge arachnid. There was immense pity in Toomaaris's eyes as his blue-white light forced the creature backwards into the centre of the chamber, its limbs flailing in frustration. Kier ran towards Josh, her nails digging into the fibrous web to free his face. Kier felt, rather than saw, the movement beside the door through which the Virenmor had left. A black shadow moved out from beneath the extinguished torch, the darkly cloaked figure that had not revealed itself in the line. Her hands dug further into the gluey web trying to free Josh as she shouted a warning to Echin.

The black cloak fell to the floor revealing a slim female figure that had last been seen in Dublin. "Loretta!" Kier cried and then gasped in wonder as the scientist shimmered into the shape of a white unicorn. The glowing Tane came forward towards Echin, who reached his hand to stroke the head of the ethereal creature. The huge spider took its chance, lunging at the Mourangil, even as it was blinded and pained by his light. The unicorn's head dropped, just as the enraged Magluck Bawah heaved upwards to deliver its venomous wound. The horn raised as the creature attempted to lower itself upon Echin, piercing the spider's abdomen. Quickly, the unicorn retreated, shaking away the stain of contact. The long limbs of the spider collapsed, its head rolled backwards, and the empty eyes signalled that the blow had been fatal. From beneath the body came a hissing drool of black liquid. Echin and the unicorn stepped away from the deceased arachnid, which had once been Galinir and was now no longer the rampaging energy of Magluck Bawah.

Kier felt the rumble of dislodging stone and cried out as she scrambled with the taut coils around Josh's body. The unicorn's horn touched the finely woven web, which fell apart in an instant, releasing Josh who was now prostrate on the floor, his chest heaving as he gulped in air. Kier and Echin were quickly by his side, helping him to his feet and by the time they had turned back to the hall Loretta stood once again before them.

Slowly, steadily, the game set fell apart. The construct that Danubin had created disassembled stone by stone until finally they stood in the marble hall of the mansion. The building creaked and the white, elaborate chandelier fell to the floor. Faer, Tormaigh and Samuel flew out of the opening that had previously been the tunnel through which the Virenmor had entered. Faer glistened, his jaw line almost crystalline, the blue of his eyes lightening fierce. "She shut us out," he told them. "A trap for humans only." Tormaigh, straight as an emerald spear, green shards glinting on the hard angles of his body, shook his head. "They left through the same passage through which you just entered," Loretta told them. "Less than twenty minutes ago." Faer and Tormaigh turned to give chase. Samuel looked at Loretta and nodded. Her serious eyes were filled with purpose, as she moved towards the marble table, steady even though the whole room now rocked, her fingers finding the button that she was seeking underneath the table. The slight swoosh of sound, as the study opened, brought Kier's eyes towards the room opposite to where they stood. Slabs of ceiling began to hit the floor as Josh moaned, barely able to stand; Echin and Kier pulling him from danger.

"We need to get out," Echin told them calmly.

Kier murmured, "No kidding," to herself as they ran. Glancing back, she hesitated when Samuel and Loretta, instead of following them through the open passage, made their way into the concealed study.

"Keep going," Echin instructed, and she turned her attention back to Josh, following the track that led back down to the river where Samuel had moored their boat. Carefully they lowered Josh into the back of the boat just as Samuel and Loretta ran out from the building and down towards the river.

Kier had seen properties demolished, heard the distinctive hiss of rubble crushing to the ground but that was not what she saw now. The building folded inwards like an empty box, popping like a gigantic balloon as it did so, but the obdurates that surrounded the corrupt space remained ominously still standing. The Virenmor, and for that matter Faer and Tormaigh, were nowhere to be seen.

"The mensira has collapsed without Danubin's mental architecture." Loretta allowed herself a few moments to catch her breath and when she spoke again her tone was caustic. "She chose to use her own home to provide the physical interplay, it will take her months, if not years, to rebuild."

"Thank you," Kier began but Samuel's stern tone cut through her intention to express relief and gratitude for the Tanes's vital intervention.

"Well," he turned to Loretta. "What are you going to do?"

Chapter Thirty-two

Klim watched Evan trying to persuade Silex to go with him into the kitchen.

"Your kind are always forgetting to eat, Silex. You don't look quite yourself, come and have something while Klim works on finding Swift."

The impish eyes flashed but the usual acerbic comment was avoided by Gabbie 's exclamation. "Well, I'm starved! I'll get some eggs going!"

"I'll sort out the bacon," declared Evan.

Silex glanced back at Klim who veiled his eyes, turning towards the stairs.

"It's sometimes easier if I do this alone," he said, his tone carefully neutral, his eyes on the whitewashed wall of the narrow staircase. He heard the Mourangil follow the others into the kitchen. Once he was in Swift's room, he became aware of how disturbed her mind was. Unlike Gabbie, Swift had a natural tidiness, stemming, he guessed, from her days on the street. Her few possessions would always be carefully stored. She automatically knew where everything was and preferred to carry whatever was most valuable on her person. Swift's clothes were strewn across the floor, empty bottles of water piled by her bed; it frightened him that she should behave so out of character. He could only reason that she had left the Stone of Silence behind to avoid her being found, even by Gabbie and Evan. That didn't add up. Something, he told himself, was very wrong. He took the Stone of Silence from his pocket and placed it in the centre of his outstretched palm. The flawless diamond coloured the spartan bedroom, throwing prisms of light over the plain walls. He gasped as the stone became a mini projector, he was seeing a picture of a place, a beach, El Silencio he guessed. The name came to him from Swift's recollection of the day that she had found the Stone of Silence, the same day she was kidnapped by those working in Peru for his uncle, Alex Jackson. The story played itself across the whitewashed wall and Klim was transfixed, finding himself furious at the arrogant and drugged youth who had once been Swift's friend. The ultimate betrayal, he thought disgusted, to give Swift up for money to those who trafficked in human beings.

Klim barely heard the soft step of the tiny Mourangil as she entered the room. He turned towards her, startled as she slipped inside the door. The images vanished from the wall and the Stone of Silence dulled to its usual glass like outline.

"What have you learnt?" she demanded in her crisp eastern accent.

Mildly Klim shook his head and replaced the stone inside his pocket.

"Only that the Swift I know has changed a great deal from the last time we met."

"In what way?" Silex coaxed.

Klim shook his head. "I think we need to talk more with Evan and Gabbie," he decided, heading for the door.

For a second Silex looked as though she would block his path, sliding across the open space; then, with a shift of her lithe body she turned and exited before he reached it. Gabbie's light chit chat, as she plated eggs and bacon for them all, held a note of desperation for Klim who knew her so well. Silex ignored the plate that Evan placed before her.

"Any luck?" Gabbie asked patting the seat beside her.

"Nothing yet," Klim told her guardedly, sliding alongside her on the bench.

"And how much time do you think we have boy?" Silex flashed adamite eyes and her hand swooped to knock over the glass of juice that he had begun to pour.

Evan frowned, "Silex! Please, your body is hungry that is all," his voice was gentle.

"I told you old man. I don't want to eat!"

The Mourangil left the small kitchen, slamming the door behind her. Dismayed, Evan turned back towards Klim and Gabbie, "If she doesn't feed her human form it will revert to its Mourangil state," he told them shaking his head.

"She seems so angry," commented Gabbie. Klim raised his eyebrows silently reminding her of the times she had exploded without reason, and often not meaning to do so. She drew her elbow back, digging into his chest, her smile breaking the tension of the room.

"You knew her before she came to Y Wasgod Oren, Evan?" Klim enquired.

Evan sighed and nodded, shoving away his plate and cupping a large mug of coffee. He automatically assumed the rolling bardic voice he used for storytelling.

"I met her when I was thirty, when I first discovered I was a Stozcist." His grey eyes gleamed with the memory of youth for a moment and then clouded with sadness. "Echin found me after my parents were killed when half a mountain fell on my village." He hesitated, placing his mug back on the table. "I was six and away with my grandmother on the other side of the valley." Gabbie pressed her hand over his and Evan lifted his shoulders. "Echin helped rebuild the school and taught us for a year or two. He was like a father to all of us who had lost our parents and we would follow him about like sheep. I worked on my grandmother's farm and after he left the school he'd come back to visit until, in my twenties, I finally noticed it was I and not he who was getting older."

The two listeners said not a word, their eyes fixed on the bard in the poignant silence.

"It was then that I first learnt of our planet's unseen indigenous race and that my teacher and hero was not even human!"

Evan looked shamefaced. "I rebelled of course. Now and again Echin would come back but I'd wreck every visit with my anger. I'd be devastated after he left. It was a pattern we followed for some years. In that time, I met and married Bethan and we had Angharad." He looked up and Gabbie smiled encouragingly.

"Then when I was thirty and clearing some land to make a garden pond, I discovered my gift. I didn't have the materials to make that pond the way I wanted it but by the time I had finished I'd fashioned the stone to my imagined expectations. Bethan was astonished at the workmanship, and I beamed with pride. She thought I had studied secretly as a stone mason!" He laughed at the memory. "It was how I made my living for a time afterwards," he added absently. "That night Silex arrived in the workshop I used in the garden. She coached me through the first flowering of life as a Stozcist. Between her no-nonsense attitude and great love for Echin, she skilfully engineered my adjustment to the new situation and when Echin returned she helped re-align our relationship."

Klim saw that Gabbie's expression reflected his own renewal of
respect for the difficult Mourangil. Getting up from the table,
Evan shook his head sadly, his words barely audible. "And yet
now," he said to no one in particular, "in this most turbulent of
times, her presence gives me no comfort."

With enormous hunger but little enthusiasm, Klim and Gabbie ate
breakfast together in the gloom of the cold walled kitchen. Trying
to reassure his friends as best he could, Klim stood up and made
his way to the front door, heading in the opposite direction to the
path that he had seen Silex take a short time before.

*

Inside the crysaline Swift felt the deep embrace of Moura. The
particles of her body merged within the wondrous cells of a
material that she knew was prized by the Mourangils above all
others. She had woven the substance from the granite bedrock of
the island, knowing its intimate construction, feeling its pattern.
Her previous contact with the crysaline in Caral had been brief
but enough for the Stozcist to recreate its substance. It was little
over a year ago since that moment and yet that time already
seemed like another existence. Since then, the Mourangils had
shown her that she was no freak of nature, but an intricate part of
the planet's gift to mankind. Echin had said that only a Stozcist
could have found and removed the Perfidium from this

luminously white cloth like material. Swift now knew, without egotism or embellishment that only she, the last Stozcist, could have done so. Evan was like a father to her, but she saw the limitation of his power, even as she quietly acknowledged the growth of her own.

The crysaline had easily given up its story to her, telling of its origin in the compressed layers below the planetary crust. An area inaccessible to the Mourangils and Devourils and yet she could bring this wondrous stone fabric into being, transform solid rock into the protective substance that infiltrated the cells of her own body, to prevent them becoming subdued by her time beneath the surface. Swift had wedged herself below the obdurate. Not even the Waybearer could tell her if Nephragm, in the form of Silex, could reach her. The destruction of the man Terence Mace had both thrilled and appalled her and its residue had left a trail for Nephragm to follow. Of this she was certain and now, above all, she was determined to prevent herself being used to harm those whom she had come to love. For without a doubt that was the intention of the malignant influence that now stalked the surface nearby.

Enduring the terrifying journey through the obdurate and creating the crysaline meant that she had eluded the search of the island. Only when she became aware of the vibration of Echin, prevented from reaching her by the obdurate, did she see her danger. The crysaline fibres gave her insight into the Mourangils and she felt the sharp dislocation of some of those who had previously supported Echin in his surface journeying. The influence of Belluvour was like a sewer that coursed beneath the layers of their presence, leaking its fetid contents into those areas where the jewelled beings had begun to darken. It was more than possible that the obdurate, its great shadowy weight above her, could host a Devouril if they found where she was hiding. She tried to suppress the knowledge that she would need to embrace the shadow once more if she were to reach the surface. Swift let herself dwell on a new possibility. She could remain suspended in the crysaline, let go of memories, fears, past hurts. The soft white material was like a womb, it would nurture and feed her cells. She was at peace within its folds, already grown comfortable in the molecular structure of her own facsimile.

*

"What will you do Loretta?" Samuel repeated his question, the steel in his voice accenting his tone from a soft brogue to one of fearsome interrogation. He tucked his hands within the folds of a capacious black shirt. For a second the image of a shining unicorn overlay Loretta the woman, who now stood heron like, unmoving, on the edge of the bank. Only the emerald-green eyes betrayed the war inside, darting from one to the other of the small group. Kier silently allowed her held breath to leave her body, she dared not speak or move. Echin and Samuel were also silent and waiting.

It was Josh who broke the frozen moment, his dazed face melted into an ice cracking smile when he saw Loretta. Painfully, he reached his hand towards her. Loretta lifted the pouch that was hanging around her neck and handed it to Samuel. Then she stepped into the boat, gently taking Josh's hand, manoeuvring herself to cradle his head as he passed once more into unconsciousness. Quickly the others followed, and Samuel made his way to the controls at the front of the boat. The small motor stuttered and hiccoughed into a steady hum as the cleric steered upriver. Kier looked up at the sky, stars shining clearly, as they made their way along the dark sheet of water.

They travelled in silence. Kier became mesmerized by the fitful ripples of smooth water illumined in the small splash of light from the side of the boat. Most of the seating area was occupied by Josh and Loretta and Kier had wedged herself into the remaining space. Echin stood with Samuel, his eyes searching the embankment. In other circumstances, it would have been an enchanting journey. The toxic aftertaste of their encounter with Danubin however, shadowed their quiet progress through the starlit night. Lulled to sleep, Kier later awoke to find her head cushioned on her elbow, absorbing the rocking motion of the boat as Samuel and Echin moored it beside a Disney style cottage. To her surprise it was now fully daylight and that meant she had been asleep for much longer than she thought. Primroses and geraniums framed the archway of the small building, dotted with wooden slats, and built from Welsh slate. The wooden windows were pristine white. A neat lawn sloped downwards to a small stone wall and a traditional wooden gate.

"Where are we?" Kier managed, her mouth feeling as dry as dust.

"The Teifi has its own particular places, open only by special invitation," Samuel answered, "and this is one of them."

"We're talking about the river?" she replied, raising sceptical eyebrows.

"We're talking about the River Teifi," he corrected.

"Ah," she said, noting the smile on Echin's face as he tied up the boat. Kier silently gave thanks that she had slept on the boat. She was not given the chance to see inside the fairy tale cottage, for Echin had whispered her away to return to Tinobar. The sensation of his hand on her arm as Samuel and Loretta took Josh inside the house, had irritably left her no choice in the matter. As a result, she made more of a fuss about the fact that she, once again, was directed by his intention.

"What do you want me for Echin?" She was surprised by the challenge in her own voice.

"I need you to help with Siskin," he told her in a frustratingly detached tone.

"Of course," she nodded her assent, feeling hopeful and hopeless in the same instant. Hopeful that she could travel within the wonderful embrace of his being once more and hopeless that her ever deepening love for Echin, the man, could ever be returned. As it was, she gave herself up to the journey, wrapped once more in the intimate cellular embrace of this creature who seemed to understand humankind more than they understood themselves. In what seemed like a few moments of light filled embrace she found herself beside him, outside the gates of Tinobar. Madeleine shuffled out to meet them. "Did you find the stones?" Her anxious face relaxed as Echin nodded, striding before the healer into the secreted place.

"Take special care Madeleine," he instructed. "Danubin is seeking you."

"I know, I have moved our location three times since you were last here. She has grown Toomaaris, her knowledge threatens us all."

"Are we betrayed?" Echin asked her.

"Only by the stones that she no longer holds in her possession," Madeleine replied.

"She has the Chalycion," Echin told her.

Madeleine stopped walking, her insubstantial features a fold of sorrow.

"That is a great blow," she told them quietly, her head shaking from side to side. "But it would have been so much more terrible if she had also continued to hold the Iridice and Amron Cloch." She held out her hand and Echin placed within it the stones retrieved by Loretta. Madeleine examined each one for some time before handing back the milky jewel that Klim had once shown to Kier, his father's stone. Madeleine held up the purple-brown amethyst to align with a shaft of sunlight that teased its way through the wooded dell. The light appeared to solidify into a golden rod that travelled through the woodland, winding through the filmy occupants of Tinobar to rest beneath a massive beech tree where Siskin sat resting. The light fell on the musician, the Lute. Long blond hair scattered untidily about his unshaven face, squinting as he raised his hands to cover his eyes. Kier deftly weaved through the injured and their healers calling out his name; she flung her arms around Siskin's neck just as he pulled himself upright. Only in that moment did she realise how much she had missed his strong yet gentle presence. The hug she received in return left no doubt, that he too had felt the fracture of their separation. The brown eyes had lost much of their strain. He was thinner however and she was assailed by a sense of some grief inside him that she suspected was only held at bay by Tinobar. The beech tree tinkled; the branches were filled with tiny golden pipes that sat in the centre of the leaves. She knew that most of its music could be heard only by Siskin, as if he had his own set of headphones secretly plugged into the organic orchestra.

Madeleine and Echin arrived beside them, and the healer smiled her approval. Echin, enigmatic as ever, nodded towards Siskin. Madeleine held out the amethyst in her palm and gave it to the musician. Kier gasped as the purple stone turned golden brown as her friend held the glistening jewel, its glow now reflected in the light of his eyes. A chord of music: part harpsichord, part drum, part flute, wavered; phrases that seemed to gather their fellows so that a graceful interplay of chords effortlessly surrounded Siskin and Kier. She had no idea how long they had stood there together, linked in the embrace of sound, but finally, when the last note eddied away, they were standing alone in an empty field.

"I think we need to climb the hill," Siskin suggested, the assurance now back in his voice.

Kier nodded and they set off together, reaching the top just as Echin emerged from a white stoned lime kiln.

"Ready?" he asked matter-of-factly, as if he were driving them to an evening out.

"Ready," Siskin confirmed.

*

"The sudden collapse of industry giant *Lendersole Games*, has shocked and rocked the financial community," Josh read aloud. Folding the tabloid newspaper, he put it down on the small table covered by a white lace cloth. Kier had been shocked to find two days had passed outside, during what had seemed to her only a brief stay in Tinobar. She shrugged off any memories of her return to Pulton last year, also from Tinobar, to find that her brother had disappeared. It was the first time that Josh had felt well enough to come downstairs and even now his ashen face inscribed the story of his ordeal. "She used the fact that I'm a Creta, probed and reflected my perception of the Virenmor to create terror for us Kier." He spoke to her but mainly for himself as he began the process of analysing what had happened in Danubin's mansion.

Kier nodded her understanding, thinking of the malignant presence that had first appeared in her dream. She had seen for herself the strange overlay of the two people who were both Danubin: the young, smart, business-like person and the dreadful, malevolent looking crone. It occurred to her that this was common for Josh, to see two physical representations of one individual.

"She used the same dimensional cross over, as you as a Creta achieve, but with a different setting, purpose and plane," Loretta stated.

Kier frowned and the other woman smiled.

"Josh explained a little of his entry into a self-created field of energy, the cross over into another dimension that reflects the world in which we live but is not that world." Kier was certain much of that conversation would have been lost on her.

"The Mourangils," the Tane continued, "could not enter the field of thought that made the illusion of the medieval hall; the pathways Danubin has developed can only be used on a human signature. In this event she cleverly used this fact to shut you off from potential help. All the others could see, once Samuel had provided light, was that the two of you had completely disappeared."

"How did you come to be there Loretta?" Siskin asked the Irish girl.

"It's complicated," she replied, glancing at Kier and moving towards the window. No one spoke and she turned back to them, sighing, her eyes seeking those of Josh.

"I offered to help Samuel get inside the mansion to atone for the fact that it was through us that Danubin broke down the secrets of Amron Cloch and almost destroyed you. It was never our intention..." She looked around the room but met little encouragement. Siskin's face was an implacable mask. She bit her lip and continued. "That's what I told Samuel anyway. I let Danubin check me out, I'm still listed in the college as a student. I did everything possible to be noticed and became part of the 'elite gamers', finding the most corrupt and violent solutions. Sean's fury was only partly faked when she singled me out. She brought me to the mansion and installed me as her personal assistant. Things were getting pretty close to unbearable when you finally turned up."

"That took a great deal of courage," Kier commented neutrally. Loretta moved nearer to Josh. "As I said, that's what I told

Samuel," her voice now almost a whisper.

"And the real reason?" questioned Josh.

"To recover the stones," interjected Siskin before she could go on.

With an uncomfortable glance at Josh, Loretta nodded.

"For what reason?" demanded Josh.

"Their Tane forms are dying," Kier said simply. "They think the stones will help. They may also have had ambitions to try to form the Myriar themselves using Mactire's drawing."

Loretta turned sharply towards the other woman.

"How did you know?" she demanded. Kier ignored the question.

"From what I have learnt the Myriar is exclusively in the hands of the last Seeds and Candillium, if she ever arrives," Siskin told them.

"I saw no trace of her in the Vortex," Loretta told them. "Danubin seems to think that Candillium or one of the Seeds was killed by Belluvour's influence about ten years ago. We did not wish our future to be left in the hands of humans we did not know, care for or respect," she countered.

"So, you betrayed Samuel and almost did a damn good job of wiping us out!" Josh turned his face, hot with anger, away from Loretta.

The green eyes flared. "We saved you from the Tolbranach and I could have left that spider pit with the Virenmor!" she seethed.

"What were you doing in the pit in the first place," Siskin asked neutrally.

Loretta slowed her breathing and turned towards the musician who waited calmly for an answer. "Even Danubin could not guarantee control of Magluck Bawah. If it had turned on the Virenmor she was perfectly prepared to distract it with myself, or one of the others while she escaped."

"Nice," Siskin commented. "So, she used the same principle that allowed her to engineer those political murders through game play?"

"Exactly," nodded Loretta.

"Why couldn't Samuel enter the illusion?" Kier asked Loretta, "After all he was able to go with Josh into the painting in Wicklow."

Loretta looked surprised. "Don't you know who Samuel is?" she asked, brows furrowed, a slight smile on her lips. "Nor did I until I came here," she acknowledged. "He's a Riverkeeper."

"What?" Josh was startled, shaking his head. "I should have worked that out!"

Kier frowned and Siskin shrugged. "What's a Riverkeeper?" he asked.

There was sadness in the emerald-coloured eyes, and her tone softened as Loretta sat down at the table.

" A Riverkeeper is a very rare and gentle creature but also incredibly forceful. He was human once but that is not his signature at this time."

Kier glanced towards the river only a short way from where she was sitting.

"No melody or mind print," Siskin nodded, now understanding. "That figures."

"A Riverkeeper," Loretta continued, "was at some time born as a human being. In their first life, they achieve a state of being that negates any need to continue to re-incarnate. Moura has a particular affinity for this kind of human, she invites them to stay physically linked to her in this plane of existence, becoming an intrinsic part of its physical structure. In this case Samuel is kinetically linked to the River Teifi. That is why Danubin and Magluck Bawah are unable to reach you where its flow has most influence. Samuel is able to live a Tane's existence in human form," Loretta explained.

"Like you?" Kier quizzed.

Loretta's eyes dimmed, "My kind are more intrinsically Tane than human," the elfin like woman answered.

"So, is that why he can move things without touch?" Siskin asked.

Loretta nodded, "It's part of his kinetic empowerment."

Kier stood up and laughed, putting her hands over her ears, "As Gabbie would say, my head hurts!"

Josh agreed, "No more technical stuff, but I do want to know if we've stopped her?"

He deliberately directed his question towards Kier and Siskin.

"We must have had some effect, Josh; she's lost that mausoleum for a start." Kier decided.

Loretta nodded her agreement, also addressing Kier and Siskin. "Danubin will be livid and seriously inconvenienced. She's very clever, the mensira manipulation is way beyond anything I've seen."

"And now she has the Chalycion," Josh stated ruefully. "All those years the Stone keepers held it safe, including my mother, and I let her take it. If only I had held on." His fingers flicked momentarily across the area of his throat where the Chalycion had rested.

"You baited the trap Josh," Loretta told him gently. "She knew that you would use the stone to repel Magluck Bawah."

"She nearly had me," Josh continued, this time looking directly towards Loretta who still sat at the table with him, her luminous eyes fixed on his face. The long straight hair now returned to a mass of copper curls.

"Echin told me you could have taken the stones for yourself and left us to die," Josh said softly.

For a long moment, the two were locked in their own private understanding. The ache in his eyes was answered by the longing in hers. Finally, he took Loretta's hand and gently kissed it. Whatever war they had been fighting, Kier decided, had at least for now, come to an end.

*

The trees that banked the opposite side of the river were heavy with summer laden leaves. There was a chill in the air that spoke of coming autumn as Kier sat cross legged on the grass and breathed in the fresh fragrance of wild thyme. A noon sky made looking up difficult and she shaded her eyes, finding to her surprise that her hand had dampened with unshed tears. She was changing. All that she had long suffocated by relentless activity, which had stirred to life in the reference room of the book shop, which had stood alone in the dark funnel of Nephragm's hatred, all of it wanted to breathe at once. Two moorhens, showing their red tipped beaks, bobbed out from the shelter of reeds across the water. A flock of waders, silvery in the sun, sparkled like magic dust and spread out over the hill that overlooked the cottage. She pulled in clean, energising air, knowing without moving, that Echinod Deem stood behind her. She turned, surprising from him an expression of intense – what had it been? Regret perhaps? It had been only a fleeting moment, a glimpse of his unveiled self. She had shared his being on a cellular level above the clouds, had felt his jewelled Mourangil form press against her skin, but she had no way of knowing his thoughts. "What happened in Lioncera?" she asked.

He came to sit beside her on the riverbank, hands across his knees, eyes following the restless swirl of the current.

"We are fractured," his voice choked as he turned towards her, holding her gaze. There was such grief in his expression that she did not press further, waiting for him to continue. He did not, only turning his face back towards the river, the sinews in his jaw tight as he pulled up his chin. The water stirred strongly as the breeze increased its chill reminder of the end of summer. Kier shivered. Slowly Echin raised himself upwards and reached down for her hand. Silently he pulled her up to stand beside him and together they slowly returned to the cottage.

Chapter Thirty-three

Klim found his way to the same spot where Gabbie had spent long hours watching the sea climb and fall against the cliffs, ever marking its presence in the worn rock. He saw the white splotches, splayed by a bird colony that had now left rows of untidy moss strewn remains, an empty city of nests. He saw no sign of the otters that had enlivened her smile as she told of their busy movement in the nearby waters. He thought of Gabbie's face at their forlorn breakfast, how she had looked shockingly tired. He had wanted nothing more than to hold her in his arms and let her sleep against his shoulder. If he had let that and more happen however, he was certain he would have lessened the already fragile connection with Swift. As much as they were all linked together, should he reach out for Gabbie in the way that he wanted to, find the hidden softness she kept only for him, he was sure he would lose the sense of Swift's location altogether. And Swift needed him, of that he was certain.

Silex had headed inland towards the densely wooded area of the island, and he could see no sign of her. Her abrasive presence, as a puzzled Evan had acknowledged, had brought them little comfort. Klim decided that he wanted to look for Swift without her aggressive supervision. His natural stealth had been sharpened by his time working with Siskin, whom he sorely missed. He made his way carefully back to the broken stone, noting how difficult it was to reach without being observed from the summit. The stone had been placed at a spot that gave the best view of the island. He reflected that it had probably stood proudly for thousands of years before being cast aside so destructively. He felt sure that this was where Swift had entered the ground below, but he did not believe that she would have toppled and smashed the stone. Gabbie and Evan had told of the hours she had spent communicating with the rock in her own unique way. Evan had given him to understand that the stone had a link with the Mourangils that he had been unable to fathom. If not Swift, Klim asked himself, then who else would have wanted to sever the connection between the stone and the ground beneath?

He looked around the green summit, from which could be seen the other island's reaching out to sea, towards every compass point. The Mourangils, Evan had told him, had ensured that Magluck Bawah could not reach them here. So, if not Swift, he asked himself, who then had smashed the stone? A fear grasped at his belly, Danubin had followed them so closely all this time, could she have found a way to alight on the island unseen? He took out the Stone of Silence and picked up one of the broken shards from the old stone nearby. The clouds swirled about him as he concentrated. Whiteness, cold yet warm, alien yet integral. He let go of the breath he was holding, He was certain that Swift was alive and in direct line with where his feet were at that moment, planted on top of the hill.

*

It was as if a silver rope reached down to her from above the surface; the crysaline stirred, motioned to respond. Klim, his beautiful, powerful mind, had found her and the startling touch of his presence pulled her awake. It was time. Slowly she began to unravel the crysaline from her cells. Her heart filled with trepidation at the thought of having to pass once more through the obdurate. Belluvour had engineered the design so that a Mourangil could not embed in its structure; the dark heart of this rock repelled the light filled crystalline beings, but she was not Mourangil. The obdurate was a snake pit of venomous hatred but it could not deny entry to a human Stozcist. Strangely the malevolent stone had taught her more about her gift than any other experience.

The molecules of her body shifted to a transparency that could align with the dense bedrock of the island. Above this had been positioned the obdurate. She saw how Echin had circled the ocean, manoeuvred the currents so that Magluck Bawah could not surface here. She also saw, with her heightened understanding beneath the surface, that this protection had been weakened by the strong pull of the obdurate above, lying in the more superficial layers. She knew her time was short; unprotected by the crysaline she was vulnerable to the sickness that attacked her underground and that this would be made worse by the prolonged period she had spent there already. Once the sickness overwhelmed her senses it would begin to destroy her human body and make her more stone than human. It made her think of the films she had watched, the fairy stories where, through magic, individuals were literally turned to stone. She wondered if they had been the early Stozcists. Now began the delicate balance of consciousness, like trying to stay awake to direct a dream. The obdurate vibrated; the sound of the executioner's blade as it sliced, pendulum like, through flesh. The malevolent rock was a maze of such cellular swings that would fracture her being in an instant. Woven between all of this however was a silver cord, the other end of which, was held in psychic rescue by Klim above. Swift stilled her molecular presence and reached towards the tensile light. She focused her being and slowly, imperceptibly, began her return journey through the marauding density of the dreadful substance above.

*

The wind had gathered overnight. Kier watched as Josh brought together the fragmented pieces of an old board that had washed down river. The cottage had a small kitchen with a granite work surface and on top of this were splashes of red Arabic characters and the dismembered images of a passenger plane, painted on the pieces.

"Sort of landed at our doorstep," he commented to Kier. "Saw it from the window this morning; thought I'd come down and investigate."

There was a hollowness in his tone, one that said he was looking for something to fill the space that had opened up after Loretta had returned to Dublin that morning. Together with the loss of the Chalycion, her absence had signalled the end of the brief respite from his self-punishing anger and regret. Kier smiled as she saw the small figure of Samuel sauntering along the riverbank.

"How's Angharad?" she asked, as she opened the back door to greet him with a smile. He had deliberately not taken the others with him on his visit to see Evan's daughter.

"Good, even happy," he replied. "Though she misses Evan."

"Will she ever get back to the village?" Kier asked.

A secretive smile played around Samuel's lips. "It seems she and the children have settled very well by the river. She has met someone."

"Just happened to meet, eh?" Josh was smirking.

"I may have introduced them," Samuel admitted. "He's a good man, a widower with no children."

The news lifted Kier, "I think Evan will be pleased. Does he know him?"

"Not yet," Samuel said thoughtfully. "I was glad I could give her news of everyone."

"All the news?" Kier asked shrewdly. Although there was no doubt that Angharad would not succumb willingly to Danubin's machinations again, Samuel was being cautious.

"Enough," he replied, signalling towards the battered sign that Josh had recovered and effectively ending that line of conversation. After a short examination of the pieces of board he looked out at the wind swirled river water.

"The Teifi," he told them matter-of-factly. "It's telling us where to look for Danubin." The fondness in his eyes told its own story of his communion with the weaving flow of fresh water. Kier had no problem in seeing Samuel as the Riverkeeper that Loretta had described. A sound that was subtle, magnetic, and circling the whole cottage; a single lengthy intonation, vibrated through every cell in Kier's body.

"Haven't heard that one before!" remarked Josh.

"Definitely not," Kier added, reaching underneath her cotton sleeves to smooth the tiny, raised hairs on her arms. "Would have remembered!"

"Siskin?" Samuel accurately surmised.

Josh nodded. "He's been up all night studying it." The tiny, light blue flicker of his eyes showed that it was another reminder of the loss of the Chalycion. "I mean Amron Cloch," he added unnecessarily. The trio moved into the main room and Josh went upstairs to call Siskin.

"How is he?" Samuel asked quietly.

"Not good," Kier replied softly.

Her attention was captured by a motion in the river. Peering out she watched as the three Mourangils, all bone dry, emerged from the Teifi. Tormaigh was the first to enter, his long thin frame bending to fit underneath the lintel of the kitchen.

"Damascus!" he announced.

Echin and Faer entered just as Josh arrived downstairs with Siskin. "Danubin's in Damascus," Echin elaborated.

"The sign from the river!" Kier looked over at Samuel and Josh who explained his unusual and significant find that morning, bringing in and reforming the pieces of board on the table.

A green crystal shard glinted at Tormaigh's elbow, Kier had come to recognise these signs of exhaustion and strain in the Mourangils. The blue of Faer's eyes had paled and Tormaigh looked gaunt.

"Before we do anything else," she announced decisively, "I'm going to make you some food."

Siskin accompanied Kier into the kitchen and began slicing cheese as she buttered bread.

"There's been no news from the island, in Mengebara," the musician's tone was serious.

"Yes, I'm worried," admitted Kier, "plus I miss them," she added. Siskin nodded his agreement as he helped her load up a tray and followed her into the living room with jugs of water.

"It's decided then," Echin said as they entered and Kier found herself bristling at his lack of consideration for her and Siskin's opinion. Her companion voiced her own feelings. "What happened to democracy?" Siskin asked lightly. "Don't we get a say?"

"Of course!" Echin replied, glancing at Kier. "Thought that you'd never ask."

"Chance would be a fine thing," she quipped, also keeping her tone light.

Tormaigh and Faer gratefully began on the sandwiches and Echin settled into an armchair.

"I want to help look for Swift," Kier stated firmly.

Echin smiled, "I remember you said that once before," he told her. Kier recalled the meeting in the book shop that had eventually led to her helping to save the girl's life. It had also resulted in bringing herself, Siskin and Klim to Lioncera.

"It's what Echin just suggested," Josh told her. She found herself even more irritated. Tormaigh, who had been concentrating on the sandwiches and was sat like an awkward frog, cross legged on the floor, looked up. "Am I still going to Damascus?" he enquired. "I never feel as odd in that part of the world."

"You're always odd!" Faer laughed. "We Mourangils have never needed to learn fast, but Tormaigh is slower than most."

His words broke the building tension and Kier straightened.

"I thought," Echin began, and after a slight hesitation added, "just as a suggestion, that we ought to split into two groups. The most pressing need is to recover the Chalycion, and I suggest myself, Josh and Tormaigh head to Damascus."

Echin began to look worried. "Klim and Silex should have found Swift by now. We have heard nothing from either, therefore Faer will accompany Kier and Siskin to the island." Finally, he added, "If you think it a good idea?"

Siskin gave a wry smile and nodded, "What about Samuel?" he asked, looking at the cleric.

"I am sorry my friend, but I must stay with the river for a while," Samuel responded.

"How are we getting there?" Siskin asked.

"It takes a huge amount of energy for a Mourangil to carry another being within their form and it is a mark of their love for you that they do so." Samuel told them.

Faer looked evenly at his human companions as he added, "But it is also our privilege." Kier said nothing, remembering how Tormaigh had carried so many of them from Tinobar.

"Josh can be carried between us to Damascus," Tormaigh commented, looking at Echin. "I think Faer will manage to the island with Kier and Siskin."

Faer nodded, "But after a little rest," he told them.

Kier said nothing but found that she too was nodding her assent. The thought of being separated from Echin again meant that she did not trust herself to speak.

"Sorted," was Josh's comment.

Faer left them to embed and renew his energies. Kier had to stop herself crying out after him, for a terrible urgency assailed her. "Swift," she whispered, "where are you?"

Chapter Thirty-four

Hope renewed itself in Kier following the invisible journey wrapped within the remarkable being that was Faer. The buoyant optimism, his organic, arrow true personality had resonated with the molecular transformation that enabled her energetic being to be transported to the Welsh island. Added to this was the memory of a melody; simple yet profoundly powerful, innervating, vibrant, that was the presence of Siskin with Amron Cloch. He glowed with new health and energy as he helped her to balance when Faer set them down. Even this early in September, summer in the remote island appeared to have already given up the baton to a tearful autumn. Faer had brought them to a cave in what appeared to be a far corner of the island. The ground outside was scattered with fading green and brown leaves, washed down by wind and rain.

"All is not well," he warned them immediately. "The protection that was wrought in this place, over several weeks, has almost vanished."

"Can we reinstate it?" asked Siskin in his soldier's voice, the black woollen hat pulled close around his head.

Faer shook his head, he too favoured a tight-fitting woollen hat and Kier was glad she had put on a hip length jumper as a cold breeze sneaked over her skin. "Sadly, no. The current weave is too intricate," he explained. Seeing Kier's blank face he added, "Toomaaris manipulated the way that the sea flows around the island. He needed to stop a Devouril from inhabiting the huge obdurate just above the bedrock, and also to prevent Magluck Bawah from detecting your presence. It appears something or someone very powerful has managed to reverse that effect."

"We need to move fast then," Siskin stated, adjusting his watch.

"Above all else we need to move with stealth," Faer returned. "I fear Nephragm is here."

Kier blanched, "Are you sure?" Her voice trembled.

"No," Faer admitted, "but he would be one of the few with the power to undo the island's protection and we have no evidence that he is, in fact, with Danubin."

*

Silex entered the kitchen as Evan was clearing away the dishes. She turned to look into the small living room where Gabbie had curled up on the armchair like a child, fast asleep.

"Don't wake her," Evan spoke more firmly that he had ever done to Silex. The impish figure looked towards him with interest as Herald growled at his feet.

"Down boy," Evan instructed. He adjusted his tone, making it softer as he stepped back to view the still sleeping figure. "The poor child has had little rest these last weeks."

He dried his hands and walked past Silex to cover Gabbie with a blanket and then gave his attention to the coal fire in the grate. For a moment, the feel of the rocky black fuel reminded him of his childhood in the mining village and, as a young man, of his relationship with Silex. He turned, his eyes soft with remembrance, to observe the hard gleam of hate in the beautiful green eyes of the Mourangil as she watched Gabbie's sleeping figure. Evan dropped the coal scuttle in shock and hid his confusion, collecting up the scattered dusty pieces from the tiled hearth.

"What's the noise about?" Gabbie reproached sleepily as she sat up, alarm written in her wide eyes and narrowed eyebrows.

"Where's the boy?" Silex demanded, her expression once again neutral.

The alarm on Gabbie's face did not lessen as she looked around, noting from the clock on the mantelpiece that hours had now passed. "I don't know," she admitted uncomfortably, looking towards Evan.

"Come with me," commanded Silex. Gabbie nodded, wiping the sleep out of her eyes.

"We'll all go," Evan said firmly, "but have a drink first Gabbie. Klim will probably return soon anyway, he's been gone long enough!"

"How long?" the Mourangil demanded.

Evan glanced at the clock, "About four hours, he left just after you did."

The Mourangil looked unsettled, "We will of go now," she ordered, heading out the door.

Gabbie shrugged her shoulders and started searching for her shoes. Evan brought woollens from upstairs that he insisted Gabbie put on, before following the stern redhead who stood waiting for them impatiently at the start of the path heading inland. Herald bounded out behind Evan and occupied the space between Gabbie and Silex.

*

Klim had not noticed the cold, nor the damp that crept through his jeans and cupped his knees as he knelt, transfixed. Swift's courage was magnificent as she focused unerringly on the silver cord that he had created as a link between them. The dark oppressive

energy that surrounded her grasped continually to obliterate the
molecules of her being. She had to keep her awareness whole in
order to move through the dreadful, dragging shadow; avoiding
the deadly slip into a sleep that would allow her to be
dismembered within the obdurate. Klim buoyed her focus with
his own powerful mind, as they inched her upwards, almost to the
level of silt and soil, just a metre or two below the surface.

"Come on Swift," he whispered, "we're almost there."

The cold touch of Silex, her hand curving around the edge of his
neck, shattered Klim's concentration. Angrily he turned to gaze
into the jade eyes, where he saw the same essence, the same
despoiling evil that he had found in the obdurate below. Dropping
the two stones he tried to jump up, but his legs, stiff with cramp
and cold, toppled him sideways. Gabbie was by his side in an
instant, her small arm, surprisingly strong, supporting him. Once
he was fully straight, she moved to pick up the stones that he had
dropped.

"Leave them," Silex commanded, but Gabbie had already
gathered each one into her small fists. "I said leave them!" roared
Silex.

Klim, his limbs now more obedient, placed himself between the
two female figures. His mind had become a whirling maelstrom
of distraction, desperate to snatch back the link he had lost with
Swift and determined to protect Gabbie from the rising surge of
black anger from the Mourangil.

"Silex," Faer's voice winged across the exposed hilltop, still littered with the smashed stones; his call seemed to echo from each fragment. Behind him came Siskin and Kier. Klim's heart sang, he willed the renewed sensation of hope that their appearance had brought into the deep well of thought, where the connection with Swift had been broken. Faer's face glinted hard edges of feldspar as he came nearer to the small redhead, whose eyes had blackened into deep funnels of profound malevolence. "Nephragm!" Faer cried, leaping towards the slight figure. Mercury like she slithered out of his reach into the tunnelled earth. Herald appeared on top of the hill followed by Evan, both panting with effort. The excited hound bounded across, knocking Faer to the ground.

"Faer!" Evan shouted. "The sea changes!"

Faer glimmered white crystal for a moment and then his human form stood solidly before them once again. He walked to the edge of the grassy mound where the sea smashed against the rocks, the turbulent current whirled madly and unpredictably back and forth. Windblown, it hurled rotting remains from deep within the ocean onto the bedraggled surface of the island.

*

Swift flailed, all of her concentration focused on keeping a sense of her human body alive, within the swirling refuse of emotion engendered by the obdurate. The link with Klim, so suddenly torn, meant that she had plummeted backwards into the black glassy shards of darkness that threatened to entrap her within their hard, voided shell. She had been almost beyond this terror, which was like swimming upwards in pitch, body bound, only her feet free to steer the way. Klim's powerful mind had illuminated a channel through, when with great effort she pushed to recreate it and saw a white glimmer ahead. One last effort; if she could marshal her scattered concentration, she would be beyond the influence of this dire prison.

Abruptly, like a shark plunging beside her in an ocean, she felt the presence of a Devouril. The moment of recognition in El Silencio, when she first discovered Galinir's malignant existence, fused with the present shock of awareness. Panic threatened to consume her as she drew in her cellular make up. Fear began to overwhelm her, for this was no nightmare from which to waken up. In its own malevolent element, her chances of defeating this creature were minimal and should she be overcome by the Devouril, she would simply cease to exist. The molecular potential of her physical existence would become absorbed within the obdurate forever. The crysaline had protected her from the sickness endured by a Stozcist when they were underground for any period. Now in this swamp of despair it had become weakened. If the Devouril rounded upon her, keeping her within the obdurate for any longer, then the sickness would be fatal. It came to her that the only way to avoid confrontation was to fully embrace the filthy mire of substance that was the obdurate.

She remembered how she had squeezed the man Mace into solid rock, felt the crush of his spirit, the murder of his evil mind. She knew that in this place the piercing blade of guilt would run rampant. It had already begun its ugly tear on the focus of her mind and would surely make her visible to the Devouril. Freezing her consciousness, like held breath, she allowed herself to sink into the foul obdurate, holding her being in stasis, waiting for the Devouril to pass. Nephragm-Silex, the creature itself was in agony! Swift caught the awareness as it roiled within the obdurate, her own subtle presence ignored. Having dared to take the body of a Mourangil in its human state, Nephragm had thought to bring, within himself, enough of Silex into the obdurate, to counter the vast tide of toxic energy against him. The plan had failed and using all of his power, he now had to flee quickly from the foul rock. Swift, her own resources also almost depleted, summoned a mighty effort, willing herself back towards the channel woven by Klim's silver cord.

Chapter Thirty-five

"The Kejambuck!" cried Kier pointing. "It's above Siskin!"
Faer leapt beside the musician and the creature sprang upwards,
followed in seconds by the Mourangil. There was a fractional
stillness, the hiatus of a page turning, as all eyes searched the
area.

"Get below," yelled Kier. "Magluck Bawah will make for this
hill." Her eyes frantically searched the skies for some winged
terror that Danubin might send. They scrambled downwards onto
the grassy plain that led towards the cliff edge. Silex's distinctive
body staggered from a small cave, infiltrating their group, and
grabbing Gabbie against her body.

"It seems I cannot shed this shell of Silex." The foul tones of
Nephragm spoke from the once distinct and graceful face, now

torn to reveal hard, coal like shards beneath the ripped skin of cheekbones and forehead. Nephragm had intended to use Silex as a mask. Instead, he found the Mourangil's human body, in essence so structurally like his own, had welded into his form. Kier saw Swift, unable to stand, crawl out of the cave behind Nephragm and Gabbie; the stirring of stones bringing her to the notice of the Devouril. He pulled Gabbie to one side, still facing the others, but bringing his free hand near enough to pull the exhausted Swift to her knees, entangling fingers around her long black hair.

"You," he flung Gabbie forwards and now fully concentrated the venomous flow of hatred towards the young Stozcist, who lifted her pained dark eyes towards him. Faer, at that moment landed in the middle of the group as Nephragm began to gather a dark cloud of air around himself and Swift. The obdurate had exhausted him and he was unable to swoop her up in his being as he intended. In that fraction of time Gabbie, the nearest to the Devouril, flung herself against him, rubbing the Stone of Silence into the face of the once Mourangil. Swift's diamond shone star bright, dissipating the black cloud. Gabbie fumbled for Arwres and pressed it into the hand that still held Swift. Nephragm screamed as the stone burnt flesh; shocked, he fell backwards towards the mouth of the cave.

Klim and Siskin grabbed Gabbie, whilst Kier and Faer lifted Swift away from the Devouril's reach.

"Hold," whispered Faer. "If I reach for him, he will embed and though I can give chase, I cannot destroy him in his elemental form."

"He can't embed," the barely conscious form of Swift whispered. Nephragm, trapped between Mourangil and Devouril, in a body that now ravaged his true physical being, waited, gathering strength, at the mouth of the cave.

"You will not kill me," he told Faer. "Murder is not within you."

"But I will." The words were within a tone, a sonorous, lingering bell of sound emanating from Siskin, who stood with Amron Cloch glowing amber in his palm.

The Devouril cringed and fell to the floor, his torn hands gripping madly around his head to shut out the Lute and Amron Cloch.

A low growl, chilling, rasping, came from behind them at the edge of the cliff. Herald bounded towards Siskin; teeth bared. Evan shouted towards the dog, throwing himself across the animal's path. The enraged dog, now the final energy of Magluck Bawah, tore viciously at his abdomen. Evan buckled and fell to the ground, his hands clutching to contain spilled entrails. Kier ran to his side, tearing his shirt in an effort to staunch the horrific wound.

"Herald!" shouted Gabbie, who had grown close to the animal during her stay on the island.

"It's not Herald anymore," Klim yelled back, hitting out with a fallen branch as the animal launched itself towards Siskin. The onslaught was halted for only a moment as the hound groped to its feet. Faer snatched Amron Cloch from the open hand of Siskin and threw it at the collapsed figure of Nephragm. Immediately the rabid dog launched itself towards the head of the Devouril-Mourangil, now in human form. Whimpering sounds interspersed with rasps of pain as the two creatures tore savagely at each other.

The two dark entities were embroiled in a wrestle of death; howling in pain, they scourged each other's stolen flesh. Magluck Bawah and Nephragm moved instinctively away from Amron Cloch, and Siskin moved in quickly to retrieve the precious jewel. Soon it became impossible to distinguish one from the other as fetid, oily matter seeped into the grass. The two destructive powers merged into one black mass that discoloured the ground immediately beneath the flailing entities. Swift and Gabbie were either side of Evan. The Stozcist reached towards Gabbie, who placed the Stone of Silence in her outstretched hand. The jewel had become clear and clean again after its horrific contact with Nephragm. Swift placed it above the torn tissue and Gabbie folded Arwres into his huge fist, closing it gently with her own tiny hand.

Kier gasped as the oily blackness spread outwards and moved further towards them. Faer shimmered and became a white jewel of light that domed the small group. Kier trembled at the sounds she had heard before in Pulton, when the earth had torn beneath her feet. Above them, the mound disintegrated, spewing clay and rubble over the now shapeless shadow beneath. As the hill came crashing down Swift covered her ears and Evan stirred, his eyes opening in horror. "The obdurate has cracked, the island is disintegrating," yelled Swift.

Evan moaned and twisted. Kier saw that his face was still deathly pale, but the edges of the ugly wound had tethered together. Shards of feldspar appeared in the shield that Faer had created as the island imploded with shocking speed.

"Samuel!" Klim shouted, pointing out to sea.

In the midst of the hissing gruel of the sea, Kier followed Klim's direction and picked out the gentle cleric. He was steering a boat towards them on a single current of calm. Faer had created a small patch of protected solid ground but Kier felt the strain of effort this required, as he held them impervious to the catastrophic motion created by the collision of Magluck Bawah and Nephragm the Devouril. Samuel brought the boat in line with the remains of the previously lush island. Klim and Siskin gently lifted Evan into the rear of the small vessel; Gabbie and Swift scrambling to take up their positions behind him. Faer signalled for Kier to follow, allowing his form to fold into the air as soon as she was safely on the boat. In seconds, the small piece of protected land was swallowed in the heaving water, that even Samuel now struggled to navigate.

Kier sank down into the bow, her eyes returning to the vanishing island. She sprang up with a cry for Samuel to stop and before the cleric had turned to answer, she was out of the boat and into the water. It was like thick tar; her breath was quickly ragged as she reached the only remaining piece of ground that Faer had held with such effort. There, in the centre, lying upon a fragment of the standing stone, were the four circles that she had known from infancy. Just as the rock tipped, she snatched the engraved stone, pressing it into her grasp as she struggled to remain afloat. Samuel's boat lurched backwards, despite his attempt to draw nearer. Kier sank downwards, her limbs threshing wildly and uselessly in the vicious undercurrent. She could hear Samuel forbidding the others to enter the water in a fierce command. At the same instance, the circles on the stone burnt her palm, so that she could feel the outline of each. Desperate for breath, she raised her fist above her head and was propelled upwards, gasping as air pummelled her lungs in its rush to reach them. The right hand, which contained the stone, visibly glowed. She pointed it towards the boat, creating a golden passage of smooth water. As she swam, it was as if she was bathing in the last rays of a magnificent sunset, that held its light until finally, she was hauled over the brim of the boat by the strong arms of Siskin and Klim.

*

In the cottage by the River Teifi Evan slept fitfully upstairs, where Samuel sat in vigil beside his bed. In the room below siskin played a wooden pipe, creating a melody that seemed of another age.

"Are you sure about Evan?" Gabbie asked Swift.

"He is no longer a Stozcist," was the sad reply.

"I wonder how he'll feel about that," Gabbie pondered, consternation dimming her sapphire blue eyes.

Kier had no idea but hoped that he could share a more secure future with his daughter. The gift that he had used so selflessly down the years had allowed him to use the Myriar stones to heal the dreadful wound inflicted by the stolen form of Herald. Now it had emerged that it would be his final act as a Stozcist. She thought about Echin and the others, her mind seeking Mengebara for news. There was none, nor any response from Josh to the awful details that Klim had posted. She thought of Silex, the impish Mourangil, so impassioned, and wondered what affect her loss would have on the mysterious beings that remained invisible to the vast majority of the human race. Siskin began to sing, a hauntingly beautiful song of mourning for all that had been destroyed. For Evan's gift, for the Mourangil already lost to them and the one taken, for the creatures whose innocence had been so abused. And finally, for Magluck Bawah. As the last note lingered, Kier's hand slid to where the stone she had retrieved now hung in a pendant around her neck.

"Look for the Stone of Mesa in the toxic residue of grief," she quoted.

"Magluck Bawah," Siskin agreed.

"What does it mean?" asked Gabbie.

"In the Vortex," Kier explained, "under all the rage and raw energy, I felt the creature's limitless suffering. I think that's why I was able to see the Stone of Mesa locked inside." She stopped to consider her words carefully, to align the thoughts that had hovered in her consciousness since Dublin, and that the stone she now wore around her neck, had endorsed. "The Undercreature was, I believe, the result of a planetary sorrow so profound that it became physically manifested in Magluck Bawah."

"Is that really possible?" queried Siskin.

Swift nodded her head in sad agreement, looking towards Klim.

"Yes," she shivered, "it's possible."

Klim remained staring out of the window, silent.

"The Myriar that Moura created for us," Kier continued, "could not be ungiven but tragically that gift propelled the Mourangils into civil war. I believe Magluck Bawah was the result of the cataclysmic convergence of the planet's intention and Belluvour's destructive force."

She turned, hearing footsteps on the stairs. Samuel joined them at the close of the evening as cloud filled skies dimmed to darkness outside. The Riverkeeper, though so close to his precious Teifi, closed the blinds.

"How is he?" Kier asked.

"Sleeping," he replied, easing himself into a space beside her.

"Do you think she's still angry?" Gabbie said quietly.

"Who?" Klim had turned back towards the others.

"Moura," Gabbie sighed. "Perhaps she wishes she had never given us the gift in the first place."

"What do you think Samuel?" Siskin had stopped the quiet strumming of his guitar. "Does our planet still look for the Myriar to be finally realised?"

"Who amongst us, can read the ebb and flow of Moura? Even the Mourangils do not always see her purpose," answered Samuel. "But little Gabbie, all I have felt of that purpose in my time here, tells me that the formation of the Myriar is both more and less than when Moura first entrusted Toomaaris with the task of implanting this gift in Ordovicia. Less, because its original intention did not come to be. More because it has survived the grinding maelstrom of human existence to become..." He turned his gaze to the shrouded window and then to Kier. Gently Samuel turned over her hand, where on the outstretched palm, still red and faintly glowing, was the imprint of the planet Mesa with its three circling moons. He looked at each of the small group in turn.

"Well," he told them softly, "we have yet to see what it will become."

ACKNOWLEDGEMENTS

My special thanks to Claire Lawton for driving with me to old haunts, older graveyards, and the muddy corners of my imagination. Thank you also to Dave Watson for patiently sharing his insight into the gaming world. Veronica, for your literally huge support, I cannot thank you enough. I am also grateful to Gweneira Raw-Rees for policing my Welsh. I still have a few phrases from our time at university, but they wouldn't last long across the border. A particular thank you to Alan Duncan for his work in proofing this second edition and for his brilliant support. Finally, thank you again Conor Watson for providing your wonderful artwork.

Printed in Great Britain
by Amazon

76200415R00227